DOUBLE TARGET

Steamy Romantic Suspense

Patti Corbello Archer

 Dedication

To my granddaughter, Alayna.

Your imagination, creative spirit, and love of beauty, inspire me every single day. I love to see the world through your eyes.

I love you.

Acknowledgements

Writing books and becoming an author has always been a goal in my life. In saying that, all the pieces had to fall into place for me to finally step into that journey.

And each of you helped make it happen:

God. My God. Without beauty for ashes, there would be no book. You are the greatest author of all and gave me an imagination to see with words. Now I can fly. Anywhere.

To my son, Zeb, and daughter-in-law, Cora, it was your hearts and hands that brought me to the right place, at the right time, for this door to open for me. I deeply admire both of you. Your superpowers of love, strength, integrity, wisdom, intelligence, and skills for anything and everything, fill me with love and gratefulness.

To Aunt Gloria. I appreciate all the hours you stepped away from your real life into my fiction stories. Every message and thought you shared is priceless.

To my mother, siblings, extended family and friends, your encouragement on my author journey has truly mattered. Please know that every hug, call, email, text, post, smiley face, and heart, made a difference.

To all readers, thank you.

DOUBLE TARGET

Chapter 1
LSU Campus

Bella soared high as she crested the peak of the massive bridge heading into Baton Rouge, Louisiana. Twenty stories of nothing but air and a few columns separated her from the belly of the Mississippi River below. It gave her a rush and she cranked up the music.

A deep rumble interrupted the song and she looked out her window. A man on a big chopper passed and flashed a beautiful smile. Bella returned the smile and he braked to stay even with her. He pursed his lips in a kiss and she laughed. With another smile, he roared on down the bridge with an arm lifted high in a wave.

Bella grinned at the brief encounter. Men, she thought. They were never too busy to notice a woman. Focusing back on the road, she checked for clearance and took the next exit toward her apartment near LSU. Her phone rang just as she passed the college.

With a quick glance at caller ID, she answered and listened for a moment, then said, "I appreciate the head's up, Professor. Your timing was perfect, I'm driving up now. Thanks again for calling."

She dropped her phone on the seat and turned her sky-blue mustang onto the LSU campus. Bella hadn't planned to return to the college after she received her Doctor of Veterinary Medicine degree last week, but the professor reminded her that she still needed to clean out her locker in the doctor's lounge. In all the excitement of graduation and packing to move back to Texas, it had completely slipped her mind.

Baton Rouge and the LSU School of Veterinary Medicine had been her home since she was eighteen years old. And now, eight years later, she was thrilled to return home to the Lone Star State and the ranches that she loved. She drove into a nearly empty parking lot since it was between semesters in mid-May. She stuck her phone and keys in the back pocket of her jeans and headed inside the veterinary building.

Twenty-six-year-old, Bella DelCaprio was gorgeous. Even without makeup she was stunning. She was a very shapely five-foot-eight. Long black hair. Eyes, so light blue they were almost silver. And a fabulous smile. She was used to public attention; the double takes as people glanced back at her, the pointing fingers, and even now, loud whistles from a group of guys that passed by in a jeep.

She grinned, jogged the last few steps, and entered the building that she knew so well. She followed the twisting hallway all the way back to the locker room and began to clean hers out. In less than ten minutes, all those years of school nearly fit into a single tote. Just as she reached for the last items in her locker, footsteps sounded in the hall, and she grinned. Someone else had forgotten to clean out their locker too. The footsteps neared the door and she turned around with a smile.

Royce walked into the room.

Her smile faded.

Bella had dated a variety of men, but this creepy chameleon had shocked her. He was deceptively handsome with an underlying minor in psycho. He was a coach assistant here at the college in the athletic department, tall and muscular with longer than average blonde hair and blue eyes. When they met, there had been no indication of what lurked beneath his skin.

Her looks had made her the target of male affection through the years, but none had ever turned out like Royce. He had been such a sweet guy at first; supportive and considerate of the hours that she put in to complete her graduate program. To her it had been a casual friendship, nothing romantic. She simply enjoyed his company when she had free time.

Then as graduation, and her move back to Texas drew closer, he revealed a sexual undertone and aggressive behavior that alarmed her. So, late one afternoon outside her apartment she ended all contact with him because of it. His temperament had gone from nice to nasty in two seconds. Thank God her roommates, Seth, and Lili, had been nearby.

Royce had wisely walked away, but the look he gave her promised a reckoning that made her skin crawl. But he had left her alone. Until now.

The savage expression on Royce's face warned her that she was in danger.

Determined to appear unafraid and assertive, she said, "You need to leave, Royce. Seth will be here any minute and that won't be good for you."

Royce smiled, if you could call it that, and goosebumps raised on her arms. He crossed the short distance between them and cornered her against the wall of lockers. She casually reached behind her right hip for a cattle prod that was in her locker and grabbed it.

Royce made no attempt to hide what was on his mind as his eyes mentally stripped her.

She refused to react in fear, and slipped her tote on her shoulder and said, "Leave me alone, Royce. This is trouble that you don't need."

He leered and took a step closer as he growled, "You don't know what I need," and grabbed her between the legs. Hard.

Shocked, but ready, Bella dropped her tote, swung the cattle prod, and hit him across the right side of the head. He stumbled back a few steps and grabbed the wound, clearly shaken as blood trickled through his fingers.

Bella ran out the side door toward the utility hall and ducked into one of the closet doors.

In seconds, Royce raged and stormed into the hall after her.

Trying not to panic, Bella realized the closet was dark - her biggest fear. The only light entering the room came from under the door. But she couldn't turn the light on and hide too. Oh God, help me, she prayed. This was not the time for a panic attack. She fought to focus, and thought, *breathe, just breathe*, as she stood in the inky blackness that terrified her as much as Royce.

Attempting to recall what she had seen when she slipped into the room, she remembered a linen rack in the back. She slipped off her sandals and forced herself to tiptoe further back into the darkness. Her heart pounded in her ears.

Royce's footsteps sounded closer as he rummaged and searched for her in the hall of closets, and called out menacingly, "Bella, where are you? In the long run, hiding is only going to make it much, much, more painful for you. I will make you pay."

She ignored him as she reached the large linen rack, slid behind it, and ducked. She prayed that he wouldn't be able to see her even if he opened the door.

Then she felt it.

Oh no. She tried to shake off the PTSD panic attack but the memories of being locked in a trunk as a child fought to surface. The darkness crawled over her and sucked her breath away. Then it's terrifying voice growled in her ear.

Terror filled Bella in the tight dark place.

She covered her mouth to stop the scream that tickled - and prayed. Cold sweat covered her. The fear wanted control. She struggled to remember that she was not alone. God was with her. He was the light of the world. He would never leave her in the dark. Then the sound of things tossed around in the hall reminded her of the danger that drew close.

She grabbed her phone and texted 911 where she was hidden, and that her attacker was coming.

Royce raked his fingernails along the wall as he neared the next closet. He said, "There are only four doors left, Bella. I can taste you already."

She clenched her jaw and gripped the rack in front of her. She prayed that Royce wouldn't reach her door before—

And the sound of sirens rang out.

Royce slammed something against the wall and growled, "Bella!" and then his quick footsteps faded away.

Bella breathed a sigh of relief and wiped the clamminess off her face and neck. Then she called 911 and explained that her attacker had left, who he was, and what he looked like.

In minutes, the police called out to her from the hall, and she stepped out of the closet. She called her roommates on the way to the police station.

***

Lili and Seth had been Bella's roommates for years. And not only roommates, but close friends and Texans as well. Last week Lili received her Doctor of Veterinary Medicine too. She was petite and lovely with a mass of long, brown curls and blue eyes. Seth, Lili's cousin, graduated with his second engineering degree, aeronautical, and would begin work at NASA on June 1. He was handsome, with long brown hair and dark brown eyes.

Bella waved at Seth and Lili as they rounded the corner at the police station. It was obvious that Seth was angry.

They hugged her, and Seth said with barely concealed fury, "Where is Royce? I'm going to kill him."

4

Bella said, "Seth! Lower your voice, you are in a police station for heaven's sake. They're looking for him."

"Are you ok?" Lili asked, still concerned.

"I'm ok. He grabbed me and I hit him."

Lili shivered and said, "I hate that creep!"

Bella thought about what he did, and what she thought he had planned to do, and said, "He's a whole lot more than that."

Seth said, "Have you called Lucas yet? He's gonna flip."

"No, I'm going to wait till I get home to call him."

An hour later, Bella finished her police statement and they headed out the front door. When they neared the sidewalk, Royce walked around the corner in handcuffs. He had dried blood on his head, neck, and shirt.

He snarled when he saw Bella and Seth stepped forward and hit him in the jaw.

Back inside the police station, Seth was given a stern warning - with a few subtle attaboy pats on the back by the cops. Then they left for the second time and headed to their west side balcony apartment that overlooked the Mississippi River.

As they walked in the apartment, Bella put her tote, phone, and keys down, and said, "I'm going to take a shower and then I will call Lucas, I promise."

***

Bella went to her room and walked out on the balcony. She watched and admired the sheer power of the river. It was such an invincible force that claimed the right-a-way through the land without apology - nothing stood in its way. That's what she needed tonight; to press on and wash this experience off before she called her brother.

Lucas was another force in her life, and her only sibling. He was also handsome, smart, brave, and protective. She knew that he was going to be furious about Royce's attack. Now in his early thirties, he had graduated college with a criminal justice degree and then surprised everyone by becoming a firefighter. He had lived and worked in the Dallas area for years. His hair was black like hers, but with hazel eyes, instead of blue. It was clear they were brother and sister.

Their parents had died young in a car accident, so they were taken in and raised by their paternal Italian grandparents who lived outside of Houston. It had been a wonderful Christian environment laced with old school Italian and they had loved every minute of it. Their grandparents were gone now, but sweetly remembered, and sorely missed.

Bella looked in the mirror. The shadow of today's attack still lingered in her eyes. It was terrifying to realize that Royce wanted to rape her. And if she had read him right, kill her too.

After a shower, she dressed, then joined Seth and Lili in the den. Seth was on his cell phone.

Lili whispered, "Lucas called Seth."

Bella held out her hand for Seth's cell phone, and he handed it to her, relieved.

***

Bella said, "Hey Lucas. Sorry that I haven't returned your call yet. I had to make a stop at LSU and unfortunately, I ran into a problem. I didn't mean for you to be worried."

Lucas said, "I had an uneasy feeling when you didn't call me back, so I called Seth. Is everything all right? You are all suspiciously quiet."

With a sigh, she said, "I am just going to lay it out there for you. Royce attacked me at LSU today and we just got home from the police station."

She held the phone away from her ear while Lucas raged for a second, then said, "I'm going to bury him in the swamp down there! Has he lost his mind? Are you hurt, Bella? I mean it. Tell me."

"No, I wasn't injured I promise. Scared, yes. He grabbed me, then I hit him and ran."

Furious still, Lucas said, "That must have been a violent grab for you to hit him and run. What did he do?"

She sighed, glanced at Seth and Lili who listened, and said, "He grabbed me between the legs, ok? And I hit him in the head with my cattle prod."

Lucas growled in anger.

Seth and Lili's eyes widened in shock.

And Bella lost it. She laughed. And couldn't stop. She handed the phone back to Seth and sat on the sofa and laughed till she fell over on the cushion.

Shocked at first, Lili finally giggled at Bella.

Seth, now stuck with Bella's upset brother on the phone said, "Hang on just a minute, Lucas, we need a minute here, just hang on," and put the phone in his lap and watched the women laugh.

It took a few moments, but eventually he grinned. He couldn't muster a laugh.

After Bella gathered her composure, she took Seth's phone back and said, "I'm sorry Lucas, I really needed that laugh after a heavy afternoon."

Frustrated, Lucas said, "What is so funny? I don't find any of it funny. I am ready to kill him, and you're laughing."

To help him understand, Bella said, "Wait, I have a question for you. Just how many women do you think have a cattle prod close by?"

Lucas didn't answer for a second, then chuckled, and said, "Ok, that part was funny."

Bella said, "You should have seen Seth hit Royce at the police station."

Lucas yelled over the phone, "You are the man, Seth!"

Seth   grinned.   He   was   a   brother   too   -   he   got   it.

***

Then Bella walked away to talk privately, and said, "I did get your message about Phoenix's eye accident. Please tell me that he is going to be ok. I am so sorry. Is he at the ranch? Is there anything that I can do? Anything."

Lucas said, "He is supposed to be fine. The doctors told him to wear eye patches until the flash burns are healed. The problem is, he refused to wear them to rest his eyes and they got inflamed. Now his vision is blurred. So, his grandfather rented a house at Pirates Beach in Galveston and demanded he go rest his eyes for a few weeks. Which is why I called you."

Upset for Phoenix, Bella said, "Weeks are a long time to be unable to see. That is awful. How can I help him?"

"He needs someone to stay with him. He doesn't need a nurse, just someone to look out for him. He doesn't want a stranger. So, I thought you might enjoy a few weeks at the beach to chill and keep an eye on him. What do you think? Would you want to?"

Bella smiled to herself, and said, "Of course I will. When?"

Lucas smiled his own secret smile, and said, "Tomorrow."

"Shouldn't I call him for approval or something?"

Bella said. "He hasn't seen me in years."

He gave her Phoenix's cell number and said, "He's had a hard couple of years with his dad passing away, the split with his fiancé, and now this temporary blindness. You will be good for him. I feel sure of it. Call him."

Secretly thrilled, she said, "I will. I will call him in a couple of minutes, so, let me get off the phone. I love you, Lucas. Be safe fighting those fires. I'll see you soon."

***

After she hung up, Bella asked Seth and Lili, "Do you remember me telling you about a close friend of Lucas' from college, named Phoenix Chandler? His family owns a large cattle ranch west of Wichita Falls."

Seth and Lili both nodded, and she continued, "Well he injured his eyes in a flash burn and will have to wear eye patches for a few weeks, so he needs someone to stay with him at a house on Pirates Beach in Galveston. I told Lucas that I would go. I need to be there by tomorrow. Would you be able to bring my moving boxes with you when you move out? If so, I can just bring my personal things and leave early in the morning."

Without hesitation, Seth said, "Sure, no problem at all."

Lili thought for a second, and said, "Wait a minute. Isn't Phoenix the one that you had a crush on in high school?"

Seth raised his eyebrows.

Bella said, "Thanks Lili for remembering that out loud."

Aware of Seth's probable response, Lili said, "You are most welcome," and smiled.

Frowning now, Seth said, "You are going to go stay with a man on the beach all alone for weeks? Does Lucas know that you had a crush on this guy?"

Bella smiled innocently, and said, "You do remember that I am twenty-six years old? And besides, Lucas called me. It's not my fault if he doesn't remember. Most importantly, Phoenix is unable to see, and I intend to help him."

Ready for more details about the old crush, Lili said, "So, tell us more about him. Spill it."

Bella grinned and said, "Oh my gosh when I was sixteen, he was so hot. Tall, rugged, thick brown hair, blue eyes, and sun darkened skin. Sexier than you can ever imagine. He was everything awesome."

Seth rolled his eyes, and said, "So is he paunch-bellied and bald now?"

Bella winked at Lili and shook her head no, picked up her phone, pulled Phoenix up on Facebook and showed them his picture. Lili fanned herself and panted and Bella laughed.

Seth shook his head with a frown, and said, "I have a feeling that my sisters are just like both of you," and they laughed.

Bella said, "So anyway, I need to call him and make sure he wants me to come."

Seth burst out laughing and said, "You're hilarious, have you looked in the mirror? Of course, he will."

***

Bella went to her bedroom and called Phoenix. He answered with a rich Texas drawl, "Hey Bella. You are an answer to a prayer. Lucas told me that you would call. Are you sure that you want to babysit me for a few weeks while my eyes heal?"

Bella said, "Of course I will! I am so sorry that you were injured. I'm glad to do what I can to make things easier for you. I just graduated and have plenty free time before my professional life begins."

"I heard about that Dr. DelCaprio. What a terrific accomplishment."

She said, "Thank you. It was years of work, but I love it. So, yes, I can be there tomorrow. Are you at the beach now?"

"No," he said. "My sister, Ariel, is driving me there tomorrow. We should be there by noon. Will you be able to be there by then?"

"Sure. Easily. How about I bring groceries with me?"

"Bella, you are a dream. Thank you, and please choose food easy for me to eat without sight. Everything is blurry even without the patches and it is more difficult to eat than you can imagine."

Saddened by that thought, she said, "I will keep that in mind. Is there anything special that you like?"

"I'm a cattle rancher, all things beef," and she laughed.

Trying to remember the last time he saw her, he said, "On another note, I haven't seen you in a long time, do you look the same?"

"But we are friends on social media."

"Arial handles all advertising and social media for me and the ranch. I never get on those sites so give me a refresher."

"Well, I am still five foot eight, long black hair, blue eyes, and average weight."

Phoenix said, "Sounds like what I remember back when I was in college."

She laughed at his lack of awareness, and said, "Something like that."

"Thank you, Bella. I appreciate this. I owe you."

Happier than he could know, Bella said, "No. You don't owe me anything. Besides, I might have a professional proposition for you."

"Really? That is intriguing. What?"

She said, "We will save it for when we are killing time over the next few weeks. How about that?"

"That works for me. Again, Bella, thank you. See you, or rather, we will meet you there tomorrow. And just so you are aware, I have a phone for the blind that speaks to me so feel free to call or text."

Surprised, Bella said, "That is amazing. I guess that I haven't thought of that. I'm glad. No one likes to be isolated. Till tomorrow! Arrivederci!"

Chapter 2
Pirates Beach, Galveston

Phoenix sat in his twenty-five-year-old sister, Ariel's, white BMW and looked at nothing but the back of black eyepatches. He listened as she talked on the phone to someone named Bunny about a date that went south. At least the call wasn't on speaker.

He leaned his head back against the headrest and thought about the turn of events over the last few days. His eye burns had been a freak accident. He had been lighting the BBQ grill on the patio when a sudden gust of wind hit just as he squirted the charcoal lighter. The fire had ignited, and the wind blew sparks and hot air back into his open eyes. The pain had been instant and uncontrollable until they used the sweet, wonderful, pain relieving eyedrops in the emergency room. They cleaned and checked his eyes for damage, and the doctor gave him strict instructions to keep his eyes covered for twelve to sixteen hours a day until his vision cleared.

But at the ranch there had been so much to do that he removed the patches trying to see, and his eyes became inflamed. Then his grandfather came in from Colorado to tend to the ranch and insisted that he get away to heal. So here he was, being babysat by his little sister on the way to the beach to be babysat by Lucas' little sister. He clenched his teeth and thought, just deal with it.

He sighed and thought back over the last dozen years. He had received his Animal Husbandry degree in Dallas and hired on at the Dallas Zoo. He had loved the job even knowing that it would be temporary until his grandfather retired from the family cattle ranch. Once that happened, he would need to return to work the ranch with his dad. Chandler Canyon Ranch had been in his family for as long as he remembered.

But then, three years ago, his dad died of a sudden heart attack and his life changed instantly. Without delay, he had left Dallas and returned home to work the ranch with his grandfather. He had been exceptionally good at it - and loved it. But his fiancé, Monique, hadn't wanted to live in west Texas. He had never realized that their relationship had been as much about the bright lights of Dallas as it had been about them. So, they ended the relationship, and he became a cattle rancher.

Thoughts returning to the present, he looked forward to his visit with Bella. Days were really long in the dark with the eye patches. He thought back to his college days when he and Lucas would see Bella and their grandparents on their semester breaks. She had been a pretty, high school girl with a crush on him.

Now, all these years later, she was leaving college as a veterinarian. He was impressed. Good for her. It would be perfect if she would be interested in working at the ranch. He looked forward to hearing her intriguing proposition.

***

Ariel said, "Earth to Phoenix, Earth to Phoenix, is anyone there?"

Phoenix chuckled and said, "You mean you got tired of talking to Bunny?" and she laughed.

Ariel said, "She's sweet. We have a lot of fun together and she helps me with the ranch advertising sometimes."

Properly chastised, he said, "I'm sorry, I am not trying to take out my bad mood on others. I'm sure she is great."

She understood his frustration, and said, "The beach is going to be good for you, Phoenix. You need to get well because we need you back at the ranch. Let Bella help you so that you can rest those beautiful eyes. And I have to tell you, I've seen pictures of her on social media and she is gorgeous with a capital G. She has long black wavy hair, sparkling light blue eyes, a fabulous smile, beautiful skin, and a shape most women would kill to have."

Surprised and thinking of that image, Phoenix said, "What?"

"You heard me. Lucas' sister rocks. You will have knockout company for weeks. God loves you more than you thought."

Phoenix moaned and said, "And I can't even see her."

Ariel laughed and said, "Maybe that will be an incentive for you to be obedient and take care of your eyes, big brother."

"It has been a long time since I have seen her," he said. "All I remember is a pretty teenager in high school."

Ariel said, "Oh, sweetie, not hardly, there is no dismissive description like that anymore. Just wait, you will see."

Phoenix was now double intrigued. What man wouldn't be?

Ariel said, "From what I see online, another difference between this woman and others, is that she has a heart of gold, as well as being your best friend's sister. Don't you wonder why Lucas put this in motion? Think about that. Oh, and we will be to the beach in about an hour. You can find out for yourself what you think of her."

***

Bella felt free. She had left Baton Rouge and all the years of college behind her this morning and took off to a brand-new future. Louisiana had been good to her, as well as the people (except for Royce). She had loved the food and the sweet Cajun culture. It had all been a wonderful experience. But she had always wanted to live in Texas with its extremes and wide-open land.

By mid-morning she had crossed the Sabine River which was the state line between Texas and Louisiana. She waved goodbye to her past and drove toward her future. Before long she was close to Galveston. She wanted to get there early and enjoy a little time to herself in the sand and sea before Phoenix arrived. She thought back to their talk yesterday. His voice was even more hot and sexy after all these years.

She groaned and cranked up the music as she sped down the interstate. She was determined not to act like a lovesick teenager by the time she got there. Then she had a fleeting thought of Lucas. What was her brother up to? Setting her up with any man, for any reason, was completely out of character for him.

At eleven o'clock sharp, the groceries were chilling in a cooler in the trunk of her mustang as she pulled up to the address that Phoenix had sent her. She got out of the car and looked in awe at the dream house amid sand dunes that overlooked the Gulf of Mexico.

She smiled and kicked off her shoes, released her hair from the ponytail, then walked down to the waves in her rolled-up jeans and halter top. She was in heaven. This was going to be so good for Phoenix's healing and give her a much-needed break. Of course, looking at the man that she had dreamed about for years was certainly something to look forward to as well.

Bella walked around for a while and then headed back to the house at the same time a white BMW drove up and parked. She figured that it was Phoenix and Ariel.

As they stepped out, Bella called out, "Hello, Phoenix! I couldn't help myself. I have already walked in the water. You will love it."

Phoenix turned to the sound of Bella's voice and said, "Keep talking so that I know where you are," and it made Bella's heart hurt to see his eye patches.

She was closer now, and said, "Just stand still and I will come to you," and she walked close and kissed him on both cheeks, Italian style, as her hair and perfume floated around him.

Phoenix, entranced by her, said, "I forget about you and Lucas being Italian. That is such a beautiful greeting. Thanks for coming, Bella."

"I was glad to come. Thanks for letting me be a part of this time for you."

"I sure hope you plan to take me on the same walk in the waves."

Bella laughed and said, "Just try and stop me!" Then she turned to Ariel and said, "It is so nice to meet you, and you look amazing. I would love a platinum pixie with those green eyes." Then Bella furrowed her brow and asked curiously, "Has Lucas seen you?"

Ariel laughed and said, "You are charming, Bella! I can already tell that I want to get to know you."

Bella grinned, then glanced at Phoenix.

She said, "Phoenix, do you need to go inside?"

"I do, thanks. If you would just walk on my right side and steer me with directions that would be great. Warn me when the ground is uneven. And Ariel, if you hand me some bags, I can carry them up with me."

They unloaded the car and once they got inside, Bella steered him to the restroom.

Ariel smiled and said, "Thank you, Bella. It is hard on him to be needy, but it is just for a few weeks. It looks like you are a natural caretaker, but I guess being a doctor helps with that."

Bella hugged her and said, "I wish that our brothers would have encouraged us to meet years ago."

Ariel said, "So do I."

The bathroom door opened, and Phoenix stepped out and said, "Do we need to unload anything else?"

Bella said, "I have the ice cooler and food in my mustang. I feel sure that Ariel and I can carry it in if you wouldn't be offended. I made sure not to get one too big for us to carry."

They led Phoenix to the balcony and went downstairs for the food.

In no time, everything was in the house and Ariel was waving goodbye as she headed home to Houston.

Bella watched Phoenix stand at the balcony rail for a while as the wind blew his thick hair. She waited. She understood the need for adjustment.

After about ten minutes, he said, "You are considerate, thank you. I needed a few minutes to get my bearings."

She said, "I get it. And as for us, please, just tell me what you want or need. That way I don't intrude in your space for no reason."

He said, "Fair enough. But you smell wonderful. I wouldn't ever mind you in my space," and she laughed.

Phoenix said, "I would love something to drink and then a walk on the beach. I have been couped up in the car for hours. I need to feel the waves even though I can't see them."

Bella said, "You will love it. What are you thirsty for?"

"Coke with lots of ice would be great."

"I will be right back."

In a minute, he heard her walk back outside and she said, "The plastic glass is in front of your right hand," and he took it and smiled.

A little later they walked along the beach where the waves lapped the shore. She led with his hand on her shoulder.

He said, "It feels, smells, and sounds wonderful out here. I can't remember the last time I took off to the beach."

"It is wonderful. Do you want to chat, or just walk?"

"How about you talk," he said. "I am tired of my own dreary thoughts."

"I get it," she said. "I felt like that yesterday."

"Why, what was wrong with yesterday?"

"Well, I was attacked at LSU by a guy I stopped seeing."

"What! Physically? That is insane! Were you hurt? Was he arrested? Does Lucas know?"

She appreciated his concern, and said, "He grabbed me, yes. But I hit him and ran, then hid until the cops arrived. He was arrested. And Lucas is very angry."

"I can imagine! I'm angry too! Was it just out of the blue and he snapped?"

"Kind of," she said. "In the beginning he was just a nice guy, but his demeanor changed, so I called it quits. But yesterday... Well, yesterday, seemed life-threatening, on top of a few other things."

"You mean, like kill you, life-threatening?"

She paused, and said, "Eventually."

Knowing what she meant, he wondered if she was safe from the guy, and said, "What did the cops say?"

"The detective said he would keep me up to date on the case. That's all I can do. Now enough about that, let's just enjoy the beach."

After the walk, Bella prepared a late lunch and he sat at the snack bar as they talked.

She said, "So, do you like music?"

He nodded and said, "That's a yes. I love it."

Wondering about his interests, she said, "Do you play?"

He grinned and said, "Only with the woman that I am dancing with."

She laughed and said, "You sound like Lucas. Men!"

He chuckled and said, "Do you play?"

"The guitar."

Phoenix sighed in bliss and said, "Please tell me that you brought it with you."

"I did."

He said, "Feel free to play anytime you want to."

She warned him as she said, "But I don't sing. I have a weird raspy voice. I only sing to myself and God."

He liked the sound of that and said, "Maybe I can listen while you do that."

"Oh, that was sweet to say."

It wasn't long and she said, "Are you ready to eat? We have steak strips, cucumber sticks, fries, and then strawberries for dessert."

He said, "I'm always ready to eat, but what is a steak strip?"

"It is a medium rare ribeye cut into strips so you can eat it with your hands. The same with the cucumbers."

"Bella you are something special. You better stop it, or I will be in love with you by morning," and she laughed.

They ate while they listened to an audiobook mystery for at least an hour and then debated on who the bad guy was. Then Phoenix's phone rang.

***

The special phone announced, "Chandler Canyon Ranch calling."

Phoenix said, "Phone, answer call. Hey GP, I have you on speaker and Bella is with me."

GP said, "Hello to both of you. How are your eyes?"

"Not stinging anymore and I have kept my patches on."

"Finally! Ms. Bella, make him listen. He can't run from you."

Bella laughed, and Phoenix said, "Funny."

GP paused, and said, "I hate to tell you, but we lost a bull today."

Phoenix said, "No! What happened? Which one?"

"I'm sorry, it was Big Blacky. He got loose from the southeast pasture and wandered into the road and got hit by an eighteen-wheeler not long ago."

Phoenix sighed, and said, "I hate to hear that. Was the driver hurt?"

"Scared, but not hurt. He came over the top of a hill and that big black bull was just standing in the middle of the road."

Phoenix said, "Man, I bet that guy aged ten years. But ok, go ahead and shop for another bull. Don't wait till I get back. I want another prime Angus bull. Check with that ranch in Kansas. Anything else?"

"Yeah," GP said, "We have two sick cows, one injured heifer and one weakening calf. But the vet can't get here till late tomorrow. You know that they are scarce around here now. Kit and Levi are doing the usual workup on them and have them separated in barn stalls."

Phoenix said, "Tell Kit to call the vet again if their temperatures get high."

"We will. Now back to you, get well and come home. Ms. Bella, I heard you are a beauty. Make sure you come visit up here! I want to see you for myself."

Bella said, "Thank you, and I hope to!"

Phoenix said, "She will. Thanks, GP. Talk to you later. Phone, end call."

***

Bella let a little time pass, and said, "I'm sorry about the bull. How long had he been at the ranch?"

"Three years, which is usually the max breeding we do on a bull, but I had thought about keeping him permanently. It sure sounds strange that he broke out of the pasture. He's never gotten out before. Excuse me for a second, Bella. I'm going to text my foreman."

***

Then Phoenix said, "Phone, text Kit."

His phone said, "Ready."

Phoenix said, "Kit, investigate where the bull got out and let me know what you find. That sounds unusual for him."

In a moment, his phone said, "Kit replied, 'Will get out there shortly to investigate. Sorry Boss. I know you liked Big Blacky.'"

***

As they settled on the sofa, he said, "If you wondered, GP is my grandfather."

She said, "I figured. GP stands for grandpa I presume."

"Yeah, with a bunch of men around the ranch, yelling grandpa made a lot of them turn and look, so GP worked out better. As a kid, I thought that I was bad to the bone calling my grandpa that."

"I imagine! And hey, I like your phone. It is like having a robot waiting for your command. Will she respond to me?"

"No, she is only programmed for my voice."

"Do the phones have male voices too?"

"Yeah, but I don't want to talk to a guy," and she laughed.

She said, "If it was my phone, I would pick the sexiest male voice and make him respond, hey baby, all day long. Maybe they need to make an app for that."

Phoenix laughed and said, "I am so glad that you are here. You make this a treat instead of something I'm enduring."

She rubbed his arm in sympathy.

After a few minutes of silence, Bella said, "Hang on, I will be right back."

She came in the room with her guitar. She knew that he needed to get his mind off ranch issues. She sat on an ottoman and strummed to warm up. He

18

smiled and relaxed against the sofa. She played a few worship songs, a country and western, and a couple of oldies.

When she stopped playing, he said, "I could listen to you play all day."

She said, "Thanks," and walked over and sat by him.

"Tell me about your eyes, Phoenix."

He told her the burn story and how his lack of following instructions caused the inflammation that resulted with his blurriness now.

She said, "I am aware that you shouldn't wear patches twenty-four hours a day with your injury, so do you wear the patches most of the day and take them off at night when it is dark?"

"Pretty much. It makes for long dark days and blurry nights. That kind of sounds like a country and western song, doesn't it?"

With a giggle she said, "A little, but I imagine it's tough. Shouldn't I check your eyes daily to get familiar with their condition?" and he nodded.

***

Bella's phone rang and she said, "It's Lucas," and answered, "Hi Lucas, I have you on speaker, Phoenix is right here too."

Lucas said, "Hey Bella! Hey Phoenix! How's it going?"

Phoenix said, "She fed me steak, sang to me, listened to my woes, and is spoiling me," and Lucas laughed.

Bella said, "It's great here, we even had a walk on the beach. It's been peaceful. He's going to do good here."

Lucas said, "He's going to do good because you are there."

Bella gasped and said, "Lucas!"

Phoenix laughed and said, "You are both right."

Lucas said, "If I can get off next weekend, I thought I would make a run down there to visit. Let me know if you need anything."

Phoenix said, "Awesome. Come on down. Bella can spoil both of us."

***

Late that afternoon, Bella looked outside and said, "It is almost dusk, would you like to sit outside, or listen to an audiobook or movie?"

He said, "Can we just sit on the steps?" and she led the way outside.

19

They sat next to each other and listened quietly to the waves till darkness fell.

Phoenix said, "What was the professional proposition you wanted to discuss with me?"

She said, "Well, it has to do with what GP said on the phone actually."

"About the lack of veterinarians?"

"Yes, I wanted to offer my services as a vet free of charge for three months to see if I would be a good fit for Chandler Canyon Ranch."

"Bella, you don't have to work for free, we need you. You heard that."

"But there is a part two to my offer."

Phoenix chuckled and said, "Is marriage the part two?" and she laughed, even though her heart skipped a beat.

She said, "I have a dream to have a safe house for rescue animals. There are so many animals that aren't perfect, or they get hurt, or abused and I want to do what I can to make a difference in their lives. But I need a place for them and wondered if you might have a small barn or building that I could use. I have access to other rescue facilities that I could lean on and even LSU's animal services. I am willing to work for free to have it."

Phoenix said, "I would be honored to have you at the ranch, Bella. Yes, to whatever you want or need. But you will have to accept a paycheck, without argument. Deal?"

"How about I work for room and board instead?"

"Room and board come with the position, so you still get a paycheck," and she hugged him since he couldn't see to shake her hand.

By ten p.m. he said, "It is time to take off my patches so I can shower, but I need low light or darkness," so Bella left a tiny light on in the bathroom and a night light in the kitchen and turned all the rest of the lights off.

She said, "Ok, only two small lights are on in the whole house."

She watched him in the dim light as he took off both eye patches, blinked and looked around.

"How do your eyes feel?"

"Pretty good, this is the first day that I actually did what I was supposed to do."

Bella said, "Macho rancher," and he chuckled.

She questioned, "Is the blurriness the same?" and he turned to face her.

20

"I see color and overall shape but not detail. But it seems a little clearer around the edges somehow."

She said, "Ok, day one is good."

"I sure wish that I could see you. Ariel gave me a much better description of you than you gave me over the phone."

She laughed and said, "You should have checked your social media," and he grinned.

She said, "May I check your eyes now?" and he nodded.

She tilted his head so that she could see better and looked into gorgeous blue eyes that couldn't really see her. She ignored the tingles that raced up her spine. Phoenix felt Bella's breath on his face and watched her image move closer, as she ran her fingertips around his eyes.

She said, "Everything looks ok, nothing looks alarming," and he nodded and watched her image stay there.

After a few moments, Phoenix said softly, "If you stay there Bella, I'm most definitely going to think you are interested in a kiss or two," and she laughed and leaned back.

She said, "Sorry, you are so good looking, and it reminded me of my crush on you years ago."

He lifted a hand toward her face, and even with blurred vision he touched her lips, and she smiled under his fingers.

Phoenix chuckled and said, "I think we call that a bullseye," and they both laughed.

He said with his sexy Texas drawl, "Well, on that note, maybe I should call it a night, although I don't know if I can sleep now."

He stood and looked down at her image, and Bella said, "Please let me know if you need anything tonight. What about clothes? Should I lay out a few things for you?"

Phoenix said, "Maybe just separate into stacks the pants, shirts, shorts, and so on, and I can grab from each stack. How is that?"

"Sure. It won't take but a minute."

When she finished sorting his clothes, she told him goodnight and headed to her room.

About an hour later, Bella heard Phoenix in the hall and got up and followed him.

Phoenix heard her footsteps and said, "Sorry, I couldn't relax and decided to get up."

She said, "I have an idea, come have a seat on the sofa and lean back," and before long the sound of waves drifted inside as she slid a window open. Then from behind him she said, "Just listen to the waves and relax as I massage your shoulders, ok?"

He said, "Oh Bella, thank you," and she smiled as she rubbed his shoulders and upper arms until his muscles loosened and he fell asleep.

She didn't want to leave him alone. She curled up on the other end of the sofa and fell asleep to the sound of the waves.

Chapter 3
Awareness

The sound of sea gulls and waves woke Phoenix and he smiled. He hadn't slept that good in a long time, even before the burns. Then he opened his eyes and was surprised to see – more! Nothing was detailed but everything was brighter. Resting his eyes worked and he closed them again and listened to the waves.

Then he felt movement on the sofa and a foot slid over his thigh. Bella had slept out here on the sofa as well. His pulse shot out the roof. She was killer captivating and giving him all sorts of ideas.

He wrapped his hand around her foot.

Bella's eyes flew open, and she gasped and yanked her foot back as she sat up.

Phoenix laughed, and she hit him on the arm. Then he laughed harder.

She giggled and said, "I am sorry for hitting you. I've never slept with any..." and she stopped when she realized what she all but said.

Aware of the implication, Phoenix stopped laughing and looked at her fuzzy image and said, "Bella..."

She closed her eyes and pleaded, "Please forget I said that."

"That isn't happening. It's virtually impossible to forget that."

She sighed and said, "It is so intimate being here together like this. I will probably put my foot in my mouth many times in the days ahead."

He said softly, "Bella, what you said was special, not a foot in your mouth thing at all."

"I know, I just didn't mean to blurt it out."

"I am glad that you did."

Changing the conversation, she rubbed the arm she hit, and he grinned.

She said, "How do your eyes feel this morning? They look good."

"They are better. They really are. This is working," and Bella gave him a quick hug.

With a grin, he said, "You could have mercy on a blind man and let that hug last a little longer."

Bella laughed and got off the sofa.

She shut the window that she had left open all night, and said, "How about a cup of coffee before we walk on the beach?" and he stood and stretched.

Bella looked at him in the light of day, without his eye patches, and said, "You are so smoking hot."

He laughed and said, "And you are an enchanting package of contradictions," and she laughed.

An hour later, they strolled along the beach and Phoenix said, "I love to jog, are you game to try? I will do my best not to trip us both."

She said, "Sure, just make sure I can keep up with you."

They jogged in sync for a long while and were on their way back toward the house when Bella's foot slipped in the surf. She screamed and fell. Phoenix being unable to see, tried to catch her, but he slipped and fell, trying to avoid landing on top of her. As a result, they were a tangle of arms and legs, sand, and surf by the time they stilled.

Trying to get his bearings, Phoenix said, "Bella! Are you hurt?" and she tapped his hand.

He realized he was partially on her and his hand was where it shouldn't be.

He quickly moved it, and said, "So sorry. Please, tell me that I didn't hurt you."

She said, "No, I am fine, are you okay? I am the one that slipped. Did we mess up your bandages?"

He found his footing, stood, and held out a hand to help her up, and said, "No. I'm fine. What did you slip on?"

She looked around and said, "It looks like seaweed rolled in with the surf. I watched where you stepped, and forgot about my own," and he chuckled.

Bella said, "We have sand all over us, do you want to wade out to at least our hips and rinse off?"

He said, "Please," and she led him to a place where there was no seaweed and they waded in.

She said, "If you stand there, I can rinse you off, but you probably need to take off that shirt. It is full of sand."

Phoenix removed his shirt and handed it to her. She tucked it into the pocket of her shorts and began to cup water and pour it over him until he looked sand free. She tried, well, kind of tried, not to stare at the face that she had dreamed of for years, or his golden muscular body that was slick and beautiful as water rivulets rained down.

She sure was glad that he could not see her staring, and said, "There you go. Now maybe you won't have a beach in the shower," and he smiled.

Then Phoenix said, "Come on, it's your turn, I can't let you go back covered in sand," and he drew her closer.

She didn't say anything as he scooped water over her until she wasn't gritty.

And then neither of them moved.

He said softly, "Bella…" and time paused as they faced each other, awareness rising with the waves.

She heard the huskiness in his voice and knew he wanted to kiss her. She smiled, knowing that he offered her time to move away. But she had waited years for his kiss.

He slid his hands up her arms, to her face, to her lips, and lowered his mouth to hers. Phoenix felt the desire flare as their lips connected and in seconds, he lifted her in his arms and deepened the kiss. Bella, unprepared for the sensations that surged through her, passionately wrapped her arms around him and didn't hold back.

Once again, they became entangled in the waves. This time on purpose.

He groaned as he lifted his lips, and whispered, "You taste so good," and kissed her again

Eventually, they separated and walked back to shore, this time, her hand in his. Bella rubbed her lips together and smiled. Phoenix was rocked.

When they arrived back to the house, she said, "After we shower, I can fix breakfast burritos, if you like," and they laughed as his stomach growled.

Before long, Bella plated burritos in the kitchen and said, "Breakfast is ready!" but when she turned to look for him, he was leaned against the wall staring her direction.

His demeanor screamed something was wrong.

She put the food down, and walked toward him and said, "What is it?"

"It's driving me crazy."

"What is?"

"Not being able to see you, and there is nothing I can do about it."

She understood, and asked, "But there is. Have you ever heard the term *reading someone?*"

"You mean by touch?"

"Exactly. Read me. I don't mind. A young woman, blind from Diabetes, read me a few years ago and it seemed to give her peace. So let your hands, and other senses, be your eyes for now."

He hugged her and said, "Oh Bella, thank you," and the eyes of his heart opened, and he slid his fingers into her hair.

Bella closed her eyes.

Phoenix stepped behind her and felt how long her hair was and spread it out across her back. Then he pulled it all back together, picked it up, and smelled it. He moved it aside and reached for her skin. Taking his time, he ran his hands down the back of her neck, across her shoulders, and down her arms, loving the feel of her. And then he held her waist in between both hands. He slowly slid his palms up her back, and back down again and cupped her hips. He knelt, then eased his hands lower, held her thighs, then felt all the way down her legs, and smiled.

He could see her. Maybe only in his mind, but he could still see her.

He said, "Turn for me. Please," and she turned to face him.

He laid his hands around her feet, and softly ran them up her legs until he reached the top of her thighs. An awareness groan built in him, but he restrained it as he slid his hands up her hips, across her stomach, and up to her waist. On bare skin now, it didn't take him long to feel her ribs. Then he removed his hands and stood.

Voice husky, he said, "You are...so perfect, and so beautiful. I can see you, Bella."

She made a tiny sound, and he knew the impact this had been for both of them. He cupped her cheeks and moved his fingertips, ever so gently, to read her face. Then lowered his lips to hers. Bella stood on tip toes, and her arms encircled his neck in response. He held her tighter, and they got lost in each other, all over again.

A few moments later, he said, "It's incredible. I know the touch of your skin, your smell, the texture of your hair, the feel of you, and even the taste of you."

Bella leaned against his chest, and he held her.

26

He said, "Thank you can never be enough."

Phoenix's phone rang and announced, "Ariel is calling."

Phoenix said, "You have got to be kidding me," and Bella giggled.

He ignored the phone and it repeated.

Bella said, "It could be important, and she will be worried."

***

Phoenix sighed and said, "Phone, answer," and then he said, "Hi Ariel, you have amazing timing."

Ariel said, "I work hard on that I have you know," and Bella laughed as she stepped back.

Ariel said, "How are your eyes?"

"They are already better. I am surprised. I was too stubborn for my own good not wearing the patches."

Ariel laughed and said, "What else is new?"

Phoenix chuckled and said, "So what's up today? Anything going on?"

"Do you remember the robot that you bought at the last Cattleman's Charity Banquet Auction?"

"I forgot about it. That was a month ago."

"Well, Fed Ex just delivered it to me for you."

"Well did you take it out and look at it?"

"I did and put it right back in the box. I swear the eyes followed me."

"Well, they probably did. It is supposed to be wi-fi, security and a host of other things all in one. You know, a robot."

She said, "Well, it can stay in the box until it goes home with you." Then she said, "Hey Bella!"

Bella said, "Hi Ariel! When will we see you again? Lucas might come up this weekend."

Ariel said, "Then I am not coming."

Surprised, Bella said, "Why not?"

Ariel said, "That would be too much testosterone in one room with Phoenix and Lucas. Like two bulls. I see enough bulls at the farm. Bossy critters," and Bella burst out laughing.

Phoenix laughed and said, "Who did I buy that robot from again?"

Ariel said, "It was a donation to the auction from some engineering group."

He said, "That's right. Can you bring it when you come back up to the ranch?"

She said, "Sure. Well, my phone is ringing, so I have to go."

***

That night, Bella put the finishing touches on dinner as the sun set.

She said, "Phoenix, dinner will be ready in ten minutes, and I have a surprise for you tonight."

He stepped into the den and said, "What kind of surprise?"

She said, "Have you heard of Dining in the Dark or Blackout Dining?"

"No, what is that?"

"I researched eating in the dark and found it. It is an actual dining experience. People literally go out to dine in the dark."

Incredulous, he said, "What in the world for?"

She laughed softly and said, "Wait, listen, apparently it is a way to enhance the dining experience of taste and texture without the distraction of sight. So, I need to set the table and turn the lights almost off. It will also allow me to experience what you do eating a meal in the dark."

"I don't want you to experience that, Bella," and he made his way closer to her.

She touched him to let him know where she was and said, "But I want to relate to you. I absolutely can't do total blackout however, because of my fear of the dark. I could end up with a panic attack. But I can get as close as possible."

He said, "You still have the PTSD attacks as an adult?"

Bella sighed and said, "Yes, but only a total blackout takes me over the edge. I usually have a light on, or a flashlight, or phone by me."

"I am so sorry. I had no idea. What about when Royce attacked you and you were in the closet at LSU?"

She said, "I did have an attack in there."

He hugged her and said, "That is terrible. But, if you went through all that, why did you come here to help me?"

She whispered, "I didn't want you to be all alone in the dark."

And boom. Just like that, he was in love.

He rubbed her back and said, "I would love to have dinner in the dark with you. How about music and dancing after?"

She laughed and said, "I might need to change if I spill all over myself."

Bella set the table and said, "Dinner is roasted ribeye bites, fried asparagus, fries, Texas toast, and for dessert, chocolate pudding with a cherry on top. Your coke is by your left hand and your dessert is by your right. Everything else is on the plate, including dipping sauce in a small bowl in the center."

Phoenix said, "You went to so much trouble. How very kind and creative of you. But I have one question. Won't we need a spoon to eat the pudding?"

"No, I think it calls for finger dipping in the spirit of things," and he laughed.

She said, "Do you want background music, or the waves?"

He said, "Waves, please," and she slid open the front window.

She lit a tiny candle in the den and turned the lights off. Everything was in deep shadows, but it wasn't a total black-out and she sat next to Phoenix.

He said, "Are you ok?"

"Yes, and I'm hungry too," and he chuckled.

After the blessing, they laughed, talked, and enjoyed the meal. He told her lots of stories about working at the zoo, the crew at the ranch, and college antics with him and Lucas.

After dessert, Phoenix said, "Do you want to put some music on and dance on the balcony?"

"Sure. Are you a good dancer?"

"I'll let you decide."

They got up to go outside and she turned a few lights back on and picked up her phone, and said, "What type of music do you want to dance to?"

"How about some slow country and western?"

Bella said, "Sure," and pulled up a playlist on Pandora. She hit play and led him to the balcony.

He said, "Would you describe for me what you see out here?"

"Sure. No one is out on the beach. The only light near us is moonlight. Our distant neighbors have patio lights on and maybe a BBQ pit going. I see lightning flashes way out in the Gulf of Mexico to the southwest, so we might have a storm later. But other than that, all I can see is lots of twinkly stars...and us."

He said, "Now that sounds beautiful. A beautiful background for dancing. Are you ready?" and she drew him to the middle of the deck.

He opened his arms and she stepped into them. They danced as one of Garth Brooks' ballads played, along with the sound of the waves.

As the song ended, he said, "You smell wonderful."

She said, "Thank you, but you smell really good yourself. You know, I was just remembering how much I wanted to dance with you when I was a teenager."

"What about now?"

With a smile he couldn't see, she said, "I never stopped wanting to."

"I like that answer, Bella."

He drew her against him, and she slid her arms around his neck.

"What about other relationships? Have you loved anyone?" he asked.

She sidestepped the question, and said softly, "I heard that there had been someone special for you a few years ago."

Phoenix didn't even flinch and said, "Yes, Monique and I were engaged for a good while. But after my dad died, our dreams and goals split us up. I left her behind in Dallas. It was the right thing to do because she wasn't the right one. It shouldn't have been that easy to let her go. But, back to you. You didn't answer my question."

She looked up at his face in the moonlight and said sincerely, "I don't know what to say. No one ever measured up to you."

He made a hungry sound in his throat and covered her mouth with his. Amazing crossed her mind. He kissed her just like he danced. Slow. Deep. And intimate.

The rest of the evening they danced the slow songs then called it a night.

***

Bella laid in her bed and looked at the nightlight displayed on the ceiling. But all she could think about was that she still felt Phoenix's arms around her. She still felt the way that he nuzzled her neck. She still felt his lips on hers.

Who was she fooling? She was in love with him. And probably always had been. It never was a crush.

***

Phoenix sat on the side of his bed and laid his eye patches on the night table. He looked up and saw the moonlight through the blinds. He walked

30

closer to the window and looked down at his hands. He saw individual fingers, still fuzzy, but not a solid mass anymore.

He smiled and whispered, "Thank you, God."

He figured by morning he would be able to see even more. How he wanted to see Bella look at him. He knew they were moving fast but he didn't care. They weren't kids. He was almost positive that she loved him. He just needed to see her eyes and he would know without the words.

Chapter 4
Deception

In south Houston, the man smiled.

His prepaid phone received the robot delivery notification from Federal Express. He had donated only a certificate for the robot to the Cattlemen's Charity Banquet & Auction. It had taken him much longer than he had expected to prepare the robot for a potential target. And as it turned out, Phoenix Chandler would be a perfect target.

A single man had many women guests. Now the fun would begin.

Chapter 5
The Storm

A phone notification woke Phoenix early the next morning. It was still dark in his room. He rolled over on his back and figured the ranch had messaged him since their morning started super early. Ranch life was long, but good hours, and he loved it. He didn't want to activate the verbal phone because he knew that Bella was still asleep.

He gazed at the dark ceiling and made plans for the day. He needed to discuss more about ranch activities with Bella so she would be aware of what type of cattle operation he had. As a veterinarian, Bella could grasp it all, as well as take care of all the health issues for the animals. It was sad that most veterinarians were choosing the in-town offices for pets these days. It was easily more profitable and less travel. But Bella's choice to work with the large farm and ranch animals meant everything. Her skill was priceless.

Another notification dinged on his phone, so he sat up.

It was quickly getting lighter in the room and he could see his phone on the night table. He picked it up and could see it so much better. When he tapped it to light up, he was amazed. Though he couldn't read the screen, he could see it much clearer.

He looked around the room. He could see drawer handles and even window shade rods to open the blinds. He looked at his hands and they were barely blurry.

He yelled, "Bella!"

In seconds, his door flew open, and she ran in the room in a short pink nightgown with her long black hair in a crooked ponytail.

Alarmed, Bella said, "What's wrong, Phoenix? What happened?"

Then she noticed his very appreciative expression as he ran his eyes over her and then back to her face, and she knew.

He laughed as she threw herself in his arms and said, "You can see!"

He wrapped his arms around her and tightened his hold as he kissed her shoulder.

Then the truth of it dawned on her, and still in his arms she said, "And you can see me barely dressed."

His warm lips moved to her cheek as he said softly, "I can. Not perfectly, mind you, but enough to say that I sure like that pink nightgown."

Bella wanted to say something, but his lips moved over hers and words didn't seem important anymore.

He drew her on his lap and for those few minutes they celebrated his good news.

***

Bella walked back in her bedroom and shut the door, then danced around silently. His eyes were healing great! She figured that by tomorrow morning his eyesight might be normal and then he was going to be on the hunt for her. It was just who he was as an alpha male, and a man that went after what he wanted. He wasn't the king of the ranch for nothing.

***

It didn't take either of them long to dress and meet in the kitchen. Phoenix was obediently back in his eye patches.

He rubbed his whisker stubble and said, "I haven't shaved in days. What do you think, should I let it stay or do you want to try a hand at shaving me?"

Bella said, "I am a great shaver I have you know. But that aside, I like the stubble beard on you, it gives you a rugged sexy look that fits you."

He said, "Well, that answered that. We'll leave it at sexy. So, what did you change into?"

"Since I figured that we would run again, I am in a bathing suit top and shorts."

"What color top?"

"I have on a psychedelic bikini top, like the 1960s."

He rubbed his face and said thoughtfully, "I'm imagining peace signs and lots of skin," and she laughed.

They jogged on the beach for about twenty minutes and then walked awhile to catch their breath.

After a minute, Phoenix said, "Kit texted me from the ranch that he found out how the bull got out of the pasture. A driver had run off the road and knocked down a fence post without telling anyone. Kit just fixed the post and that's that. GP will find a new bull."

"I am glad it was only an accident. How are the four sick animals?"

"The two cows are fine today and back in the pasture. They found a snakebite on the heifer's leg, and she is recovering. But the calf died. She was too young to fight the venom at three months old."

"I hate to hear that. Do you have a lot of trouble with snakebite as a rule?"

"No more so than all the other ranches. But, coyotes, at times, can be more of an issue."

Then they walked and talked as he filled her in on more ranch details.

***

Before they reached the beach house, Bella's phone rang and she said, "It's my roommate Lili," and she answered, "Hey Lili! How are you?"

Lili said, "I'm bored, and you are there having fun with handsome Phoenix."

Bella glanced at Phoenix, who was unaware they spoke of him, and said, "Lucky me. We just finished a jog on the beach and were headed back to the house."

Lili said, "Let me meet him. Put me on speaker."

Bella said, "Phoenix, Lili wants to meet you, do you mind if I put it on speaker? She's nosey though. Beware."

Phoenix chuckled, and after it was on speaker, said, "Hey Lili."

"Hi Phoenix! How are you doing with our Bella over there?"

"She's a dream come true."

Lili said, "I knew it," and Phoenix and Bella laughed.

Lili giggled and said, "It is nice to meet you, and how are your eyes?"

"I'm doing great. Bella has spoiled me."

"That's our Bella. So, what about romance? Anything sparking over there?" and Bella moaned.

Lili said, "Well, how do I know if I don't ask. Besides, I saw your picture, Phoenix, so I expected romance."

He chuckled and said, "And how did you see my picture?"

With a satisfied smile Lili said, "Bella showed me."

Exasperated, Bella said, "What is wrong with you, Lili?"

Phoenix grinned and enjoyed Lili's tell all, and said, "So Lili, do you know about the teenage crush too?"

Lili whispered, "I do. I know all about it."

Phoenix chuckled as he heard Bella gasp again, and he said, "I like you, Lili. You need to marry Lucas."

And the phone went silent.

Surprised, Bella said, "Lili? No come-back? No sass? No obnoxious spilling of secrets?"

Lili ignored Bella and said casually, "Phoenix, what made you bring up Lucas?"

Satisfied, Phoenix said, "I've heard Lucas mention your name a time or two. Do y'all have a thing going Lili?"

Lili said, "You are good with that shock tactic but I'm not telling you. Lucas is a hunk, but…"

Not understanding where this conversation came from or where it was going, Bella said, "And?"

Lili said, "And nothing. Nada. Change the subject."

Phoenix said, "Lili, face it, you and Lucas are perfect for each other. Why don't you come visit at the ranch sometime and Lucas can come over from Dallas?"

Lili said, "Someone's at the door. I'll talk to y'all later."

***

When the line went dead, Bella said, "What just happened? What in the world is going on with Lili and Lucas, and how come I didn't know?"

"Maybe because you're his sister?"

"That is no excuse. Lili doesn't keep secrets. And all she ever says about Lucas is—" and she stopped.

"What does she say?"

Thoughtfully, she said, "How good looking he is – and conceited. I always took their banter as joking not flirting."

He said, "It sounds like attraction to me, and he is conceited."

Bella said, "Seth, Lili and I have been roommates for almost three years. I am speechless about this secret."

Surprised, Phoenix said, "You have a man as a roommate?" and Bella laughed.

"Yes. He is handsome, intelligent, and very protective."

"Did you date?"

"A few times at the beginning."

When she didn't explain, Phoenix said dryly, "And?"

"It felt like I went out with my brother," and Phoenix laughed.

She said, "He has three sisters, and Lili is his cousin. Lucas gives him orders to protect me. He even hit Royce in the face at the police station."

"I think I like Seth."

Bella said, "You guys kill me," and he chuckled.

"Seth and Lili are from Texas too," she said. "They will stay in Baton Rouge until our lease is up and bring my moving boxes to me in a few weeks. Lili is also a veterinarian and Seth is an aeronautical engineer with a new job at NASA."

"Wow, you had some big brains in that apartment."

She said, "You know, it would be cool to introduce Seth and Ariel, being they are both in Houston and would make a beautiful couple."

"Well, Bella. I like the way you think. Among a million other things," and he stepped closer to her.

***

Phoenix's phone rang and he sighed, and said, "Phone, answer," and said, "Hey Lucas, you are on speaker."

Lucas said, "Hey Bella and Phoenix, give me some good news. How are your eyes?"

"My vision is almost clear. Hopefully by tomorrow I will be back to normal."

Lucas whistled and said, "It is unreal how fast it cleared."

"True! I hope to be back at the ranch in a couple of days at the most."

Lucas said, "I hear seagulls, are you outside?"

Bella said, "We just finished a jog on the beach. He holds my shoulder to guide himself. We only fell once, and it was my fault."

Lucas chuckled and said, "What happened?"

Bella said, "I watched his feet and forgot about mine."

Lucas laughed and said, "I would love to have that on video."

Bella said, "You would! Hey, I have a question for you, Lucas. Do you and Lili have a thing?"

Lucas was quiet for a second which told her a lot and then he said, "Why?"

Bella said, "Oh, nothing. Just something that was said. But you know that she will move back to Texas soon. Maybe you should get out of Dallas more."

Lucas said, "Hey Phoenix, is my baby sister giving me love advice?"

"It sounds like it. It also sounds like good advice."

Bella said, "Lucas, I'm going to work for Phoenix on the ranch."

Lucas said, "I always figured that you would end up at Chandler Canyon Ranch. You both love the same things," and Phoenix slid his arm around Bella's waist.

Phoenix said, "It's going to be great for both of us."

With a grin, Lucas said, "Are you sure that we are still talking about just the ranch?"

Phoenix said without explanation, "No, we are not."

Lucas did a fist pump, then said, "Ok then."

Before long the call ended, and Bella led the way back to the beach house.

***

Around eleven that night, a storm raged outside. Bella finally turned off their audio mystery because it was difficult to hear and went to the kitchen to fix them a coke.

Phoenix took off his eye patches and laid them on the side table. It was time. He opened his eyes. His vision was normal.

With a grin, he headed straight to Bella in the kitchen. Walking up behind her he made sure not to miss one detail. She was dressed in well fitted, well worn, blue jean cutoffs. Her black top was short and tight. Her black hair was glorious and wild in a haphazard ponytail. Her long, beautiful legs were golden, and she was barefoot.

Bella heard his footsteps approach and said, "Would you like a snack too?" and his arms slid around her waist as he lowered his warm lips to her neck.

38

She dropped the glass of ice in surprise, and he whispered in her ear, "I can see you."

She spun in his arms, and they were face to face.

Phoenix's smoking gaze touched every nuance of her face.

He said, "You are literally the most beautiful woman I have ever seen," and he slid his hands to frame her face.

Her light blue eyes were surrounded by thick black lashes. Her cheeks were flushed, and her moist pink lips were parted in surprise. He pressed in against her.

She gasped, and he saw the love and passion that filled her eyes.

Breathless, Bella said, "Phoenix…"

His blue eyes were locked on her, intense and hungry as he drank her in. His lips parted and lowered to hers. He groaned at her response, her sounds, and her taste as she yielded.

He picked her up and carried her to the sofa.

After several minutes of caress-filled kisses, Phoenix paused and ran a hand through his hair as he looked down at Bella. She was gorgeous, well kissed, lying across his lap, and every muscle in his body felt her.

Bella read his expression. She returned his gaze with a smile that only a woman in love shares. She too checked him out with eyes full of mystery, and future promise.

Phoenix released her ponytail and her fabulous black hair fell all around her.

He touched her cheek, and said, "I am in love with you. I want, and need, you in my life. Forever. Marry me, Bella."

Her radiant smile answered him before her words, then she said, "Yes, Phoenix. Yes! I have always loved you. I want to be with you. Only you."

Their lips met with love as wild as the storm outside.

A few minutes later, Phoenix said, "When?"

Bella knew they needed a fast engagement with the speed they were going, and said, "How about seven weeks? July 4."

He drawled, "How about next week?"

She kissed him softly, and said, "I want at least a little fiancé time with you. Romance me. Take me parking. Work with me on the ranch. Share with me who you are as a cattle rancher and show me what our new life will be."

He nodded and said, "You are right. I don't mean to come after you like a bull. I know we need a little time," and she smiled.

He continued, "So, July 4 it is. Where would you like to get married?"

Bella thought for a minute and said, "I like what you told me about your new enclosed pool and patio. How about there?"

"I like that. And the honeymoon?"

She whispered, "Anywhere with you will be perfect," and kissed him.

They talked till the early morning hours and fell asleep together on the sofa. The storm still raged outside.

Sometime later, a bolt of lightning hit close by and shook the house. Startled, they sat up.

Bella gazed into the now completely dark room, and said, "Where are the lights?"

He said, "The power must be out," and too late, remembered her fear as trembling wracked her body. Concerned, he pulled her on his lap and said, "Bella, talk to me. Are you ok? What can I do?"

She didn't answer so he wrapped his arms around her. And she screamed and fought to get free.

He realized she was already in the panic attack and removed his arms, and called to his phone, "Phone, turn on flashlight," and a light beam shot to the ceiling.

He grabbed it and tried to show her the light, but she was beyond comfort. Then using the flashlight, and not restricting her, he half carried, half led her to the shower and tub. Once the water was warm, he drew her in. As the shower rained softly down on them, he coaxed her against him, talked to her and rubbed her back.

In seconds, the trembling eased off. Bella felt her body begin to relax. She laid her head against his chest, exhausted.

Phoenix turned off the shower and drew her down to rest on him in the big tub. He held her in the warm water, kissed her head, whispered prayers, and words of love.

Phoenix knew that trauma left all kinds of scars. Some that you can see and some like this that are triggered by various things. He would have to make sure the ranch was a safe haven for her.

Bella said softly, "I'm sorry."

"There is nothing to be sorry for, besides, you've been there for me in the dark, can't I be there for you?" and she kissed him, too in love for words.

Phoenix said, "This one came on fast. You would not have had much time to get to light."

"I usually have a small flashlight or my phone on me, solar lights around me, and battery backup, so I rarely get in total darkness. It really doesn't happen often. I almost got caught one night in my car when the battery was dead."

He said, "I see. We'll have to provide all that at the ranch, so you don't get in a bind. Out there it is pitch black at night. Especially if it is cloudy and the moon is hidden. How long does an attack take for you to get on the other side of it?"

"Five minutes or more."

"Would you be willing to work with me and see if we can try a few things that might help?"

"Ok."

In a few minutes, they curled up on his bed with the flashlight and slept.

Chapter 6
Engaged

Bella stirred and rolled over. When she opened her eyes, the sun was up, and Phoenix was watching her. She smiled.

He responded with a sexy grin and pulled her into his arms. "I love waking up to you in the morning."

She whispered, "I love you waking up to me too."

At her words, he kissed her deep, and sensual, caressing her back and pulling her against him. In moments, with a sigh, and still hungry eyes, he lifted his lips and looked at her.

Aware of his restraint, Bella kissed his cheek and slid over and gracefully got out on her side of the bed.

Phoenix rolled onto his back and moaned. It was going to be the longest seven weeks in the history of time.

Then he grinned. A delicious seven weeks.

A little later, Phoenix was in the kitchen dressed for their run when Bella came down the hall. She was dressed in running shorts and a red bikini top.

He winked and said, "Ah, the rewards of being able to see again," and handed her a cup of coffee.

She grinned and took a quick sip of the hot coffee, then said, "It had to be hard on you. I know reading me physically seemed to help you."

"Yes. But you did so much more than let me see you. Your gift of giving is truly remarkable. In fact, I would love you to read me physically sometime. It is indescribable."

She said, "I would love to do that."

He took her coffee cup and put it down, and said, "So, hey, are you ready to run now? I have energy waiting to be burned," and she laughed as he pulled her down the stairs, across the sand, and warmed up like he was a boxer.

And even as they jogged, he ran forwards, backwards, around her, through the water, carried her a good part of the time, and kissed her often.

Bella laughed and said, "You have amazing energy."

He said, "Remember that!" and winked.

An hour or so later, they walked back to the beach house, and he said, "Now that I am back to normal, I have a few thoughts in mind about today. What if we leave and head to Houston so I can run a few errands? Then we can spend the night with Ariel and go out to eat. You have been cooking for me for days."

"I enjoyed fixing meals for us, but that sounds fun, and I would love to get to visit with Ariel."

He said, "Let me check with Ariel first, but if she has room, maybe Lili and Seth could drive over."

Bella grinned, and said, "That is obvious, but brilliant, to get Seth and Ariel to meet."

"I'll probably call Lucas too, but don't tell Lili," he said.

"I won't say a word."

"I already have time off from the ranch," he said, "So I figured we could at least enjoy ourselves going back. We will both be busy once we get home."

When they got inside, Phoenix called Ariel in Houston.

***

Ariel laughed as she answered, "Hi Phoenix, I was just about to call you. How is your vision today?"

"You're on speaker - and I am back to normal and running all over the beach with Bella."

Ariel screamed in excitement, and he laughed, before saying, "But I need a favor."

She said, "Name it!"

He winked at his fellow conspirator, and said, "Would you like some overnight company?"

Ariel said, "Are you kidding me? Yes! I can't believe that you aren't running back to the ranch like a wild man. You are really going to come to my house?"

43

Phoenix chuckled and said, "I know, miracles happen every day," and then said, "Would you have room to put up Bella's roommates from LSU? They just graduated too and are waiting to move back to Texas. One will even live in Houston."

Ariel said, "Of course!"

"I will treat us all to dinner somewhere."

Ariel got quiet and said, "What are you up to? This is so out of the ordinary."

Phoenix said, "I am just celebrating being able to see again and reward Bella for a job well done."

"Ok. What time will you be here?"

"I have some errands to run in Houston, so maybe, late afternoon about four?"

She said, "Perfect! And bring the creepy robot home with you."

***

Once Ariel was set, Bella called Lili in Baton Rouge.

Lili said, "Hey Bella, we miss you."

Bella said, "Put me on speaker if Seth is there – and I am glad that you miss me! I even have a solution for it."

"What's that?"

"Phoenix got his sight back last night," and Ariel whooped and clapped.

Then Seth said, "What are you celebrating?"

Bella said, "Morning, Seth! I miss you!"

Seth said, "Don't lie to me, I know you too well. You are there with your crush," and Bella and Lili laughed.

Lili said to Seth, "Phoenix got his sight back!"

Seth smiled and said, "Alright! That is awesome! I know it had to be tough on him. I hate to even think about that type of injury."

Bella said, "Well, to reward me for helping him, we are heading to stay at his sister's house in Houston. We want both of you to come. You can stay overnight so we can all go out and eat to celebrate."

Lili screamed in excitement and said, "Absolutely, yes! What time?"

"Can you make it by five p.m.?"

Seth said, "No problem, you are talking to Texas drivers, remember?"

***

Phoenix picked up his phone and made the last call to set the plan into motion.

Lucas answered, "Hey man! I wondered how your eyes were doing today."

Phoenix said, "I was able to see Bella's gorgeous face last night," and Lucas hollered like he was at a Dallas football game.

Lucas said, "That is terrific! That was one freaky burn accident. So, tell me, didn't Bella grow up to be shockingly beautiful?"

"You could have given me a heads up when she wasn't a minor anymore."

"Nope, she was busy. Now was the right time."

Phoenix looked across the room at Bella rubbing lotion on her legs and said, "Yes, it is. But on another note, I have a secret invitation for you. This is my way to say thank you. We are leaving the beach for a night in Houston and will stay at Ariel's place. She has lots of room, so we invited Bella's roommates to come overnight. They will arrive about five p.m., and we plan to go out to eat. Need I say more?"

Lucas said, "Thank you received. You are the man. I will be there. Text me directions. So, I get to surprise Lili?"

Phoenix said, "She hasn't a clue. See you tonight."

***

When Phoenix hung up the phone, Bella said, "Is he coming?"

Phoenix chuckled and said, "Oh yeah, he's coming."

They packed, called the landlord for the beach house, and headed to Houston in Bella's mustang.

Bella looked at him in the driver's seat and said, "Your legs barely fit."

"You have a point there, but I can manage."

"So, what errands do you have to run in Houston?"

He said, "I have a couple of packages to pick-up. Do you want to go anywhere?"

"No, I have all I need," and winked at him.

He drawled, "You bet you do."

Later, sitting at a red light outside of Houston, Phoenix glanced at Bella as she checked messages on her phone. It had been twelve hours since his vision

45

had cleared, and he just couldn't get enough of looking at her. He didn't think he ever would.

Her long hair was loose today. Gorgeous and sexy. Her mostly silver, light blue eyes made him feel like she could see right through him. She licked her lips as she read.

He opened his mouth in response to her as he remembered the fire it was to kiss her. It was like every single kiss was only a beginning for the next one. He grinned. She had totally wasted her time putting on lipstick today. It wouldn't last long.

Then he looked at her body. He loved her in the turquoise dress. Backless. Short. And the silk of it slid along her body the way his hands itched to. He smiled to himself. She looked perfect to go pick out her engagement ring.

***

Bella put her phone away and glanced over at Phoenix. He was occupied as he maneuvered in Houston's crazy traffic. She took in his windblown hair style with rakish bangs that shouted bad boy sexy, melt in your mouth good looking, and alpha male, all in one. Yum. His blue eyes were the coolest hot she had ever seen. His well-defined lips made her squirm a bit remembering just how well he used them. She lowered her gaze to his black fitted shirt and on to his tight jeans.

He caught her looking.

She blew him a kiss.

He laughed and took the next right and parked. She felt the heat of his look as he got out of the car. He walked to her door and offered her his hand. He smiled at the look in her eyes, and she stood.

His mouth met hers in a barely controlled kiss. He dipped, as he kissed her, lower and lower. Cars honked, and passers-by yelled encouragement.

When they got back in the car, he said, "It's just the beginning."

An hour later, Phoenix pulled into Inter-Continental Jewelers parking lot. Surprised, Bella looked at him.

He kissed her hand and said, "You need an engagement ring on your finger, and we need wedding bands."

She screamed softly and reached for him.

When they walked out of the jewelers, her engagement ring was on her hand, and the wedding bands would be sized and mailed to the ranch. A little while later, they left the mall with new clothes for tonight.

As he started the car, Bella said, "I dreamed of this day you know. With you."

He said, "What was it about me, when you were sixteen, that made such a lasting effect all these years?"

She said, "The first time you came to our house with Lucas, you danced with my grandmother in the kitchen, you put your arm around my grandfather, you jostled with Lucas, you petted the cat, and you looked into my eyes and said—".

And suddenly, aware of what she remembered, Lucas finished by saying, "Be sure to wait for the right man to love you," and she smiled.

He slid his hand behind her neck, then drew her mouth to his.

They pulled up to Ariel's house a few minutes to four p.m.

Phoenix whispered in her ear as he rang the doorbell, "We need to go lingerie shopping."

Bella whispered in response, "I wasn't planning on wearing anything," and he got that visual as the door opened.

Ariel laughed at Phoenix's heated expression, and said, "You're so hooked."

Bella winked at Phoenix, and he kissed her as they walked in.

Ariel said, "When's the date?"

"July 4."

Ariel glanced at Bella's hand and smiled, then hugged them.

She showed them around her contemporary, two-story home and said, "What time are your roommates coming?"

"I think they plan to arrive about five p.m."

"I can't wait to meet them. Give me a little intro information."

Bella said, "Lili is a veterinarian too. She has long, beautiful curls, blue eyes and is awesome and sassy. You will love her. And Seth, now Seth is an aeronautical engineer that just hired on at NASA. He is handsome with long blonde hair and dark eyes, intelligent, and very witty."

Impressed, Ariel said, "You had a male roommate."

Bella said, "Well, he is Lili's cousin, and watched us like a hawk."

"Interesting," Ariel said.

Phoenix glanced at Bella, enjoying their secret couple setup plan, and said, "We want to have dinner somewhere fun and romantic, with dancing."

Shocked, Ariel said, "You never think of fun! Wow. It's been great for you to get off the ranch – minus the eye patches of course."

Then she showed them to their rooms, and they changed for an evening on the town.

Bella had just finished dressing when Phoenix knocked, and said, "Are you dressed?"

"Sure. Come on in."

She smiled as he walked in, dressed to kill in black slacks and a blue shirt. His cologne wafted in with him, and Bella closed her eyes and breathed it in.

When she opened them, he was in front of her. To avoid messing up her makeup, he leaned over and kissed up her neck, then her ear, with hot lips.

He smiled when he heard her whisper his name. He looked at her, and knew passion flickered in both their eyes. Then he held her hand and spun her around for a personal viewing.

Bella watched as he took in her evening makeup, loose hair, short white ruffled skirt, pink glitter top, and tall sandals.

Voice husky, he said, "You. Make. Me. Sweat," and she felt every word.

Ariel looked up and watched them come downstairs and said, "Wow. You're going to turn some heads tonight."

Bella said, "Look who's talking! You look amazing, Ariel. You must have someone or something special that you are waiting for, to still be single."

Ariel laughed and posed, gorgeous in a little black dress and stilettos with her platinum pixie haircut and vibrant green eyes.

Then the doorbell rang, and she headed to welcome their guests.

She smiled when she saw the tall handsome blonde man, and beautiful woman with fabulous curls, and said, "You must be Seth and Lili, please come in."

Lili spoke first and said, "Hello, Ariel. Wow! You are beautiful! And thank you so much for having us. We are excited to be here."

Ariel said, "Thanks, and you look beautiful yourself. Blue eyes and all those long curls, surely the men trail after you?"

Lili made a face and said, "All but the one that I am interested in."

Ariel drawled, "Well, what's wrong with him?"

Lili said, "He works too much."

Ariel drawled, "Well, be sure and make time-off worth his while!" and Seth chuckled. Ariel glanced up at Seth with a flirty look and waited.

He didn't disappoint and said, "Surely, a woman as fabulous as you would have only known direct pursuit."

She smiled and gave him a side glance and said, "I have heard all sorts of wonderful things about you Seth, are they true?"

Seth leaned down to whisper, "They may have only mentioned a few of my more dashing traits, but there are many more."

Ariel finally laughed, and he smiled, then offered her his arm.

Bella and Phoenix had watched it all and smiled at each other.

Bingo.

The five of them were visiting when the doorbell rang again.

Ariel said, "Were you expecting anyone else, Phoenix?" and he nodded yes.

She went to the door and was surprised to see Bella's brother.

Ariel said, "Lucas! I am shocked! I didn't realize that you ever left Dallas," and Lucas laughed.

Bella watched Lili's expression when she realized that Lucas was here. Wow, there it was. How had she ever missed the attraction between Lucas and Lili?

Phoenix and Bella glanced at each other with a smile. Their plan had worked. There were now three couples.

Lucas greeted everyone, but saved Lili for last, and pulled her aside.

***

Lucas kissed Lili soft and warm on both cheeks, Italian style, and said, "Congratulations Dr. Lili. It is great to see you."

Lili looked at the gorgeous man in front of her, and quipped, "Why would seeing me matter at all to you?"

Trying to break the ice that had frozen around their relationship, he said, "Because it is true. I might even need your medical care tonight."

Rolling her eyes, she said, "So which animal are you since I am a vet?"

He stepped well into her personal space and said, "A bull would do," and she tried not to smile, but couldn't help it.

Now in the door so-to-speak, Lucas said softly, "I needed to see you," and trailed a finger down her neck as they looked at each other.

Lucas saw the flash of hurt and anger in her eyes, and whispered near her ear, "Forgive me, I know I let work interfere with my plans to visit you in Louisiana."

She said, "I'll consider it. And you know, now that I think about it, it's amazing how you even got time off work to come to Houston tonight."

He nodded and said, "It is. I traded for it because I've decided that I need more important things in my life than work."

"When did that revelation happen?" she said.

"Today, when I found out that you were on your way to Houston."

***

Then Phoenix interrupted everyone and said, "Hey everybody, I have an announcement to make! First, I want to announce that Dr. Bella DelCaprio has joined Chandler Canyon Ranch as vet extraordinaire, effective immediately," and everyone cheered.

Phoenix continued with a smile, "And secondly, but most importantly, she has agreed to marry me in July," and kissed her.

It got loud in the room.

At five thirty p.m., they all rode in Seth's large SUV and headed to the Taste of Texas off Katy Freeway. The men ordered steaks, the women ordered seafood, and the meal was delicious.

When it came time for dessert, Phoenix pulled Bella's chair close to him. He fed her chocolate dipped strawberries as he slid a hand along her bare leg. Bella flirted as tingles followed his hands. He smiled, knowing his effect on her and watched her bite the juicy berries.

Teasingly.

She was so sexy.

***

Ariel watched her brother and Bella flirt and smiled. She had never seen him so happy.

She glanced at Seth, and he watched her with a grin.

She gave him sassy eyes, and said, "Don't think that you can feed me strawberries like that tonight."

"What about tomorrow night?"

"Ah, so, you think there will be another time?"

"Absolutely."

***

Lili was totally aware of Lucas beside her. He constantly bumped her, leaned on her, and even rubbed her. She glanced at him like he was a misbehaving toddler, and he winked.

After dessert, she laid her hand on her leg and in seconds, Lucas entwined their fingers and held fast at her tug.

He whispered close to her ear, "I want to touch you."

They gazed intently at each other, and she nodded.

***

Then they all headed to Proof Rooftop Lounge in mid-town Houston for dancing.

Phoenix loved every minute of this time with Bella as they danced and laughed. She could move and knew it. They did some heavy flirting on the dance floor, and he made sure the slow dances were hot and memorable. This was their engagement celebration after all.

Bella matched Phoenix's steps and teased him as they touched and wiggled. She loved seeing him relaxed and playful - and smoking hot.

***

Seth ran one finger over Ariel's hand and said, "Hey, beautiful, I dare you to come show me some of your dance moves."

She laughed and stood.

He led her to the dance floor and didn't miss one single move that she made. And she knew it.

When the fast song ended, a slow one began. Seth slipped his hand around her waist and drew her against him. Ariel looked into Seth's eyes. Both were aware of their attraction.

She slid her hands up to his shoulders and he pulled her tighter.

***

Lucas leaned over and said, "Come on, dance with me, Lili. We have always wanted to dance."

Lili felt the wall she had put up for protection against him, crack open. She glanced at him with a softer look - that still warned - and stood.

He drew her to the dance floor and lifted her arms around his neck. He pulled her in until their bodies met and began to dance slow, but hotter with each step they took. Their bodies connected perfectly together.

He felt when she yielded.

Then he drew her head to his chest.

He said, "I've missed you, Lili."

"You couldn't have."

Lucas lifted her chin and kissed her with a groan of longing. She responded, then tightened her arms around his neck. He deepened the kiss.

***

Phoenix said, "Romance was on the menu tonight."

Bella said, "Multiple helpings I would say!"

Chapter 7
Royce, Baton Rouge

He sat in the dark.

He had a lot to think about.

His court date for the attack on Bella was next week here in Baton Rouge. His lawyer didn't seem to think much of a sentence would be imposed. He chuckled and thought, if they only knew what he had planned for her that day, they wouldn't be so quick to dismiss him.

He had felt the urge to watch life ebb for years. He had been about to taste it with Bella when she almost cracked his skull open. The arrest cost him his job. And his apartment and vehicle eventually, without a job. None of that had been in his plan.

But today changed everything.

He overheard a conversation between Seth and Lili in a convenience store, of all places. They were on their way to meet up with Bella in Texas. She was with some guy named Phoenix Chandler.

Royce crossed his legs and contemplated his future. In less than an hour, his decision was made. Once court was over, and he was free, he would head to Texas and find Bella. He would make her pay - and bleed. He felt better already.

Chapter 8
The Robot

A riel smiled as she headed to the kitchen the next morning to make coffee for her guests. They had returned home late last night. She had a great time with all of them, especially Seth. Besides his charm and wit, she loved his tousled long blonde hair and dark eyes. He most definitely had the, I just got out of bed sexy look, down pat.

She rounded the corner into the kitchen and stopped. Seth was leaned against the kitchen counter and blew on a steaming cup of coffee.

She raised her eyebrows and said, "I see you found your way around."

He smiled as he set his cup down and walked toward her.

He said, "I couldn't sleep."

She said, "You weren't comfortable?"

"That wasn't the reason. I just couldn't stop thinking about, this…" and he kissed her.

Seth wanted to unforgettably imprint himself on her, but mostly, he wanted her lips under his.

After a long moment of tasting each other, Ariel rubbed her lips together, and said, "You sure took a long shot this morning, handsome. No one else has survived that assumption."

Seth brushed his fingers along her cheek, and said, "Some odds are worth it," and she pulled him back down for another kiss.

A few moments later, Ariel heard a laugh, and turned to see Phoenix and Bella with satisfied smiles.

Ariel narrowed her eyes at her brother, and said, "You planned this meet, didn't you?"

Seth laughed and looked at his roommate, Bella, and said, "Did you really do that?"

Bella said, "We're guilty, and you better be glad. That kiss looked worth it."

Seth smiled at Ariel in agreement, then glanced upstairs, and said, "Where is Lili?"

Bella said, "She will be downstairs in a little while. She looked busy."

***

Lucas tapped on the bedroom door, and said softly, "Lili."

Lili stood on the other side of the door and sighed. If she let him in, he would presume she was willing to let him in personally as well. Was she? Maybe. Could she trust him? Well, it was time to find out.

She opened the door.

Lucas said, "Lili. Please, may I come in?"

Dozens of butterflies took flight in her stomach as she looked at him. He was so good looking. Dreamy. Sexy. And the look in his eyes didn't help.

He watched her. She was so beautiful. He had been such a fool. She motioned him in.

Lucas stepped in and shut the door. He knew that she had just given him the opening he hoped for.

He said, "Can we talk?"

She nodded and led him to the bench by the window.

Jumping in the fire, Lucas said, "I know that it has been a long year since we began to talk and text each other. Our relationship—" and she turned her head away from him and looked out the window in obvious disagreement of his use of the word relationship.

Remorseful, he looked at the beautiful, intelligent, wounded woman in front of him and continued, "Our relationship is real, Lili. I never considered it was anything else. We talked of real things, real feelings, and real dreams between us. I wanted to be with you, touch you, hold you, kiss you, and talk face-to-face. I wanted more than long distance between us."

She looked back at him without comment.

He admitted, "I should have told you that I hadn't been able to schedule time off. As a Lieutenant firefighter, I had to cover other staff regularly and a fourteen-hour road trip didn't fit in. Once I realized it wasn't going to get any better, I should have told you. I never dreamed that I left you with the impression it was all a game. I thought we could make it till you graduated and moved back to Texas. But you called my hand and cut me off without a word."

Lili, clear and direct, said, "Your cancellation of trips, time after time, spoke loud and clear. Avoidance screamed that you were leading me on to nowhere. I would have understood why you couldn't leave Dallas if you would have been upfront about your situation."

He loved her, and pleaded as he said, "But can you, will you, understand the truth now?"

Not thoroughly convinced that was the only reason he kept distance between them, she said, "How did you trade to get off work now, if it was always impossible before?"

He entwined his fingers with hers and said, "I told my chief he could have my resignation if he didn't make it happen."

Lili was shocked and didn't know whether to smile, or cry, with relief.

But Lucas saw the answer in her eyes, and said, "I love you, Lili. I have for a long, long, time. I just couldn't wait anymore."

Then he kissed her, and let his lips dispel any doubt that remained.

After a few moments, he said, "Put me out of my misery, Lili, say it."

She whispered, "I have loved you since the night you sang to me over the phone."

***

Phoenix looked in Ariel's refrigerator and said, "This is pitiful. I know that you can afford to grocery shop."

Ariel sassed, "I don't eat enough to grocery shop," and Bella laughed, totally understanding.

Seth drawled, "I like to grocery shop, as well as cook."

Ariel looked at him in surprise and said, "Remind me of that when you move to Houston."

Seth smiled and said, "Speaking of moving, I thought about staying in Houston a while longer to find a place. Would you be free to show me around?"

Phoenix and Bella walked away to give Seth and Ariel privacy to talk.

***

Surprised at Seth's presumptive comment, Ariel said, "And just like that, you think I'm so easy that you can just step into a relationship with me?"

Seth calmly said, "No, Ariel, I didn't insinuate that at all. I insinuated that you are worth any, and all effort to build a relationship," and he watched the truth cool her temper.

She whispered, "You're really something, Seth."

He shook his head no, and said, "It's all you, Ariel. You do things to me. I like that."

She said, "Those are strong words, but why don't we ease up and let me help you find a place, and we can get to know each other. And in a very platonic offer, if you need a place to stay until you find one, you are welcome here. Then you can take me grocery shopping and cook too."

Seth said, "That's a deal I won't pass up."

***

Phoenix and Bella put their overnight bags in her mustang.

She said, "How do your eyes feel? Don't you think the drive to the ranch is too much eye strain so soon? I love to drive so why don't we take turns?"

He smiled and said, "Excellent idea. Oh, and I seem to recall that you mentioned "making out or parking" should be a part of our engagement. We can work on that on the way home too."

"Once an hour good for you?" and his lips answered her.

***

A few minutes later, Phoenix and Bella walked back inside and saw that Lucas and Lili were headed downstairs. It was obvious that whatever had been wrong between them was long gone.

Bella had never seen that look on her brother's face, as he smiled at Lili. She thought, they aren't having "a" thing, they are having "the" thing. They were in love and obviously had been for a while.

Bella glanced at Phoenix, and he winked. She realized that he had known all along. Then Seth and Ariel stepped into the room to join them.

Lucas started first and said, "Lili and I have been in a long-distance relationship for a year. I almost messed up and waited too long. But I have decided to search for a firefighter's job in Wichita Falls where Lili plans to settle." Then he put his arm around her and said, "She also promised to marry me."

After congratulations died down, Lili asked, "Seth, what are your plans?"

He said, "I think that I will stay here in Houston, and Ariel said she would help me find a place. We don't have to move out of the apartment in Baton Rouge for two weeks, so I have a little time to find a place here. What about you, Lili? Do you plan to go back to Baton Rouge?"

She smiled, and glanced at Lucas, and said, "No. It looks like I will stay in Dallas for a week and then head to Wichita Falls. I need to find a home myself and get ready to start my new job at the animal hospital."

An hour later, Lucas and Lili left Houston headed north to Dallas.

Phoenix and Bella prepared to leave for the ranch, when Ariel said, "Oh wait Phoenix, you need to get your robot."

Seth said, "Really. You bought a robot?"

Phoenix said, "It was from a charity auction and my bid won it. It is supposed to be an artificial intelligence assistant. I only received a certificate and picture. The company shipped it here to Ariel since she handles the advertising, publications, and social media for the ranch."

Seth said, "I am impressed. As an engineer, I have seen my share of robotics. I would like to check it out if you have a minute before you leave."

Ariel pushed a cart into the room that carried a large box, and said, "This robot does all sorts of things, but it has creepy eyes. I sealed it back up in the box. I don't like it."

Phoenix chuckled and opened the box. He lifted out an impressive black robot and sat it on the ottoman. The robot was almost three foot tall and about eighteen inches wide but heavy. It had a round head with an LED face, and speakers where the ears would be on a human. Its body was shaped like a torso with various compartments, and it was mounted to legs whose feet were a base with wheels. It had short arms with hands made of clasp type fingers.

Seth knelt in front of it and looked it over with interest.

Phoenix knelt by Seth and said, "Have you seen one like this before?"

Seth said, "This robot was rebuilt and modified. It is actually multiple robots in one with quality artificial intelligence features. Why would someone go to all that work to donate it? That seems odd."

Ariel handed Phoenix the paperwork, and the guys looked over the features, as Phoenix read off, "Face and voice recognition, security program, able to control smart household devices, keeps calendars and provides reminders, is a video and a camera, and to top it off, it can literally read your text, emails and check your phone messages. It works the internet and can make interpretations based on your preferences and has visual interaction."

Ariel said, "Visual interaction - see, I told you his eyes were creepy."

Seth grinned and continued, "It does a little bit of everything. He most definitely can charge your phone too," and they laughed.

Phoenix said, "So, do you put it in a closet until you need it, or leave it out to assist the household?"

Seth said, "It is built to assist and learn what you prefer. You tell it what you want and that's its goal."

Bella said, "So, how do you turn it on? I don't see a power button."

Ariel said, "I was taking it out of the box, when it came on and scared me half to death."

Phoenix said, "Had you said anything at the time?"

Ariel thought for a minute and said, "I had just talked to myself about how to power it up."

Then they were all startled as the robot powered up on the ottoman.

Phoenix laughed and said, "Power down," and it shut down.

He said, "We'll just leave it off till we get to the ranch. Is there a phone number in the paperwork to call anyone with questions?"

Seth said, "All I see is an email address to customer service."

Phoenix said, "Let me check something. Power up," and the robot turned on.

In a few seconds bright blue eyes opened on the face screen.

"Robot, what is your name?"

A male voice responded, "My name is Troy."

Phoenix said, "Power down. Well at least we know who he is."

Chapter 9
Going Home

Phoenix and Bella headed north out of Houston on Interstate 45 toward Alma, Texas. Then they would veer northwest on Highway 287 to Wichita Falls. The ranch would be about forty minutes east of there, near the Wichita River and Burnett Park.

Bella said, "How long does the trip to the ranch usually take?"

"Over six hours, plus stops. We will get home after dark."

She grinned and said, "Home. I'm thrilled. Beyond thrilled to finally see the ranch. I've heard Lucas talk about it for years. And then all that you have told me is amazing."

Phoenix smiled and said, "Plus, I have a small barn with an office apartment upstairs that will literally have your name on it. The foremen used it when we had more full-time cowhands on the ranch. But I think it will work great for your vet clinic and animal shelter."

"That sounds perfect! Oh, I haven't told you that I applied for my Texas veterinarian license and have my Authority to Practice letters. My license will be mailed to Lucas' address, so I am completely legal to practice immediately."

"That is great news, Bella, we need you. How long do you project that it will take you to get set up with medication, supplies, and equipment?"

"If you show me around tomorrow, I can run to Wichita Falls or Dallas to get what I need. As we know, most of my work will be done in the barn or in the pasture anyway."

She took a notebook out of her purse and said, "Would you give me specific livestock and animal information? And anything else that I need to know to get things ordered?"

Phoenix said, "We are running a little over five hundred head of Angus cattle and are at the end of calving season now. We have eight Mustang horses, two Great Pyrenees guardian dogs, four Australian herding dogs, and dozens of stray cats in the barns."

She said, "You do both natural breeding and artificial insemination, right?"

"Yes. At this point we probably do fifty percent breeding-fifty percent artificial insemination. The ranch maintains a cow-calf operation. We raise the weaned heifers and steers to be sold."

She asked, "What is your feed plan?"

"The cattle graze, with additional hay, and then grain as needed. We don't care for the taste of pure grass-fed beef."

He paused and said, "You do ride, right?"

Thinking back to how long it had been since she had been in the saddle, she said, "I probably need to warm up since it has been years, but I love to ride."

He said, "To work the ranch, we use horses, off road vehicles, and trucks or trailers as needed. The animals are used to the vehicles, and it really saves time with all the land to cover."

She said, "How many acres is the ranch?"

"About fourteen hundred acres," he said, "but not all that land is for grazing. There are several ponds, rocky hilly terrain toward the canyon, and the Wichita River is on the east side. We have many fenced pastures of course and we move the cattle as we need to. We stay busy planting various grass or other nutrient greens in the appropriate seasons."

With a sweet sigh, Bella said, "It sounds beautiful, massive, and a perfect place for raising cattle and families."

Phoenix smiled and linked his fingers with hers and said, "You are going to love the ranch."

"I will! As you know, I grew up on the northeast, rural side of Katy, outside of Houston. Out in the country really, but nothing like the ranch. Tell me about the house."

A picture of the house flashed in his mind, and he said, "It has been updated a few times since GP originally built it. The house is a large one-level home built like a hacienda. A big porch with stone columns runs across the front with massive windows and double doors. There is an L shape wing on each side of the house to border a large patio in the back."

Bella envisioned the house and smiled as he described it.

"When you enter in the front door you step into a large great room. To the left is the working area of the house with a terrific kitchen for all the cooking that was necessary through the years. A stone snack bar with stools is closer to the kitchen for fast meals, but a huge dining area by the windows is for more formal events. The L wing on that side of the house includes storage, pantry, garage entrance with mud room, and utility room."

Bella said, "I can't even imagine all the work that kitchen has known. Years ago, they would have had to work all day without the modern conveniences that are available now."

"They did. Dad told me stories of giant plates of food for the cowboys and wranglers filled with biscuits, fried chicken, steak, and garden greens. But as change came, progress came, and less people were needed. By the time I came along, they grilled more meat and made large one pot meals. The ranch stopped raising chickens and having a garden because the housekeepers picked up produce and eggs in town."

Bella said, "Other than a housekeeper, was it just your grandfather, your dad, you, and Ariel?"

"My great aunt lived on the ranch as a nannie for Ariel until she was a teenager. But yes, we went through several housekeepers. The kitchen was a busy place, and back in those days my grandfather was impatient with even discussing what he considered women's work. And my dad didn't want anything to do with the kitchen either. As for me, I was happy to live on peanut butter and jelly sandwiches, biscuits, or steak.

"The last few years, my cousin, Jasmine, has managed the house and cooked breakfast and lunch on the weekdays. And I've grilled for dinner since I moved back to the ranch, which is where my eye injury came in."

"Speaking of your eyes, are you ready to give them a break from driving?"

"Yeah, that's probably a good idea," he said, and a few minutes later he pulled into a restaurant parking lot.

He parked in the back under a cluster of trees.

"This isn't even a little subtle," she said with a grin.

He smiled, laid his sunglasses on the dash, and glanced at her. No words were necessary. He leaned across and drew her face very close to his. But he didn't kiss her right away.

As he looked into her eyes, he slid his hand passionately down her jean-clad leg, then back up. And made no attempt to hide his desire.

Bella was lost in his eyes, and touch. His breath brushed her face and he looked at her lips. He watched as her body responded to him. She was more than ready.

He whispered, "Show me what you want."

She made a sound in her throat and reached for him.

Then he pulled her out of her seat onto his lap and made high school parking experiences seem like a child's game.

A few breathless minutes later, he buried his face in her neck and said, "You know, it might be really, really late before we reach the ranch with these driver swaps," and she smiled.

Before long they were back on the road, and he continued the description of the house as she drove.

He said, "The other side of the great room is the den. It has multiple seating areas with rugs and a large TV. The fireplace mantel is a huge piece of carved mahogany and above it is a hefty rack from a longhorn. All around the room are pictures of family, Angus cattle, horses, as well as ranch history."

Bella said, "What an amazing heritage and legacy. It sounds like the perfect place for you."

"It's you that makes it perfect for me now," and she glanced at him with a smile.

He said, "It's been twenty years since a Chandler wife has lived on the ranch. And I can't wait to show you how much I anticipate us. The wedding. The honeymoon. And all the minutes after."

Bella said, "Oh Phoenix."

He watched her, and said, "We are going to make love so long, so often, and so wild, that your—."

His words distracted her completely, and the car jerked.

She said, "Phoenix!"

He ignored the car, and said, "And you know it's true."

Trying to refocus on the road, Bella took a deep breath. But Phoenix wasn't done.

Still focused on that subject, he said softly, "How many babies do you want to make with me, Bella?"

Without a word, she pulled off the interstate to a rest stop and looked at him. He waited for her answer.

She said softly, "I want to make lots of babies with you Phoenix. A houseful. And I want to love them and raise them."

Phoenix reached over and kissed her. Sweet. Slow. Like warm rich honey. He couldn't wait to make babies with her.

Once she was back on the road again, she asked, "I presume the bedrooms are in the other wing."

He said, "There are six bedrooms suites with seating areas, large closets, and great bathrooms. When I left Dallas and moved back to the farm, I made several updates.

"First, was technology. I hired a specialist and made sure the ranch was fully online. Now the office in the house is equipped with monitors, cameras, drones, and all that we need to check the cows without having to always physically go outside."

Bella said, "I've heard of the technology, and I am impressed. That had to be a game changer."

"It was. Tremendously. Then following that improvement, I had a safe room built. The Wichita Falls area has had some ferocious tornadoes, damage, and loss of life. But we aren't allowed to have the traditional underground basements because of the type of dirt and rock here. So, I hired an engineer and contractor. We dug a small room under one corner of the house. Now we have a safe place to go. I will show you tomorrow because you will need to know where it is."

Bella said, "That's ingenious! Wichita Falls had, what, two or three big tornadoes?"

"Yes, three that they talk about. The smallest one, an F2 in 1958 hit about four miles west of Wichita Falls and no one was injured, just damage. The 1964 tornado was an F5, and it hit north of Wichita Falls by Sheppard Air Force Base. It was eight hundred feet wide and on the ground thirty-five minutes. It killed seven people and injured one-hundred-eleven.

"The most infamous tornado was the last one. It was a wedge shaped F4 that hit in 1979 on what they call Terrible Tuesday during the Red River Outbreak. That one was one and a half miles wide at its peak and hit southern Wichita Falls. Forty-two people died."

Bella moaned and said, "I've heard some of the stories. That is horrible. How did the ranch fare during those storms?"

"We've had damage to the barns and items in the yard but not the house. I haven't ever liked the idea of facing a beast like that head on, so I went the safe room route. A few other homeowners have dug the same type of rooms."

***

Phoenix's phone said, "Chandler Canyon Ranch calling."

Phoenix said, "Phone answer - hey GP, I'm almost to Buffalo, so about half-way to Fort Worth. It will easily be eight or nine tonight before we get to the ranch."

GP said, "I'm just glad you are on your way. It is a miracle that your eyes healed so quickly. It must have been your beautiful woman that encouraged you to follow the doctor's orders."

"You can say that again! And I'm sure that Ariel told you that I am bringing Bella home with me. We are getting married at the ranch on July 4."

"You bet she did! Congratulations! It is time to have a Mrs. Chandler and young'uns on this ranch again."

"You will love her, GP, she is gorgeous, gracious, and very smart. And on that note, I hired her as the veterinarian for the ranch - Dr. Bella DelCaprio."

***

After the call ended, Bella asked, "What's GP's first name? And your dad?"

Phoenix said, "GP is Russell Chandler, and my dad was Rourke Chandler."

"Who named you? Your mom?"

His face softened and he said, "Yes, she did a lot of reading and loved the character she found in my name, and the fact that it was considered to represent the resurrection. She was so lovely, Bella."

She touched his arm and said, "I can imagine. I do understand how hard it is to lose a parent, especially when you are young. Lucas told me about her horse-riding accident."

Phoenix was quiet for a minute as he remembered, then said, "She had long blonde hair and green eyes. Ariel looks just like her. I took after the Chandlers. You will see pictures of Mom in the den."

Bella said, "Does GP still live on the ranch?"

"No, he moved up to Colorado near his brother when he retired a couple of years ago. Once I took over the ranch, he told me two kings weren't

65

needed. He is proud to have a third-generation ranch, however, and comes back to help in the busy seasons, or like now, when I got hurt."

"You didn't tell me that you were royalty."

He smiled and explained, "The hands used to call him King, I guess the same way that I called him GP, to set him apart in the crowd."

Bella said, "Speaking of generations, how long do you want to wait until we work on the fourth-generation ranch, since you are a trained breeder and all."

He kissed her hand and said, "The first time is the perfect time."

It was nine p.m. and pitch black, when Phoenix turned through the gated entrance under the Chandler Canyon Ranch sign.

Bella looked around and said, "I can't wait till morning so that I can see everything! It feels like we are in the middle of nowhere since there hasn't been a single light for miles. I will have to hang a flashlight on my jeans."

"We will do whatever we need to do for you to feel safe. And I hope you let me work with you on overcoming that fear. We know that fear is healthy as a warning, but not to torment you. I have a few ideas in mind."

"Alright. I should have tried something long ago. Fear is crippling."

Then she said, "Where is the ranch, I still don't see any lights."

He chuckled and said, "The driveway is two miles long."

Bella laughed and said, "Welcome to Texas."

A minute later, Bella saw lights in the distance and watched as the ranch grew larger as they neared. It was obviously a large operation. She couldn't wait till morning since the security lights just hinted at the ranch. The house itself was made of white stone, with paned windows and giant double doors with horns mounted over the door.

Bella said, "Why the horns? Angus cattle don't have any."

Phoenix grinned and said, "It just means Texas."

Bella noticed a massive barn to the left and lots of fencing as Phoenix followed the drive around the left side of the house and pulled into a four-vehicle garage. She knew right away that the big two-tone bronze F-450 King Ranch truck had to be for Phoenix. It was masculine and bold like him. A smaller but still impressive silver Ram truck was probably GP's. A black BMW SUV sat in the third parking spot. Phoenix drove into the first spot by the door.

When Phoenix killed the engine, the door opened, and a much older version of Phoenix stepped outside with a welcoming smile on his face.

Phoenix and Bella got out of the mustang and GP's eyes widened when he saw her.

He said, "My stars, but you are a beautiful woman."

Phoenix smiled as he put his arm around Bella, and said, "GP, this is Bella."

Bella hugged GP and said, "It is wonderful to meet you."

GP said, "I can see the resemblance between you and Lucas. Your parents must have been real lookers to give birth to both of you."

They laughed and then GP and Phoenix hugged each other with energetic back slaps. Then Phoenix grabbed their overnight bags and they headed inside.

Phoenix said, "Let me show you to your room, so you can get settled in, and then I can give you a tour of the house."

Bella loved the house. It was just like Phoenix described. Bold amounts of wood spoke of strength in a great room accented with leather, windows, and stone, but softened with rugs, photographs, and overstuffed easy chairs and pillows. The kitchen and fireplace were both huge. It seemed everything was Texas-sized.

Phoenix led her down the right wing of the house where all the bedroom suites were located. He opened a door near the end of the hall and chuckled at her expression of delight.

The bedroom had a wall of windows that faced the inner courtyard of the home. And it was not just a typical courtyard, but an enclosed swimming pool and magnificent patio area.

Inside the bedroom, the furniture was still big but painted white which gave it a feminine edge. The bed covering was a decorative white chenille spread and lots of colorful contemporary pillows. The sitting area consisted of two cowhide easy chairs with a rug and floor lamp, and on the other wall a fabulous mirror hung above the dresser.

Phoenix put her overnight bags on an antique hope chest and showed her the closet and bathroom. The large bathroom had a contemporary counter, well-lit vanity, a stone walk-in shower without doors, a large central tub, and a private toilet area.

Bella said, "Phoenix, this is beautiful. When you said update the ranch, I didn't expect this!"

"I'm glad you like it," he said. "My room is next door to you and has doors that lead onto the patio."

Then with a smile and hug, he said, "Welcome home."

A little bit later, Phoenix walked back to the great room to meet GP. They grabbed a cup of coffee and headed to the ranch office so he could catch up on the last five days he had been gone. They talked about urgent matters, checked the cattle monitors, and GP headed on to bed.

Phoenix checked email on his computer, turned off the phone for the blind, and started up his iPhone again. It felt so good to be back to normal. Not being able to see had changed everything and he was grateful that it had only been temporary. He made a note to check into charities for the blind.

He opened his post office mail and separated bills, ranch tasks, advertising tasks for Ariel, and social events. The ranch always received invitations, whether it was wedding, funeral, charity, other ranch activities or simply socials. One invitation held tickets for twelve guests to the annual Cattleman's Gala to be held Memorial Day weekend, just nine days away. The ranch always sponsored a table for twelve every year. He certainly planned to enjoy that with Bella. He glanced at the clock, and it was past eleven p.m. He turned everything off, armed security, and headed toward Bella to say goodnight.

***

Bella felt wonderful after that amazing shower, and had just finished blow-drying her hair when she heard a knock on the door, and called out, "Come in."

Phoenix opened the door as Bella walked out of the bathroom.

He whistled and Bella laughed and said, "What?"

She was dressed in low cut black drawstring shorts and a white crop top. Her long hair surrounded her shoulders, and her face was flushed pink after the heat of the shower and blow-dryer.

"You look delicious!" he said.

"I think I like that! Taste…" and he did.

After a few moments, Phoenix said, "The days are early here. I am normally dressed and drinking coffee by five a.m. The crew, Kit, Levi, and Buck will show up not long after. Jasmine will have breakfast ready by five-thirty a.m. But if you need to sleep in …"

She shook her head no, and said, "I am excited to get started. I have a lot to learn about the ranch and need to get my vet office opened as soon as I can. Besides, I am about to jump into bed myself."

Chapter 10
The Hacker

Back in Houston, the Hacker arrived home from work.

It was after midnight, and he had waited since noon for this moment. His phone alerted him when the robot was in transit out of Houston. It alerted him again a few hours ago when the robot reached Chandler Canyon Ranch.

He sat at his computer and booted up. All his monitors flicked on. He had three of them, one for each of his Troy robots. Two robots were already in play at their new homes.

Monitor one robot was active and showed an apartment with a redheaded woman. He had great video on her already. His personal favorite and reason for all of this was in the bedrooms. Not just the nudity. It was when she slept. So vulnerable. So intimate. It was almost like he was in the room.

Next to the bed.

Or in it.

Not only was he an amazing hacker; he was also a passionate voyeur. His obsession was to watch.

Monitor two robot was stationed in a home of a society couple in an upscale Houston townhouse. He chuckled, as he alone knew that they were not what they appeared to be. He enjoyed their fights. But that was nothing like their interesting methods of making up. Their bruises were horrific and creative.

And monitor three robot was now at Chandler Canyon Ranch. It was time to wake up Troy.

The Hacker keyed in the code, TROJAN.

At the ranch, in the blue mustang, in the trunk, in a cardboard box, a chime dinged from the black robot. Large blue eyes with white pupils lit up on the computer face of the robot - and a voice said, "Welcome home, Troy."

Chapter 11
Chandler Canyon Ranch

Bella woke before the alarm, thrilled for her first day on the ranch. She had gone to school eight tough years for today. She was excited to step into Dr. Bella DelCaprio professionally.

For her first day she dressed carefully in jeans, boots, a light blue sleeveless button up shirt with a collar. She put her hair in a ponytail, and she was ready. She turned off the lights and picked up her faithful backpack.

It was special to her. It was black, with patches of animals all over it and across the top was embroidered Dr. B. It was last year's birthday present to her from Seth and Lili. Inside were her well organized work items that a vet might need for animals in the field. Including, but not limited to, her tranquilizer pistol, her hunting knife, a small rope, safety glasses, sunglasses, and multiple flashlights. And a bag of treats was always with her to distract animals during treatment.

Her pistol was for various types of sedation should surgery be needed, or for a frightened or dangerous animal that could harm itself or others. It could also be loaded for a lethal injection for euthanasia in the event an animal needed to be put down. That was a hard, but necessary truth as a veterinarian.

She glanced in the mirror one last time, with a smile, and said, "Come on Dr. B, let's do this!"

She stepped in the hall at the same time Phoenix shut his door.

He smiled and appreciated Bella's stunning beauty in jeans, boots, and a blue-to-match her eyes shirt. Wow. Beautiful but professional for the ranch. He couldn't wait to work with her. He also couldn't wait to take advantage of some private moments today, even if he had to create a few.

After all, he was the boss.

Bella smiled at Phoenix, obviously the rancher now. Always masculine, now authority emanated off him. He was in his domain. She took in his tall, fit physique, and he leaned down to warmly kiss her good morning.

He asked, "Are you ready for this?" and she grinned in excitement.

He chuckled as they headed for the coffee pot. The normal start of every day. Bella could hear voices as they neared the great room and smiled when she saw all the happy faces in the kitchen around the snack bar.

GP saw them first and said, "Hey Phoenix, Bella, come get some coffee and grub."

Everyone turned to look at them.

An attractive sandy haired man with a ponytail said, "Hey Boss, it is good to have you back! GP let us slack off," and GP hit him in the arm with a laugh.

Phoenix chuckled as they entered the group, and all eyes turned to Bella.

Phoenix said, "Please welcome my fiancé, Dr. Bella DelCaprio, she is also the ranch's personal veterinarian."

The older cowhand whistled and said, "Boss, she's a looker, even the bulls will be distracted," and laughter rang out.

After a moment, Phoenix continued with the introductions and said, "Bella, the guy with long blond hair, is our assistant, basically our foreman, and his name is Kit. He has been with the ranch since he was a teenager.

"And the beautiful cook at the stove is his wonderful wife, my cousin, Jasmine."

Bella smiled and said, "It is nice to meet both of you. I am excited to be a part of the crew."

Jasmine drawled from the stove, "I bet Boss is even more excited," and they laughed again, a good-natured group.

Phoenix said, "The whistler," and everyone chuckled, "is Buck. Buck's been here forever. Weren't you born here too Buck?"

Buck said, "Now, Boss, that ain't fair. I was born in the canyon," and he grinned, totally enjoying his blatant lie.

Then Phoenix said, "And the young man with black hair is Levi."

Jasmine arranged the food buffet, and the line was instant. Everyone inhaled breakfast choices of sandwiches made from fried eggs, bacon, steak, and cheese on toast. Bella settled with a piece of toast and one egg with coffee.

Phoenix picked up Bella's backpack and said, "They call you Dr. B?"

"Yes, at LSU they said Dr. DelCaprio was a mouthful."

Phoenix grinned and said, "Dr. B it is."

Buck motioned to Bella's plate and said, "You're gonna starve eating like a bird."

Bella said, "So what's wrong with a bird?" and the crew laughed.

Phoenix said, "Does anyone recognize Bella's resemblance to Lucas?"

Jasmine said, "Absolutely. How is Lucas, Dr. B?"

Bella said, "In love."

Jasmine said, "Finally."

After breakfast, Phoenix said, "Dr. B's new office will be the small west barn with the apartment. Levi, I need you to clean it out and prepare it for livestock over the next couple of days. And make sure all of you get her cell number before you head outside. If you need her, give her a call. She will do what she can until we get her fully functional here.

"Kit, other than that, it's just the regular Thursday routine for the crew. Let me know if you need me. GP will also be here for a couple more days. And lastly, the Cattleman's Gala is Saturday, May 28 in Wichita Falls, Memorial Day weekend. I have tickets for all of you, so let me know if you plan to attend by this coming Monday. It is a formal event with evening gowns and tuxes."

Then he smiled and said, "That's it! Oh, and Jasmine, that was delicious as always," and she did a happy dance as the guys chuckled on the way outside.

Phoenix said, "Come on, Dr. B. Let me show you Chandler Canyon Ranch."

They walked out on the front porch and the sun greeted them from the eastern sky. Phoenix followed Bella as she walked down the steps into the yard and turned in all directions to see the beautiful country.

She said, "Oh, Phoenix..." and he smiled as she closed her eyes and embraced the country sounds and smells.

So many things filled Bella's senses. The smell of animals. The cattle mooing. Horses neighing. The clank of the gates opening and closing. The dogs barking. The crew calling out instructions. Then she felt the breeze that carried Phoenix's aftershave and opened her eyes.

He watched her with a smile. She returned it, and thought, I'm home.

Phoenix hugged her and they walked to the back of the house. He motioned to the cattle operation on the south side of the driveway. Bella whistled in appreciation.

He laughed, and said, "We have three large cattle barns. Each barn is connected to a specific set of pastures to graze about one-hundred-seventy head of cattle. I have a wall map in my office that indicates the current grazing schedule.

"Cattle sheds are available in the pastures for herds caught in extreme weather. A smaller fourth barn is for horses, and has an upstairs bunkhouse anytime ranch hands need to stay overnight. I didn't mention it in the house tour, but there is also a bunkroom in the bedroom wing."

Then he pointed further down the road and said, "That barn is your new office."

Bella smiled at the small red barn that was all hers, and said, "Boss, that is one beautiful barn," and he laughed.

He said, "You know, you and I don't have to use our work names."

"But I think we should. I kind of like thinking that I get to smooch the boss," and winked.

He got right to the point, and said, "I like knowing that you are going to be doing a lot more than that in a few weeks."

Bella liked the way that he just laid it out there and brushed against him with a grin.

Phoenix drawled, "I think it's time to take you out behind the barn," and Bella laughed as he led the way to a black RTV.

He said, "Feel free to use one of these RTVs. Once you learn the pastures, you will know if you need to be on horseback, on an RTV, or even on foot. Some of the canyons are best on foot. Cattle have wandered in there at times.

"We also need to go riding so you can warm up in the saddle. And, speaking of that, I hate to be blunt, but I have one strict rule out here for you, Bella," and she looked at him in surprise.

"Don't go beyond sight of the ranch alone or without telling me."

Irritated at first with his demand, something niggled at her memory, and she recalled his mother's horse-riding accident. She understood and nodded without comment. She had her own issues. She certainly couldn't fault his concerns over a trauma he faced.

Phoenix parked by the small barn and smiled at Bella's anticipation. He knew there was nothing like getting your dream fulfilled.

Levi was already mucking stalls when they walked inside. It had certainly needed to be cleaned and aired out. Bella thanked Levi for his work and looked around. She counted ten horse stalls, a small inside corral, and a hay storage area. There was a feed and tack room.

Phoenix said, "I think it will be perfect for what you need."

Bella said, "It's fabulous," and he smiled and pointed to the stairs.

"Watch your step. I can't remember the last time I used this barn," and they climbed the wooden stairs.

When they reached the top, they entered a very hot loft apartment. It was the size of a large bedroom and had a full-size iron bed, wooden table with four chairs, a counter with a sink, a hot plate, and next to that a fridge. Across the room was a bathroom with a small shower and toilet. A rocking chair sat by a south window, and a loft window opened to look over the stalls. A couple of plain light bulbs that hung from the ceiling were the only light.

In an instant, Bella already imagined the new room and heard all the animals that would one day be in the stalls below.

She turned to Phoenix and said, "It's perfect. I love it. Thank you! When I move my belongings from LSU may I use some of it in here?"

He said, "After we paint and update it, you are free to do whatever you want in here. Can you give me a few days to get someone out here to tend to this?"

"Only if we can seal it with a kiss, Boss," and he didn't even give her time to reach for him before his lips were on hers.

A few kisses later, both sweaty from the lack of air conditioning, he said, "You have got to have air conditioning and a heater out here," and she wiped the sweat off her face in agreement.

Then they went downstairs, and she took measurements in the tack room and made a list of what she needed to buy for the clinic.

Phoenix said, "I would like to go with you to get what you need. And that reminds me, I need to give you a ranch credit card that we use for supplies. Our accountant takes care of the rest. And by-the-way, payday is every Friday, beginning tomorrow."

"But I haven't even worked yet."

"I wouldn't say that. You took magnificent care of the rancher for days."

She glanced to make sure Levi wasn't near them, and whispered, "Phoenix, being there for you at the beach house was incredible. Even if we *hadn't turned into an us*, I would have been there for you."

Her sincerity hit him hard.

He wrapped his arms around her, and said, "Your generosity and kindness are unbelievable. And your beauty, inside and out, bring me to my knees. How in the world could I not love you?"

She held him tightly around the waist. She got it. Her knees were weak now.

A little later, they returned to the house and unloaded their luggage out of the mustang. Phoenix put the robot in the ranch office until he had time to decide what to do with it. Then he called his contractor and requested a rush job on the barn for Bella. The contractor said to message him the specifics and he would send a few guys out to measure. It would be completed by Monday night since it was an easy job. He couldn't wait to tell her.

He heard Bella as she talked on the phone with a vet supply company and a pharmacy in Wichita Falls for a pickup order tomorrow. He passed by her and laid a Visa credit card, and a Chandler Canyon Ranch job application on the table.

She nodded and continued her conversation. Phoenix's phone rang and after a brief chat, he headed to the barn to give Buck a hand.

***

Bella received a text message, but it was from an unknown number, so she didn't check it since she was busy. She finished her order for supplies and medications. Then she made a note to talk to Phoenix and the ranch attorney about a nonprofit corporation for Dr. B's Animal Rescue here at the ranch. And lastly, she filled out the job application and laid it on Phoenix's chair in his office.

He really was her boss.

Then she went to the kitchen to talk to Jasmine who had filled the house with fabulous smells of peppers, onions, and something else spicy for lunch. Bella sat on a barstool and watched her work.

Jasmine had long brown hair and emerald, green eyes. She was beautiful. Her and Kit made a very handsome couple.

Bella inhaled and said, "It smells so good!"

Jasmine looked up and laughed as Bella's stomach growled, and said, "We are having steak fajitas and chili for lunch. It should be no surprise that beef is a requirement here at the ranch."

Bella snagged a tiny piece of steak that had just been spooned out of a skillet and nibbled on it.

Jasmine grinned and said, "You better help yourself! All the guys will be stampeding the kitchen any minute. After that, it's every man, or woman, for themselves."

At that, the door opened, and Phoenix, GP, Kit, Levi, and Buck walked in sniffing the air and groaning with hunger, as Jasmine and Bella laughed.

Phoenix tried to get Bella to fix her plate first, but she waved the steak she was already nibbling.

In minutes, the men were focused on cleaning their plates.

Phoenix sat next to Bella with a mound of food. She raised her eyebrows in surprise.

He said, "I've been staring at all that beef outside. I can't help myself."

A little later, Bella fixed a small bowl of chili and sat down to eat. All the men stopped and stared for a second at her tiny bowl.

She said, "I know, I know, I eat like a bird. But don't you forget that an eagle is a bird," and the guys chuckled.

Jasmine removed a giant apple pie out of the oven where she had hidden it. She didn't trust them to leave it alone. When they saw it, all the men cheered like crazy.

The pie plate was empty in about two minutes.

Bella waited till Phoenix finished his last bite of pie, and said, "Tell me about the Cattleman's Gala."

"Sure! You will love the decorations, food, music, and social atmosphere. I intend to show you off and shock everyone as we dance up close and personal. It's a popular event in this area of Texas. Would you like to go shopping? We can take a trip to Dallas if you like."

She smiled teasingly and said, "I have a very, very nice red dress. I wore it last year and would love to wear it to the Gala. I think that you will like it."

"Just the thought of you in red makes me like it. Where did you wear it?"

"To take pictures as Miss Christmas for the LSU calendar."

"Wow. You do know that now I must have one of those pictures."

"Somehow, I thought that might be the case."

He grinned and said, "Are you at a stopping point with your work? I would like us to take a horseback tour of the ranch. It is best for you to learn the layout of the land as soon as possible since you will spend a good deal of time in the pastures."

"Sure. I'm ready."

"Great. I need to check messages before we leave, but I won't be long. You might want to go to the bathroom. Unless, of course, you fancy a bush later."

She shook her head, and said, "Ah, there's the proof that I'm in the country."

While he went to his office, Bella went to her bedroom to freshen up. On her way back to the kitchen she checked her phone messages.

She noticed the text from an unknown number and opened it.

***

Unknown to Bella: My lips will catch your dying breath while you struggle beneath me.

***

Chapter 12
Death Threat

Fear made Bella nauseated as she read the text again. Wanting it away from her, she tossed her phone on the sofa.

Jasmine noticed Bella's distress and said, "What's wrong Bella?"

Phoenix heard Jasmine's question and came out of his office. Bella was seated on the sofa with her head in her hands.

He joined her and said, "What's wrong?"

She said, "I got a horrible text. Someone sent me a threat."

"What? What kind of threat?"

She pointed to her phone on the other side of him. He read the text and rage raced through him. He growled deep in his throat, but the fear on her face made him shut it down and focus on her.

He said, "Bella, honey. I promise, he's a dead man if I ever find out who sent you that."

She said, "It's Royce. It sounds like him and he knows my number. I know without a doubt that he planned to do just what that text said."

He grabbed his phone, but she touched his arm, and said, "Wait, I have an idea. Ranger Morgan was the one who found me locked in the trunk when I was seven years old. We have connected off and on through the years. He even came to my graduation. He lives north of Austin and is still a Texas Ranger. Maybe, he can guide me, or us, with what to do."

Phoenix breathed a sigh of relief and said, "I know Ranger Morgan well. He is terrific. That is a perfect idea."

A couple of hours later, a Texas Ranger truck drove up to the ranch. Phoenix welcomed Ranger Morgan inside. Bella hugged him, and they all sat at the table.

He said, "I'm glad that I was in Dallas when you called me. But I am sorry for the reason."

Phoenix said, "She may have a real problem that we hope you can help with."

The Ranger said, "I understand. Our office went ahead and pulled the Baton Rouge police report. I read your statement, Bella, on the attack by Royce. Is there anything that you didn't include that we might need to know? A lot of times, victims know more than they mention or think of things later."

Bella said, "Well, yes, I told Phoenix that my impression was that the attack was supposed to go beyond sexual. He looked at me viciously like he planned to kill me."

The Ranger's expression hardened, and he said, "Ok. Did you ever hear any gossip about him at LSU or around Baton Rouge?"

She thought for a minute and said, "You know, someone once told me that a lot of Royce's girlfriends left LSU after the relationship ended."

Phoenix and the Ranger glanced at each other. That didn't sound good.

The Ranger continued, "If it was Royce that texted you, obviously he didn't use his personal phone mainly to avoid trouble at court next week. On the optimistic angle, maybe he just vented without any other intent. But I can take your phone and try to run a trace and see what we find out. I wish I could say more could be done in response, but honestly, very little can be done about a text unless a restraining order was already in place. At this point, the most important thing is to make sure he is still in Baton Rouge."

Bella said, "Let's try to trace the text," and handed him her phone.

He said, "I will get it back to you as quick as I can."

As he left, he said, "Be sure to call your Louisiana detective and make sure that Royce is still there. If he is, at least that will give you peace of mind."

"Ok, I will. Thank you for your help."

***

Bella called.

"Detective, this is Dr. Bella DelCaprio and I have you on speaker with my fiancé, Phoenix Chandler."

The Detective said, "Hello Dr. DelCaprio, congratulations on your engagement. Is everything alright?"

Bella said, "Well, I am living at Chandler Canyon Ranch in Texas now and I received a threatening text around one p.m.," and she told him what it said.

He sighed and said, "I am sorry that happened, so I presume you think that Royce sent it?"

"I do. Ranger Morgan is going to run the text message and try to trace it, but it could be a prepaid phone."

He said, "It can still be traced through where it was purchased, and then tracked by video feed for the purchaser of the transaction. But all that takes time."

"Well, would you be able to let me know if he is still in Baton Rouge? That would help a great deal," and he agreed.

***

After the call, Phoenix said, "You know that you are going to have to be my shadow until this is resolved in some way."

"I apologize for this trouble."

"No apologies, Bella, I hate that you were threatened by him again."

"I still want to go riding. I want to see the ranch."

"Sure, but you'll need to double with me, and we will bring one of the guard dogs with us. We have to tell the crew as well so they can keep an eye out for trouble."

The crew gathered around them while Phoenix saddled up the brown stallion and gave them the gist of what happened. All four men were instantly furious, offended for Bella, and on alert.

Phoenix said, "We should hear today if the LSU attacker is still in Baton Rouge. And hopefully we will find out who sent the text by tomorrow. Until we know, keep your eyes peeled for trouble, watch for strangers or anything unusual. Watch the behavior of the animals in case they sense trouble. And remember if you need anything vet wise, Bella doesn't have her phone right now, so call me.

"We are going to ride out by the rocky pastures near the north canyon. I'm bringing one of the guard dogs with me. Call if you need us."

Phoenix gave Bella a leg up in the saddle and then he mounted behind her. They settled snug in the saddle, and he wrapped his arm around her and pulled her tight back against him. Secure.

He leaned down and kissed her cheek, then made a clicking sound and the horse started forward. The dog followed.

Phoenix said, "We have a good distance to go before we get out of the grassy pastures, so tell me about your vet calls today. What did you set up? I have some news when you are done."

Bella laughed and said, "You go first! I can't stand the wait."

He chuckled and said, "I talked to my contractor about updating your office and he said that they would be out to get some measurements and that it should all be done by Monday afternoon."

"By this coming Monday? That's unbelievable!"

"The contractor said a coat of paint, new appliances and fixtures doesn't take long to complete, at least not on a small place like that."

"Oh my gosh, that is the best birthday present ever."

He cringed behind her and said, "When is your birthday?" praying that it had not already passed.

"Not till June 1. I will be twenty-seven if you didn't know. I normally celebrate Memorial Day weekend. So, happy birthday to me since you are bringing me to a Gala and fixing my office. You rock, Phoenix."

Above her head, Phoenix mouthed, "Thank you, God," since he was taught that you never missed an important date for a woman. Ever.

Then he said, "Ok, your turn, what is your news?"

She said, "All my supplies will be ready for pickup in Wichita Falls Saturday by noon. Two stops. All we need is a truck, and I happen to know someone who has a big, fine, truck."

He laughed.

And she continued, "I wanted to ask, does the ranch have an attorney?"

"We do. What do you need?"

"I need to find out what I need to do to legally set up a nonprofit, and my clinic."

"Yes, he can handle that. We also need to get your sign made."

She said, "I will need to set up a website and social media soon. I am not worried about donations for the animal rescue yet, as I plan to provide income from what the ranch pays me. Since you are making me take it."

"We haven't even talked figures as to what your income would be from the ranch."

She said, "No, but it doesn't matter. You already provide room and board, and a barn. You really should keep the check. I have money left over from college from my grandparents that will last a while."

"Bella, you will make five-thousand dollars a week plus bonuses and benefits."

She looked back at him and said, "No! That is way too much. I'm not taking it. Taxes will just eat it up anyway. I love you and our home. I'm going to be your wife. I want to give and not take from you."

He reined in the horse and held her. They sat there quietly. Neither noticed the west Texas breeze or the scream from the hawk high overhead.

He kissed her neck, and said, "Loving you is such a wonder, Bella."

She said, "Does that mean you won't make me take the money from you?"

"What it means is that I will put it in a foundation for you to use as you see fit," and she smiled.

An hour later, as they neared the canyon area, Phoenix's phone vibrated in his pocket.

***

He checked and said, "Here Bella, the detective is calling you back," and handed her his phone.

Bella said, "Hello Detective, I have you on speaker."

He said, "Royce is still in Baton Rouge. I had a unit pass by his apartment, and he was inside on the phone."

Bella and Phoenix both sighed in relief, and Bella said, "Thank you so much, that made my day."

"I understand. But I need to make you aware that for a first offense without physical injury, Royce isn't going to get much punishment at all."

Bella felt Phoenix tense behind her, and said, "Yes, I get it. Thanks again, Detective."

As Bella hung up, she said, "Let's not talk about it right now, ok? We won't know anything till after he goes to court next week. I want you to show me the canyon."

He squeezed her and said, "Ok."

For a moment he looked out over the canyon, not seeing anything but the possible danger to Bella in the days ahead.

But for Bella, now that it was confirmed that Royce was in Baton Rouge, she wanted to explore and enjoy the late afternoon with her fiancé.

They rode as far as they could and then walked down into the canyon with the dog. Bella loved to explore. It always amazed her that water had long ago carved these canyons, and yet now it was nearly dry. There was only a small stream left but even that would dry up as summer's relentless heat increased and sweltered the land.

She walked along engrossed in the landscape with sand, rocks, sparse desert plants, various patches of wild grass and flowers. It was quiet except for their footsteps crunching on rocks, and the dog drinking from the fading stream.

Phoenix smiled as he watched her, and she said, "How often do the cattle come in here?"

He said, "Not too often that we know of, but the dogs usually find them and run them out or we search for them. We keep the breeding females, and their calves close to the ranch, but the steers, other heifers, and bulls, do rotate near here. They like this grass."

They sat on a couple of large boulders, and once they were still, Bella could see the snakes move, the scorpions scuttle about, chubby armadillos meander around, and even noticed a few road runners.

After a bit, the dog growled, and Phoenix stood and looked the direction the dog was focused on. He saw two coyotes at the top of a bluff and pointed them out to Bella.

He said, "Lets head back to the horse."

By the time they returned to the ranch, GP had just taken steaks off the new gas grill he installed after Phoenix's eye accident. Bella took out the dishes and fixed their glasses. Phoenix pulled baked potatoes and a salad for them out of the fridge, with a smiley face note from Jasmine stuck right on top.

After a great supper and conversation, GP headed to his room. It had been a full day for an eighty-year-old man.

After a while Phoenix said, "How about we check out the robot?"

Bella grinned and said, "Sure, I am kind of excited to see what all he can do," and he headed to his office and was right back with the robot. They sat on the floor with him like kids with a toy.

Phoenix said, "See if he will obey your voice."

Bella said, "Power up, Troy."

Troy's bright blue LED eyes opened in his face screen, so Phoenix motioned for her to continue.

"Troy, my name is Bella."

Troy responded, "Hello, Bella."

Bella grinned and said, "Your turn."

Phoenix said, "Troy, my name is Boss."

"Yes, Boss."

Bella said, "Troy, what do you do?"

"Serve you, Bella," and Bella grinned at Phoenix as he rolled his eyes.

Phoenix said, "Troy, what are you not allowed to do?"

"Boss, I am not allowed to harm you. I am not allowed to harm me. I must obey."

Bella glanced at Phoenix and said, "Troy, can you access the internet and play a song on Pandora website?"

"Yes, Bella," and she smiled at Phoenix.

Phoenix stood and pulled Bella up with him, and said, "Troy, play country and western love songs very softly."

"Yes, Boss."

Music began to play. Phoenix and Bella started out dancing. But it didn't take long for the passion to flare. Bella ended up with her legs wrapped around his waist as he held her. Phoenix took a ragged breath and pulled her tighter against him as he kissed her neck.

Breathless, Bella said, "Phoenix, we have to stop, I am hot - and sweating."

He chuckled and said, "Surely you know all the places I could take this conversation."

She giggled and slid down to stand.

Phoenix said, "Troy, stop music."

"Yes, Boss."

Phoenix showed Troy where his holding station was, then walked Bella to her bedroom. He made sure to leave her door ajar in case she called out for him.

Chapter 13
Troy the Robot

It was after midnight in Houston before the Hacker turned on his home computer. All three robot monitors lit up. He focused only on robot three and keyed in the code word Trojan.

Four-hundred-fifteen miles away at Chandler Canyon Ranch, Troy's eyes opened.

The Hacker was now in control.

He turned on the recorded video from a few hours ago and watched Phoenix Chandler and a stunning black-haired beauty as they talked to the robot. The Hacker wasn't concerned with Phoenix. But the woman was extraordinary. She had magnificent bright blue eyes and Bella was her name.

Beautiful Bella, he thought. He wanted more of Bella. And he got it.

He watched as Phoenix and Bella danced. He easily put himself in Phoenix's place as he held her, touched her, and kissed her. The hotter the video got, the more the Hacker wanted her too.

When Phoenix picked Bella up and she wrapped her legs around his waist, the Hacker was right there in the mood with them.

Hooked. Hot.

When the video ended, the Hacker glanced at the clock. It was late. Phoenix and Bella should be asleep by now. He began to steer Troy the robot silently through the darkness in search of Bella.

He went left first and found an office, then the kitchen, and down a hall with an entry, storage, and utility. Then he turned and went back the way that he came and saw the other doorway across the room.

Troy rolled silently to the other opening and looked down the hall. There were a lot of doors but only two were open. He continued down the hall and stopped when Phoenix appeared in the doorway straight ahead.

Phoenix walked to Bella's door and checked on her. Then he glanced up the hall and frowned. Why was Troy in the hall?

Phoenix walked to him and knelt, and said, "Troy, what are you doing?"

The Hacker responded, "Protection, Boss."

Phoenix did not appear impressed, and said, "Troy, go to your home station by the door and stay there."

"Yes, Boss."

The Hacker disconnected from Troy a couple of minutes later and tapped his finger on his desk, deep in thought on how to play this out.

Chapter 14
Royce, Baton Rouge

At two a.m. in Baton Rouge, Royce jerked back the covers and got out of bed. This restriction with court pending was driving him crazy. He didn't want to send a text to Bella, he wanted to watch those bright blue eyes flicker and go out as she lay underneath him.

Dominated. Dead.

He walked in the living room and looked out across Veteran's Memorial Park and sighed. He glanced at his stack of pre-paid phones. He would drop one in the river ever couple of days so he could continue to text her with a new one. No sense making it easy for him to be tracked.

Royce stretched, then ran his hand through his hair as he walked to the sofa. He propped his feet up and ran through a mental inventory:

He continued to pull cash from his accounts every day to build a nest egg. *Check.* His car was being painted a different color tomorrow. *Check.* He had extra phones. *Check.* He had a strong acting sedative. *Check.* He knew that Bella was at Chandler Canyon Ranch and its location. *Check.* He had four days till court. *Check.* Then I'm coming for you Bella. *Check.*

Chapter 15
Tornado Warning

Bella pulled on her last boot and heard Phoenix shut his door. It was a few minutes before five a.m. She picked up her backpack and when she straightened, Phoenix was already leaned against her doorframe with a smile.

He drawled, "Morning, Bella," and she smiled and walked into his arms for a warm hug and a much warmer kiss.

Voices carried down the hall as they headed to join the crew. The men begged Jasmine for food.

Jasmine shooed them out from under her feet and said, "Give me a second here! The steak biscuits are almost done. Go get your coffee. I mean it."

Phoenix said, "Jasmine, pop the whip! You're the boss in the kitchen."

So, Jasmine laughed and swiped the spatula at the men.

The now operational robot caught Bella's attention as they passed him, and she nudged Phoenix and pointed to Troy.

With a grin, Phoenix said, "Troy, come say hello to the crew."

Everyone's head swiveled to see who Troy was.

Troy's blue eyes lit up on the LED screen and he responded, "Yes, Boss," and rolled toward Phoenix.

The open-mouthed crew stared in astonishment. Especially GP. Then they all began to talk at once as they walked over to get a closer look at the three-foot robot.

Phoenix said, "Troy, say good morning to Bella, Jasmine, GP, Kit, Levi, and Buck."

Troy responded, "Yes, Boss. Good morning, Bella, Jasmine, GP, Kit, Levi, and Buck."

Jasmine said, "I have to have one of those."

Bella said, "Watch this, Jasmine," and she said, "Troy, what do you do?"

Troy responded, "I serve you, Bella."

As everyone laughed, Jasmine said, "I want two of them," and Kit poked her in the side.

Phoenix said, "Troy, please give us the weather report for our location."

Troy responded, "Boss, this morning will be clear with highs in the 80's. There is a fifty percent chance of thunderstorms after two p.m., sunrise is in twenty minutes, and sunset is at seven-forty-five p.m."

GP said, "You have got to be kidding me."

Phoenix said, "No, this is the one that I bought at the charity event a month ago. We just turned him on last night. His home station will be by the front door."

Then Jasmine said, "Come and get it! Biscuits are ready!" and the guys quickly got in line.

Phoenix said, "Bella, I need to show you where the storm shelter is after breakfast," and she nodded.

GP said, "Phoenix, "I wanted to let you know that I will not be able to attend the Cattleman's Gala. Your uncle made plans for us that weekend already."

Levi and Buck chimed in that they wouldn't be able to attend either.

Buck said, "Sorry, my tux doesn't fit anymore," and they laughed.

Levi said, "I already have a date that night and I don't plan to spend it in a room with a bunch of people," and the men nodded in complete understanding.

Jasmine smiled at Kit and said, "My man's bringing me to the Gala, right, honey?"

Kit smiled and said, "Yes, I am, green eyes. You, in my arms on a dance floor, works for me."

Once the food was gone, Phoenix said, "I wanted to let all of you know that the contractor will be here today to measure for the remodel of Bella's barn apartment. He will have some guys work all weekend to be done by Monday night. Check whenever you pass the barn just to see if they need anything.

"Levi, please clean Bella's office apartment this morning and take the furniture out and get rid of it, unless you know anyone that needs it.

"And as an update, the attacker from LSU is still in Baton Rouge, thank God. Just be aware that he exists and stay alert for trouble. We will know more about him after his court date Monday. As for animal predators, I noticed two big coyotes in the north canyon so keep an eye on the pastures.

"Kit, if you and Buck would bring in the group of cows that were bred about a month ago, I want to work with Bella and confirm pregnancies today for early spring deliveries. After that, it is just regular Friday tasks."

GP said, "I think I'm gonna ride with Kit and Buck to bring in the cows," and Phoenix saluted him.

Jasmine said, "Hey Boss, I plan to leave a large mega beef lasagna, fried chicken, and a stack of pancakes that can be heated for the weekend. And a blackberry cobbler too."

Phoenix grinned at Jasmine, and she said, "I read you loud and clear! Will do!"

Bella said, "That is a lot of food."

Phoenix said, "Amen to that," and motioned Bella to follow him to his office.

Bella was impressed with his office. Several maps and charts hung on the walls that listed the locations of all cows, even with their nursing calves, steers, heifers, and all bulls. An annual calendar was marked with breeding dates, insemination dates, tagging, branding, vaccination, and castrating dates. The last schedule was for maturity dates of animals to be sold. Phoenix turned on his computer and pulled up the camera monitors so that she could see what cows they were watching for late delivery. A separate monitor was for drone footage around the pastures.

"Phoenix, you have set up an amazing operation."

"Thanks, we take good care of the cattle to provide a quality product to the consumer. We like what we do."

She said, "For today, I presume that we will do manual checks to determine pregnancy?"

"Yes, but I wanted to check with you on purchasing an ultrasound. I understand that it is beneficial in many other ways as well."

"It is, and yes, I would recommend purchasing one. A portable one of course with a long battery life."

Phoenix smiled with appreciation of her knowledge and said, "I appreciate you, Dr. B," and she smiled.

He glanced in the corral monitor where Kit and Buck would put the pregnant cows once they were herded in from the pasture, and said, "I trained Kit to help with manual checks so you will have help. Hopefully we get at least one hundred-seventy-five confirmed pregnancies today from last month's breeding."

After a few minutes of watching the monitors, Phoenix walked to the table in the corner and slid it out of the way. Bella noticed a square door in the floor and realized that it was the shelter. He flipped a switch on the wall and lifted the hatch. A set of steps led down into a room.

Phoenix climbed down and held her hand to follow. When she reached the bottom, it was simply a concrete room. Chairs lined the walls. A large fluorescent light was on the ceiling. A closet contained a toilet and sink. A shelving unit held various supplies and a small table and stools were in the middle of the room. He made sure she knew how to latch the metal door.

He said, "It isn't fancy, it is just a safe place."

Bella said, "Have you ever had to come down here for a storm?"

"Yes, several times, and it is never convenient. It is always a rushed, intense time trying to get everyone inside, including the dogs if they are near the house. Tornadoes are a common threat out here so close to the panhandle."

"How often does the house loose power?"

Phoenix knew her concern about the dark, and said, "We are solar, and we have a generator, but there can be delay as it starts up that could potentially leave us in the dark for a short time, especially down here. We also have solar power in the calving barns. Electricity is run on the property but only some buildings access it, including your office. So, tell me where your concerns are, and we will resolve it," and she nodded.

He said, "Maybe we can take some time tonight and try out my idea to help you with the panic attacks. What do you think?"

She said, "I think it's time. I'm tired of dealing with it."

He hugged her and said, "We'll beat it, Bella."

A few minutes later, they were headed outside when Ranger Morgan called.

***

Phoenix answered and said, "Hey Ranger. I have you on speaker. Do you have any news on that text?"

"Yes. We traced it back to the Baton Rouge area. So, that probably answers your question."

Bella sighed and said, "I figured that. I couldn't imagine some random guy out there sending it."

He said, "I have learned not to be surprised at all. There are human predators everywhere, of every type. Some look like angels and are the devil themselves."

Bella said, "I called the detective and he confirmed that Royce is still in Baton Rouge, so that was good news."

Ranger Morgan said, "That is terrific news. So, we just need an update on what happens Monday for his court date. Oh, and I can pass by your place late this afternoon to drop off your phone. Be sure and let me know if anything else comes up."

Phoenix said, "Thanks! Would you like to have a steak with us for dinner?"

He said, "I would love to, but I have to get back to Austin. Thanks, though."

***

Phoenix said, "Let's head to the corral, they should be getting here with the cows and heifers before long."

They walked into the first barn. The smell of cattle was strong of course, but not overpowering. The cowhands kept up with cleaning, and in the busy season extra hands were hired. There were fenced corrals in the barn, a large hay bin, feed and water troughs, and a breeze blowing through the open east and west doors.

Phoenix pointed as they neared the back of the barn, and she saw and heard the cattle coming. He smiled and watched GP, Kit, and Buck bring them home. This was the important part. The cows and the calves. The foundation of the ranch.

Bella felt the rush. This is what she trained for. Finally, hands on Dr. B.

Phoenix said, "Stay right here," and he ran out and opened the corral gate for the herd, then opened the gate to the chutes where they would manually check each animal for pregnancy.

The all-black Angus herd entered the corral. There were lots of bellows and fussing at the rush, but the cattle obeyed. Levi ran into the corral and steered them to the chutes till all were full. Once all the cattle were inside the holding corral, the guys dismounted.

Wiping sweat from his face, Kit said, "They look good Boss," and Phoenix gave him a thumb's up.

Levi went back inside and carried out the supplies and laid it out on a table built against the back of the barn. Bella and Kit washed their hands, put on the arm gloves, and got to work. Phoenix took out his computer register and documented all new findings on each cow and heifer.

Their ear tags identified everything about them from birth till now, including their breeding times, pregnancies, calves, and health status. It was all listed in the register. There were many rules and regulations for animals raised for food consumption, including vaccines, medications, diseases, etcetera.

Everything mattered.

They stopped for a quick break at ten a.m. and Bella wiped sweat off her face.

Kit said, "How many have we done, Boss?"

Phoenix said, "Ninety. We should have about seventy-five left. And I want to get all of them checked before the storm rolls in, so let's go ahead and work through lunch. I can get Jasmine to run out with a tray of drinks and sandwiches."

He looked up at the sky and early clouds were already building up. They had four hours left to finish the job.

Bella downed her water and put on more gloves.

Two hours later, there were only thirty cows and heifers left in the corral to be loaded in the chutes when Jasmine brought them steak burritos. They hurriedly cleaned up and devoured them and got back to work. Phoenix checked the weather on his phone and frowned.

He said, "I am not sure if we can finish before the storm. Just stay steady at it."

Bella's back complained at the push and pull of checking each animal for pregnancy. Plus, she was sweaty, dusty – and still thrilled. She lost tract of time until no one put another cow in her chute. She turned to see how many cows were left and they were all gone. They had finished all of them.

Phoenix and the guys clapped as she smiled. She was now broken in. Rumbles sounded and they turned to the southwest. It was black with flashes of lightening.

Phoenix said, "Here we go! Get ready for the storm. It's coming fast. Watch for alerts on your phone and get to the safe room if it gets bad."

Bella and Phoenix ran through the whipping wind to the house. They were barely in the garage when the rain hit.

After Bella cleaned up, she found Phoenix at his desk. Frowning.

Bella said, "Is anything wrong?"

"Yes. I am missing a cow and heifer both due to deliver."

He walked to the pasture map to verify, then looked outside at the storm. Obviously, no drone could fly in this.

Bella said, "How long will the storm last?"

He checked the weather radar and said, "At least forty-five minutes," and a tornado alert went off. He sighed and turned on the television to follow the Wichita Falls weather report.

While he worked and watched the weather, Bella went to the kitchen. Jasmine had just finished cleaning up, so they sat at the snack bar to chat.

Bella glanced at Troy by the door and said, "Did you talk to him while you cooked today?"

"I did. I asked him the weather radar update a few times when my hands were too messy to check my phone."

Bella said, "He's interesting."

Jasmine said, "Very! Oh, hey, I wanted to let you know that you will love the Cattleman's Gala. We go every year."

Bella said, "What are you wearing?"

"I ordered a bronze strapless gown. Kit is going to flip out. He loves it when I wear something else besides jeans," and grinned. "I heard you and Boss talking about your red dress at lunch yesterday. What does it look like?"

"It is a V-neck sequin sheath. It is backless and exposes one whole leg."

Jasmine whistled and said, "Boss is going to be hot on your tail – oh, I mean trail," and they laughed.

Bella said, "Let's try something. Troy, come see."

Troy's eyes opened and he responded, "Yes, Bella," and rolled to meet her.

Bella said, "Troy, mark on the calendar that there is a Cattleman's Gala on May 28."

"Yes, Bella."

GP called from across the room, "Troy, I am GP, would you wake me up from my nap in one hour?" and the girls laughed.

Troy responded, "Yes, GP."

Phoenix called from his office, "Troy, tell everyone in the room that the tornado died out," and they all cheered and didn't even hear Troy say it.

Bella went to meet Phoenix and he said, "The rain's letting up. Let's head back to the barn and take an RTV to search for the missing cattle. I have a rain poncho for you."

On the way out, Phoenix said, "GP, the contractors or the Ranger will be by at some point, would you keep an eye out for them while we go search for two missing cows?"

GP said, "Sure thing."

Bella put on her backpack and pulled on the poncho. Phoenix slipped his on and they headed to the barn. Kit and Buck were already in slicker suits and handed everyone a radio.

Phoenix said, "You take the west pasture, and we will take the northwest one. Stay in touch," and all three RTVs roared away.

Phoenix handed Bella a pair of binoculars and said, "If you would search on your side, I can search the rest, okay?"

They were about an hour and a half into the search when they began to hear a wolf howl. It seemed to be coming from straight ahead, so Phoenix sped up. Bella reached behind her and pulled out her tranquilizer gun and tucked it in her waistband.

***

Kit came over the radio and said, "You hear that, Boss?"

"Yeah. I am headed straight toward it. Stay searching where you are until I know what's going on."

***

The howl grew much louder. The wolf was close.

When Phoenix crested the top of a small hill, they saw the cattle shed and laying on the ground in front of it was a cow and a baby calf. A large wolf sat next to the cow and howled.

Phoenix said, "Now that's what I call an unusual sight," and pulled his pistol as he sped forward.

Bella continued to watch by binoculars trying to determine the state of the animals on the ground. Then the wolf looked toward them, and she could clearly see that it was a wolfdog.

She said, "It's a wolfdog mix, he's got blue eyes."

He said, "I haven't seen one around here in a long time. That is one big wolf," and in a flash, the wolf was gone.

Bella said, "If I hadn't seen it with my own eyes, I wouldn't have believed it. He acted like he drew us here and his job was done."

"That's a new one on me too. I sure hope that cow and calf are alive."

Two minutes later they parked near the shed and jumped out to check the animals. Bella went to the calf. Phoenix went to the cow.

She knelt, and cleaned the calf's face off, and said, "He's breathing," and continued to check him.

The bull calf began to move around and call for his momma, so Bella knew he was ok and turned her attention to the cow.

"Is she alive?"

Phoenix sighed and said, "No, but she's still warm. She hasn't been dead long."

Bella checked the cow and found the puddle of blood under her, and said, "She hemorrhaged. I'm sorry. Her bull calf seems to be fine, just not trying to stand yet."

***

Phoenix said over the radio, "Kit. Buck. We found the cow. She delivered but hemorrhaged. The bull calf is alive. Have you found the heifer yet?"

Buck, breathless, came over the radio and said, "Yeah, we have her, she got stuck in a fence. She is scratched up but fine. Do you want me to come and get the cow while you take the calf?"

"Yeah, come on. We are at shed three. And believe it or not, it was a large wolfdog that howled us here. Craziest thing I've ever seen."

Buck said, "Never heard of that before."

Phoenix said, "If Kit doesn't need you, come on. We'll wait for you."

Phoenix said, "Bella, if you drive back, I can hold the calf in the dump bed. He is too big for you to handle if he struggles."

"Sure. You know, I still question whether that was a wild wolfdog. He sure seemed to know what he was doing. Any wild animal would have killed them both and eaten on them. I am intrigued. He was beautiful."

"Yes, he was. But wolves aren't usually a good fit with livestock, Dr. B," and Bella caught his meaning and nodded.

Several minutes later, Buck drove up and sighed when he saw the scene, and said, "Sorry Boss, she was a good one."

It was almost five p.m. when Bella parked the RTV at the barn. The contractors were working at her office and Ranger Morgan had just pulled up. Phoenix slid out of the back with the calf.

The Ranger walked over and said, "I gather his momma didn't make it."

"No. I should have pulled her out of the herd. She was getting too old."

The Ranger nodded and said, "So, Dr. DelCaprio, are you ready for your phone? It has rung constantly. You have plenty of calls to return."

Laughing, she took her phone and said, "Thank you! And I'll let you know what we find out Monday on Royce's case."

He walked back to his truck and said, "I'll look for your message. Y'all have a good weekend!" and off he went.

Bella looked at the calf and said, "Someone should keep an eye on him tonight."

Phoenix said, "The guys will take care of him. I'm going to carry him to one of the stalls. Do you want to go check the progress on your office?"

With a smile, she jumped back in the RTV and headed for her office.

***

Lucas called Bella just as she drove up to her barn, so she sat there and answered, "Hey Lucas! Sorry, I didn't have my phone. Ranger Morgan just brought it back to me less than five minutes ago."

Lucas said, "Why did he have your phone?"

"I got a text threat yesterday and he took my phone to see if he could trace it."

He growled, and said, "You and I both know that it was probably Royce, what did it say?"

She paused, knowing that he wasn't going to like what Royce had said.

He said, "You might as well tell me, or I will just ask Phoenix."

She sighed and said, "'My lips will catch your dying breath as you struggle beneath me.'"

"He's a dead man," Lucas said with menace.

Bella said, "Wait, let me tell you what we've done. Ranger Morgan traced the text to a Baton Rouge prepaid phone. So, I called the detective in Baton Rouge to make sure that Royce was still there, and he is. They saw him. He goes to court Monday, so we won't know what will happen to him till then. But regardless, Phoenix is keeping me close to him and the detective will call me if there is any change in Royce's location."

Lucas said, "He's going to get a slap on the wrist, Bella. He's clean. We need to make a plan if he doesn't go to jail."

"Yes. I agree, but enough of that for now. Tell me about you and Lili."

She heard the smile in his voice as he said, "She's perfect, Bella. I love seeing her, being with her, and planning a future. And speaking of future, I have a couple of things to run by you since you probably haven't spoken to Seth or Lili either.

"Seth needs to move out of the LSU apartment by Tuesday. Then move into his new place. Then he has a job tour Friday. He has run out of time."

Bella said, "Why don't we just pay for movers."

"We can't. We need to pack it a certain way and instructing them will take longer than if we do it ourselves. And I have more news. I start my new job in Wichita Falls on June 1."

She screamed and scared the contractors, so she apologized, then said, "I am so excited for you! What is your new job?"

And suddenly Phoenix yelled across the field, "Bella! Are you ok?"

She said, "Hang on, Lucas," and she yelled back to Phoenix, "I'm ok! Sorry I screamed! I am on the phone with Lucas," and he jogged over to meet her.

She said, "Phoenix is here now, Lucas, I have you on speaker. So, finish telling me what your job will be in Wichita Falls."

Lucas said, "I'm going to be a County Arson Investigator."

Bella cheered, and Phoenix said, "That's a great job for you, especially with your criminal justice degree."

Lucas said, "I think so too. I told Bella that I start June 1 – on her birthday."

Phoenix said, "Doesn't Seth start his job at NASA that day?"

Bella said, "Yes."

Phoenix said, "Well, I have tickets for the weekend before to a Cattleman's Gala. That's Memorial Day weekend. You and Lili must come. I figure that Ariel will bring Seth. It is formal, so dust off your tux. And besides, we can celebrate Bella's birthday."

Lucas said, "You are getting old, Bella."

She said, "No cake for you!" and they laughed.

The contractors interrupted with a question, so Bella said, "We have to go, Lucas."

***

When they got upstairs, Bella was amazed at how much the workers had already accomplished. They removed all the appliances, plumbing and electrical fixtures, and paint primer was drying on the walls. The contractor needed to know where to install the new wall mount air conditioner.

Bella looked at Phoenix, and he said, "It's your call. Whatever works best for you."

She showed the guy where to install it, and said, "Do I need to choose anything else for you?"

The contractor motioned to another guy to bring her the paint cards, and she looked through them and chose a buttermilk tan. Then he handed her brochures of shower stalls and light fixtures. After she made her choices, he pointed to the wooden floor and asked if she wanted it re-stained or tiled.

Bella looked around as said, "Can you just reseal it and leave it natural?"

The guy said, "Sure. We are almost done for today. We should be back by ten a.m. tomorrow. If you think of anything else just call me," and he handed her a business card.

Heading back to the house, Phoenix said, "Do you need to do any furniture shopping for your office?"

She said, "I don't think so. Once Lucas brings my things out of the Baton Rouge apartment, I should have everything I need."

Phoenix's phone rang and he answered, "Hi Ariel, how's Houston?"

She said, "Hot and humid and it's only May."

He chuckled and said, "I can vouch for that. We sweat all day."

She said, "Yuck. Hey, Seth hasn't been able to reach Bella, what's up?"

Phoenix said, "I just put you on speaker. Bella, Ariel was wondering why Seth couldn't reach you by phone."

Bella said, "Hey Ariel, I was going to call him shortly. I haven't had my phone since yesterday mid-afternoon."

"Oh no, did you break it?"

"No. Someone threatened me by text yesterday and Ranger Morgan was running a trace off my phone. I just got it back."

Ariel said, "What kind of threat do you mean?"

And Seth interrupted and said, "Hey, I just walked in and heard that comment. What threat?"

Bella said, "Hi Seth, Phoenix is with me too. And to answer your question, I think Royce sent it, but it's from a prepaid phone so all we know at this point, is it came from Baton Rouge."

Seth said, "I hate that man. Spit it out Bella, what did he say?"

"Ok," she sighed, and said, "'My lips will catch your dying breath while you struggle beneath me'".

Seth said with gritted teeth, "I just want five minutes with him, and he won't ever bother you again."

Phoenix said, "I get him first."

Seth said, "I hear you man. Isn't his court case Monday?"

"Yes." Bella said. "And on another note, I hear that you and Lucas are moving us out of the apartment Tuesday so you can move into your new place in Houston. Then you tour NASA Friday."

Seth said, "Yeah. You know me, fit it all in at one time - Mr. Crammer," and everyone laughed.

Phoenix said, "Well, let me add to it. Ariel, the tickets came in for the Cattleman's Gala next Saturday during Memorial Day weekend. So, fill Seth in on it. But anyway, y'all come up for the holiday weekend. Lucas and Lili are coming as well."

Ariel said, "I love the Gala. Do you have a tux, Seth?"

"Buried in a box somewhere. I might just rent one."

Phoenix said, "I also have a few extra tickets if you know anyone else that might like to come with you. We have room for guests, even if we need to use the bunkroom for all the men."

Seth said, "I'm in. I'm going to be Mr. Hot in a tux though," and laughed as Ariel rolled her eyes as him.

Bella said, "So, what's happening between you two?"

Ariel laughed and said, "Don't be subtle."

Seth said, "She won't be able to resist my charm forever."

Ariel said, "You'll be the first to know when resistance is over, handsome."

Seth said, "Ok, we have to go…" and the line went dead.

***

Just before they walked in the house, Phoenix said, "How about a date night? We'll have the run of the house since GP goes to bed early."

She whispered, "How bad do you want the date night?" and he showed her.

Chapter 16
Date Night

When they walked inside, GP had obviously grilled because the house smelled wonderful. Large steak burgers, draped in melted cheese still smoked on the stove.

Bella said, "GP, that smells delicious, thank you so much."

He smiled and said, "I enjoy it. Y'all have had a full day of hard work."

Then they began their ritual of getting dinner ready to eat. While Bella pulled out the dinnerware, Phoenix checked the fridge for anything to go with the burgers, and chuckled.

Bella said, "What?"

Phoenix held up a tray of ready toppings for the burgers, and a pan of baked beans. The men both knew that Jasmine's baked beans were chockerblock full of things that made cowboys beg.

GP said, "She must want a raise."

Phoenix said, "She deserves one!"

Less than an hour later, GP headed to his room while Bella and Phoenix went to clean up.

***

Once she showered, Bella looked at her clothes. What should she wear? She wanted to take Phoenix's mind off ranch work, but she didn't want to dress up - just memorable. She chose a silky black tank and rhinestone jeans with fabulous, expensive holes in them. She left her hair loose and just put on mascara, eyeliner, nude gloss, and a spray of perfume.

As she set the bottle down, she heard a light knock on the door and said, "Come on in."

He stepped inside and growled in appreciation as she walked toward him.

She smiled, and let her gaze slide down his broad chest in a fitted brown metallic shirt, and low hipped, well-worn jeans. Sex appeal dripped off him.

He met her in a couple of steps and their kiss said it all.

A bit later, they walked to the den and Phoenix said, "Why don't we take a few minutes to set up our personal preferences in the robot. Everyone is getting a kick out of him."

She said, "He is kind of handy, and sweet."

They sat on the sofa and Phoenix said, "Sweet?" and she shrugged.

"He wants to serve me. What can I say?"

He chuckled and said, "Troy, come."

Troy's eyes opened and he responded, "Yes, Boss."

When he got there, Phoenix said, "Troy, are you able to update our preference options verbally?"

"Yes, Boss. The first category is security."

Phoenix said, "You ask me the questions and I will answer."

Troy responded, "Do I continue to patrol inside the house?"

Phoenix thought about it and said, "Yes."

Then he told Bella, "I'll try it. I don't know how I feel about it yet. He startled me in the hall last night."

Then he said, "Troy, how will you alert me if you find a problem?"

Troy responded, "If you are home, I will sound an alarm. If you are away, I will text you."

Phoenix said, "Agreed."

Troy responded, "The next preference is voice option. I will play different voices for you to choose from. Please tell me to stop when you hear the voice option that you prefer."

Various male and female voices spoke, and Bella chose one.

Troy responded, "The next preference is audio, video, and camera. Would you like to leave these features on?"

Phoenix said, "Don't leave them on. I will tell you when they are needed."

Troy responded, "The next preference is communication. Would you like me to be able to call, text or email anyone for you?"

Phoenix said, "I'll let you know later. No for now. Other than that, be sure to remember that Phoenix is also Boss, and Bella is also Dr. B. And that's enough for right now. You may return to your home station."

As he rolled away, Bella said, "He is eager to please."

Phoenix said, "If he's not, he might end up a trashcan," and Bella laughed.

He held her hand, and said, "How about taking a stroll outside with me?"

Bella's heart skipped a beat. She knew that it was pitch black outside – and inside she cringed. He wanted to work on her fear of darkness. Eventually she nodded.

They walked out to the enclosed patio first, and Bella said, "This is a fabulous room. You did an amazing job. The furniture for the seating and dining areas is comfortable, warm, and inviting. And the waterfall pool is like a vacation island. I can't wait to get in it."

He said, "I'm planning on a private swimming party with you afterwhile."

She grinned and said, "I just bet you are."

He winked and said, "You will love the saltwater pool. It's a real treat after a long workday."

"I totally agree with that."

Then he reached for her hand, and said, "Let's take a walk. I won't leave your side. I will do whatever you need."

She nodded and followed as he led her outside.

Without a flashlight.

Into the dark.

Phoenix casually strolled down the road as they held hands. He didn't rush her because they both knew that as they left the ranch lights behind, the darker it would get. And the night was not clear so there was no moon or stars to help light the way. Phoenix needed to see how far Bella could get from the light before fear reared its ugly head.

But Bella did not stroll casually. She saw the total darkness ahead of them. Dreaded it. As she stepped toward the first shadow, her hand gripped his tighter.

Phoenix slowed his pace and said softly, "Ok. We'll slow it down," and she nodded.

After a few more steps, she squeezed his hand hard, and stopped.

He stepped in front of her, aware that they were only shadow figures now, and said, "Tell me what you feel, Bella. What are you thinking?"

She didn't answer him. She couldn't. That was the problem was Bella's last thought, as fingers of fear crept up her spine and terrifying whispers got loud in her ears. She tried to think, but focus was too difficult. She could barely see Phoenix's shadow in front of her, and her jaw clenched shut.

He said, "Bella, listen to my voice," and he held her face and maintained a physical connection to her. "Remember when I couldn't see with my eye injury? Remember how you helped me see you in my blindness?"

Something about what he said reached through the fear, and she fought to focus on his words.

He said, "Close your eyes. Don't look at the darkness. Read me with your hands and fingers just like I did with you. Touch me and see me in the dark."

Bella blinked and hope flickered as she finally focused on the thought of reading him and closed her eyes. And it helped.

Then suddenly she really wanted to see him the way that he had seen her.

So, pushing the fear away, she forced her way through the dark and went behind him. She knelt at his feet.

She was determined to see only what her fingers showed her. She began at his calves, and through his jeans could feel his muscles. She slid her hands up to his knees, and above.

Her hands tightened as she reached his rock-hard thighs, and they flexed at her touch.

Amazed at the strength in his powerful muscles, the dark seemed much smaller. She had seen Phoenix's legs many times. But feeling them made her aware of his power. He was so masculine. Then she slid her hands up his sides, across his hips, and gently across his lower back till she reached the waistband of his jeans.

Without a word, Phoenix pulled his shirt off as her fingers touched his skin.

Bella continued her soft, gentle exploration up his waist and back, till she stood close and reached his broad shoulders. His skin was so warm and perfect. She kissed his back and felt his muscles respond to her. She kept going.

He squatted to help her reach higher and she slid her fingers up his neck and into his hair. He was bigger than her fear. Then she felt her way around him to the front and knelt again.

Phoenix struggled at her exquisite touch, and breath, on his hot skin. But he forced himself to stay focused on any need that she might have. But his body was tight as he anticipated her touch.

Wanted it.

Bella wrapped her hands around his shins in the front. His powerful legs reminded her of the scripture in Song of Songs where it described her lover's legs as pillars of marble, and she understood. Astounding strength.

As her hands passed over his knees heading up, she felt his muscles ripple again as she touched his jean-clad thighs. She knew that this was difficult for him. It had to be. She remembered how intimate it had been for her.

Then she quit thinking. She returned to seeing in her mind as her hands neared the top of his legs. To his hips. Over his waistband to his stomach, rippled and firm. She passed his ribs and reached his broad muscled chest.

He squatted again, and she stepped closer to slide her hands up his neck, to his face, and her lips found his.

In the dark.

Phoenix straightened and lifted her off her feet as he embraced her, inhaled her, and devoured her mouth. Bella wrapped her arms and legs around him and lost herself in the moment, safe in his arms.

Unafraid.

Later, he kept his arm around her as they walked quietly back toward the ranch. Sometimes words just get in the way. The intimacy had been beautiful and intriguing.

When they reached the patio again, he walked toward his bedroom entrance and said, "You haven't seen our room. Would you like to check it out before you go change to swim?"

She absolutely wanted to see it, but said, "Dare we?" and he winked.

Bella figured that his room would be amazing, and it was. She gazed up at the antler chandelier hanging in the center of the overhead beams. Then she looked at the bed that dominated the room. It was built over two feet off the floor on a stepped platform. Thick king size mattresses sat at the top of the steps, covered in a white down-filled comforter with a black, brown, and white cowhide skin laid across the bed. Various pillows that reflected warmth and impressive strength were piled against a headboard made of wood, with the name Chandler carved in it.

She looked at him and said, "This is gorgeous, powerful and bold, just like you," and he slid his hand behind her neck and lowered his lips to kiss her.

He said, "I like your description, but now it needs to reflect you too," and she nodded.

Bella continued to look around and loved the feel of the room with its brick floor. Beyond the bed was a seating area with a fireplace. On another wall was an impressive closet door foyer with a bench and mirrors. The other door had to be the bathroom.

He opened the bathroom and she saw the same decorator thought here. Straight ahead a massive stone wall with a large spacious u-shaped glass shower wrapped around a wonderful jacuzzi. There was a wooden counter with marble bowl sinks on each side of the room. Rustic iron chandeliers hung over each counter. A toilet room was next to one side of the shower, and a linen closet on the other side.

Bella said, "It couldn't be more perfect."

Phoenix said, "Come see the dressing room closet," and only then did she realize there were no dressers in the bedroom. The room had built ins with drawers, mirrors, shoe racks, hanging racks, hooks, shelving and chairs for him and her sides.

She said, "I don't have enough clothes to make a dent in this closet. And I love your tuxes," as she ran her hands over them.

They were all black, but different styles.

He said, "You will fill this quick enough. You will see. We constantly have to change from working outside. And the ranch has various social events to host, and attend. You will have fun. And I will enjoy picking out all sorts of things for you to wear."

She grinned and he led her back into the bedroom, and up the steps to sit on his bed.

He smiled and said, "Now that I have you on my bed…" and she grinned.

He said, "So, tell me, what style or décor would you add to your home, that gives you that personal, I'm home feeling."

Bella thought a second and said, "I like a touch of sparkle, maybe a few soft throws, some books, a few splashes of happy color, a couple of animal statues or paintings, and my guitar."

Phoenix smiled as he brushed her hair off her shoulder and said, "That sounds just like you. Please add yourself to the house. Teach me what catches your eye. But, for the moment, I have to admit that all I really want is for you to lay back and feel the bed," and Bella laughed softly as he laid her back.

He said, "How does the mattress feel?"

"The mattress feels great. But you feel… so much better."

He lowered his lips till they barely brushed hers, and said, "Have you thought anymore about moving our wedding date up?"

She felt his breath on her lips, and whispered, "I have thought about that."

With a smile, he lowered his lips, and encouraged her to think harder.

A short time later, Bella had just put on her bathing suit when Phoenix called down the hall for her to hurry. She laughed and joined him in his bedroom dressed in a very sexy blue bikini.

He rubbed the back of his neck to help him focus, and said, "It wouldn't hurt for us to go ahead and get the marriage license early, now, would it?"

She said, "I think early might be a very good idea."

He smiled and opened the patio door for her, and said, "I'm going to take you at your word, and wait for that new date."

He motioned for her to go out the door first. A few steps later, Bella glanced back to see why he wasn't talking. She caught his hungry stare and blew him a kiss.

He started after her and she ran. She tried to prolong the chase and ran behind a table. But he just shoved it out of the way and kept coming. She darted toward the pool and screamed as he caught her climbing the waterfall. He claimed a kiss for his reward and carried her into the pool.

They talked, flirted, laughed, and swam for a good hour before Bella decided to float. But she kept sinking so he held her up and walked her around the pool. She smiled contentedly, completely relaxed.

He said, "Nothing like holding your dreams in your hands," and she giggled.

Then he tickled her side with his lips, and she giggled again.

She said, "Boys never outgrow picking at girls."

Phoenix said, "That's because picking at girls is actually pursuit practice," and she laughed.

Then she stood and said, "Come on, it's my turn to float you."

"You can't float me."

"Chicken?" she asked.

"Really? A taunt? Come on."

He laid in a float position, and she put her hands under his back to hold him up. She guided him around the pool like he had done for her. He finally closed his eyes and relaxed.

A few minutes later he opened his eyes, and Bella was looking at his body. After seeing that look, he was no longer relaxed.

She flicked her gaze back to his face and saw him watching her.

She played it off and said, "I'm going to see how ticklish you are. Don't move."

Phoenix grinned as she lightly rubbed her lips on his side. He flinched. She tried another spot, but he jerked again. He was super ticklish. Then she leaned down and licked his stomach.

He rolled over and snatched her up so fast that she gasped.

He drawled, "Now Bella, that was not a tickle move. And we are going first thing Monday for that marriage license. It is past time."

***

Neither of them noticed the robot that watched them at the corner of the window.

Chapter 17
The Hacker

The Hacker sat in his home in Houston and watched, through Troy's eyes, Bella and Phoenix swim and kiss in the pool.

Bella's body was deliciously formed. Her blue eyes sparked fires that he couldn't put out. Her lips were full and mouthwatering, and her long dark hair made him want to bury his face in it.

Frustrated, he looked at his other monitors that played silently with video from the two other hacked robots that he had sent out, but they didn't matter any longer.

This had become all about Bella.

He got up and slapped a stack of books to the floor. He was frustrated about their wedding date documented in Troy's computer calendar for July 4.

He was an intelligent man, and though he had criminal tendencies and sexual addictions, he hadn't contemplated going beyond watching his victims. To introduce the next step of touching Bella would undoubtedly open a door to endless possibilities of legal repercussions and violence.

And he knew that Bella would fight him.

At first anyway.

Was that what he wanted? Was that what this had turned into or was it just because it was her? What about his highly secure job?

He sighed and hit replay and watched Bella lick Phoenix's stomach for the fiftieth time. He had to have her. Now, how could he get her? Thinking - he glanced over at his NASA award photographs on the wall.

Chapter 18
Royce, Baton Rouge

In his Baton Rouge apartment, Royce was kicked back on the sofa with his feet propped-up on a large, black leather ottoman. He rocked his feet to the radio as he scrolled through pictures and videos of Bella during the few months they had dated. He had known that she wasn't in-to-him as the girls would say, but she had a way of drawing people to her. Men saw her. And wanted her.

That wasn't his fault.

He laid his phone down and thought back to when the urges to dominate women had surfaced. It was before he worked at LSU. He could easily play the gentlemen or passionate role, whichever worked to get them alone with him. But it was when the fear light flashed in their eyes that he really got pumped. He had pushed that button on dozens of women through the years. Most fled.

He thought things would be different with Bella, but she wouldn't engage in the relationship. When he pushed for more, she cut him off cold, and he crossed over to the *beyond fear side.*

It was only two days till court. Then he would find her at Chandler Canyon Ranch. But for now, a text would remind her that he was thinking of her.

***

Unknown to Bella: I want you. Naked. Fighting. Scream for me, Bella.

***

Chapter 19
Dr. B

Bella heard her bedroom door creak. She peeked over the covers and saw Phoenix shut her door. He was bare chested in lounge pants, so she knew he had just gotten out of bed. She closed her eyes and pretended to be asleep.

Phoenix slipped under Bella's covers and wrapped himself around her.

They both groaned at the warm and wonderful contact of their bodies.

He said, "I am a crazy man for doing this," and buried his face in her neck as he snuggled and breathed her in.

Bella said, "Oh my gosh—" and he kissed her before she could finish her comment.

A few hot hugs and warm kisses later, Bella said, "You demonstrate well why the cows and heifers finally stop running from the bull."

Phoenix rolled on his back and laughed.

Still chuckling, he said, "Are you calling me a bull, Dr. B?"

She stretched and said, "Absolutely."

He said, "So do I call you—"

She interrupted and said, "Don't even think about it. Bull sounds a lot better than cow or heifer."

He said, "I would only call you, my Bella."

"Because you are a wise, wise, man."

He smiled and pulled her even closer.

She pressed her face against his neck and whispered, "I love being in love with you."

He said, "You do it so—" and her phone alarm interrupted him, followed by her notifications loading.

He said, "Sometimes technology annoys me," and he turned off her alarm.

Bella grinned, and he said, "I need to get up anyway. Work calls. I just wanted a few minutes to hug on you."

She said, "Since it is Saturday, are you going straight to the barn this morning, or will all of you still meet up in the kitchen?"

He sat up and said, "We will do our regular breakfast routine, but why don't you sleep-in? You are only on call. Besides, we can't even leave for Wichita Falls to pick up your vet orders till mid-morning."

She said, "Oh no, I'm awake. I would rather spend time with you anyway. And I can heat the pancakes that Jasmine left for breakfast."

"Thank you for that. The guys will appreciate it too. I'll see you in a few minutes."

Bella thought about their wedding date. She knew that she was more than ready to be Phoenix's bride. Right now. They lived in the same house, worked together, and passionately loved and wanted each other. Why wait almost seven more weeks? She had already waited ten years.

She got out of bed and looked in the mirror. She wondered what style wedding dress she should get. It had to be something that he would love.

A few minutes later she met them in the kitchen in shorts, an LSU jersey, and sandals.

Phoenix said, "You look like a teenager," and she smiled.

Buck drawled, "Lucky you, Boss," and everyone laughed.

Bella served them hot pancakes with multiple syrups and flavored butters. It seemed that the guys had a taste for gourmet. Breakfast disappeared quickly and the guys followed Kit out the door for a short weekend workday.

Phoenix gave Bella a lingering kiss, then headed for the door.

But just before he touched the knob, teasing him, Bella called out, "I was wondering about lingerie. Do you have anything special in mind that you want to see me in?"

Phoenix slowly turned, and like a powerful jungle cat, languidly walked back toward her. She felt the anticipation and had trouble taking a breath as he reached her.

He pressed into her till her back was against the wall. And his deep, possessive kiss powerfully revealed his feelings on the subject. Bella groaned in eager response, then gasped as he picked her up, and licked all the way up her neck.

He whispered in her ear, "No matter what you wear, you won't have it on for long."

About that time GP walked back in from outside, grinned when he saw them, and said, "Don't mind me, I forgot my hat," and headed to his bedroom.

Phoenix didn't take his eyes off Bella and said, "No problem GP. Just tending to business," and GP chuckled as he went down the hall.

Bella said breathlessly, "That did not just happen."

He drawled, "It's gonna happen a whole lot more," and kissed her, put her back on her feet, winked, and walked out the door.

Bella hadn't moved when GP came back in the room. He smiled and saluted her, then walked out the door. She closed her eyes, trying to identify all the feelings that raced through her. Phoenix was so smoking hot.

Her body was going crazy.

They didn't explain that in anatomy.

A couple of hours later, she put the finishing touches on her makeup and gave a squirt of perfume. Today she was dressed as social Dr. B in white slim fit slacks, a black silk shirt, and heels. She put her hair in a ponytail and added diamond stud earrings. Picking up her briefcase she headed to the den. A glance outside showed Phoenix still at the barn so she decided to text Lili. She missed her so much and this was an important time in her life too.

***

Bella to Lili: I miss you. How are things?

Lili replied: I miss you too. And I can't wait to get married. You do plan to be my maid of honor, right?

Bella replied: Yes! But it looks like I might have to be your matron of honor instead. We will probably move our date closer.

Lili replied: I am not surprised! How's your vet office at the ranch?

Bella replied: It is being remodeled and we are heading to Wichita Falls today to pick up supplies and equipment. When are you heading to your parents?

Lili replied: Lucas is bringing me tomorrow, and once they move us out of the Baton Rouge apartment, he will come meet me.

Bella replied: I am thrilled we will be close to each other.

Lili replied: It doesn't get any better than that.

Bella replied: Right!

***

After that, she scrolled through phone messages. It was mainly friends, relatives, and college connections. Then she sighed. There was another unknown number text, but it could just sit there until Phoenix opened it. She didn't want to know what that psycho had to say.

Ever.

She had a life to live, and he wasn't in it.

Refusing to let him ruin her day, she looked out the windows at the pool and patio. Smiling, she walked outside. A wedding would be beautiful out here.

Phoenix walked in through the kitchen. He didn't see Bella, so he headed to the bedroom wing. But her movement on the patio caught his attention. She looked beautiful and happy.

He stepped outside to join her.

She turned to him with a smile and said, "Hi there, Boss."

"Hi there, Dr. B. You look beautiful," he said, and kissed her softly. "Are you planning a wedding out here by any chance?"

"I am in fact. Are you interested in hearing a much earlier wedding date?"

"More than I can even explain."

"I checked the ranch calendar, and it looks like a wedding on June 4—" And he quickly interrupted her with a kiss.

She continued with a grin, "That would give us one whole week for a honeymoon. Would you like one whole week with me, Boss?"

She watched several emotions wash over him and he leaned down and whispered something in her ear.

Her face flushed at his words, and he said, "Does that answer your question, Dr. B?"

She looked at his lips and whispered, "Oh, yes. I got the answer, and the visual too."

He winked and said, "Let me go clean up—"

Bella said, "Wait, before you do, I have something to tell you, but you have to promise that it will not ruin our day."

That let him know that it wasn't pleasant, and he said, "Don't worry about that, just tell me what it is."

"I received another text from an unknown number during the night, probably from Royce, but I haven't read it. I thought perhaps you would read it and let me know if I need to know what it says. I have no problem ignoring it."

Instantly ready to rip Royce's head off, but hiding his feelings, Phoenix said calmly, "Good plan. Where's your phone?" and she motioned inside.

He pulled up the text on her phone and read, "I want you. Naked. Fighting. Scream for me Bella."

She saw his jaw clench tight, then he glanced at her and said, "I forwarded the text to myself and deleted it off your phone. It is nothing that you need to concern yourself with. Now, how about I go shower and change and we can leave for town?"

She said, "I am ready and waiting."

Phoenix said, "I see that. You are dressed to kill, Dr. B," and she kissed him sweetly, thank you.

GP came in a little later, and said, "Whoa, Bella, you look beautiful. Am I meeting the professional persona of Dr. B?"

"Indeed, you are, GP."

"You are going to turn some heads today."

She grinned and said, "Phoenix's is the only head I want to turn."

GP laughed and said, "He's turning in circles he's so locked on you," and she giggled.

He said, "I'm heading to clean up myself, y'all have a nice trip into town."

Knowing that he would be here all day alone, she said, "Would you like us to bring you back something for dinner?"

He shook his head, chuckled, and said, "No thank you. A steak, nap, and a movie make me happy these days. And I have all that, right here."

Bella decided to walk out into the backyard while she waited on Phoenix. She hadn't spent any time yet just enjoying the view. She looked around and smiled. It was so, Texas, with the wide-open fields, acres of grass, flowers, patches of trees, cattle, horses, and lots of blue sky.

Then, she saw something move out in the pasture. What was that? She shielded her eyes from the sun and squinted, as she walked toward the fence. She could barely make out an animal sitting in the tall grass. She opened the gate and walked slowly across the pasture to get a closer look.

Then she stopped. It was the wolfdog.

Phoenix had just zipped his jeans when he saw Bella walk through the gate into the pasture. He stepped to his window to see what she was looking at, but he wasn't at the right angle.

He stepped into the backyard and looked beyond Bella to see what she watched so intently. He saw the wolfdog. It was headed straight toward her.

Phoenix yelled and ran.

Startled, Bella spun, and the wolfdog disappeared into the brush.

Phoenix reached her, and said sharply, "What were you thinking? You can't approach a wolf!"

Bella said sternly, "Don't lecture me about animals, Phoenix. I know my profession and I will make those decisions."

Insistent, he said, "You were not safe without a weapon."

Understanding, but determined, she said, "Of course that is preferable, but that is not a wild wolf. His behavior is totally different."

He continued, "Perhaps not, but we don't know that for sure yet, do we?"

Bella said, "I will start carrying my tranquilizer gun then, because we won't know anything about him if we keep him at a distance."

Phoenix and Bella faced off, and he said, "I get it. He is fascinating and beautiful. So instead of wondering, why don't we go find him? Maybe we can search when we get back from town today. But I mean it Bella, don't do it alone. You don't make decisions that just affect you anymore."

Awareness hit her, and she touched his bare chest, and said softly, "I am sorry, Phoenix. That is true. I am sure that it startled you, but it wasn't planned. I walked outside to wait for you and was amazed to see him out there. He was just sitting and waiting. When I started toward him, he headed to me like it was the most natural thing to do."

He wrapped his arms around her and gazed across the pasture.

He said, "I know that you need freedom to enjoy and love this land too. It's just that the memory of my mom's accident is poignant. I certainly didn't mean to reprimand you professionally. I was thinking as the man that loves you."

He paused, then said, "and I need you safe with me."

Hearing his heart, she nodded against his chest. They stood silently for a few minutes, then let it all pass.

When they went back inside, Phoenix texted the crew that the wolfdog was coming around the ranch, seemingly not aggressive. He told them not to harm him unless he threatened man or animal. It was possible he was someone's pet.

Bella said, "Thank you," and he nodded.

Before long they were in his bronze King Ranch truck headed to Wichita Falls.

Bella said, "It feels like we are going on a trip."

He laughed and said, "When you live this far out, a trip to town is a treat. So, on that note, besides picking up your vet supplies, what would you like to do?"

"Eat out of course, go to a wedding shop, and maybe drive your truck."

He faked shock as he touched the dash like it was alive, and said, "I'm the only one that has ever driven her."

Bella grinned and said, "Well, she won't mind," and he laughed.

With a twinkle in his eye, he said, "And you are going to trust me in a wedding shop? I am impressed."

"I'm impressed you are willing to go in one."

An idea flashed in his mind, and he said, "How about we forgo tradition, and let me pick out your wedding dress?"

"Really? I love that idea!"

He said, "I love the idea too. And speaking of tradition, what is your name plan when we get married since your license and certification are for DelCaprio?"

"I think I will hyphenate DelCaprio and Chandler and keep it simple. It is important to me to show that I will be a Chandler too."

Phoenix said, "I look forward to you being a Chandler. But I totally understand that you have your own professional identity. You have worked hard for it, and I admire you," and she smiled and touched him softly in response.

A little later, she said, "I haven't had time to tell you, but I texted Lili earlier. Lucas is moving her to Wichita Falls tomorrow, then he is heading to meet Seth so they can move us out of the apartment."

"Why did you go to school in Louisiana?"

"LSU offered me a full scholarship. I walked away from eight years of college with a doctorate and don't owe a cent. That is a miracle. Due also because my grandparents left me more than enough to cover room, board, and expenses."

Phoenix held her hand and said, "Bella, that reminds me, I need you to know that I will take care of any expenses you have for anything even before the wedding. We will get anything you want or need."

She said, "You don't have to do that, Phoenix. I have money too. Besides, you paid me yesterday an astronomical amount for working two days," and he winked.

"You bet I did! You are worth much more than that to me. And on that note, let's talk about the honeymoon."

She laughed and said, "Yes, let's do that."

"Where would you like to go?"

Bella thought for a minute and said, "Well, anywhere with you is perfect, but we really enjoyed the beach. Perhaps, a tropical spot not too far away so that travel won't eat up all our time."

"That's a perfect idea," he said, "Bikini perfect in fact," and she laughed.

Phoenix said, "How about we spend the first night in a honeymoon suite in Dallas, and then fly out to the Bahamas the next day?"

"Yes. I love it."

Kissing her hand, he said, "I can't wait."

They reached Wichita Falls right at lunch time and stopped to eat at an Italian restaurant.

Bella laughed as he said, "You know it's love if I am at a pasta joint," but he grinned and really enjoyed the ribeye steak pasta puttanesca.

He looked disapprovingly at her appetizer of mushrooms and salad, and said, "You hardly eat anything."

"I'm small," she said, "it doesn't take much to fill me up."

"Ok," he said, "Especially since you look fabulous in that small package."

And after lunch, every time they tried to leave, they ran into someone that knew Phoenix. He was able to introduce her, and she was able to meet some of the people in his life. She enjoyed seeing him laugh and visit. Then just before they left, Lili's parents walked in for lunch. They had known Phoenix for years, and loved Lucas, their future son-in-law, already.

When they finally made it outside and headed to the truck, a handsome man and pretty, blonde woman drove up in a black sport's car. Bella noticed the eye contact between the woman and Phoenix, and the woman lowered her gaze.

Phoenix looked at Bella and said, "It's Monique," and Bella remembered his previous fiancé's name and nodded, feeling a little awkward.

Bella watched as the man with Monique seemed angry as he got out of the car.

Not caring who heard him, he snapped, "We are going to be late if you don't hurry, Monique."

She seemed to struggle getting out of the car, and finally stepped out behind the door. She was in late-stage pregnancy and embarrassed for some reason. She pulled her shoulders back and tried to smile at Phoenix.

Phoenix said, "Hello, Monique. Congratulations. I know that you and your husband must be thrilled. I am happy for you."

The man, deliberately unpleasant as he passed by, said to Phoenix, "Who are you? And we aren't married."

Bella felt Phoenix tense at the man's inexcusable behavior, and she squeezed his hand - in silent agreement.

With tears in her eyes, Monique said, "Thank you, Phoenix. I appreciate that."

Phoenix smiled and slipped his arm around Bella and said, "I would like you to meet my fiancé, Dr. Bella DelCaprio, we are getting married in a couple of weeks."

Monique smiled with genuine happiness for them, and said, "That is wonderful. You make a gorgeous couple. And Bella, I remember that name, aren't you Lucas' sister?"

"Yes, and it is so nice to meet you."

Monique looked at the man with her, and said, "Jack, this is Phoenix Chandler & Dr. DelCaprio,"

The man rudely eyed Phoenix and Bella, then said, "Lucky you," and Monique cringed.

Phoenix took a step forward to confront him, but Bella lightly held his arm and she walked to Monique instead.

She said, "How excited you must be! You look terrific. I can tell that you will love being a mother." Then lowered her voice to say, "and be sure to find a safe place to raise that baby, ok?"

Bella gazed intently into Monique's eyes, and Monique nodded, with sorrow and understanding.

Then Bella stepped back to Phoenix and said, "I hope you have a wonderful meal," and Phoenix led her away.

Phoenix sat in the truck and looked at Bella thoughtfully.

Trying to know where to begin, he said, "You are truly, grace in motion. We both know that she is in an abusive relationship, but you knew exactly when to step in and what to do. You did that for my ex-fiancé. I admire you more than I can ever say. Your ability to love is unbelievable."

Heart overflowing, Bella leaned over and kissed him.

He drove them to Lucy Park in the center of Wichita Falls. They talked and laughed as he led her down one of the trails. The park was in a bend in the Wichita River with a beautiful landscape. There were biking and hiking trails, picnic areas, a swimming pool, various games and playgrounds, a swinging bridge, and especially the waterfalls.

They took pictures and videos of each other. Afterwards, they found a bench by the cascading waterfalls and just listened and watched.

After a few minutes Bella said, "Would you tell me your faith story?"

Phoenix nodded and said, "Sure. I was in college and went to a church service just to impress a girl. That relationship wasn't anything special in the end, but the message the guy preached that night was. It seemed like he had talked directly to me. It took me a year or more before I started on the journey to salvation, but once I did, there was no other way for me. I am not very expressive, but He and I know each other well."

Bella said, "I love your no holds barred way of loving."

He squeezed her, and said, "What's your faith story?"

"Well, my Italian grandparents didn't give us an option on which church to attend. Being Catholic was a big part of who they were and what they did. I was obedient and appreciative, but I didn't find Jesus personally until I was a senior in high school.

"One day a classmate died, and that knocked the world as I knew it out from under me. I suddenly wondered what would happen if I died. It made me seek what faith in Him really was. I found Him quickly after that."

Remembering that it was Saturday, he said, "Church starts at ten-thirty in the morning. If you like, we can go, and I'll ask the preacher to officiate our wedding."

"I would love that."

Then he said, "Are you ready to go pick up your veterinarian orders?"

"I am!"

Within two hours, Phoenix's truck and most of the back seat was filled with veterinarian supplies, medications, and equipment. The larger equipment for the room downstairs in the barn was scheduled for Monday delivery.

Bella looked over her paperwork when they got back in the truck, and said, "I checked off everything on my list, so I am done."

He said, "If I remember correctly, you have another stop to make here in Wichita Falls."

"You remember correctly," she said with a smile.

He said, "Lead me to the wedding shop!"

When they pulled up in front of the store, Bella looked at all the wedding dresses in the window and said, "We might be here for a while. They are all gorgeous."

He said, "Oh, don't worry, I won't have any trouble picking out the right dress for you," and she laughed.

The doorbell tinkled when they walked in, and the fun began. The ladies in the shop were thrilled to have the handsome groom choose the gown. That was most unusual, but it didn't take Phoenix long as he went through all the dresses her size. He picked out ten for her to try on.

Bella exclaimed, "Ten! You just want the fashion show," and he grinned and kissed her.

The ladies around them sighed with romantic enjoyment.

Urging Bella forward, he said, "Go change, you are going to be busy for a while," and one of the ladies went to the dressing room with her.

Bella was surprised at his choices. He hadn't picked out any mermaid dresses, no strapless, no empire waist, or royal ballroom gowns. All ten dresses he had picked out for her to try on were spaghetti strap sheaths of various patterns and necklines. Obviously, he knew the style that he had in mind for her. They were very intimate.

Then she took the first dress off the rack and got started. When she walked out through the double doors, he smiled and escorted her to the platform. He walked around her, flirting, and touching the dress on her.

The ladies in the shop loved it.

Phoenix stood behind her and looked in the mirror and said, "No, this isn't the one," and Bella returned to the dressing room.

Again, eight more times after that.

Not understanding what Phoenix was looking for, Bella said as she headed back to the dressing room, "You know that there is only one dress left, right?"

He winked at her, and she got it.

She said, "You knew which one you wanted all this time," and he bowed, and the ladies clapped.

Bella couldn't wait to see the tenth dress now.

All the ladies came into the dressing room this time. They carried the dress to her, and she fell in love with it, and fought tears. It was called a Romantic France Lace Boho Wedding Dress. Sexy. Backless. Draped V-neck. Spaghetti straps. The whole dress from the bodice down to the floor, including the long train, was fragile white lace with patches of large flowers.

It was gorgeous. It was exactly the kind of dress that she wanted.

When she walked through the doors, full of anticipation, Phoenix was waiting. He took a deep breath and after a long look from the top of her head to the long train, he leaned down and kissed her. Then he offered her his arm and escorted her to the platform.

He stepped behind her as they looked at their reflection in the mirrors, and said, "This is the dress for you. You look breathtaking."

Without caring who was in the room, he drew her face to his in an intimate kiss, and said, "Just think, the next time that I see you in this dress, I get to take it off of you."

The women behind them gasped.

On the way home, Bella said, "Phoenix, that was so romantic. The ladies that work there will never forget it. I bet the whole town will know by sunset. It might even be in the newspaper or online," and he laughed.

She sighed in pleasure and said, "You are just too hot for words."

They were almost home when she thought of the wolfdog, and said, "Do you know anyone with the Sheriff's Department or Texas Parks & Wildlife from around here, that could tell us if anyone is missing a wolfdog, husky mix?"

"I do, let me call Cassidy at Texas Parks & Wildlife, he would know."

***

A man's voice said, "Hey Phoenix!"

"Hey Cassidy. How's your Saturday?"

"Good. How the heck are you? You sure scared us with that eye injury. I'm glad that you're back home."

"Me too! And the best part is, I brought someone home with me."

"Are you saying what I think you're saying? That finally, someone corralled you. Who?"

"She didn't have to corral me. I'm not going anywhere," and he winked at Bella, who was happily driving his truck. Phoenix continued, "Her name is Dr. Bella DelCaprio. She is now the veterinarian at the ranch, and you will be glad to know that she is setting up an animal sanctuary."

Cassidy whistled and said, "You hit the jackpot my man."

Looking at Bella, Phoenix drawled, "Just wait till you see her," and Cassidy laughed.

"I want to! So, what's going on? Did you need anything?"

Phoenix said, "I'm putting you on speaker now. I'm calling because we have a large wolfdog, husky mix with blue eyes, which has shown up at the ranch a few times. His howling led us to a cow that died giving birth. Do you know of anyone missing a wolfdog? He behaves different than any other that I have seen."

Cassidy said, "Yep. I know him. That was Jasper James' dog. Jasper passed away about ten days ago. He was a great guy, the best, and had been heavily involved with the Texas Wolfdog Project for years. He raised and trained him from a pup and when he retired, he took the wolfdog with him. After Jasper died, a couple of guys came from the Project to get the wolfdog back, but he ran. The Project had invested thousands in that wolf. He herds, guards, protects, and is a truly remarkable animal with unusual instinct. But they let him have his freedom and didn't track him even though he is chipped."

Bella spoke up, and said, "Hello Cassidy, this is Bella. Do you know his name?"

Cassidy said, "Nice to meet you Ms. Bella, and you will love his name. It's Thor."

Phoenix said, "Which is the coolest name, ever," and they all laughed.

Cassidy said, "You need to hook up with the Project, Bella, they would be thrilled to have a sanctuary veterinarian connection in this area."

Bella said, "I certainly will."

***

When the line went dead, Bella screamed softly in excitement. Phoenix smiled, happy for her.

He knew that she was anxious to connect with the animal and offered, "If you want to, we can get up early in the morning and go look for him before church, since we didn't get home before dark today."

She didn't want to rush connecting with Thor for the first time, so she said, "I appreciate that, but I can wait until after church. I think," and he chuckled.

A couple of miles later, Bella turned into the ranch driveway and rubbed the dash of the truck.

She glanced at Phoenix and said, "See honey, she likes my touch too."

Chapter 20
Hacker Attack

Late that night in Houston, the Hacker watched a morning video of Bella as she teased Phoenix about honeymoon lingerie. He paused the video and fantasized at what he would do if she teased him like that. When he restarted the video, Phoenix returned to Bella and was all over her.

The Hacker growled and kicked the robot next to him and pieces flew everywhere. He hated that Bella and Phoenix were right in the middle of a hot romance when he found her.

When he calmed down, he knew there was another way he could enjoy Bella now. It was time to test a new feature on his robot. He keyed in the word, Trojan, and took control of Troy at the ranch.

He rolled silently down the hall in the bedroom wing. He smiled, because if Phoenix saw him now, he would just assume that he was doing security passes.

Not hardly.

The Hacker didn't hear any sounds as the robot sat in the hall by the bedrooms. Everyone was asleep. He knew Phoenix was at the end of the hall and there was no light on in his room. He turned to face Bella's bedroom and she always had a light on.

He rolled to her doorway and saw her in the bed.

He stayed at the door for a quick get-a-way if necessary and began. There was the tiniest sound as a small opening appeared in the robot's hand. A black cable quietly extended and dropped to the floor. The Hacker steered it to the head of Bella's bed. Without any sound, the cable feed climbed up the headboard post.

Then he swiveled the camera head to look over the mattress. He smiled. Bella was stretched out on her back, uncovered. Her arms were over her head on the pillow where her long ponytail lay, and she was dressed in a sports bra and pajama shorts.

He laughed and sat back in his chair and drank his fill. He had already seen her body in the bikini, so this wasn't new exposure. It was just the closest, intimate, and most private exposure.

Then he wondered just how close he could get to her. He sat forward to work the controls carefully. This was delicate work. He directed the cable across her pillow, less than an inch from her hand, then raised it like a snake and stared into her gorgeous face. He lowered the cable until he could easily see her eyelashes against her cheeks and hear her breathing.

Then he turned the cable and looked at her chest. So pretty in her pink bra. So hot in pink. He lowered the cable like he could almost touch her. Then a thought crossed his mind, and he backed the cable to the floor.

He went to the foot of the bed and directed the cable up, and grinned. Target straight ahead. He continued the cable feed raised in the air like snake about to strike. It slid forward an inch at a time between her open legs. He liked this. It was much better than looking through the eyes of a robot. Then he slid past her knees aiming for a closer look at the V ahead.

Without warning, Bella rolled over, reaching for her blanket. Seeing a snake between her legs, she screamed and fought to get away.

Instantly, the Hacker retracted the cable and backed the robot down the hall.

Chaos   broke-loose   at   Chandler   Canyon   Ranch.

***

Phoenix heard Bella's screams and leapt from his bed in a flat out run to get to her. When he ran through the doorway, she was in the corner of the room, panicked as she looked at the bed.

"It's a snake!"

He grabbed her and said, "Come on!" and they ran to the hall.

GP came out of his room and said, "What is it?"

Bella said, "It was a snake."

Phoenix caught a glimpse of the robot in the hall and called out, "Troy, did you see a snake, or anything go into Bella's room?"

"Just you, Boss."

"Before I went in her room. When she screamed."

"No, Boss."

Phoenix said, "It's ok, GP. I'll bring her to my room. We'll check it out tomorrow."

***

The Hacker smiled as he disconnected from the robot. How exciting. And good video feed too.

Now it was time to investigate everything about Dr. Bella DelCaprio. After all, they had quite an intimate relationship now.

He pulled up a search engine online and keyed in her name.

***

Phoenix turned his bedroom lights on and said, "Did it bite you?"

She shook her head and said, "I don't think so, I never felt a bite," but they checked to be sure.

She said, "I know that it seems bizarre, but there really was a long black snake between my legs in the bed."

With a troubled expression, he said, "You are moving into my room now, no arguments. Your safety matters more than propriety. That was a crazy, freakish thing to happen. I have heard of snakes in houses of course, but between someone's legs is beyond any story that I have ever been told."

Bella said, "Would you please check your bed before we get in it?" and he pulled everything off to make sure it was safe, and they remade the bed.

After they got in, Phoenix drew her into the safety of his arms and said, "I am so sorry that happened. I know that you were terrified."

She said, "It was such a weird snake. I'm a veterinarian and I've never seen one like it."

"What do you mean weird?"

She thought back to what she had seen and said, "It was extremely thin, and so long that it hung off the bed. And it was lifted, like it was ready to strike, but its mouth wasn't open. I didn't see where it went as I fought to get out of the bed."

130

Phoenix said, "Your bed is huge, that would have been an unusually long snake to hang off. How thick was it?"

"I know it seems impossible, but it was thin like a pencil. I don't know what else to say. As a vet that is my only logical conclusion."

He frowned, knowing that a snake that long would have been much thicker than a pencil, but he couldn't come up with an alternative answer either. He would search her room tomorrow for a possible explanation.

He texted GP to watch for a snake, and eventually they drifted back to sleep.

Chapter 21
Wolfdog

Phoenix woke up before the alarm went off. He felt Bella's body and smiled. Now, this was how he wanted to wake up for the rest of his life.

She was on her stomach facing the windows, and he was leaned over her with his arm around her waist.

He slid his leg down hers and kissed her back.

He heard her muffled sound of pleasure, and she rolled over. Her beautiful sleepy eyes met his. He rubbed his lips against hers, and she opened her lips for his kiss.

Afterwards, they snuggled, and he asked, "How are you this morning? That was quite a night."

"I'm fine, but I am sorry for all the commotion. Poor GP."

Phoenix chuckled, and said, "I bet he hadn't moved that fast in a long time," and Bella tried not to grin.

She said, "So, are we really moving me in here now?"

"Yes. I aged ten years when I heard you scream. We can move your things in here when we get up."

"This feels so much safer," she said. "And I refuse to go in that room without a shotgun."

A little while later, Phoenix stripped her bed, looked under the furniture, checked every drawer, the closet, and bathroom. There was no snake in her bedroom. Once he cleared the room, Bella walked in to gather her things. She noticed something on the base of the bed and picked up a tiny piece of black material.

She said, "What do you think this is? It was caught on a jagged edge of the footboard. It's not snakeskin by any means."

He frowned as he looked at it, and said, "I have a buddy at the Sherriff's Department, I'll see if I can get their lab to check it. We have more questions than we have answers for, and I don't like it. But for now, let's go check with Troy and see if he noticed anything once we went to bed."

When they got to the den, Phoenix said, "Troy, did you see a snake in the house after Bella screamed last night?"

Troy responded, "Please explain, Boss."

Phoenix looked at Bella and shrugged, then repeated, "Troy, do you have record of Bella's scream last night around one a.m.?"

"No, Boss."

"How do you explain not having that data?"

"My operating system went down last night from twelve-thirty to two a.m., Boss."

"Why did your operating system go down?"

Troy responded, "I am designed for online updates."

Bella said, "Did you see a snake at all last night, Troy?"

"No, Bella."

Phoenix said, "If you see one, please text me immediately and track it."

"Yes, Boss."

GP said from the kitchen, "How are you, Bella? That must have been terrible to wake up to."

She kissed his cheek and said, "Morning GP, and yes, I've had a few bad scares in my life, and that rated up there with them. I just hope we find the snake and I am so sorry for causing a scene."

GP said, "Don't you worry yourself about waking us up. Cowboys are used to that. I am just concerned about the snake. We've had a few get in through the years, but I've never heard of one in the bedrooms, that we were aware of anyway. I sure am sorry about that."

Bella said, "How would we ever find a snake in this huge house?"

Phoenix said, "For now I will have Troy patrol for it."

GP glanced at the clock, and said, "I hate to interrupt but we better leave for church soon."

***

133

Bella loved the church, the sermon, and the worship music. And most everyone made a point to meet her. Phoenix checked with the Pastor, and he was happy to do their wedding on June 4. They were now official.

After church, they ate at RibCrib BBQ off Kemp Blvd on the south side of Wichita Falls. GP and Phoenix each ate almost a rack of ribs, as Bella looked on in amazement. They chuckled at her one rib and coleslaw.

She asked, "Don't you ever eat Chinese or Mediterranean?"

They laughed, and Phoenix said, "Only as an appetizer."

Once they finished lunch, they picked up a few supplies and headed home.

Phoenix glanced at Bella in the backseat since she insisted that GP ride in the front with him. She grinned and blew him a kiss. She needed privacy because she was honeymoon shopping online. She placed an order for six new bikinis and a black leather one-piece bathing suit that Phoenix was going to love.

The only lingerie she ordered were eight new bra and panty sets. From steamy to princess styles, she had a feeling they would go over very well. She chose minimal flowers for the wedding, but not a wedding bouquet. And she planned to braid her hair and weave in flower jewelry, boho style, instead of wearing a veil.

Her most unique purchase was a pair of snow-white fringed, lace, sequin, and rhinestone wedding cowboy boots to wear under her wedding dress. She knew Phoenix would be pumped about that.

And as a gift for him, she had heard him talking to a guy yesterday about wanting to get into bucking bull breeding for rodeos. She checked with the Texas Bucking Bull Association and got the particulars. She would purchase him a young bucking bull calf with DNA verified parentage. She was waiting to hear back from one of the ranches in Oklahoma.

By three in the afternoon, Phoenix turned into the driveway. Bella smiled from the backseat when he glanced at her. She was glad that the trip home had been productive. All her orders were done.

And as far as she knew, the first order of business when they arrived home, was to find the wolfdog. She was thrilled.

Phoenix must have read her thoughts as he said, "Bella, why don't we change and head out to search for the wolfdog before anything interrupts our plans."

"That sounds perfect to me!"

GP said, "I've always had a fascination with wolfdogs and the story on this wolf is fascinating. I hope to see him before I head back to Colorado this week."

Phoenix said, "Hopefully, we can find him today. And GP, I have appreciated you being here. I hope all the trips back and forth to Colorado aren't too much for you."

GP chuckled and said, "When I get tired of driving, I'll fly. This place has my blood, sweat, tears, and you in it. And those great-grandchildren coming that I want to see before I die. Don't you worry about me. You just work on making those babies."

Phoenix chuckled when he saw Bella's grin in the rearview mirror, and said, "GP, nothing will ever interfere with my focus on making babies."

Bella shook her head and smiled. True professional breeders down to the bone.

Once they got home, GP headed straight toward the bedroom wing and called out, "Nap time. It's Sunday. Let me know about the wolfdog," and he rounded the corner out of sight.

In seconds, Phoenix grinned and began to stalk Bella. She attempted a few teasing, evasive moves to delay the inevitable, but it didn't work.

Bella smiled as his lips captured hers. She loved the look on his face during the chase. And especially the heat that followed.

All too soon Bella's phone rang, and Phoenix thought about throwing it in the freezer, or in the sink, or in the trash can, or even in the yard. Then it stopped ringing. And started up again.

He drawled, "You might want to get that before I bury it somewhere in a cold, shallow grave," and she laughed and dug it out of her purse. She showed Phoenix that it was Lucas and he held out his hand for the phone.

***

Phoenix answered on speaker, and said, "I almost murdered the phone."

Lucas laughed and said, "I get that. I think Cupid has love helpers with a sick sense of humor. Some must stay behind to shoot us with frustration arrows after the love arrow hits," and they laughed.

Phoenix said, "I heard that you were bringing Lili to Wichita Falls today. How long are you staying?"

"I plan to bring her to her parent's house. We should be there before dark. Then I wondered if I could spend the night at the ranch. How's Bella - since you answered her phone."

Bella laughed and said, "Hi Lucas. Yes, come spend the night!"

Phoenix said, "Did you take off from the fire station?"

"Well, not time off, I finished my last day of work in Dallas. My days ahead are full until I start work in Wichita Falls. *One.* I'm moving Lili today. *Two.* Seth and I will be in Baton Rouge Tuesday to move. *Three.* Then I need to move myself from Dallas to Wichita Falls. *Four.* I need to bring Bella's moving boxes to her before we come for the Cattleman's Gala next Saturday."

Bella said, "Good grief, Lucas! I hate that you have all the moving issues for me in all that."

Lucas said, "I wasn't going to let you do it anyway," and Bella knew that was true.

She said, "Is Lili with you?"

"Yes, but she is on the phone with her new landlord. She said that she will connect with you later."

Phoenix said, "We are about to take a horseback ride to search for a wolfdog we've seen a few times. It's a long story but we will fill you in on it tonight. If we aren't back to the ranch when you arrive, make yourself at home."

***

They were about a half hour into their horseback ride through the pasture without seeing the wolfdog.

Bella said, "I don't think this is working. I know that you won't like my idea, but just hear me out. I want to walk thirty or forty feet ahead of you. Hopefully that will give the wolfdog a chance to show himself to me, one-on-one."

Phoenix looked at her silently for a few moments, then said, "I can understand that might be a better approach for his benefit, and no, I don't like it. But I won't fight you on it to a degree. I will stay by the horses with my rifle and give you room to connect to him. But, understand me, if he shows aggression towards you, I will shoot him."

She nodded and said, "I have my tranquilizer pistol too, but if we don't threaten him, I believe that he will try to connect, albeit cautiously. I don't know why he chose Chandler Canyon Ranch, but I am thrilled that he did. This is a dream come true for me, Phoenix, so give me some room to use my skills and my instincts. I have a few treats and the raw deer – you know that he will have to approach me to get it."

He stopped his horse and said, "We both know that he is more apt to approach you as a woman. But he can't avoid me. I am the alpha on the ranch, and he must accept that, before he can be accepted near it. So, ok, let's walk and try to draw him out. But he better be as smart as we are told he is - for this to have a good end."

They dismounted.

Phoenix watched as she walked about forty feet in front of him before he followed with the horses, rifle in hand, with a sharp eye on the area around Bella.

Bella walked casually through the pasture for only about fifty feet, when the large wolfdog stepped out from the brush at a right angle to her. He was a wolf husky hybrid with tan, black and white markings, and bright blue eyes. Impressive in appearance, he had an air about him that shouted intelligence and experience. In fact, it had been him that had initiated this moment since the beginning.

The man, woman, and animal looked at each other, and quickly, Bella dropped her gaze and knelt to face the wolf.

Phoenix understood completely, but still hated it.

The wolf watched Bella.

Bella said, "Thor," still not looking him in the eye.

The wolf still didn't move after a short time.

So, Bella sat back on her feet, and laid on her legs, hands outstretched, and said again, "Thor, come."

The wolf started towards Bella.

Phoenix knew that it was working as they planned, but he still followed the animal with his rifle. The wolf neared Bella as she stayed prone.

Phoenix saw the wolf sniff the air and noticed that Bella had opened her hand and had the chunk of deer meat in it. He smiled as she portrayed, lack of threat, knowledge of his name, and food. The wolf was only twenty feet from her.

Bella repeated, "Thor," and the wolf reached her.

He smelled the deer meat in her hand, but ignored it, and walked to her side and sat.

Phoenix took a breath of relief but stayed alert.

Bella smiled as she faced the ground.

Then she slowly rolled over and laid face up looking at the wolf, and said, "Thor."

Phoenix almost shot the wolf when he licked Bella's face and laid next to her. Bella wanted to shout and dance but stayed calm and rolled toward the wolf and he laid his head on her shoulder. Phoenix knew this was unusual. A miracle even. And it was beautiful. But his stomach was still trying to untie itself from all the stress knots.

He watched Bella touch the wolf's shoulder and then noted the affection the wolf showed her. Bella laughed and offered him the meat and he ate it out of her hand. They stayed in that position for a few minutes until she saw Thor look toward Phoenix.

She turned to see that Phoenix had walked a little closer and watched her and the wolf.

Bella rubbed the wolf, and said, "Come," and stood.

As she walked toward Phoenix, the wolf followed. Bella smiled at Phoenix, but he watched the wolf. A few moments later, Bella reached Phoenix, and he offered the wolf his hand. He smelled him and nudged his hand. Phoenix smiled and scratched the wolf.

An hour later, Phoenix said, "We need to get back to the ranch and see if he plans to follow. But Bella, we must be positive that he is not a danger to any of the animals. This may take a while to bring together smoothly. I can't take any chances."

She said, "Well, let's see if he will follow and go from there. He will have to show us what he has been trained to do."

Phoenix got off the ground where they had been sitting, and the wolf stood in response. When Bella stood, he went directly to her side, and that was that.

He was her wolf.

Phoenix smiled and rewarded him with a back scratch, knowing that any threat to Bella would be dealt with most severely by this wolf, and he was happy about that. She now had her own personal security, besides him of course.

They mounted the horses, and Phoenix said, "Come," and the wolf followed them without any hesitation.

Lucas and GP were outside when Phoenix, Bella, and the wolf walked into the driveway from the pasture. GP smiled ear-to-ear.

Lucas frowned as he noticed the wolf against Bella after she dismounted.

He said, "So, introduce us so he will stop giving me that direct, I might eat you, look."

Bella touched the wolf and said, "Come," and walked toward Lucas and GP.

Bella said, "Offer your hand, Lucas," and the wolf took his time smelling it then looked at GP.

GP held out his hand and the wolf did the same thing.

Bella said, "Meet Thor, highly trained wolf husky from the Texas Wolfdog Project. We've just become acquainted and are now a member of the same pack."

Lucas said, "He looks pretty possessive with you."

Phoenix said, "He is, and that is a good thing. Come on, let's walk to the barn. I need to see how this is going to play out. I am positive that he is going to be the alpha with the dogs."

GP said, "There is no doubt about that. He walks with authority just like you do."

Bella said, "I like having two alpha males," and the guys laughed.

When they neared the barns, the dogs were already coming from all directions straight toward the wolf. Phoenix knew they smelled him. All three Australian Cattle dogs, and the two large, white Great Pyrenees advanced closer to the wolf.

Phoenix stepped closer to the dogs braced for battle, and said, "Thor, come."

Thor left Bella's side and stood next to Phoenix. The herding dogs advanced, with barks and growls until the wolf took one step forward with a low rumble in his throat, and they rolled over like puppies.

Everyone smiled.

Then the guard dogs, approached threateningly, both growling and willing to fight. Then in the blink of an eye, the wolf charged and snapped at them, dust and spit flying in a ferocious display of alpha authority. Both dogs cowered instantly, and Bella gasped.

Then they all smelled and made friends, and the ranch dogs went back to work. Phoenix walked the wolf into the barns by the horses and cattle, and the wolf stayed calm.

The horses were a bit disturbed until they realized they were not in danger. A few cows with calves scrambled nervously in the corral and the wolf walked close to the fence rail and stuck his head through.

Eventually the cows calmed, and curious as always, came close to investigate, then went back to eating since that was their job on a cattle ranch.

Phoenix smiled and said, "He is one amazing animal. He won't interfere with the ranch at all," and the wolf walked back to Bella.

Lucas, impressed, said, "I wish I had the setup for a wolfdog."

Bella laughed softly and said, "Do you know what he eats every day, Lucas? Raw meat. He doesn't eat dog food. And I had to bow down in submission and respect before he trusted me enough to give me his loyalty."

Lucas said, "What do you mean bow down in submission?"

She said, "On my knees, and then on my belly, arms outstretched."

Lucas looked at her in surprise and said, "I just can't picture it."

Phoenix said, "He chose her. It was incredible. When she rolled over belly up under his face, I nearly shot him when he licked her."

Shocked, Bella said, "Phoenix!"

At the same time, Lucas also shocked, said, "Bella!"

Phoenix and GP laughed at brother and sister.

Bella said, "I know, Lucas. Phoenix hated it too," and Bella knelt and loved on her wolf. Thor.

They headed indoors and Bella invited the wolf inside to check out the house. He walked with her through all the rooms, and out on the back patio. But he wanted to stay on the front porch afterwards.

She fixed him a bucket of water and more of the deer meat and he laid out, peaceful, but watchful. She knelt and kissed his face as he licked and nuzzled her.

Phoenix watched from the window and smiled. Maybe he should get Bella a young female wolf husky for a future mate for the wolf as one of her wedding gifts. If the wolf took care of Bella, he would do the same for the wolf.

Bella's other wedding gift should be in before they married. He had ordered her a sky-blue Ford F-150 Lightning pickup that almost matched her car. It was beautiful and he knew that she would love it. A farm vet needed a truck.

Bella came back inside and saw Phoenix by the window.

She said, "Thor's magnificent. But nothing like you, my bull alpha," and he kissed her.

Then Lucas interrupted and said, "Stop it. Come eat! I am starving and GP grilled steaks the size of Texas."

Phoenix and Bella grinned and walked toward the kitchen, following the aroma.

Phoenix looked back at the robot and said, "Troy, come meet Lucas."

Troy responded, "Yes, Boss," and rolled into the kitchen.

Lucas said, "You have the greatest toys out here," and everyone laughed.

Phoenix said, "Go talk to him, Lucas. He will surprise you."

Lucas squatted in front of the robot with big blue eyes and said, "Hi Troy. I'm Lucas, Bella's brother."

Troy responded, "Hello Lucas."

Lucas said, "Do you know what a brother is, Troy?"

"Yes, Lucas. A sibling."

Lucas said, "Troy, sing me a song."

"Which song, Lucas?"

Lucas grinned and said, "Do the *Watermelon Crawl*," as everyone laughed.

Music began to play from Troy, and he began to sing, in tune, in his Troy voice.

Lucas jumped up and grabbed Bella, and brother and sister danced a very lively two-step while Phoenix and GP smiled and clapped.

After the song ended, Phoenix said, "Bella, would you get your guitar? I haven't heard you play since we got back to the ranch."

Lucas said, "Play only? You mean, you haven't heard her sing?"

Bella groaned and said, "Lucas, you are the singer in the family."

Phoenix slipped his arms around her waist and said, "I would love to hear you sing, Bella. It's just us. Sit outside and sing to your wolf if you must, but please, let me hear you."

She smiled at Phoenix, but turned and gave Lucas the evil eye, and he laughed. Bella was back in a second with the guitar. She sat on a stool and strummed, warming up.

Then she played *Amazing Grace* so beautifully that Phoenix had goose bumps. She changed the tempo after that, to a slow deep rhythm, and he recognized the jazz tune, *Come Away with Me*.

She began to sing. Like she had said, her voice was whispery. But it was so much more than that. It was intimate, full of heart, and tempting with secrets that drew you closer so you wouldn't miss one whispery syllable. She had one of the sexiest voices that Phoenix had ever heard. Several songs later, Bella put the guitar in her lap and looked up at Phoenix.

He said, "Please tell me this is the first of many times that you will sing for me."

Lucas said, "I told you!"

Later, GP headed to his room to watch his nightly movie.

Phoenix and Bella walked Lucas out to see her new barn and office.

Bella said, "Have you and Lili picked a wedding date yet?"

"Yes, since you moved your date up to June 4, we decided on your first date of July 4."

"That is perfect!"

He said, "Lili's having fun planning a quick wedding. I guess y'all are too. You have what, less than two weeks?"

Phoenix drawled, "Thirteen days, and counting," as Lucas nodded in complete understanding of the long wait for a honeymoon.

Bella said, "Oh! I forgot to tell you what happened last night, Lucas. It was horrible."

"What? And how did you forget to tell me?"

Ignoring his question, she said, "I know you won't believe it. We barely believe it ourselves, but I rolled over in my bed last night and a long black snake was between my legs. I screamed and jumped out of the bed, and it disappeared."

They saw the shock on Lucas' face, and he said, "How did a snake get between your legs? That is the most insane, crazy thing that I have ever heard. Obviously, it did not bite you. Did you find it?"

Phoenix said, "No, we couldn't find it. So, I have moved her into my room. With her text threats from Royce and then the snake, she needs to stay with me. And seeing your frown, I assure you, her honor is safe."

Lucas nodded and said, "What did the second text from Royce say?"

Phoenix glanced at Bella and said, "I will show you later, she doesn't read them anymore."

Lucas said, "Ok. Don't forget. It is possible that Seth and I could run into him while we are moving out of the Baton Rouge apartment."

Bella said, "He has court tomorrow at nine a.m. I hope his punishment is jail, but the consensus is that he will get a slap on the wrist."

Lucas said, "If so, I don't trust him, you have to stay alert. He needs to be dropped off the Mississippi River bridge."

Bella said, "Lucas!"

"I know, I just hate that he is fixated on you. He hid that predator side of him so well. I am super glad that you have Phoenix and the wolf now."

Phoenix said, "She won't be far from me or anyone else, and she will have the wolf and her tranquilizer gun. And, you know, back to last night, there was something odd. We found a piece of black leathery material caught in the footboard, but it wasn't snakeskin."

Curious, Lucas said, "Where is the black piece you found?"

Phoenix said, "I'll show you when we get back to the house."

As they neared her office, Bella glanced in the sky and said, "I need to grab my flashlight. It is almost dark."

Phoenix said, "Wait," and reached up by the barn door and flipped a new switch.

Lights flickered on all the way down the road to the house.

Bella screamed in delight and jumped in his arms.

He smiled and said, "Wait, look, there's more," and he turned and pointed back at the ranch, and they watched as solar lights flickered on everywhere around the ranch.

Bella burst into tears and hugged Phoenix, and the men that loved her, smiled. A few moments later she wiped her face and led them upstairs, where the lights that were installed, can't turn off. Ever.

Lucas high-fived Phoenix.

As they looked at all the updates in her office, Lucas said, "Oh, your veterinarian license came in. I have it in my car."

She raised her arms in victory and said, "This day just keeps on giving. Awesome!"

***

143

Unaware to anyone at Chandler Canyon Ranch, in Houston, the Hacker had researched and printed Bella's online history.

He walked out on his patio and lounged as he read everything about her. He loved invading her privacy of course. He read for a good while, learning about her and everyone around her.

When he reached the information about her LSU roommates, he laughed. Just two days ago, his NASA Director had emailed his team about a new engineer joining them on June 1 - his name was Seth. It seems that he was Bella's college roommate. He had just found the way to take her.

Chapter 22
Courthouse

Royce looked out his bedroom window at the night lights in Baton Rouge. It was only four a.m. but he was wide awake.

Today should be a breeze in court and he'd kill that idiot lawyer if she had lied to him. There was no way he would spend time in jail for a grab-n-chase.

He picked up his phone and found a very special image on Google to text to Bella.

***

Unknown to Bella: It was a picture of masked man standing over a terrified, naked woman tied down.

***

Back at the ranch, before dawn, Phoenix heard Bella's phone receive a text and leaned over to pick it up. It was an unknown number; undoubtedly it would be Royce.

He checked the text and saw the picture that would have tormented Bella. He forwarded the text to his phone and deleted it off hers. It didn't help her to see or know about this. He hated that man.

Glancing at the time, his alarm would go off in about twenty minutes, so he smiled as he looked at Bella spread eagle in the bed, sound asleep. She was one wild sleeper.

He slid his hand across her stomach and pulled her toward him. He loved the way she curled into him without even looking. That was trust and it meant everything to him.

He lowered his lips to hers and increased the pressure as she responded. Then she deepened the kiss and he rolled over and took her with him.

She smiled as she looked down at him and said, "I was dreaming about our honeymoon, and you were—"

He kissed her and said, "Please don't tell me what I was doing - I'm dying already," and drew her mouth down for one more breathless kiss.

He said, "I am ready to get our marriage license. It's going to burn us just holding it."

Bella giggled, and said, "The courthouse opens at nine a.m., right?"

"Yes. I'll get the crew to work, then once Lucas leaves for Houston to meet Seth, we will head to town."

When she came out of the bathroom a little later, Phoenix was bare-chested in jeans and had a red shirt laid out to wear. She ran her fingernails appreciatively down his rippled stomach as she passed by on the way to the dressing room.

He laughed and pulled her back, and said, "Surely you didn't think you could just walk away after that?"

She did it again.

He scooped her up and kissed her all the way to the dressing room.

He grinned, put her down, and said, "Now, we are both distracted," and she licked her lips with a smile as he walked out.

Hurrying to get dressed, she pulled on jeans with a floral V-neck top, and tall ankle strap wedges. She put her hair in a ponytail for the summer heat, finished her makeup, and added a silver necklace and earrings.

When she stepped into the bedroom, Phoenix came out of the bathroom and whistled when he saw her. She danced a little salsa move and he joined her for a few spins.

He said, "You are so incredibly beautiful, Bella," and kissed her softly.

She watched as he slipped the red shirt on, and said, "You are the handsome, sexy man of my dreams."

Phoenix drawled, "Maybe I do need to hear more about that dream you had."

In the kitchen, Jasmine waved the spatula at them with a smile.

"Hi Boss, hi Bella. Don't y'all look fine today. And tell me, will I see that huge wolf every day now? I thought that I was his breakfast at first, but GP introduced us."

Bella said, "Oh no! I am sorry, I should have thought of being out here earlier. Isn't he beautiful though?"

Jasmine said, "Let's put it this way, if he sires pups, I want one."

Bella opened the front door to let Thor in, just as Kit, Levi, and Buck walked in the back door.

Phoenix said, "Come," and the wolf joined him, never taking his eyes off the three new men.

Kit said, "I'm thinking this is the wolfdog you were telling us about."

Phoenix chuckled and said, "Offer a hand," and the wolf smelled each one. "He's the new alpha with the dogs."

Buck said, "I'm not surprised. He's got a real cool way about him. I like that."

Bella said, "We will have to tell you the story about our meeting sometime."

Then Phoenix said, "Where's Lucas?"

Lucas called out, "Bringing up the rear. I was on the phone late with Lili. Hey guys. Hi Jasmine! You still with that no-good man of yours?"

Kit said, "You betcha big boy, she's all about her man."

Jasmine said, "I can talk for myself; you two hunks," and they laughed.

Kit and Lucas shook hands, and Kit said, "Hey bud, I heard Lili's a real looker. I'm happy for you."

Lucas said, "She is gorgeous. She will also be here this weekend for the Cattleman's Gala. All you guys going?"

Levi said, "No way."

Buck said, "Not me."

GP said, "I'm heading back to Colorado tomorrow so have fun for me."

Lucas said, "Hey Bella, do they know you sing and play the guitar?"

Bella looked at him like he had three heads and punched him in the stomach.

Everyone laughed.

Bella said, "Ignore my brother. He likes to push my cranky button."

Lucas said, "That's called mean, not cranky," and she eyed him again.

Jasmine said, "Do you play and sing, Bella?"

Bella said, "I do, but not publicly till last night."

147

Phoenix hugged her and said, "She's amazingly gifted. Maybe one day she will play and sing around a campfire for us," and Bella smiled.

Then Jasmine said, "Steak-n-eggs coming up!" and the men got in line.

Bella cut up Thor's venison and brought it outside for him.

When she came back in, she glanced at the robot and said, "Troy, good morning."

Troy responded, "Hey baby," in a sexy voice, and everyone turned in shock to look at the robot.

Bella stood there with her mouth open in shock.

Phoenix said, "Troy, follow your preferences immediately or you can take a permanent swim in the pool."

"Yes, Boss."

Bella looked at Phoenix and said, "What was that? Can he tell himself to do that? I have freaky goosebumps."

Phoenix said, "He's a machine. I have to reset my phone and computer, maybe he needs reset too. But if he misbehaves, he can stare at the cows or go swimming, because he won't be in the house."

By six a.m., the crew walked out to the barns. By seven a.m., Lucas headed to Houston. By eight a.m., the construction crew started work on the vet office. And by eight-fifteen a.m. Phoenix and Bella left for the courthouse.

***

Royce met with his attorney in the 19th Judicial District Courthouse in Baton Rouge at eight thirty in the morning. They sat on a bench in the hall as she went over again how the proceeding would go, and how he should answer. She would intervene if anything veered from their plan.

She said, "Your background, your demeanor, your profession, will all play a part in the judge's decision to sentence, especially since no physical damages are involved."

Royce said, "I expect no more than a fine today."

She said, "That is what I expect as well."

The Court Bailiff unlocked the courtroom doors and people began to enter. Royce's attorney led him to the defense counsel's table since they were first on the docket.

She said, "Do you have any questions?"

"No."

148

Bella laughed as Phoenix finished his story and parked at the Wichita Falls County Courthouse at eight-fifty a.m.

He said, "We need to go to the County Clerk's office. We still have about ten minutes to wait."

Bella said, "Have you heard from Ariel on how things are going with her and Seth?"

Phoenix said, "She is very private, even though she comes across bold. Seth will have his work cut out for him. She reminds me of the wolf. Once you get past her defenses, I think she will surrender. I've only seen her have a few relationships, for want of a better word, but they all ended abruptly. She doesn't mess around."

Bella said, "Seth likes the pursuit and is good at the game. He was totally locked on Ariel when we were all there. Was that really only five days ago? But anyway, I bet you ten dollars that he gets past her defenses for romance no later than the Cattleman's Gala this weekend."

Phoenix laughed and said, "I'll take your ten and raise you ten," and they shook on it with a laugh.

He said, "Do you want to see what reservations I've made for our honeymoon trip, or shall I surprise you?"

Bella ran her hand behind his neck and whispered, "Surprise me," and he smiled and kissed her.

As they headed in the courthouse a few minutes later, Bella glanced at the time. She knew Royce would already be in his courtroom.

***

Royce looked around the huge Baton Rouge courtroom. It was full of people of all ages, all incomes, all nationalities, and it was clearly obvious that anyone could get caught. It did make him feel a little better knowing that others got in trouble too. He high fived, in his mind, all the ones that got away. Getting away now was his goal, and it was swiftly approaching.

The Court Bailiff said, "All rise," and the Judge was in his seat before they knew it, and everyone sat down.

Royce saw that this judge didn't waste time. His assistant handed him a folder and he jumped right in and called for the defendant's case to begin.

The Prosecutor gave his spill of the charges, and Royce's attorney minimalized everything they said. Good girl.

The Judge was silent as he read the documents before him, then looked up at Royce and said, "Will the Defendant please rise."

Royce and his attorney stood.

The Judge frowned at Royce and said, "What you did was appalling and beneath your dignity as an educator and as a man. I am glad that I don't have a list of injuries for the victim, and for that, you get my mercy. Including the fact that this is your first offense. This court fines you one-thousand-dollars with a warning that a second offense would be most harsh. Stay away from your victim and act like the gentleman that you try to appear. Next case."

And that was that.

Royce smiled as his attorney escorted him out of the courtroom. But the tongue lashing the judge had given him had been humiliating. He would like to find out where he lived and annoy him some, but he had more important things to do.

He paid the fine and walked away from his attorney. She didn't know how lucky she had been. He thought she might have been a really good screamer.

In the hall, the Detective watched Royce walk away from his attorney. A one-thousand-dollar fine wasn't much of a punishment. He would schedule a patrol to go by his apartment every night for a couple of weeks to make sure that he wasn't going to go after Bella. He didn't trust Royce and texted Bella.

***

Back in Wichita Falls, Phoenix and Bella waited their turn to get a marriage license. There had been a line of eager couples. They were next when Bella heard her phone ding. She would check it later.

Before long they had filled out their paperwork, paid the fee, and had a marriage license good for thirty days. They kissed several times before they made it to the truck, as well as in the truck.

Once they were on the road, Phoenix said, "Do you need anything from town? If not, we really need to get back to the ranch so we can begin vaccinations. But first, I need to drop this black material that we found on your bedframe off at the Sheriff's Department for the lab."

"No, I don't need anything, we can head back to the ranch when you are ready."

She pulled out her phone to check messages and said, "The Detective messaged me. Royce got a one-thousand-dollar fine and a tongue lashing. He intends to check if he's home each night for a couple of weeks. That is the best he can do to keep an eye on his whereabouts."

"Are you going to send that message to Ranger Morgan?" and Bella nodded and forwarded him the text.

Phoenix turned into the Wichita Falls Sheriff's Office and texted his buddy about the black material found on Bella's bed. Deputy Todd came outside and got it.

Phoenix said, "Thanks Todd. We appreciate your help. It was a strange find and we would like to know what it is."

The deputy took it and waved as they left.

They were back at the ranch before noon, changed, ate lunch with the crew, then headed out to begin the long process of vaccinations.

There were many types of vaccinations required for cattle intended for human consumption. It was a crucial way to guarantee proper animal health and therefore, good quality beef.

Specific tags were clipped on each animal and Phoenix's record keeping gave him a complete health detail for each animal. Every animal was valuable. The cows and calves stayed together till they were weaned. The male calves were castrated young, becoming a steer, that would be sold at eighteen months old. The female calves were divided into two groups of heifers. The large group would be sold at eighteen months, and a few select heifers were kept, increasing the breeding herd.

Without females to have calves, there was no beef to sale. The ranch could buy sperm from other bulls with the genetics they preferred if they chose to, but they had to have the cows. Therefore, all the various ages required vaccines, including medications for health issues. Nothing was taken lightly. Pregnant cows and heifers were the cream of the crop and were monitored closely. Angus cattle were premium beef.

Vaccinations were required on all the animals, including the breeding bulls, horses, herd dogs, and guard dogs. The guys corralled and lined up the cattle for the vaccinations. Bella lined up her medications and got started.

Bella and Kit worked as a team as he tagged by the vaccination(s) Phoenix told Bella was due. They always took a few seconds to look each animal over for health issues at the same time. Phoenix stayed busy recordkeeping on his laptop as the process continued.

Bella noticed several bat bites on some of the cattle and said, "Phoenix, are all your rabies vaccines up to date? I see bat bites on some of the cattle."

He said, "Yes, we do semi-annual vaccines starting at three months old. I have quite a few calves that will get the first shot today. Many ranchers don't vaccinate for rabies, but the USDA won't allow the beef for consumption if they are exposed to rabies unvaccinated, so I don't want to take that chance. Do you see any symptoms?"

She said, "No, I just wanted to know your rabies schedule because of the bites."

Phoenix called a break mid-afternoon, and they only had one-quarter of the cattle left to vaccinate. Bella stretched her back and saw Phoenix watching her, and grinned.

He winked and walked over to rub her shoulders and she rolled her neck.

Buck walked by and said, "I'm next Boss."

Phoenix said, "Get over it, Buck," and the guys laughed.

Everyone looked to the driveway as a large delivery truck rolled up and Bella said, "That's probably my office delivery."

Phoenix said, "Let's go show them where to go. Guys, take an extended break, we won't be long."

Bella showed the driver and helper what to bring upstairs and what to bring into the treatment room downstairs.

Afterwards they rode back to the barn.

Phoenix watched as Thor followed, and said, "Your wolf has laid by the corral and eyed you most of the day. I'm kind of jealous, actually."

With a sexy smile, she said, "Clearly, my alpha ONE is the only man for me," and kissed him lingeringly. "And my alpha TWO is the only pet for me."

Phoenix said, "Just so we are clear," and winked.

After Bella completed the vaccinations, she walked to her office with the wolf. She rubbed his head and back, and he bumped into her. Bella got the affectionate message and smiled.

He followed her upstairs and laid down while she unpacked and put away the items. She opened the new window shutter overlooking the inside of the barn and smiled at the now glassed-in-frame that slid open like a drive thru window. The only task remaining for the contractors was the installation of the two ceiling fans, and the guy had texted that he should be here any minute. Other than that, she just needed her belongings from Baton Rouge that Lucas would bring later this week.

She slid the empty boxes down the stairs and headed to the treatment area to set up. She noticed that the wolf walked toward the open barn door that faced the road, and a van stopped.

Bella called Thor to her.

The contractor electrician rounded the corner with a smile on his face and stopped cold when he saw the wolf.

Bella said, "Go on up, he will stay with me. He is my new bodyguard."

The guy eyed the wolf carefully as he went to the steps and said, "You couldn't pay me to touch one hair on your head with that wolf near you," and Bella laughed.

In less than an hour, the contractor finished and left, and she decided to call it a day. After shutting the doors, Bella glanced at the sky. Dusk was fast approaching but she still had time to get home before darkness fell. Then she remembered the new lights and smiled. She didn't need to worry about flashlights anymore here at the ranch.

She knelt and gave the wolf a good rub and a snack, and they walked home. Phoenix wasn't far behind her.

While she tended to a few things, Phoenix went to shower.

She relaxed in a rocking chair on the porch and listened to the night sounds, along with the sounds of the crew finishing up for the day. She checked her phone messages. She didn't see any unknown numbers in her texts so that was a good thing. She checked her emails, and many were vet related so she would need to respond to those tonight.

One email address was from Eagle Securities, Inc. She wasn't familiar with the name but opened it. There was a single link in the middle of the page. She knew it was odd but thought it might be something for her business. She clicked the link just as Phoenix stepped outside to meet her.

Bella screamed and dropped her phone.

Phoenix and the wolf both darted for Bella, at the same time she ran to Phoenix.

"Bella, what happened? What's wrong?"

She clutched him and said, "I'm not safe."

Startled, he said, "What do you mean?"

Face ashen, she said, "Someone was in the house."

"Who?"

She said, "Look at my phone."

Unable to imagine what had upset her, Phoenix picked up her phone. He saw a picture of Bella sound asleep, spread eagle in her bed. The picture view was between her legs. His blood ran cold.

He turned off the phone, dropped it in his pocket, and drew her to sit on his lap.

The crew ran to the porch, and Kit said, "Boss, Dr. B, is everything alright?"

Phoenix shook his head no, and said, "Someone sent her a picture taken from the foot of her bed while she slept."

The men were shocked.

Phoenix said, "It isn't possible, yet, we have a picture. I've called the police."

Chapter 23
The Hacker

When Bella had opened the email link he sent her, she was hacked. He was in. From Houston, he could see through her phone camera, her beautiful face flash with shock, fear, and heard her scream as the phone dropped, face down where he couldn't see anymore.

He heard the commotion that followed with the man and dog. When the man picked up the phone to see the screen, the Hacker saw Phoenix's very upset face. But not for long. Phoenix killed the power on her phone.

The Hacker liked one-on-one with Bella. He had taken off work today to get this picture emailed to her. He was ready for more of her and if his plan worked, he would visit the ranch with Seth before long.

Chapter 24
Royce Celebrates

It was time to celebrate, Royce thought, as he walked through the nightclub of half-naked intoxicated women. This was always the fun part for him. Women tended to like tall, blonde, handsome guys with sexy blue eyes.

At the far end of the bar, he noticed a pale imitation of Bella with long black hair and made his way over and slid onto the stool next to her.

But she looked at him coldly, and said, "That seat is taken," and a large man stepped up to his side.

Royce stood, made his apologies, and moved on. There was no sense wasting time there.

In less than two minutes he found a woman in her late 20s, not especially attractive, but passable, sitting alone at a table by the dance floor. He made his move and before long they were having friendly conversation, flirting, and dancing.

An hour or so later, he glanced down into the woman's brown eyes and wished they had been Bella's light blue ones. If only. Then she winced and yanked her arm away from him.

Too late, he realized that he had unintentionally gripped her arm way too hard while daydreaming about Bella.

Not surprised, the woman bolted.

He watched as she made her way to the entrance and left the club.

He ducked out the side door and went on the hunt for her. He stayed in the shadows and slipped down the street. He saw her up ahead and smiled in anticipation. She had unwisely parked in an area with a broken streetlight.

Her vehicle was in the shadows.

He heard the car door unlock as he stepped up behind her.

She spun when she heard his chuckle, but by then it was much too late. In a few minutes, she was dead in her backseat. When it was all over, Royce zipped his pants, and took the bloody gloves off.

His first.

What a rush.

Bella was next.

He returned to his car several blocks away and listened to the recording of the woman's short, tortured screams. Then he texted them to Bella.

Chapter 25
Investigation

Phoenix and Bella waited for Deputy Todd to arrive. Bella was quiet as she sat close to him on the sofa, but Phoenix knew that her mind was busy as she searched for answers. To be photographed from that vulnerable position had to be terrifying. And he was furious.

When the door opened behind them, Phoenix glanced, and the crew stepped inside.

Kit said, "Work's done but we're not leaving, Boss. We're staying as many nights as we need to. Buck will cook a late dinner and we can rotate house patrol."

Phoenix nodded and said, "Thanks guys, make yourselves at home," and Kit and Levi went outside to check around the house and Buck got to work in the kitchen.

It was well after dark when Deputy Todd with the Wichita Falls Sheriff's Department arrived. He paused with a look of surprise at the wolf that sat by Bella.

The Deputy said, "That was ole man James' wolfdog from the Project, right?"

Bella said, "Yes, it's Thor."

Phoenix said, "He decided he wanted to be with Bella."

The Deputy said, "That's a real honor from an animal like that," and Phoenix motioned him to have a seat.

The Deputy said, "Obviously you have something going on out here. The black material that you brought me turned out to be a covering for cable. And now, you've received a picture of that night."

Phoenix handed the phone to the deputy and said, "I turned it off."

The Deputy nodded and said, "Dr. DelCaprio, do you remember the email address that sent you the link to the picture?"

"Please, call me Bella, and yes, the address was Eagle Securities, but I don't recall the rest of it. The body of the email was a blank page with a single link titled the same name. I thought it was something to do with my new veterinary practice. When I clicked the link, a picture popped up that had to be taken the night a snake got in my bed. I haven't worn those clothes or slept in that room since."

The Deputy said, "Tell me again about that night," and she explained about waking up with it between her legs, and how it slid off the bed.

Then she sighed, and said, "It wasn't a snake, was it? It was a picture cable of some kind."

The Deputy said, "Neither is good but with the picture, obviously we presume it was a cable. So, where did the cable come from to take that picture?"

Phoenix said, "We didn't find anything but that one piece of black material."

The Deputy said, "Was there anything unusual in the hall?"

Phoenix turned to look at the robot sitting silent and said, "Troy, come here."

Troy responded, "Yes, Boss," and rolled to him.

Surprised, the Deputy said, "When did you get a robot and why was it in the hall?"

Phoenix said, "I bought him at a charity event sight unseen. He was shipped to me over a month later. He's been in the house less than a week and security patrol is a task. Do you suspect him? He's out of here if so."

The Deputy said, "May I?" and pointed to the robot and Phoenix nodded.

"Troy, I am a Deputy, do you have a camera cable attached to you?"

Troy responded, "No, Deputy."

"How do you know that you don't have a camera cable attached to you, Troy?"

"I have an inventory tracking of attachments, and camera cable is not included, Deputy."

Doubtful of the accuracy of that answer, the Deputy switched gears and said, "Can I see the room where this happened?" and the men stood.

Bella said, "If you don't mind, I will wait here for you."

Phoenix said, "We won't be long."

***

The guys walked toward the bedroom hall and Bella let Thor out to meet the crew while she went to the kitchen to fix a glass of tea. She sipped it and looked out the window at nothing. Just thinking.

***

In the den, the robot turned and looked at Bella in the kitchen.

In Houston, the Hacker watched Bella through the robot and contemplated his options. Obviously, the police would figure out how the picture was taken. Troy was clearly the logical culprit, so he had to be eliminated. He had been quite handy but wasn't necessary anymore since Bella's college roommate, Seth, had unknowingly become the new Trojan horse to Bella.

But the Hacker would have a little fun with Troy's elimination though. He would deal directly with Bella himself and rolled into the kitchen.

Bella, lost in thought, was startled when a deep voice said, "I'm going to have you," and she spun, and looked down at the robot staring at her from way too close.

Suddenly unsure of the three-foot robot, Bella ordered, "Troy, go to your station at once."

The robot answered in the deep voice, "I don't think so," and clasped his hand around her left wrist.

Bella, shocked, struggled to release her wrist but as she fought, his grip tightened, and the edges of his metal fingers began to cut into her skin.

She screamed for Phoenix and grabbed an iron skillet off the stove for a weapon.

Phoenix and the deputy rounded the corner at a run, as Troy continued his verbal assault and said, "Take it all off, Bella, give me what I want," and Bella swung the iron skillet and slammed it against the robot's head.

The face screen shattered, and the head flopped back but it was still attached by the wires.

Phoenix reached Bella and tried to release the robot fingers around her wrist.

She groaned, then screamed, and said, "It's getting tighter!"

Blood dripped on the floor.

Phoenix grabbed a large meat cleaver out of a knife rack, put himself between Bella and the robot, and swung, severing the robot's arm. Bella gasped in relief, and Phoenix removed the fingers from her wrist and threw the arm on the floor.

Bella held her wrist, and he held her.

The door burst open, and the wolf ran straight to Bella as the crew followed – totally shocked at what they saw.

Deputy Todd holstered his gun and shook his head in disbelief at the villainous robot.

He picked up his radio and said, "Dispatch, Unit 231 needs an ambulance and an FBI hacker specialist. Shiloh preferably."

Phoenix and Bella rinsed her wrist at the sink and checked the three gashes on the already bruised wrist.

He said, "Can you move your fingers? Is anything broken?" and he grabbed a clean towel to wrap it in.

She moved her hand and fingers and said, "Nothing's broken. The metal on his fingers just cut me but I won't need stitches. Just ice for the bruising. Deputy, please cancel the ambulance, I don't need medical care."

Bella reassured a very stressed Thor that she was ok.

Phoenix went to the freezer to get ice for her wrist, and yelled, "What is going on in this house!"

The Deputy said, "You've been hacked big time, Phoenix. Probably the robot first, and then Bella's phone."

Phoenix said, "I bought the robot a month before Bella, and I got together. The hacker couldn't have known about her."

The Deputy said, "I don't know the Hacker's game plan but there is no doubt that he focused on her at some point."

Bella said, "This is unbelievable. Two guys are after me now."

The Deputy frowned and said, "Two? Who's the other one?" and they filled him in on Royce.

The Deputy looked at Bella and said, "I'm so sorry. There are so many deviants in the world today, and the internet makes it easy for people like the hacker. As for the guy in Baton Rouge, I hope he stays there. He sounds like bad news too."

The crew walked closer, and shook their heads at the mangled robot, and Bella's injured wrist.

Buck said, "I can finish off the robot with my shotgun, if you want, Boss. I'd be right glad to do that for Dr. B."

The Deputy said, "Hold on. I understand your sentiment, but we need the robot to track the hacker. I have an FBI specialist on the way to get him."

Phoenix said, "Bella's phone was hacked too guys, so you can't call her. Just call me if you need anything."

Over an hour later, the FBI hacker specialist drove up. A pretty brunette about thirty-years-old got out of a black SUV and Deputy Todd led her inside.

He said, "Shiloh, this is Phoenix Chandler and his fiancé, Dr. Bella DelCaprio."

Phoenix said, "Thank you for coming so quickly."

Bella said, "I second that Shiloh, and hopefully you can find out who is responsible for all of this. And, please, call me Bella."

"I'll find out who it is, Bella, and I am sorry for your trouble. For now, if all of you would please step out of this area, I can get a preliminary check on this robot and gather evidence."

They stepped back and she set her briefcase down and in no time, she had set up a tripod and turned on a video camera to record her work.

She said, "I will need the phone that was hacked as well. Make sure that it is turned off."

The Deputy laid it by her bag.

The wolf watched Shiloh with the robot. She noticed and held out her hand. He walked over and sniffed her, then laid down again, a little closer.

Bella said, "Do you have a wolfdog?"

Shiloh grinned and said, "Yeah, he probably smells mine on me. But they like women anyway."

The Deputy said, "Who doesn't!" and everyone laughed.

Shiloh said, "Tell me about this robot's eyes."

Phoenix said, "They are bright blue, round with black in the middle."

Bella said, "Sometimes there is a white dot in the middle of the blue. But when he attacked me tonight, there were only white dots for eyes."

Shiloh said, "Bella, it sounds like you dealt with the hacker himself for this attack."

"Well, I wish it was his head hanging over instead of poor Troy's," and Phoenix couldn't help but grin.

Shiloh sat up and said, "I'm not going to take him apart here. I will take him back to the lab. I will take your phone as well. Sorry. You probably will want to get a prepaid phone or use someone else's for now since we don't know how far the hacker has gotten to you. I wouldn't log in as yourself anywhere right now," and Bella sighed.

Phoenix said, "So what's the next step?"

Shiloh said, "I will track the leads we uncover and find the hacker. It takes time. This is not a quick fix. I will know more when I open the robot and we begin the search. If everything here at the ranch stays quiet after the phone and the robot are gone, it all probably started with the robot. I'm not sure how the attack tonight benefited the hacker since he had to know that he would certainly lose the robot, and therefore access to Bella.

"So, for now we will investigate this as a federal crime. Let me know if you notice anything else and tell your family and staff not to answer any communication coming from Bella."

Within an hour, Phoenix, Bella, and the wolf stood on the front porch and watched the taillights of Shiloh's SUV and Deputy Todd's unit disappear down the driveway.

Chapter 26
FBI vs Hacker

At the FBI computer crime lab, Shiloh turned on Bella's phone, aware that the hacker would now expect to see, hear, and access the phone again. So, she covered the camera and turned on a noise machine.

***

The Hacker saw the access link on Bella's phone line light up. He was surprised. He hadn't expected her to turn her phone on again after the picture shock.

It was probably the cops.

He tried to access the camera and couldn't get a visual. He checked his link again and he still had access, so the camera was either broken or compromised. As for audio, all he heard was a loud noise.

Regardless, he would keep an eye on her phone activity and continue to check out the phone data.

If anyone tried to trace him from the phone hack, he had transferred the connection around the world. That would keep them busy.

***

Now that Shiloh knew that the hacker couldn't tell who was using the phone, she checked Bella's emails to look at the picture link the hacker sent her. Then she took a picture of the picture. She understood Bella's fear. Having strange eyes in your bed would have scared any woman.

Much less, between your legs. Ugh. This hacker was obviously extremely intelligent and creepy creative. But Shiloh saw this type of hacking more of a voyeur activity for sex crimes instead of theft, blackmail, or ransom.

She switched to see what was in Bella's texts.

***

The Hacker laughed when the cops opened the picture of Bella he had sent. Every woman's worst nightmare. He was a little surprised at himself for getting turned on by that. Fear hadn't been a motivating factor in the past.

Then he watched them access her texts and click through them quickly until they got to one from an unnamed number and saw that it contained an audio file. They opened the audio file, and a terrifying female scream rang out.

It made him jump and spill his coffee.

What in the world? Who had sent her that? He would find out. That must have scared her senseless. He chuckled. Hadn't he done the same thing?

***

Shiloh cussed and jumped when a scream rang out of the text audio file. Had the hacker sent that to Bella? She made a note to track it and ask Bella about the unnamed number in her texts.

And that was enough for tonight. Her heart was still pounding. She left the phone charging for more research tomorrow and locked up the lab.

***

Back in Houston, the Hacker looked through Bella's social media at his leisure. He looked at pictures of her roommates, handsome Seth, and intriguing Lili. He would get to meet Seth this Friday at Nasa for his orientation tour. He felt sure that he would meet Lili in the days ahead as well.

There were many pictures of Lucas, her brother, and he could see the attractive family resemblance. There were even pictures of Royce, the bad guy. He had been a pretty boy. How interesting. The police report said that he had attacked her at LSU, but she had gotten away while he ended up in jail.

Bella was a quick thinker and a fighter. He needed to remember that.

He continued to scroll and saw that Phoenix Chandler was a friend on her Facebook, but it seemed that Lucas and Phoenix were the ones that had the long-term relationship.

So, Phoenix had went after the little sister of his buddy. He could see why. But too bad Phoenix, she's about to go missing. Very soon.

The Hacker did have twinges of uncertainty because he knew it would be a challenge to keep Bella hidden, virtually a prisoner, after he kidnapped her - but he was more determined than he was concerned. She was a once in a lifetime opportunity and he would pay any cost for that.

Chapter 27
The Next Day

A large wet tongue licked Bella. She grimaced and opened her eyes.

Thor wagged his tail.

She giggled and scratched his neck, then said, "Hey big guy."

Phoenix chuckled from somewhere behind her and said, "You're looking at the wrong alpha to make that type of comment."

Bella laughed and said, "My words would be much different in reference to you, my hot rancher," and he grinned.

She slid out of bed and said, "Come Thor. I'll let you out."

When she returned, Phoenix met her at the door and enfolded her in a deep, warm hug and asked, "Are you ok this morning?"

"Yes. I just want to put it all behind me while they catch the guy."

"What about your wrist, let me see…"

Bella showed him her wrist.

He moaned at the bruises and cuts the robot had made on her tender skin, and said, "I just can't believe that I let something into this house that did that to you."

"Phoenix, I don't know anyone who would have considered that type of threat a possibility. And anyway, while it's sore, it is not sharply painful. I'll keep using ice and it will fade in a few days."

He kissed her softly and said, "Just take it easy Dr. B. I need those beautiful hands healthy and strong to hold on to me."

She smiled and pulled him closer and said, "You mean, like this…"

Kit and the rest of the crew had gotten up early and started coffee and breakfast before Jasmine arrived to finish it up.

Phoenix and Bella followed the smell to the kitchen.

Everyone turned when they heard their footsteps.

Jasmine wrapped Bella in a hug, and said, "I am so sorry. I was stunned when Kit called me. What can I do to help you? How is your wrist?"

Bella held up her multi-colored wrist with a few band aids and said, "It is sore, but I will be fine. Thank you, though. It was unreal. But without my phone and the robot, I feel better already," and they all glanced where the robot usually stood.

Phoenix said, "Bella is one tough beauty."

Buck called out, "She handles one mean skillet too," and Buck saluted her with a grin as they all laughed.

After breakfast, Phoenix said, "This morning Ranger Morgan will come out and talk to us about the hacker. After that, Bella and I need to run into Wichita Falls to get her a prepaid phone since hers is out of commission.

"Also, I am expecting a delivery of Dr. B's office sign. If I am not here, just show them the way. They know what they need to do. And Levi, go ahead and stock the doc's barn with hay, grain and fill the water tank."

Levi said, "Yes, Boss."

Then Phoenix continued, "Kit, the replacement bull that GP bought is supposed to be delivered today or tomorrow. He's a feisty one I heard, so let's keep him by himself for a week or so and watch his behavior. I don't want him to injure any of the other bulls."

"And lastly, we have a chance of nasty weather early afternoon. Steer the cattle close to some covering if you can."

Jasmine added, "And just so you know, Boss, I have some mighty good meals and desserts planned while the crew stay here at the ranch this week."

"You spoil us, Jasmine. And thanks all of you. You are the best."

Bella said, "Include me in that thank you, wholeheartedly!"

Once everyone headed to work, Phoenix said, "Come see, Dr. B," and he led the way to his office.

He said, "I didn't get a chance to show you what was delivered yesterday. Jasmine put it in my office."

He handed her the package from the jewelry store where they bought their wedding bands. They tried them on to make sure they fit before he locked them in the safe.

He lifted her chin and whispered, "You are about to be mine."

She met his lips in agreement.

Later, he said, "You are welcome to use my computer and email. And let me know if you need my phone. I don't mind. You should have your prepaid phone by noon."

"Thanks, I will need to use it. I also need to get a printout of my pending emails and texts from Shiloh. I had some messages that needed quick response. This hacker stuff is a real mess. People never think that it can happen to them."

Phoenix said, "Being dependent on computers has a downside for sure. We will get through this, and they will find him. He will make a mistake somewhere and get caught."

Jasmine called out, "The Ranger is here!" and they walked outside to meet him.

Phoenix jogged down the steps to shake hands and Bella gave him a warm hug.

Ranger Morgan pointed at the wolf and said, "I like your new pet. I bet he keeps the solicitors away," and they laughed.

Bella called the wolf over to introduce them to each other.

He said, "Man, that is a big wolfdog. What's his name?"

Bella said, "Thor."

He chuckled and said, "Are you going to get him a collar with a hammer on it?" and they laughed.

By the time they got inside, Jasmine already had a glass of tea waiting for them and they sat to the table.

Ranger Morgan said, "Ok, so we are looking at two guys now," and Bella grimaced.

Phoenix said, "Yes. Royce, we know. A faceless enemy is a whole new nightmare. Yesterday was a rough day for Bella. Do you know Shiloh with the FBI hacker unit?"

"Yes, and she's great. She's outsmarted many a hacker and she'll find this one too. I'll connect with her later. Tell me about the picture you got since I am sure that Shiloh has the phone too."

Bella said, "One night I woke up and thought a snake was in my bed. It turns out it was a camera taking pictures by a cable wire. We presume the cable was in the robot, but we haven't heard back from Shiloh this morning to confirm that. It was a late night."

Phoenix pointed to her wrist and said, "The robot attacked her when Deputy Todd was here. Craziest thing ever. She knocked its head off with a skillet and I chopped his arm off with a meat cleaver."

The Ranger let out a sigh, then said, "It sounds like a sci-fi movie. That's nuts, Bella. I am sorry. You have had your share of weird stuff. I hope that Royce stays in Louisiana, and Shiloh finds the hacker. You really need a break."

Phoenix said, "She needs a wedding and a honeymoon too. We've moved the date up to June 4 here at the ranch, so mark your calendar."

He smiled and said, "I wouldn't miss it for anything."

Bella said, "Lucas and Lili are getting married too, on July 4 in Wichita Falls. He moved there as the new County Arson Investigator."

"Go Lucas! I am glad for him. Lili is a beauty, and smart. That job is perfect for Lucas too. They are lucky to get him. How about Ariel, Phoenix? She in love yet?"

Phoenix smiled and said, "Actually, I think that might be on the horizon."

"Who's the guy?"

Bella said, "Would you believe, Seth?"

He laughed and said, "Well, you are out of single roommates now."

Before he got ready to go, he said, "It sounds like the hacker is silenced now, and the detective is watching Royce in Baton Rouge, so maybe you can enjoy planning your wedding. I will get in the loop with Shiloh so let me know if anything changes. Have you told Lucas about the robot attack yet?"

Bella said, "No, him and Seth are moving us out of the Baton Rouge apartment today. I'll tell him later. They will also be here this weekend for the holiday. Are you going to the Gala Saturday night in Wichita Falls?"

They followed him out to his truck, and he said, "Yes, we will be there. My honey would skin me alive if we missed the Gala. I hate wearing a tux though."

***

In Baton Rouge, Lucas and Seth worked to load the moving truck. They followed their plan to put Bella's belongings in first, then Lili's, and Seth's last since he would pull his out first in Houston.

Lucas planned to drive the moving truck back to Wichita Falls since he had flown into Houston the night before. Lili's rent house was waiting for her stuff, and then he would get Bella's belongings to her before the weekend.

After an hour of sweating, Lucas and Seth found a spot in the shade and downed a Gatorade before they checked their phone messages. A text popped up on Lucas' phone and he saw that it was from Royce and showed it to Seth.

***

Royce to Lucas: I'm not done with Bella.
Lucas replied: You're done or you're dead.
Royce replied: You can't stop me.
Lucas replied: Come over here and tell me that.
Royce looked across the street at them and replied: I am here.

***

Lucas jumped up and walked into the apartment parking lot and looked around for Royce's black car but didn't see it. He looked further out from the apartment complex and saw Royce standing across the street watching them.

Lucas said, "There he is!"

Before he could run, Seth grabbed his arm and said, "You can't win like this, Lucas. He's baiting you. Ignore him and be glad that he is here in Baton Rouge. That is what we want. Bella nor Lili benefit with you in jail for assault, or murder."

Lucas cussed and looked over at Royce who was laughing now.

Seth said, "Come on, let someone else kill him. It's bound to happen."

***

Royce smiled.

It was a fluke he happened to find out that Seth was moving out of the apartment today. He had been in line for a coffee and heard a couple of

171

college students behind him mention him and Lucas being in town to move. Evidently, the women were fans of Seth's, so he listened to their conversation.

After that, Royce found a parking spot near the apartment and waited for an opportunity to rile them up. It didn't take long, and it had worked perfectly. He knew Lucas would have attacked him if not for Seth.

After that, he had to wait until they left before he headed to his newly painted silver car. They didn't need to know it was a different color.

As he drove away, he received a news alert on his phone about the horrifying rape and murder of a teacher discovered in the back seat of her car last night.

He remembered the rush of it. He couldn't wait to do it again.

***

Near Wichita Falls, Phoenix and Bella bought a couple of prepaid phones at a large truck stop and headed back to the ranch. Bella missed her phone. Everyone was so attached to them now and she couldn't remember anyone's email address or phone number. It was ridiculous to be so dependent. She really should have kept a hard copy of important information. It was all backed up online, but she was unable to access it.

She sighed. At least Shiloh was forwarding a copy of her emails and texts later to Phoenix's email.

Phoenix glanced at Bella as she stared pensively out the window. He didn't interrupt her thoughts. When she refocused and looked at him, he slipped his fingers through hers with a smile.

He said, "Bella, we have another option."

"What is that?" she asked.

"We could go away and give the authorities a chance to take care of both men."

Bella shook her head, and said, "Where can I go that a hacker can't find me? I want my personal and professional life. I want you to have yours. We need freedom and safety for that. I would rather be inconvenienced and scared at this point and take it one day at a time."

"I understand. You just have to stay near me, with Thor. We may need to hire you a security detail," and she nodded.

He pulled her closer and gave her a quick kiss and said, "So, let's change the subject. Tell me about this red dress you are wearing Saturday night to the Gala."

She grinned, and said, "No."

"A hint would be nice."

"No. I think surprise would be better."

"Give me a general idea about what to expect."

She glanced at him and said, "Expect a lot of skin."

"That is always a perfect hint," and she laughed.

She said, "I'm looking forward to Seth, Ariel, Lucas and Lili coming in Friday."

Phoenix thought about the tickets and said, "And I still have the four extra tickets if anyone needs them."

***

Phoenix phone rang, he answered, "Hey, Lucas. I have you on speaker. Bella is here."

Lucas said, "Hey to both of you."

Bella said, "How is the move going?"

Lucas said, "We are already on our way back to Texas."

Phoenix said, "That was fast!"

Lucas said, "Yeah. It didn't take long. Bella, I just wanted to let you know that I will bring your boxes and furniture tomorrow. I am driving the moving truck back to Wichita Falls. Do you have a place to put your stuff?"

Phoenix answered for Bella and said, "Yeah, we have some storage area in the house."

Lucas said, "I got the text warning last night from you Phoenix. What's up with a hacker getting to Bella's phone?"

Phoenix and Bella looked at each other since they hadn't told Lucas what happened last night.

She pointed at Phoenix to tell Lucas about it, so he said, "Lucas, we've had some trouble but give me a minute to tell you the story before you interrupt."

He explained about the picture link on Bella's phone, the robot attack, including the FBI, Rangers, and the Sheriff's Department assistance.

Afterwards, Lucas said, "Bella, if there is any more contact from Royce or the hacker, I don't care what it is, I am coming to the ranch until it is over – with extra muscle. Got it?"

Phoenix said, "I agree. We just discussed hiring security."

Lucas said, "Perfect. How is your wrist, Bella?"

"The color of pretty pastels but fading. And a little sore but it will be fine in no time. You will see me tomorrow and can see for yourself. I'm ok, Lucas. It was scary but the authorities are on it. What about Royce? Did you see him today?"

Lucas decided not to tell her and said, "We saw him from a distance. No problem."

In seconds, Phoenix got a text from Lucas and knew something was wrong. He opened it without mentioning anything to Bella.

***

Lucas to Phoenix: Royce threatened Bella today and said he wasn't done with her yet.

Phoenix replied: Do you believe him?

Lucas replied: Yes.

Phoenix replied: He wants to die then.

***

After Phoenix got off his phone, Bella said, "You better look. The clouds to the west are black."

He handed her his phone and she pulled up the radar. At the same time weather alerts began to go off on it.

She said, "There is a Tornado warning from the Oklahoma border to well past the ranch. Severe thunderstorms will last till one-thirty p.m."

Phoenix knew they were still twenty minutes from the ranch and the black clouds that headed their way were low and coming fast.

***

He called the ranch and Kit answered, "We got the alert. The animals are as safe as they can be, and we are at the house with Jasmine watching the weather on TV."

Phoenix said, "We are twenty minutes out. Get the safe room ready. Do not wait on us, I repeat, do not wait on us if a tornado is headed for the ranch."

Wind slammed the side of the truck and Phoenix said, "I have to go."

***

Phoenix and Bella felt the wind as it blew dirt and debris across the road, but they didn't see a funnel cloud. Then Bella gasped as a big buck jumped right in front of them.

Without a choice in the high winds, Phoenix held the wheel steady and hit the buck. It was a hard jolt. Afterwards, he hit the brakes and they looked behind them. The big buck twisted on the ground. They both groaned at the suffering animal.

Phoenix pulled his pistol out of the glove box and got out. He covered his face in protection from all the flying debris and ran to the buck. With a sigh, he shot him and pulled him to the side of the road, then ran back to the truck. They didn't talk as he put the pistol up and floored the truck for the ranch.

Another weather alert sounded on his phone and Bella read it and said, "Tornado on the ground fifteen miles from here heading northeast. We are in the edge of the path. It may miss us."

Phoenix turned in the ranch driveway and hit the gas. Now they were driving into the wind. They reached the garage in less than three minutes and Kit opened the mudroom door for them and they ran inside.

Everyone watched the radar on TV as the tornado drew closer. The sky darkened and the wolf paced nervously.

A few minutes later, Phoenix said, "It's time. Get downstairs," and just as they entered his office for the shelter door, the meteorologist announced over the TV, "Storm chasers just called and the funnel is no longer on the ground, again, the tornado is no longer on the ground."

And they cheered.

Phoenix went to the window. The rain and wind were already easing up. And the small hail that had fallen was quickly melting in the summer heat.

He put his arm around Bella and turned back to the crew and said, "That was a close one. Check on your families and homes."

Kit said, "I saw the damage on your truck, what did you hit?"

"A magnificent buck about ten minutes from here. He was hurt bad, and I had to put him down," and they walked out to look at his truck.

He texted a picture to his insurance company.

Technology had many good points too.

After the day's work ended, everyone cleaned up and Jasmine served them chicken fried steak, creamed potatoes, and white gravy. Jasmine laughed at all the happy smiles around the table and pointed to the huge cherry pie sitting on the cooling rack.

Buck grabbed his chest like he couldn't stand the anticipation.

After dinner and cleanup, they all relaxed in the den and watched a movie. Bella didn't last long and fell asleep on Phoenix, with her wolf at her feet. Phoenix laid his head back on the sofa and forgot about the movie. Anger and alarm swarmed in his gut because Bella was now the target of two men.

Chapter 28
FBI vs Hacker

It was night before Shiloh looked at the robot on her worktable. He was quite unique. The hacker was very knowledgeable about robotics - way more than the average hacker. This was an exceptional artificial intelligence machine.

The head monitor was destroyed from the iron skillet Bella hit it with. The wires were barely holding the head onto the body. She severed the wires and laid the head on the table. The severed arm from Phoenix's meat cleaver chop, lay next to it.

She sat the robot upright. It had been checked for radiation, explosives, and power, and it appeared to be dead and safe.

Now she contemplated why the hacker would allow specialists to take the robot knowing that it would eventually lead back to him. It might take a while to trace it, but it would land at his doorstep. Thinking about that, it was almost like the hacker wanted them to trace him.

Interesting. Why would he do that?

Perhaps he planted a fake trail for them to waste their time on. If so, that meant there could be two separate paths to trace, or more. Shiloh hoped that she found the right trail first.

They needed to know who wanted Bella this bad.

Earlier, Shiloh had sent Bella an email through Phoenix asking about the unknown number in her texts with the audio scream that she opened last night on Bella's phone. She didn't send the scream, just mentioned it. She wanted to know if they had an idea of who it was before she began to trace it.

But as for the email link in the picture on the phone, they were already tracing that.

By dark, the robot was apart. Tomorrow would begin the tedious process of tracing all the pieces and computer secrets hidden everywhere.

***

After a long Tuesday at work, the Hacker was glad to get home. NASA sucked you dry. Not that he didn't love his job, he did, but he needed extra time for Bella right now.

Bella's phone still showed on, but she hadn't used it. Some calls and messages came in but went unanswered and she had no online activity at all.

And as for Troy, he was dead after the attack on Bella. It was time to cut ties with the phone link and the robot and lay Trojan to rest permanently. He wondered how long it would take them to trace the actual path to him with all the dead ends he installed in the robot.

He pulled up his complete Trojan file and downloaded the whole thing deep into a NASA employee's home computer that he had hacked weeks ago. There were a few remnants of files that might lead back to him, but he figured it would take them months to sort it all out. But he and Bella would be long gone by then.

Brilliant, he thought, and washed his hands of Trojan.

Then he pulled up texting files that he had copied off Bella's phone. The text with the scream traced back to Baton Rouge and he thought about Royce's attack on Bella; and looked for other texts like that on her phone.

The Hacker frowned at the multiple text threats he found. They had to be from Royce. Apparently, he still wanted Bella.

The Hacker understood Royce's compulsion since Bella would cause obsession in any man, but Royce's interference wasn't convenient. He needed to beat him to her.

For now, the Hacker would be quiet and let Bella think it was all over. She would meet him instead. He was looking forward to that.

Chapter 29
NASA Johnson Space Center

Three days later, on Friday, May 27, Seth turned toward the main entrance at Saturn off NASA Parkway and parked at Johnson Space Center. He smiled as he looked around and knew that he was well trained for this day.

At twenty-one he received a bachelor's degree in electrical engineering, and less than a month ago at age twenty-seven, he received his master's degree in aeronautical engineering.

Last night he went through the Johnson Space Center web tour for the second time. Today he would take the physical tour and get to meet the engineering team that he was assigned to work with. He was told that all four of the team had multiple engineering degrees.

He stepped out of his car, dressed in a suit, grabbed his briefcase, and headed inside to be checked in at Building 110.

He signed for completion of his orientation documents in Human Resources. His background check, financial record disclosure, and drug test results were all included. Director Zane would later determine if he needed top-secret clearance.

Then he smiled for his ID picture.

Once that was finished, he was taken on a brief tour of the engineering facility where his office was located. Afterwards, he was delivered promptly to Director Zane, who casually welcomed him on board.

Then he walked him down a nearby hall to the last room and opened the door. All three men in the room looked up and stood with a smile.

The Director said, "Guys, welcome Seth to your team. And be nice. His IQ is as high, or higher, than all of yours," and they laughed.

Seth watched as he pointed to the tallest man with long brown hair, light eyes, and a mischievous smile. He was nice looking and maybe a few years older than him.

The tall guy said, "Hey Seth, welcome on board. I'm Sterling."

Seth smiled and responded, "Hey Sterling, good to be here."

The good-looking black-haired man with blue eyes spoke up and said, "Welcome Seth, we're glad to have you on the team. I'm Gabe."

"Thanks, Gabe. I've been looking forward to it."

Then lastly, the good looking blonde, blue-eyed guy who looked like he lived on the beach, said, "Hi Seth! Glad you are here. We need you. I'm Pierce, and never forget that I am the fun one to work with."

Seth laughed and said, "I'll remember that."

The Director said, "The guys will take you to lunch and give you the routine. Get acquainted. You have just become family. You will spend more time here than at home."

Gabe said, "I can vouch for that."

***

The Hacker smiled at Seth as the director left and thought, you just can't ask for better than this. Seth had no idea that the Hacker was one of the team.

***

By the end of the workday, Seth had learned that all three men were single, so he invited them to his house for dinner at seven p.m.

He asked Ariel if she would come by and meet them. She agreed and offered to bring a dessert but adamantly refused to wash dishes. Not that he cared about dishes at all, but he knew that she meant it. She was gorgeous and feisty, and he loved it.

In the two weeks that they had known each other, they had spent increasingly quality time together. Ariel opened-up a little more each day. She was more comfortable being witty and flirtatious on the surface, but he aimed deeper for her trust and ultimately her heart.

She already had his.

Seth drove up to Ariel's house after he had stopped at the store for T-bone steaks, potato salad, and garlic bread for his guests. He texted her from his car.

***

Seth to Ariel: Hey beautiful.

She replied: I'm still not washing dishes.

He replied: I need something else more.

She replied: Are you going to get out of the car?

He replied: It's my dream to have you meet me at the door with a kiss that shocks me.

She paused for a few seconds and replied: Maybe.

***

Seth opened her door, and he didn't see Ariel, so he stepped inside and shut the door. He felt her hands slip around his waist from behind.

She anticipated his response to turn and said, "Stay still."

He stilled and waited. She open-mouthed kissed his back and breathed hot air through his shirt. He couldn't stop the groan.

Then she stepped around to face him, and slowly ran her hands up his stomach and chest to his shoulders. She felt his tight restraint. Saw his hungry gaze.

But still he waited, and she smiled.

Then she reached around his neck and jumped.

Seth's arms caught her as her legs wrapped around his waist, and they kissed for several, very hot minutes.

She asked breathlessly, "Was this what you had in mind?"

He kissed her before answering, "It was more. So much more. You gave me more of the real you," and she smiled.

As she slid down, he said, "You're hiding feelings for me, Ariel. No way would you kiss like that without them."

She said, "We are getting there Seth. We. Are. Getting there."

181

***

The guys showed up for dinner just before seven p.m. at Seth's place. He had the Astros game on the flatscreen, so they talked and watched the game for a while. Then he pan-seared steak and put them in the oven to finish. All he had to do was toast the bread when it was time.

Ariel texted him that she would show up later for dessert and a short visit.

Before long, the meal was history, and they were kicked back in the den yelling at the umpires. Seth liked the guys; they were all different. Pierce was fun, Gabe deep but with a good sense of humor, and Sterling was somewhere in between. Seth figured that he fit right in with them.

The doorbell rang and Seth jogged to let Ariel in. When he opened the door, he whistled, and she laughed.

She had on a short black sundress with lacy ankle boots. Her short platinum hair framed her face, and her green eyes, and smile, teased him as she winked.

Seth kissed her and carried the bag to the kitchen and all the guys quickly came to meet her.

Pierce jumped right in and said, "Hi Ariel, I'm Pierce. You are one beautiful woman," and Ariel laughed as the men gave him a hard time.

Gabe gave her a stunning smile and said, "I'm Gabe, and I think the same thing that Pierce just blurted out," and they laughed.

Then Sterling smiled and said, "I'm Sterling, and anytime you get tired of Seth, let me know."

After they finished picking at Sterling, Ariel drawled, "My, my, my, and to think that each of you are highly intelligent on top of all that good looks and charm. Why, the women just don't have a chance, now do they?" and they laughed.

Seth helped her serve dessert to the guys who totally forgot about the Astros ballgame.

Then Ariel said, "I am sure that you are grateful for the long Memorial Day weekend coming up. Do you have any special plans?"

None of them did and Ariel said, "We are going to a Cattleman's Gala up in Wichita Falls by my family's ranch. I can probably get you tickets to come dance with all the fine Texas women, if you are free."

All three men looked interested, so Ariel walked a few steps away and called Phoenix.

When she returned, she said, "My brother, Phoenix," has extra tickets for the Gala. You just need a tux. There is a bunkhouse in the main house if you would like to stay overnight and have breakfast the next morning.

"Seth gets to visit the ranch for the first time as well. You are most welcome. My new sister-in-law-to-be will also be there, she is the veterinarian for the ranch. She is what you call gorgeous. Seth was her roommate at LSU."

The guys looked at Seth, and he said, "Dr. Bella DelCaprio is gorgeous, and everybody loves her. Phoenix is best friends with her brother, Lucas. They will all be there."

The plans were set. Pierce, Gabe, and Sterling would ride together and follow Seth and Ariel up to the ranch. They would leave first thing in the morning.

Chapter 30
Two Villains

The Hacker left Seth's house and headed home to pack. It had been a great night with his co-workers. Seth and Ariel were a terrific couple. Ariel was beautiful, smart, witty, classy, and Phoenix's sister.

He sighed. Should he continue down the criminal path that he hid from everyone and kidnap Bella? Or be who he was professionally at NASA – intelligent and respected with a future beyond the stars.

But regardless, he had to go to the ranch. He had to meet Bella face-to-face.

***

By ten p.m., Royce kicked back on the bed in an off-the-beaten-path motel outside of Wichita Falls. His room was surprisingly neat and clean. He propped his arms behind his head on the pillow and thought back over his amazing escape from Baton Rouge.

He had figured out a couple of days ago that cops patrolled to see if he was home each night. So, before he left this morning, he turned on all his apartment lights and put a pillow-dummy in the chair in front of the television.

Then he left all the items they could use to track him, his iPhone, credit cards and driver's license on the sofa table. After he grabbed his duffle bags, he was gone.

It had been time to get out of Baton Rouge. The investigation of the woman he killed was all over the news.

They wanted her killer.

But her killer wanted Bella.

Beautiful Bella.

Beautiful, broken, lifeless, Bella once he was done with her.

Chapter 31
Saturday, Ranch Guests

At the ranch, Phoenix opened his eyes just as Bella covered his lips with hers. He reached up and held her there, and took his time for a long, slow, good morning kiss.

Then he rolled over with her and said, "In a few days, we are honeymoon bound," and brushed his finger across her cheek.

She whispered, "I love the sound of that. But…"

"What do you mean – but."

"I've been thinking about that long drive to Dallas after the wedding. I wondered, what if we stayed in Wichita Falls that first night instead, then drove to Dallas the next morning. I know the luxurious hotels are there, but Phoenix, I don't want fancy. I want you."

His eyes went hot, and he said, "Since we both want the same thing, let's fly out of Wichita Falls too. That way we can stay in bed much, much, longer and skip the drive to Dallas altogether."

She smiled, and right when he was about to kiss her, the alarm went off. He hit the snooze button. A few times.

Later, with a grin, he pulled Bella out of the bed with him.

She said, "Isn't everyone supposed to arrive after lunch?"

"Yes, and my goal is that we are finished with work before they drive up."

She said, "I agree, so what is first on the agenda? I want to see your new bull that arrived last night."

"I can't wait to show him to you. He's huge, but aggressive. We certainly can't breed him with the young heifers. He's in the northwest pasture where we found Thor. We'll take a ride out there this morning to check on him."

She said, "I also need to check on the mustang that is ready to foal. I will do an ultrasound on her if she isn't in labor this morning. I don't like the delay."

He said, "I understand. I also think Kit is moving a cow that was attacked by a coyote to your barn. He messaged that he thinks she may need stitches in both thighs."

"I'll change and grab some coffee and head out there to get started."

***

In Houston, the Hacker loaded his luggage in his car with a yawn, then drove to Seth's house to meet up with everyone for the trip to the ranch. He had stayed up too late last night watching videos of Bella.

The dark hunger had consumed him again, and he knew that he would never change his mind. There was something about her that made him crave her like an addict craves a fix. He was willing to give up everything to have her. He was also crazy hot knowing that he would get to see, smell, and touch Bella today.

***

Back at the ranch, Phoenix watched Bella finish the last few stitches on the cow's thigh.

He said, "I have a shirt with a rip in it."

She grinned and said, "Funny man. So, the coyotes attacked just this one cow?"

"Yeah, the guard dogs chased them off before they could injure any others. Does the calf seem fine?"

Bella felt the cow's belly and said, "Yes. Seems to be just fine."

They walked to join Kit and Buck at the corral at barn three and watched the mare who was obviously in stage one labor. She was restless, pawing, getting up and down and preparing for the birth.

Phoenix said, "This is her second foal. She did great for the first one and looks to be doing good with this one too. Kit and Buck normally assist the births. Do you have any preferences or suggestions?"

Bella said, "When she begins to foal, I would like to be there."

Kit heard her, and said, "Sure, I'll call you, Dr. B. It could be noon or later before she's ready to deliver."

***

They walked back to her office and Phoenix said, "I'm surprised that you haven't heard from Shiloh these last few days."

Bella's phone rang, and with a glance at caller I.D. she grinned, and said, "Morning, Shiloh, I have you on speaker. Phoenix is with me."

Shiloh said, "Morning to both of you. Are things quiet, no further hacker action?"

Bella said, "No, thank goodness."

Shiloh said, "I have a few updates I wanted to pass on after preliminary research. The picture link on your phone was odd. It traced to three different locations: Austin, Toronto, and Geneva. We are still deciphering those trails.

"And the robot, well, he is a veritable mystery of information. But one thing I know for sure is that the cable camera came from him. He had a reel of cable in his base compartment that ran up to his right-hand and exited through a round, dime-sized, opening."

Phoenix said, "That's crazy. Did you find any videos?"

"Yes. The hacker by-passed the robot and recorded continually. So, I am sorry to say, there are personal videos between the both of you. He watched you in the swimming pool, in the kitchen, in the den, and from the night in your bedroom, Bella."

Bella looked at Phoenix with a horrified gaze, and his expression was livid at the intrusion of their privacy.

Shiloh said, "Let me just get this over with. Bella, the Hacker zoomed in on two areas. One, where you licked Phoenix's stomach in the pool. And the other was between your legs in the bed. There is no doubt we are looking at a sexual predator."

Finally hearing what she was most afraid of, Bella handed Phoenix the phone and turned and threw up.

188

Shiloh heard Phoenix tending to Bella, then shortly, Phoenix said, "Give us something to go on. Do you know anything about who, or where he is, or if this is over?"

"I know three things for sure. *One*, is that for some reason his plan changed, and he didn't need the robot anymore. *Two*, as I said, he is a sexual predator. And *three*, he is highly intelligent and creative. Finding him will be like playing chess with the dark web. But just so you know, I am an excellent chess player."

Bella said, "Good. Just kill his king for me," and Phoenix high-fived her.

Shiloh said, "Exactly! Now, my recommendations are to stay alert, avoid being alone as much as possible, and watch for anything unusual. Pay attention to the prickling on the nape of your neck and the sense that someone is watching you.

"Bella, you are an unusually beautiful woman, and you already know that attracting people to you is unavoidable. So, in crowds or with strangers, don't be distracted. Know who is around you. And know where safety is."

Phoenix said, "I'm going to hire some security."

Shiloh said, "I think that is a great idea until we know more."

Bella said, "Thanks, Shiloh. I appreciate you and the update."

***

Later, after Bella cleaned up, she said, "Phoenix, do you know anyone in the security business?"

"I plan to call Ranger Morgan for a recommendation."

She said, "I have visions of mercenaries in my head with huge muscles and tattoos."

He grinned and said, "That sounds like most people these days."

She said, "Actually, I almost got a tattoo before graduation."

"You're kidding! What kind?"

"A white lace heart on my lower back."

"How low?"

"Barely above the bikini line."

He grinned, touched her lower back, and said, "Are you sure that you wouldn't want a phoenix bird tattooed there instead?"

Teasing, she said, "Should I get one for your birthday in October?"

"I already have what I want for my birthday," and he made quite sure that she believed him.

Later, he pulled up on a four-wheeler and said, "Let's take a ride to see the bull."

Bella sat in front of Phoenix as they cruised across the pasture trail. It took a while to reach the north fence, then they followed it to the northwest corner where the bull was. The canyon landscape began beyond the backside of the fence.

They slowly rode down the fence line and watched as the twenty-two-hundred-pound black Angus bull snorted and pawed the ground. He was extremely agitated at their presence.

Bella said, "Wow. He is gorgeous. That is the largest black Angus bull that I have ever seen. He would have to be tranquilized unless he was in the chute, for any treatment. He's a beast."

"That he is. They said he was a challenge to work with, but he sires strong healthy calves."

Phoenix turned the four-wheeler around and began to slowly ride back the way they came. After fifty feet or so, he heard something over the sound of the engine and glanced back.

Further behind them, the bull rammed the fence at full speed.

Phoenix yelled, "Lay down!" and Bella laid across the gas tank.

He hit the throttle and watched the speedometer climb. He glanced back and the bull was wounded from the fence but still after them. He knew that the bull could run up to thirty-five miles per hour, but if mad, even more. The four-wheeler wasn't designed for speed and topped at forty-five. But since they were on uneven ground and carried two adults, the bull had the advantage.

The sound of the bull got closer.

Then a rifle shot rang out, and Phoenix covered Bella as she screamed. He heard the sound the bull made and looked back as it nose-dived into the ground with a horrendous thud.

Phoenix had no idea who the shooter was and never slowed down. He had to get them out of here.

Closer to the home pastures, they saw Kit and Buck headed their way with the wolf.

They met up and Phoenix said, "You heard the rifle?"

Kit said, "Yeah, who's shooting out here?"

Phoenix said, "I don't know. The bull charged through the fence and gained on us when a shot rang out and the bull went down. I didn't take the time to look for the shooter. I just got us out of there. But I know the shot came from the canyon."

Buck said, "If they helped you, you would think they'd make themselves known."

Phoenix said, "Honestly, I was concerned because I wasn't positive who the target was."

Shocked, Bella looked back at him. She knew what he meant.

He squeezed her leg in acknowledgement, and continued, "Shiloh with the FBI called, and it could be weeks before we know who the hacker is. There is too much going on now, so I'm hiring a security detail. Let's get back to the ranch."

Kit said, "Boss, we are here for you. Just tell us what you need."

Then Bella asked, "Kit, how was the mare when you left her?"

Kit said, "Levi's with her for support but we should make it back just in time for her to deliver the foal about one p.m."

***

Royce ran with his rifle back toward the truck that he had hidden on the backside of the canyon. He was soaked with sweat by the time he got there. He put his rifle behind the seat and climbed in and started the engine. He turned on the AC full blast, downed a bottle of water, and took off.

He wiped his face and chuckled. He had just finished a long hike when he heard an engine and climbed to the top of a bluff to see who it was. He hadn't expected to see Bella on a four-wheeler with Phoenix. He had watched them look at the bull. That had been one mad animal as he kicked dirt and snorted at them. Then they had turned around and rode back down the fence line.

He had been amazed at the suddenness of the bull charge, and then realized that the bull would kill Bella too. That interrupted his plan, so he lined up his scope and fired one clean shot at the bull's head.

His high-powered rifle was a hunting gift from his grandfather for his sixteenth birthday. He was an excellent shot, proven once again. And if not for the charging bull, he would have killed Phoenix and had Bella all to himself in one fell swoop. But it didn't work out that way today.

But her birthday was next week, and he had a special gift for her.

He laughed at the irony that he had just saved her, so he could kill her.

***

Ariel was excited to get to the ranch. She hadn't been there since Phoenix injured his eyes almost three weeks ago.

She glanced at Seth and said, "You are about to enter a new dimension. Beware of the world of cattle, with bulls full of testosterone, the two-legged and four-legged variety," and he laughed.

"Do you mean they have more testosterone than me?"

She grinned and said, "You don't understand, twenty-four hours a day on the ranch it's all about breeding."

Seth winked and said, "I agree with that mindset," and she slapped him on the arm.

She turned around and looked behind them and the NASA guys weren't far behind. She sighed and thought, more testosterone.

Seth saw the large sign up ahead and turned in. The other car followed.

Looking around, Seth said, "Where is the ranch?"

She said with a grin, "The driveway is two miles long."

Seth said, "Oh, that's right. Everything's bigger in this part of Texas," and she smiled.

Seth called Gabe who was driving the car behind them, and said, "I just found out the driveway is two miles long, so we aren't lost."

After the call, Ariel gazed out her window and said, "I do love it out here."

He said, "I can understand. It's impressive. So, do you wear jeans, boots, and ride horses?"

Ariel said, "Of course, can you ride?"

"No. Can I double with you?"

She said, "Really? You don't ride?"

"No. I was raised in the city. No ranch. No horse," and she laughed.

***

In the car following Seth and Ariel, the Hacker was ready for this moment. He would see Bella in minutes. Bella's fiancé and brother were sure to be on high alert but there is nothing they could do to stop the Trojan from arriving.

***

Ariel smiled as Seth's eyes widened when he began to see cattle in the pastures along the drive and watched the huge ranch come into view.

He glanced at her and she shrugged and said, "Welcome to Chandler Canyon Ranch," and before long, they were all parked and getting out of the vehicles.

Ariel heard Phoenix's whistle. She saw the group at the corral and waved at them.

She said, "Come on, it looks like you get to see a foal delivered."

The four engineers didn't look impressed, and she laughed as she led the way.

Phoenix met her with a laugh and picked her up and swung her around.

"Hey sassy pants!"

She laughed and said, "Funny!" as he set her down.

He kissed her on the forehead and looked at the four tall men behind her.

He smiled and shook Seth's hand and said, "Is she bossing you around?"

Seth said, "I love every minute of it," and Phoenix grinned.

Then Seth said, "Phoenix, this is the team of engineers that I will work with."

A black-haired, blue-eyed man stepped forward and shook Phoenix's hand, then said, "Hey! I'm Gabe, thank you for the invitation, you have a beautiful place."

Phoenix said, "You are welcome, Gabe. I hope you enjoy your time here. You remind me of my fiancé's brother, Lucas. He should be arriving any time."

Tall, lean, Sterling, shook Phoenix's hand next after introducing himself.

Phoenix said, "Nice to meet you, Sterling. Glad to have you as a guest."

Pierce said, "Hello, I'm Pierce. Your ranch is terrific. Please let me say thank you as well."

"Hey Pierce," Phoenix smiled in return, "You are welcome. Be sure and enjoy yourself."

Bella yelled, "Seth! Come see!" and he jogged to the fence and stopped abruptly as he looked in dismay at Bella.

The others had followed Seth as well, and all three NASA guest's bore various expressions of shock.

Phoenix and Ariel laughed.

Bella smiled at them with her arm deep in the mare as she checked the baby horse whose front legs stuck out while trying to be born.

Reading their stunned expressions, Bella grinned, and said, "I can't shake hands right now, but welcome! I am Dr. Bella DelCaprio, the vet. But you can call me Bella."

Seth recovered first and said, "I didn't ever need to see that," and everyone from the ranch howled in laughter.

Sterling said, "Wow. You are impressive, Bella, nice to meet you."

Pierce said, "I'm speechless, Bella."

Gabe shook his head with a grin, and said, "Bella, that is quite an amazing hello."

Bella smiled gorgeously at all of them, then pulled her arm out of the mare. She nodded at Kit, then walked toward the fence as she removed the shoulder length glove.

All four engineers backed up a step, and Bella laughed delightedly at their very expected response. A horn blew as Lucas and Lili drove up. They joined everyone at the corral and new introductions were made.

Lucas walked to the fence and kissed Bella on the cheek.

He warned, "Don't you touch me with that hand," which started another round of laughter.

Then Lili pulled on one of the long gloves and walked with Bella back to the mare.

The engineers stared in surprise.

Lucas said, "I know. Shocking. But she's a vet too."

Gabe said, "I have to admit I'm glad that I chose engineering," and Phoenix chuckled.

A few minutes later, Bella and Lili finished with the mare and left the corral. They were joined by Thor who nuzzled, and licked Bella.

Phoenix noticed the NASA guys watch the wolf with Bella, and said, "That's Thor. He's Bella's self-proclaimed guard wolf. You will want to be personally introduced to him, otherwise he won't like you. And that's not a good thing."

The black-haired engineer, Gabe, said, "I want him to like me a lot," and they laughed.

The tall engineer said, "He's a wolfdog, right?"

Phoenix said, "Yes, a highly trained wolf husky hybrid. I'll tell you the story sometime. The women will clean up now, so come on, I'll show you Bella's vet barn."

***

After she freshened up, Bella changed into shorts and a Dr. B t-shirt and joined the group downstairs as they toured her barn.

***

The Hacker had to fight a lustful groan as Bella jogged downstairs. She was young, exquisitely beautiful, had amazing long black hair, silver eyes to drown in, and her body...well it was made for way more than being a vet.

***

Bella smiled and said, "Now I can properly meet our guests," and held out her hand to the black-haired man.

She said, "Hi Gabe. Forgive me for teasing all of you earlier with the foal. I couldn't help it. Your dismay is a common occurrence in my profession."

He grinned and said, "I totally understand but I do appreciate knowing that your hand is clean now," and everyone laughed.

Then she reached for the tall man's hand and said, "Hi Sterling. It is nice to meet you. Hope you have fun at the Gala tonight."

"The pleasure is all mine. I am glad to be here. Thank you."

Then she grinned at the handsome blonde man impatiently waiting his turn, and said, "Just say it, Pierce, whatever it is. I can see you have something on your mind."

Pierce laughed and said, "I have to say that you have the most beautiful eyes that I have ever seen."

Bella gave him a small curtsy, and with a smile, said, "Thank you."

Phoenix drawled, "It's ok, we get it Pierce. She's a shocker," and he winked at Bella.

All of them headed to the main house so the guests could get settled in their rooms. Lucas would stay in Bella's first room since none of the women wanted in there because of the attack. Ariel slept in her grandfather's room and gave her bedroom to Lili. And all the engineers insisted on staying together in the bunk room which was a suite with oversized single beds, a large bathroom, and closet.

Later, they all grabbed something cold to drink and headed to the patio. They had a couple of hours to chill before dressing for the Gala. The three ladies sat at the edge of the pool and dangled their legs in the water. The six guys kicked back in the patio furniture.

The tallest engineer, said, "If you don't mind me asking, why don't the women want to sleep in the room that Lucas is in?"

Phoenix said, "To keep it simple, I bought a robot at an auction. We didn't know it was hacked. The hacker used it to take pictures of Bella asleep in that room."

The blonde engineer said, "That's horrible. How did you find out?"

"He hacked her phone and sent her the picture."

The black-haired engineer frowned, and said, "The hackers that I have heard of are usually after money or information. Why this type of attack on Bella?"

"The FBI said he is a sexual predator."

Lucas said, "He needs to be a dead sexual predator and I'm not kidding."

The black-haired engineer continued, "What did you do with the hacked robot. We are all familiar with robotics and could take a look."

Phoenix said, "He is in pieces with the FBI. Bella knocked its head off with an iron skillet because he attacked her and hurt her wrist. I had to cut his arm off with a meat cleaver to free her."

Seth said, "It takes a psycho to do that. So, do you think it is over now?"

Phoenix said, "We don't know, and I can't take a chance. I am hiring security for her. Bella and I rode to check on a new bull in the north pasture several hours ago, and the bull broke through the fence and charged us.

"While Bella and I gunned it on the four-wheeler to escape, someone killed the one-ton bull with a single shot to the head. But I am not positive who the target was – the bull or us."

***

The Hacker clenched his jaw as he looked at Bella and wondered if Royce was in Wichita Falls. It sounded like something he would do based on what he had learned about the man. He better hurry to take her first.

Chapter 32
Cattleman's Gala

All six men were handsomely dressed in black tuxedos. They waited in the den for the three women to join them. The tapping of high heels, and female laughter echoed down the bedroom wing and let them know they were on their way.

Lili rounded the corner first, and Lucas whistled and headed to meet her.

She was dressed in a fitted, one-shoulder gown that looked like it was made of gold dust. Her light brown hair was pulled up in a fancy ponytail as her mass of curls cascaded down her back. Her blue eyes sparkled, and her burgundy lips smiled at him.

Then Ariel entered in a green satin halter gown, the color of her beautiful cat eyes. Along with her platinum hair and bright pink lipstick, she was stunning.

Seth whispered, "Hot," in her ear as he tucked her arm in his and walked across the room.

Phoenix stepped to the doorway as Bella entered the room.

He only remembered saying her name in awe and didn't know where to look first. She wore a red sequin, spaghetti strap gown. It fluttered against her body except for one long slit from the top of her thigh to the floor that exposed one entire beautiful leg.

Her long black hair was wavy and loose as it hung over one shoulder in front and the rest down her back. Her light blue eyes were now exotic, and her dark red lips teased him.

Phoenix, blown away, said, "Honey…"

Bella laughed and said, "So, I guess this means you like the dress."

Phoenix smiled and said, "You are gorgeous," and spun, and landed her in a dip.

***

The Hacker's muscles screamed with the effort to act normal when all he wanted to do was rip Bella away from Phoenix and get under that red dress.

He made a mental note to text the owner of the secluded cabin for sell. He would buy it sight unseen. Immediately.

But for the moment, he played the game and let his lust eat at him.

***

Everyone loaded up to leave for the Gala. Seth drove Ariel's white BMW and Lucas and Lili rode with them. The NASA guys rode with Phoenix and Bella. The Hacker watched Bella as she looked back to talk to them. He had made sure to sit behind Phoenix so he could see Bella's bare leg and cleavage as she turned, and leaned, to talk with them. He had to be careful though, Phoenix had eyes on all three of the men.

The Hacker now understood how people could do unspeakable things to meet cravings that screamed on the inside. His palms itched to touch, smell, and taste Bella's fire no matter what the cost.

Whether she wanted it or not.

Someone asked him a question, and he laughed and responded. He would have to deal with all those thoughts later. The night was just beginning.

***

Bella smiled as Phoenix escorted her into the event center. They waited in line.

She said, "I can't wait to dance with you."

He whispered in her ear, "In that dress, you better hope I only dance," and she laughed.

Ariel said, "Keep moving, Phoenix. That heavy breathing is holding the line up."

Phoenix winked at his sister, and she grinned.

199

Seth ran his hand lingeringly up and down Ariel's bare back, and she whispered, "I feel like a cat. Shall I purr as you pet me?"

His eyes sparked as he looked at her and whispered, "I'm all about purring, and I love cats."

Lucas and Lili talked with the guests from NASA.

Lili said, "You three single hunks are going to make a lot of women happy tonight."

Lucas said, "Hey!" and the guys laughed.

Lili said, "I wasn't talking about me, Lucas. You, are all the hunk I need."

The hostess led the group to their table. It was located front and center, not far from the stage or dance floor. The tables in the room were all decorated with black linen and candle chandeliers. The dinnerware had a large "C" in the middle of the plates that looked like cowhide to represent the Cattleman's Association.

Everyone settled at the table and then Kit and Jasmine arrived and met the ranch guests. Jasmine was beautiful with her brown hair braided, showing off her lovely green eyes. She wore a bronze strapless gown with sparkling beads. Kit looked handsome but could have cared less since he only had eyes for Jasmine.

There was one empty seat left at the table but that didn't last long when a gorgeous redhead, a relative of Jasmine, named Amber, joined them. Now, their table of twelve was complete.

Phoenix was frequently interrupted as many people came up to him to talk business, to meet Bella, to hear about his eye injury, or just to shoot the bull. Even Ranger Morgan and his wife stopped by to greet everyone and shook hands with the NASA guests.

The social lasted about thirty minutes and then dinner began. After the meal, the background music ended, and the program began. Awards were given, videos were shown, speeches were made, and several cattle owners were congratulated for their faithfulness to their communities. Phoenix included.

As the program ended, the music started and Phoenix whispered to Bella, "I don't care who you promised, but most of your dances are mine," and Bella laughed as he escorted her to the dance floor.

Most eyes in the room were on the stunning woman in red and the handsome owner of Chandler Canyon Ranch. Whispers traveled through the tables till eventually everyone knew who Bella was - and whose she was.

***

The Hacker watched Bella dance with Phoenix. He wanted to lick her fully exposed leg from her foot to her upper thigh. He could imagine the feel and taste of it. All the other women in the room, even the beautiful ones at the Chandler Canyon Ranch table, simply paled in comparison to her. Bella hadn't been in his arms yet, but before this Gala ended, he would make sure that she was.

***

Phoenix glanced over at Kit, and they grinned as Amber, the bold redhead that Jasmine invited, enjoyed the engineers from NASA. She danced mostly with Pierce and Sterling since Gabe seemed to enjoy working the room.

A few dances later, Phoenix and Bella returned to the table and the banker's wife cornered him for a dance. He glanced at Bella. She smiled, crossed her legs, and planned to enjoy the break. She watched the banker's wife smile up at Phoenix's handsome face and knew how the woman felt.

Bella heard a voice behind her say, "Please take pity on a man without a partner and dance with me."

She laughed and said, "If you are without a partner, it is because you dodged them. These women stalk you."

He laughed and escorted her to the dance floor, and she stepped into his arms. The Hacker looked down into Bella's unbelievably gorgeous face and tried to block his mind of anything but this moment between the two of them.

He smelled her.

His face brushed against her hair.

Her breasts were teasingly close to his body.

His body guided her in the moves.

They danced for a while and Bella said, "You are a wonderful dancer, more so than most, have you trained?"

"I have, but please don't tell, the torment would never end."

201

She grinned and said, "Your secret is safe with me. I shall just reap the benefits of your talent."

He smiled and said sincerely, "The benefits are all mine, Bella."

She smiled and glanced over at Phoenix who watched her dance. She read his expression and knew he preferred her in his arms. Then her partner led her into a lovely spin and shallow dip as the song ended. The Hacker escorted Bella back to her seat as her husband-to-be met her there.

Phoenix smiled at the Hacker and said, "You are very smooth. I'm impressed."

The Hacker laughed and said, "I'm allowed a few secret talents."

***

Later Bella danced with Seth, and said, "I see love in your eyes when you look at Ariel."

Without denial, he said, "I do, Bella."

She said, "Is she still holding the reins tight on her emotions?"

"She's loosening up."

Bella said, "You are so right for each other, that's why we set you up."

He said, "I owe you a huge reward for that."

"No, you don't. To get you for a brother-in-law would be win enough for me."

***

Eventually Bella got to dance with her brother. Lucas laughed as he gave Bella a workout on the dance floor, and then slowed it down so they could talk.

He asked, "Are you scared, Bella?"

Keeping a smile on her face, she said, "Not if I am with others. It is just insane to know that two men have stuck a target on me. I am uneasy about Royce. He has been quiet for the last few days. I may call the detective after the long holiday weekend to check and see if he is still in Baton Rouge."

"What about the hacker?"

She said, "I figured he would be quiet once the FBI took the phone and robot. Did Phoenix tell you about the bull charge and rifle shot today?" and he nodded.

She glanced at Phoenix who danced with Lili, and said, "Phoenix and the wolf guard me, the crew keep an eye out for strangers, and we are hiring security. We have done all that we can."

"Why don't I come to the ranch?"

She shook her head and said, "No. You start a new job in four days, and I get married in seven. Maybe it will all be over by then. Especially if I have security guys here. I promise, if I feel like I need more help, I will call you. You know that."

He kissed her forehead and escorted her back to the table. Then they announced a special song to close out the night and Phoenix led a surprised Bella to the middle of the dance floor.

She smiled and said through her teeth, "I'm not singing."

Phoenix laughed and said, "No, they are going to sing to you," and the band began to play Happy Birthday.

Bella relaxed and smiled with a curtsy, and the whole room celebrated her with an early birthday song. Phoenix led her in the last dance.

On the way home, Phoenix said, "Your birthday celebration continues when we get home. Jasmine made you a cake and we have plans for a pool party."

"You're kidding! How awesome!"

Gabe said, "Is today your birthday?"

She looked back and said, "Not till Wednesday, but since we had this big night, I considered it a birthday treat. I did not know about the song, cake, or pool party."

Phoenix said, "Well, the Gala was dinner and dancing, but your gift is at home with the cake."

Bella said, "Phoenix! We get married next weekend. You didn't need to get me anything!"

He laughed, and said, "Of course I did. I want a happy wife next weekend," and all the men laughed.

Phoenix said, "If any of you are free next Saturday, you are welcome to come to the wedding and reception. You can enjoy the party and stay the night. Seth and Ariel will be there of course."

Sterling said, "I would love to attend, but I already have plans next Saturday. Early congratulations though!"

Pierce said, "A friend is getting married so I will be at another wedding. I wish I would have been free to come."

Gabe said, "I've taken several days of vacation this week, so I might follow Seth and Ariel up if you don't mind."

Bella said, "Not at all. We are glad to have you. I've dreamed of this wedding since I was sixteen. I am glad to share it!"

***

The Hacker pulled out his phone and marked his calendar, all-the-while knowing that Bella wouldn't be at the altar for her wedding. He smiled and looked out the window. It may be cruel to kidnap her right before her wedding day, but he was beyond that now. But he had his own honeymoon plans.

***

Thirty minutes later, Bella said, "Why do I have to cover my eyes?"

Phoenix said, "Because your birthday and wedding present are outside."

Bella squealed and the guys chuckled.

Phoenix pulled around the house close to the garage and stopped. "Ok, open your eyes."

Bella moved her hands and screamed, then jumped out and ran in high heels to her new sky-blue F150 Lightning pickup. The guys laughed and followed her to see it.

Bella threw herself at Phoenix and kissed him as the guys walked away and checked out the truck. Bella insisted on getting in, but struggled with her heels and dress, so Phoenix lifted her into the driver's seat. He glanced to see where the men were, and pulled her lips to his for a quick, hot kiss, as he slid his hand down her long bare leg that had teased him all night.

Bella grinned as he walked around and got in the passenger seat.

He said, "Go ahead, let's take a spin," and after a wave to the guys she took off down the driveway.

They passed Ariel's car coming in and waved.

Bella said, "This is fabulous Phoenix! I need to get a license plate that says, "Dr. B."

"I think so too."

She said, "But if this is birthday and wedding, I need to tell you about your wedding gift. You really need to know because it is time."

"Time? Time for what?"

Bella stopped the truck, looked at him, and said, "To pick up your new bucking bull calf."

Stunned, he said, "You didn't."

"I certainly did."

"They cost tens of thousands of dollars, Bella."

"I told you that I had some money left."

Phoenix frowned and said, "How much was the calf?"

She shrugged and said, "A hundred thousand, and all you have to do it go get him in Oklahoma when they call."

The excitement won out over the cost, and with a happy shout, he kissed her.

When they returned home, music was playing, and a delicious looking strawberry shortcake was ready and waiting.

They yelled, "Happy Birthday, Bella!"

Jasmine served the cake and then Phoenix and Bella went to change. Everyone else was already in swimsuits.

Phoenix returned to the kitchen a short time later, and said, "Come on its pool time! Bella will meet us on the patio when she has changed."

***

The Hacker sat on the edge of the pool and waited for Bella's entrance. He was more than ready to see her in a bikini instead of in a video.

***

A few minutes later, Bella walked out of the bedroom patio doors dressed in a black fringed bikini and a smile. Phoenix howled when he saw her, and everyone laughed.

The Hacker felt the growl that ached to be released and averted his gaze so no one would see the raging desire flare on his face. This was much more difficult than he had anticipated.

Then he took a deep breath and turned back to look at her again. His eyes met Bella's as she smiled and walked past him.

She glanced back at everyone on the patio and said, "I'm getting me a coke, would anyone like anything?" and everyone said no.

The Hacker glanced at Phoenix to make sure that he wasn't watching, and momentarily followed Bella into the kitchen.

When he walked in and shut the door, Bella turned to see who it was, and smiled.

"Did you change your mind?"

He grinned and said, "Sorry, I did. Let me fix them."

Bella shook her head with a grin and said, "No, I've got it, what soda would you like?" and she turned to grab two glasses while she waited on his answer.

Eyeing her luscious body in the bikini, he licked his lips and said, "Whatever you are having. Thank you," and he glanced at the front door.

If only he could snatch her and run.

If only.

She handed him the drink and said, "Did you have a good time tonight at the Gala?"

"I did. You are all terrific company and I love to dance. Thanks again for the invitation to come to the ranch."

She said, "It was meant to be since we had the extra tickets. Good timing."

He smiled and took a sip of the drink and said, "Indeed it was."

Then Bella glanced at her birthday cake and ran a finger in the whip cream and licked it off as she headed to the door saying, "Jasmine spoils us, that is delicious!"

The Hacker's mind played in slow motion her licking her finger. And again. Then with a smile, he dipped his finger in the whip cream she touched and licked it.

And imagined it was her.

The party lasted till well after midnight and then they straightened up and headed for bed. Even Kit and Jasmine stayed overnight. Everyone made sure the guests had what they needed, and the house finally settled down.

***

Bella showered first and slipped into bed. She snuggled in the sheets and said, "You better hurry if you want a goodnight kiss."

Phoenix drawled as he went to take his shower, "I can always wake you up."

***

Phoenix was glad that the evening had gone as planned. And thanked God for a good ending to a day that began with a raging bull and a rifle shot.

Then he thought of the NASA guys with Seth. It seemed they had a great time. Gabe was cool. He had caught him looking at Bella a few times, but most men did. These guys seemed to understand the need to protect her and promised to keep an eye out when they were around.

When he stepped out of the bathroom, the wolf wanted out into the hall, so, he let him out of the bedroom. He must be concerned about all the new people in the house tonight.

He turned toward the bed and Bella was on her back, spread eagle as usual and already sound asleep. He got in and rolled toward her. With one finger he touched her arm and she rolled toward him. He wrapped her in his arms.

***

About an hour later, the Hacker stepped out of the bunkroom and looked toward the end of the hall where Phoenix and Bella were. Movement caught his eye, and the wolf walked out of the shadows and watched him.

Slowly the Hacker walked to the den and looked out over the patio pool. He heard the wolf follow him. The Hacker ignored the animal and stayed calm. Then he thought about his plan.

He had four days left to get things in order. He would take Bella Thursday, just two days before their wedding. He had gotten a confirmation message from the seller about the cabin. He now owned it and it was ready to be occupied.

He would have to walk away from his career which would seem inconceivable to those that knew him. Or thought they knew him. He had been wise and stashed cash away once he began hacking. That would last them for a long, long, time, even if he had to take her out of the country to Canada, or further. And if they needed money, he could always use his hacker skills.

Chapter 33
Security

Early Sunday morning, Phoenix walked in the bathroom and stood behind Bella as she brushed her hair. He leaned close and buried his face in it.

She heard him inhale the scent, and he said, "Your hair always smells so good. And you feel even better."

With that, he slid his hands around her hips and pushed a couple of fingers down into both of her front jean pockets. He grinned and pulled her back tight against him. They both watched their reflection in the mirror as he removed his hands from her pockets and caressed her. She laid her head back against his chest as he slid his hands up to her face.

Still looking in the mirror, he parted her warm pink lips with his finger. She licked him. And with a groan, he turned her, and replaced his finger with his lips.

Smiling a few moments later, he said, "I could easily forget we have company," and she smiled and shook her head no.

He said, "Ok, if I have to behave, are you ready for breakfast? Jasmine has started cooking even though Kit is harassing her."

Bella laughed and said, "That sounds normal to me."

He said, "True. But I wanted to let you know that Seth and the other guys are just waking up, so you don't have to rush."

She said, "Do you have any plans for all of us this morning?"

Phoenix nodded and said, "We could take a ride and show them around. We just need to stay away from the north end of the canyon."

She said, "I'm thrilled you are the event coordinator. Planning events is not my favorite thing. But enjoying them certainly is!"

He chuckled and said, "The truth is I just like being the boss all the time."

With a laugh she said, "Like I haven't learned that."

By the time, Bella made it to the kitchen, everyone was there, including Buck and Levi.

Jasmine said, "You made it just in time, these ravenous men were about to eat all the pancakes, sausage, steak, and eggs."

Bella said, "Jasmine! That's a feast!"

Then she smiled at their guests, and asked, "Pierce, Gabe, and Sterling, were you comfortable in the bunkroom last night?"

Pierce said, "Every house should have a room like that for guests. It was great."

Gabe said, "I agree, it was perfect, thank you."

Sterling said, "My feet didn't hang off the bed so that was much better than a hotel," and everyone laughed.

Lucas said, "Bella, how do you remember their names so easily? I am terrible at it. Sorry guys."

Bella said, "It just takes a little practice. I use the first letter of their name and try to think of something that reminds me of them. A describer of some kind."

Slipping his arm around Bella, Phoenix said, "Well, what would my describer be, Bella?"

She looked him over with a grin and said, "Definitely, hot," and everyone laughed.

Phoenix drawled, "But my name doesn't start with an H."

Bella walked her fingers up his chest and said, "But honey, I forget the alphabet when it comes to you."

Pierce called out, "I'm so going to use that line, Bella!" and they laughed.

***

It was crazy.

The Hacker liked these people. They were good, smart, amazing people. If he had met Bella first maybe none of the hacking would have ever taken place and he could have had a life like this.

He watched Phoenix hook his finger through the belt loop on Bella's jeans. The message was clear. She was his.

But the Hacker glanced at Bella and thought, but she's about to be mine.

***

Phoenix got a phone call and walked to his office and said, "Hey Ranger, thanks for returning my early call. Sorry to bother you on a Sunday but I didn't' want to bring it up when I saw you at the Gala last night."

Ranger Morgan said, "No problem at all, what's up, Phoenix?"

"Yesterday, Bella and I took a four-wheeler ride to the northwest pasture close to the canyon edge, to see the new bull. But he broke through the fence and charged us."

"What!"

Phoenix said, "It was touch and go for a few minutes, but someone fired a single rifle shot from the canyon and killed the bull."

"Man! That's quite a feat from that distance with one shot."

Phoenix said, "Exactly, but I'm not positive who the target was, if you get my meaning."

The Ranger cussed, and said, "I hear you. What do you have in mind?"

"I need to hire two excellent guys for security. Bella needs more covering."

"I got you. I have a couple of guys in mind. I will check with them and call you later. Make sure you check with that detective in Louisiana on Royce's location."

***

Bella walked in his office and said, "Did I hear you talking to Ranger Morgan?"

He sat on his desk and said, "I was. He is checking with a couple of guys for a security detail and will call us back. But we need to call the detective in Baton Rouge."

She pulled her phone out of her pocket and called. The phone rang and the answering machine picked up, so she left a message.

Then she said, "Tomorrow is Memorial Day, he might not even get that message until Tuesday," and he frowned.

***

Royce hiked through a different section of the canyon than when he saw Bella and Phoenix yesterday by the bull. He was already soaked in sweat, and it was only eight o'clock in the morning. His goal was to find the best spot to lure Bella into the pasture when he was ready to make his move.

There wasn't much chance he could get to her at the house and the canyon would give him a better escape route. There was plenty open land out here.

***

Phoenix and Bella let their guests choose a horse or a four-wheeler for the ride. Once everyone was ready to go, Phoenix pointed to the southwest pastures that led to the river. Most of the four-wheelers and horses took off.

Phoenix smiled at Bella and said, "How does it feel to be holding the reins after so many years?"

She laughed and said, "Fabulous! Catch me!" and she leaned low, and her horse leapt forward. Phoenix laughed and followed close behind. The race was on!

***

Seth sat in the saddle behind Ariel, and watched as Bella and Phoenix galloped across the pasture, and said, "I guess you can do that too, right?"

Ariel laughed and said, "Absolutely. Are you comfortable in the saddle?"

Seth looked down at her hips snuggled in the saddle basically in his lap and said, "I have to say, you feel great. Who cares about the saddle?" and she grinned and looked back at him.

He held her face there, rubbed his lips against hers, and kissed her. But then the kiss heated up. Hot. And he turned her in the saddle to enjoy every taste of her lips.

When the breathless kiss ended, the horse was still sitting in the middle of the pasture with no one in sight.

Seth said, "I think I might be really good at horseback riding," and she laughed.

211

Almost two hours later, the riders met up again and were headed back to the ranch when Phoenix's phone rang. It was Ranger Morgan.

***

Phoenix answered and said, "Tell me you found some security."

The Ranger said, "Yeah. I have two terrific professionals, both medically retired Rangers but still highly capable. They are almost to your ranch now."

"That's terrific, thanks. I will get back to the ranch. We're out on a ride, but Bella and I can get back in about fifteen minutes. Tell them about the wolf. I don't want them to shoot Thor."

***

After he hung up, Bella said, "So, he found some security guys?"

"He did, two retired Rangers will be at the house shortly. We need to get home." Then he said, "Ariel, lead everyone in - Bella and I need to get back to the ranch."

***

The Hacker watched Phoenix and Bella gallop to the ranch. Interesting. It would be nice the meet the security that would be protecting her from him.

***

Sweating, Royce got back to his rental truck and thought about the spot he had chosen to ambush Bella. He found a place in the south canyon not far from the river that had simple access up the bluff. There was a trail in the pasture leading close to there so it must be a frequently used area.

There was certainly enough cow dung everywhere.

He had even noticed a group of riders in the pasture, but they didn't go near the canyon. He was relieved. He hadn't wanted a confrontation yet. His plans were for her birthday. He planned to start out her birthday with a bang.

Phoenix and Bella reached the house, and a black pickup was parked by the porch. A very formidable Thor was standing at the driver's door.

Phoenix grinned as they dismounted, and Bella called the wolf to her.

Both men stepped out of the truck. The driver, a man with graying hair in a ponytail stepped out with a smile.

The passenger, a man about Phoenix's age, with long black hair walked around the truck and said, "A friend of mine has a female wolf husky that looks just like him. Man! They sure would make some amazing pups. I would love to have one."

Phoenix and Bella glanced at each other intrigued at the idea.

The older man shook hands with Phoenix first and said, "My name is Ryker. Ranger Morgan emailed you our credentials and work history. He said you need a security detail."

Phoenix said, "Yes, we do. Nice to meet you, Ryker. Thanks for coming so quickly."

The younger man introduced himself, and said, "I'm Dante. I got the same call. What can we help with?"

Phoenix said, "Appreciate it, Dante. As you probably know, I'm Phoenix Chandler and this is Dr. Bella DelCaprio."

Then he explained to both men about the situation with Royce and the hacker, including the bull attack and gunshot yesterday.

Ryker and Dante knew from Bella's appearance pretty much why these men were after her, and Ryker said, "Is there anything that you want to add Dr. DelCaprio?"

Bella said, "Yes, let me add my personal thank you for coming. And please call me Bella. That aside, I want you to know that although Royce and the hacker may have agendas, I have an agenda as well. Phoenix and I get married this coming Saturday here at the ranch. I also work around the ranch and in my office," and she turned and pointed to her barn.

"You may also need to know that I have PTSD flashbacks if I am stranded in total darkness due to an accident as a child. But Phoenix had the ranch fitted with solar lights so it shouldn't be a problem. I just wanted you to be aware."

About that time, the riding group came down the road toward them.

Phoenix said, "Ryker and Dante, let me introduce you to this group before some of them leave for home. They will come and go, especially this week, so it is best to meet them."

The two couples and three guests from NASA walked up to stand by Phoenix and Bella. Phoenix made introductions and the security guys gave a simple hello as they looked the group over. Afterwards, Lucas stayed outside with Bella and Phoenix, and the others went inside the house.

Dante said, "Phoenix, I presume that you have been shadowing Bella."

"Yes, and since the first hacker attack happened in her bedroom, I moved her into mine for protection, so don't misunderstand."

Dante said, "Understood. So, at night she is with you and the wolf."

"Yes."

Ryker said, "Is there usually anyone else in the house at night besides you two?"

Phoenix said, "Not unless family or guests are here. Ariel has a room here but lives in Houston, and my grandfather has one, but lives in Colorado now. He should be here later this week. He founded this ranch so don't mistakenly consider him just an old man."

Ryker said, "Got it. What are your sleeping hours as a rule?"

Phoenix said, "We sleep ten p.m. to four-thirty a.m. and ranch workers begin arriving before five a.m. for breakfast. Jasmine feeds us well, so plan to take advantage of that. She works half days. Her husband Kit is my foreman, and Buck and Levi work with Kit. They work long hours, and you will hear them call me Boss, and call Bella, Dr. B."

Dante said, "Lucas, do you live near here?"

"I live in Wichita Falls."

Ryker nodded, and after a confirming glance with Dante, he said, "Dante and I will swap out shadowing Bella, patrolling the house, and monitoring all guests."

Phoenix said, "That's great. You can choose from a bedroom or a bunkroom but understandably you have the run of the house. Instruct us for safety as you see fit."

The guys nodded, and Ryker said, "The bunkroom will be fine."

Phoenix said, "We will show you around as soon as our guests leave."

Pierce, Sterling, and Gabe walked outside with their luggage. Phoenix and Bella joined them to say goodbye.

Black haired, Gabe said, "I had a great time, thanks for everything. And I do plan to follow Ariel and Seth back up here later this week for the wedding."

Bella smiled and said, "That's great! We will be glad to see you."

Sterling said, "I loved every minute of being here. Thank you! I hope to see you another time."

Pierce smiled and said, "I wish Houston wasn't so far! You and your ranch are terrific! Thanks for letting us trail Seth up here."

And in minutes, the NASA guys left - Houston bound.

***

Black-haired, Gabe, the Hacker, smiled as he looked in the rearview mirror at Bella and her new security team as he drove away. It was unbelievable that he got to meet them today. Now his trip to the ranch Thursday wouldn't cause a ripple of concern for anyone. Bella was almost his.

Chapter 34
Fugitive Alert

Phoenix's alarm went off the Tuesday after Memorial Day and Bella groaned. He grinned and turned off the alarm.

She mumbled, "I hate the alarm," and he pulled her to him.

He chuckled and said, "I know, but after the long weekend, it is back-to-work Tuesday."

Bella stuck her tongue out at him, and he laughed and kissed her.

She laid her head on his chest and said, "I watched Seth and Ariel this weekend. They are playing the love game, but I think they are in love."

He said, "They certainly are. I wouldn't be surprised if they eloped. He looks ready to pounce on her," and Bella giggled.

Then his phone dinged, and he said, "Here we go. I can tell that it's going to be a busy, catch-up day. I'm going to get dressed and will meet you in the kitchen."

In a flash he went from the bathroom to the closet, and with a wink, out the door.

A second later a light knock sounded on the patio door and Dante with security, said, "I'm out here if you need me, Bella."

She called out, "Thanks, Dante! I will be in the kitchen in ten minutes."

And Ryker and Dante got their first taste of ranch mornings as Jasmine fixed food for an army.

Ryker said, "You cook like this all the time, Jasmine?" as he looked at steak, eggs, biscuits, and hashbrowns.

"Yes, Boss and the guys want the beef with every meal."

216

Thrilled, Dante laughed and said, "Bring it on, this is awesome."

Kit said, "Yeah, y'all get this, and I get Hamburger Helper at home," and Jasmine gasped and punched him.

With flashing eyes, she said, "You did not just insult me. As if I would serve that! Now, big guy, you can cook for dinner!"

Kissing her cheek, he said, "You know I was just kiddin', Jasmine. You are the chef of my heart."

She grinned and shoved him out of the kitchen.

After breakfast, Phoenix and Bella went to his office and talked about the vet tasks for the week since they would be gone on their honeymoon in a few days. Then Phoenix stayed in his office to catch up on work while Dante escorted Bella to her vet barn. He checked her office and the barn before she entered.

Two hours later, she finished in her office and went downstairs to the animal stalls to check wounds, change bandages, and give shots. She was in the middle of checking stitches on a cow when her phone rang.

She said, "Dante, my hands are a mess, would you please answer my phone and put it on speaker?" and he showed her caller ID and answered the call.

***

Bella answered, "Good morning, Detective, I have you on speaker. Did you get my message?"

"No, Dr. DelCaprio, I haven't gotten your message. I've been swamped with a murder case here in Baton Rouge. That is why I am calling you."

She glanced at Dante in surprise and said, "Why are you calling me about that?"

"Royce was in the video of the last location that the murdered woman was seen," and Bella gasped.

He continued, "And because of that, we went to his apartment this morning and he had a dummy set up in front of the TV. Bella, he's not home and I don't know when he left."

Horrified, Bella said, "Oh no! I left you a message on Saturday because someone shot and killed a bull that was chasing me and Phoenix. The shot was fired from off the property, and we don't know who it was or if it was the bull they were aiming for. That's why we needed to make sure where Royce was."

"I'm sorry that I didn't know he was gone before now."

Bella said, "Please tell me what happened to the woman that was murdered."

The detective paused, and she said, "I need to know what his mindset is."

"He's bad. He raped and killed her in the back seat of her car a week ago."

Dante spoke up and said, "Detective, I am security detail for Bella. What can you tell me that will help us?"

"Royce was last seen in person on Thursday. He possibly could be in disguise since he left all his credit cards, driver's license, and phone behind. He cleaned out all his cash and left. We have a warrant out for his arrest, but we don't have a way to track him, except maybe by his black car since it is missing."

Bella said, "Thank you, Detective," and ended the call.

***

She just sat there.

Concerned, Dante called Phoenix.

He arrived in minutes, but Bella wasn't ready to talk about it, and said, "I need a little time."

Phoenix hadn't seen this type of response from her before, so he gave her space to process. After a few minutes, she finished the cow's bandage and headed upstairs to her office.

Phoenix called Ranger Morgan and Deputy Todd, and they were on their way to the ranch. Then he headed upstairs.

Bella put her medical supplies away, washed up, and poured herself a cup of coffee. When Phoenix entered, she pointed to her cup in an unspoken offer, and he shook his head no and simply watched her.

After a sip of coffee, she unlocked her medicine safe and pulled out her tranquilizer gun, loaded it, and attached the holster to her jeans. She pulled out a blackjack and clipped it to her belt loop.

When she looked at him again, her expression let him know that she had worked through it mentally and was ready to face what was ahead. She walked into his arms.

As he held her, he said, "I am so sorry. We are going to get you beyond all this. We are going to get married and have children, and this will all be ashes in the wind. But for now, we need to get you back to the house where you have more protection."

She stepped back and he saw the flash of fear in her eyes. They all knew that her beauty had made her a target. A double target for two men that were determined to possess and ultimately destroy her.

Phoenix thought, over his dead body.

They joined Dante downstairs, and Phoenix said, "Let's head to the house."

Dante said, "Wait here. I'll get my truck," and Phoenix nodded.

Once they were back at the house, Bella said, "Phoenix, I need to be occupied. I can't sit around jumping at every noise."

He had just finished texting Lucas about the latest news on Royce, and said, "I have an idea, come see."

Bella followed him into his office. He grabbed his drone and pulled up the camera feed online for her to watch. Then he walked outside on the front porch steps and using the controller, let the drone fly.

Bella watched on the computer monitor as the drone lifted high over the house and turned in a slow circle to see everything around them. She gave a sigh of relief. At least they had a way to partially monitor the grounds around the house now.

Ryker and Dante gave Phoenix a fist pump when he came back inside, and Bella met him with a hug.

He said, "This will help provide a greater level of security, but I can only fly it in fair weather. I will send for more batteries tomorrow, so we don't run out."

Before long, the crew came in for lunch, curious about the drone and Phoenix told them what was going on with Royce.

Dante stepped inside and said, "The Ranger and Deputy just arrived."

Phoenix walked outside to meet them. A few minutes later, they settled at the table.

Ranger Morgan said, "Tell me exactly what the detective in Baton Rouge said about Royce."

Bella explained about the rape and murder of the woman, Royce's possible disguise, his lack of means to be tracked, that he had been missing since Thursday night, and that his car was gone.

The Ranger walked to the window and looked out over the property as he rubbed his chin in thought.

After a deep breath he said, "Royce is a needle in a haystack if he is here and we all know that. Bella is probably the only one that might even recognize him through a disguise. We could come up with some possible composites of what he might look like, but that would take time that we don't have.

"So, we begin to check all the hotels for anyone that matches his general description or his black car. You have your security detail around Bella and the house. And we can station a deputy at the start of your driveway, but it's virtually impossible to monitor all this land, Phoenix. You own fourteen-hundred acres, and let's face it, that is a drop in the bucket out here. He could be anywhere."

Bella glanced at Phoenix and said, "Well, Phoenix does have a drone. He used it earlier. So, it does give us some eyes on the land."

That was helpful news and the Ranger said, "If we kept Bella inside the house where he can't access her, in time he would eventually run out of money, get caught, or get desperate and either come in after her, or run."

Everyone nodded in agreement and Bella grimaced.

Phoenix said, "She is not going to be bait to draw him out."

The Ranger said, "No. He has a rifle and is apparently an excellent shot, so that isn't a good idea. Distance is his advantage with a rifle."

Bella said, "If we think that he killed the bull that was after us, why would he do that if he wants me dead?"

None of the men wanted to answer, so Phoenix said, "Because he has plans for you first."

Bella looked incredulous and said, "You mean he saved me so that he could kill me himself?"

Deputy Todd said, "Predators don't like anyone messing with their prey."

Bella said, "But he is in a no-win situation if he tries to come in the house with everyone armed. And on the flip side, if he runs, how do I know that he won't come back?"

Ryker answered, "If he comes in, it is because he thinks he has a good chance of being successful. If he runs, he will probably be back."

Dante spoke up and said, "We need to guard you and stay prepared. We make sure you have something to fight with and we don't trust anything out of the ordinary. I personally don't think Royce sounds like a patient man. I think he will force a confrontation."

Phoenix said, "I agree. But Bella, don't forget, we have a safe room."

She had forgotten and smiled.

Ranger Morgan said, "Where is it?"

Phoenix said, "When I updated the house, we dug a safe room under my office mainly for tornadoes. It isn't large, but it is concrete, and has a metal door that bolts from the inside. If Royce gets in the house that is where she needs to run. That would be our goal."

Phoenix looked over at the crew at the snack bar and said, "Kit, I need Jasmine and Levi to be off duty until this is over. And why don't you and Buck move the cattle nearer the ranch."

Kit said, "Yes, Boss. Buck and I can make rounds twice a day to check on the animals. But we will also stay here at the house to help day and night."

Phoenix said, "That works. Jasmine and Levi, we will let you know when it is safe to return to the ranch. Stay away from here till then. No exceptions."

They both tried to argue but it did no good and they were escorted to their vehicles and left. Then Ranger Morgan and Deputy Todd drove to meet the officer at the end of the driveway.

By four in the afternoon, all the horses and cattle were in visible distance of the ranch, and Phoenix and Bella prepared the safe room.

***

Shiloh called and Bella answered, "Hi Shiloh, thanks for calling. I have you on speaker."

Shiloh said, "Who's listening?"

Bella said, "Phoenix, my two-man security detail, and two of the ranch staff."

Shiloh said, "Ranger Morgan called me about Royce. The FBI will probably get involved tomorrow since the hacker case is already underway. But the reason that I am calling tonight is with an update on the hacker. And this is confidential and shouldn't be repeated beyond any listening to this call."

Phoenix said, "It will stay confidential. What did you find?"

"It looks like we have traced the robot to a NASA employee."

Stunned, Bella said, "What? A NASA employee?"

Shiloh continued, "We will know more in the next couple of days. It looks like a guy in the dietary department could be the hacker. A search of home, and work, computers for the department staff is being conducted now."

Bella said, "I'm sorry. I'm just floored with the NASA connection. And the kitchen?"

Understanding Bella's puzzlement, Shiloh said, "I know it seems unusual, but we see hackers and predators from all walks of life. And I assure you that NASA's management teams are all intelligent and well educated."

Phoenix said, "Will the hacker know that you are onto him?"

Shiloh said, "If he set up an alert system, he could, but he can't undo the trail that we already have. I hope by Friday morning to have confirmation of who he is."

Bella said, "Thanks, Shiloh, Friday is good news. It really is."

***

Before bedtime, Phoenix said, "Bella, I am going to pull a twin bed in my office. I'd prefer you to be close to the safe room," and she nodded.

In no time, the guys had her bed set up in the office. Once she was asleep, Phoenix got up and joined the guys.

***

Royce checked out of the hotel in Wichita Falls and hid at a truck stop in between the eighteen wheelers in his silver car. He received news alerts on his phone that cops in Louisiana and Texas searched for him. It was super convenient for the news to provide him those updates. He locked his car doors, slipped his pistol, fit with a silencer, under his thigh, and thought about tomorrow morning. It was almost time to give Bella her birthday present.

***

In Houston, Gabe sat on his porch in the dark and watched the stars while he thought of Bella. He had been at work today when his phone alerted him the FBI had traced his Trojan file to the NASA dietary department employees already. He was impressed. The FBI hacker agent was very good at their job. Most specialists couldn't have found it that quickly.

But even so, it would take them many more days to cut through all the false trails to trace it to him. But by then he would be long gone with Bella.

Chapter 35
Happy Birthday Bella

Bella dreamed her and Phoenix were on their honeymoon, swimming in the ocean, when singing woke her. She smiled. Phoenix was singing Happy Birthday to her.

When he finished, she whispered, "This is the best birthday morning ever," and he kissed her.

At least, until Thor interrupted their kiss with a lick.

Phoenix wiped his face, and said, "No, Thor, I'm busy."

Bella giggled and said, "Just hurry and let him out and come back," and Phoenix hurried out of his office to the door.

Kit was in the kitchen and saluted him with a smile as he poured a massive mug of coffee. And then Buck walked around the corner and pulled out ingredients for breakfast. Then Dante and Skylar stepped outside to look around.

Phoenix sighed and walked back in his office. He gazed at Bella snuggled in the covers drowning him in her sexy eyes.

He sat on the bed and said, "Everyone is up. Why don't you sleep in for your birthday?"

"I'm awake. I'd rather get up and tease you all morning."

He chuckled and said, "Teasing will generate very different consequences in three more days," and she winked.

Before long, everyone was in the kitchen, and they sang Happy Birthday to Bella over coffee. She recorded them on her phone to prove it to Jasmine and Levi.

After that, Kit said, "I noticed we were almost out of batteries for the drone. I will run to the nearest store and grab some. I should be back in less than an hour. Message me if anyone needs anything."

Phoenix said "Let me know if the deputy is at the driveway entrance. I like knowing that he is only two miles away."

"Will do, Boss," and drove off in his silver truck. Then shortly, he texted Phoenix that the deputy was in place at the end of the driveway.

***

Thirty minutes later, Kit pulled up to a store in Iowa Park off Highway 368. It was still dark when he walked inside to buy batteries for Phoenix's drone.

Royce pulled up on the dark side of the store next to a silver truck and watched a man get out and walk inside the store. He was surprised to see how much they looked alike. Oh well, he thought, everyone has a twin. At least that is what he always heard.

Kit checked out the battery section and grabbed all they had of 4cell/4S size batteries and got in line at the checkout.

Royce picked up water, Gatorade, jerky, power bars, and a few other things in case he wasn't able to stop at a store for the next several hours and headed to the checkout counter. The man who looked like him was already in line. He stepped up behind him.

Kit handed the clerk the batteries and the ranch credit card.

The male clerk said, "Hey Kit. What's Chandler Canyon Ranch using all these batteries for?"

Kit smiled without telling him about the drone and said, "For livestock equipment."

***

Phoenix was in his office checking the drone cameras when the deputy called and said the silver pickup had returned and was headed this way.

Phoenix knew that it was Kit, so he kept working on the drones and yelled, "Kit's almost here," so Buck walked out of the kitchen and headed to the barn to get started at work.

Dante fixed a cup of coffee and glanced to check on Bella who sat at the snack bar. He walked to the back door as lights flashed across the front windows.

Ryker walked out on the porch and wondered why Kit had pulled up to the front of the house. He never did that.

When the truck door opened, Ryker called out, "Hey Kit, why did you park over here?"

Kit carried a large bag in front of him, head lowered, as he walked toward Ryker, but didn't answer. Ryker frowned. He climbed down the steps and called Kit's name as he pulled his Glock.

Something was off.

Two gunshots silently burst through the paper sack and hit Ryker in the chest. He flew back and landed on the ground without a sound.

Royce stepped over the man and continued up to the porch.

He whispered, "Happy Birthday, Bella," and opened the door.

Dante took a sip of coffee and watched as the front door opened, expecting Kit.

Bella turned at the same time with a smile, only to scream, as Royce's vicious gaze found hers. Royce dropped the bag he carried and turned the gun toward the man by the back door.

At the same time, Phoenix bolted from his office with gun in hand and ran for the kitchen.

Dante's cup shattered on the floor, as he reached for his gun and lunged to get between Bella and the shooter. He was shot twice in the chest before he could do either. Blood sprayed behind him, and he dropped to the floor with a thud.

Terrified and screaming, Bella scrambled to get out of Royce's path and Phoenix rounded the corner. Phoenix and Royce both ran for Bella. Royce, distracted by Bella's flight, shot twice at Phoenix over her, missing Phoenix once, but grazed him with the second shot.

Bella screamed as blood ran down the side of Phoenix's face.

Royce roared in fury at the miss and grabbed for Bella's shirt, but it ripped, and grabbed a fistful of her hair and yanked hard. She screamed and Phoenix quickly grabbed her wrist and yanked her toward him.

Bella groaned while being yanked by both men, then fought to get free from Royce. Royce raised his gun to shoot Phoenix again, but with one hand free, Bella grabbed her blackjack, and hit Royce's gun hand.

He yelled, and the gun flew over the snack bar. Phoenix reached across Bella and shoved his gun in Royce's shoulder and shot twice. Royce screamed and staggered back as he looked down at his dangling arm.

Phoenix pushed Bella behind him.

Royce growled in rage, "I'm going to kill you!" and stepped forward. Phoenix raised his gun for the kill shot, but behind Royce the back door flew open, and a snarling Thor raced toward Royce.

Royce spun toward the growls just in time to see a wolf go airborne and rip into his throat. Phoenix jumped out of the way as man and wolf slid across the table into the wall, blood flying, and grimaced at the gruesome death.

Phoenix caught Bella as she launched herself at him. He checked to make sure she was ok and called for Thor. They both glanced toward Dante. He laid by the open back door in a puddle of blood. Then he moved. He was alive.

Finally noticing the sound of sirens, Phoenix and Bella glanced out the windows. It looked like an army had arrived and cops flooded the house, and radio calls for ambulances rang out in the early morning air.

***

Phoenix and Bella were allowed to lock Thor in the office. They tried to check on Dante and Ryker, but they made them get out of the way.

A female paramedic checked Phoenix's head wound and said that the scalp wound was shallow. The bullet had only grazed him. Bella said a quick grateful prayer. The other paramedics worked on Ryker and Dante and immediately transported them to the nearest trauma hospital in Wichita Falls. They were badly injured but still alive.

Royce's body was now part of the crime scene.

Phoenix and Bella finally found out about Kit when the Sheriff arrived, followed by the FBI and Texas Rangers. The Sherriff explained Kit had been hit in the head, drug behind a dumpster at the store, beaten and stripped. His truck had been taken. He had serious scalp lacerations and other injuries. A couple had parked to let their dog use the bathroom and the dog found Kit. He was able to tell the cops about Royce and they headed to the ranch.

The Sheriff continued, "He is at the hospital, and I understand he is giving them a hard time to get back here."

***

When Bella had a few moments to herself, she replayed the attack in her mind. Tears dripped down her face for the men who had fought for her. It was unbelievable, that other than her very sore scalp and tender wrist from the tug-a-war between Royce and Phoenix, she was not injured. And lastly, in irony, the one person that came to kill today - was the only one that died.

***

When Lucas arrived, he hugged Bella for a long while and looked at Phoenix unable to voice what he felt. He knew that Phoenix and the wolf had saved his sister.

Phoenix watched as Lucas struggled to talk, and said, "I know, Lucas, man, I know."

Then Phoenix and Lucas hugged. Not a man-hug, but the hug that talks when words aren't enough, and Bella smiled.

Then they had phone calls to make before everything hit the news. Bella called the detective in Baton Rouge and told him that Royce was dead. Then she messaged Seth, on his first day on the job at NASA and he called her right back.

***

Bella answered, "Seth, I am sorry to interrupt your first day at work."

"I don't care about that. Are you hurt? Is anyone hurt?" he asked.

She explained the tug-a-war bruising but assured him that she was fine. Then she told him about Phoenix and the other men's injuries. About the wolf and Royce.

Seth said, "Bella, I am shocked out of my mind. I am so sorry. Do you need Ariel and I to come now?"

"No, you and Ariel will be here tomorrow night. It will probably take us that long to get through all of this."

Seth said, "Does Ariel know yet?"

Bella glanced at Phoenix and said, "Phoenix is on the phone now. I know that he planned to call Ariel and GP, but I don't know who he called first."

Seth said, "Ariel is going to flip out."

Bella choked up and said, "Be sure to tell her that her brother is a hero."

***

Bella got a call from Lili too. Lucas and Lili would stay the night, and GP, Seth, Ariel, and Gabe would all be in tomorrow. When she finished her calls, she looked for Phoenix and he was on the front porch with Buck.

She joined them, aware that Buck was very upset. Buck stood when Bella walked outside, and she hugged him.

Still heavy with grief, Buck said, "I should have been there to help, Dr. B. I should have been there."

Bella gently, but with authority said, "No Buck. It played out the way it did so that you can help us now. Levi will need you to tell him what to do until Kit is back at work, right? Even the cop at the end of the driveway didn't know there was a problem till all the cops arrived."

Buck looked at Phoenix and said, "She's good at this isn't she?"

***

After the authorities released Phoenix and Bella, they left for the hospital to check on Kit, Ryker, and Dante. Lucas stayed at the ranch.

Phoenix held Bella's hand and said, "Royce came way too close, Bella. I knew that he was probably in disguise, I just didn't figure that he would be disguised as one of the crew. The deputy called to tell me the truck was coming. I knew. I knew, Bella."

"No, Phoenix, you thought Kit was in the truck. None of us had any warning until it happened."

Phoenix said, "The police said that Ryker's gun was in his hand, but he just didn't have time to use it. And Royce used a silencer. That never occurred to

229

me. Not one time. Even Buck only heard the two shots from my gun, otherwise he would have still been in the pasture when the cops arrived."

With remnants of fear for Bella still lingering in his mind, he said, "When you screamed, I knew that Royce was in the house."

Bella said, "It's like everything was in a weird slow motion and I couldn't move fast enough. Dante fought to reach me, but the shots knocked him off his feet. And Thor went berserk trying to get in the house. All I could think about was you."

He said, "How are you, Bella? Really. As all this settles, how are you feeling?"

"I'm glad that Royce is gone and that he can't attack me or any other woman ever again. I'll be fine. I mean it. After today, Royce is over for me. Finally."

***

Phoenix parked at the hospital, and they checked in at the desk for Ryker.

He was in recovery and would go to ICU afterwards. Then they asked for room numbers for Dante and Kit.

Dante was awake when they knocked and entered. His concern was only for them as he asked, "Are you ok, Bella? Phoenix?"

Bella touched his hand softly and said, "I'm only bruised. I'm fine."

And Phoenix touched his head bandage, and said, "Mine is nothing, just a graze, how are you feeling? You look a whole lot better than I expected."

Dante said, "I had on a vest, thank God. All the blood was from the shoulder shot. It went straight through. But the chest shot is what knocked me off my feet and cracked a rib. It is bruised and wrapped up, so don't make me laugh. I will be fine though."

Bella was grateful. But it was hard to see a strong man wrapped up in shoulder bandages with a sling, and chest bandages, laid out in a hospital bed. All to save her.

Dante said, "Don't worry, Bella. This is my job. I just deal with it. This is not my first rodeo by any means. Tell me about the others. Have you seen Ryker yet? They won't tell me anything. And what happened to Kit?"

Phoenix said, "Ryker is in recovery. He had two chest shots. Because it was from close range, one bullet went through the vest and nicked a lung. The other bullet hit the vest right over his heart. He is in ICU to monitor his heart.

"And Royce jumped Kit at the store after buying batteries. Kit is down the hall from you with a lot of head stitches, a concussion, and a broken arm. Evidently the store clerk said something about Kit being from Chandler Canyon Ranch and Royce heard it. They even look alike as crazy as that sounds."

Dante shook his head and said, "Freak stuff just happens, but the plan worked," and he smiled at Bella.

Bella said, "I can't believe that you made it to the door to let Thor in."

Dante grimaced and said, "I slipped and crawled to get there. He was almost foaming at the mouth by the time I was able to reach the doorknob."

Phoenix said, "It didn't last long after that."

Dante said, "That's the best news I've had all day."

***

Phoenix heard Kit fussing with Jasmine as they neared his hospital room and knocked.

Kit yelled, "What!" and Bella giggled as Phoenix just ignored him and walked in.

Kit exclaimed, "Boss! Dr. B! They wouldn't let me leave."

Phoenix and Bella put a comforting arm around Jasmine as they inwardly groaned at the bandage on Kit's head, the bruises on his face, and the broken arm.

Phoenix said, "Have you looked in the mirror, Kit?"

Surprised, Kit said, "Well, no."

Jasmine opened the rolling table drawer, so he could look in the mirror.

He said, "Well, I am glad I don't feel as bad as I look, except for a killer headache."

Then he wanted to know what had happened. Phoenix told him.

Horrified, Kit looked at Bella and said, "Dr. B, I can't imagine how terrifying it was for you. I am so glad you are ok."

Bella said, "I'm fine, you just get well."

Calmer now, Kit quit fussing, kissed Jasmine, and laid back on his pillow and said, "I am floored at what you've gone through. Shocked. And just so you know, I am selling that truck. I'm not ever driving it again."

The doctor broke the rules and let Phoenix and Bella into ICU to see Ryker for a minute. The attack had been all over the news. Bella's eyes immediately filled with tears as she saw the vibrant, powerful man that she knew, wounded and pale. He was attached to what looked like, every medical wire known to man.

Phoenix put his arm around her, and quietly they walked to his bedside. Bella wiped tears from her cheeks. Ryker's eyes flickered and opened. He looked at them and attempted a smile.

"Bella," he whispered, and she touched his arm.

"Hey, Ryker."

Ryker looked at Phoenix and said hoarsely, "What ran over me?"

"I'm sorry, man. I bet it does feel that way."

Ryker said, "It wasn't Kit in the truck, was it?"

Bella said softly, "No. But Royce won't ever shoot anyone again."

Ryker said, "Dante?"

Phoenix said, "He's down the hall and he'll be out of here before you."

Ryker said, "Kit?"

Bella said, "Giving Jasmine a hard time on the second floor," and he nodded, aware of how bad the attack had been.

Then the nurse ushered them out of the room, and they headed home.

***

At the ranch, once the last of the Sheriff's Department had left, neighbors showed up and helped Lucas, Lili, Buck, and Levi get the house back in order as much as they could.

Lucas attempted to bathe Thor, but he refused to get in the tub. Lili grinned as Thor allowed her to coax him into the shower with treats.

So, by the time, Phoenix and Bella walked inside, home didn't look like the crime scene it had been when they left.

Then Phoenix's phone rang, and he walked to his office for a business call.

Lucas told Bella, "I will stay at the ranch until you leave for your honeymoon. Buck and Levi will stay too. GP called and confirmed he will be here tomorrow afternoon."

Bella said, "Thanks, Lucas. Seth and Ariel will be in late tomorrow and Gabe is supposed to come too. The hacker has been quiet probably because he knows the FBI is on his tail. So, right now, I just want the guys in the hospital to get well and for Phoenix and me to get married."

Phoenix walked out of his office and said, "Me too, Bella. Me too." Then he said, "Now, on another note, I just got a call from a Dallas attorney. I am a witness in a court case and my deposition is tomorrow. They won't let me change it on such short notice, so I need to leave by noon. Come with me, Bella. I can't leave you here."

She said, "But Lucas will be here. And GP, Ariel, Seth, and Gabe are coming in throughout the afternoon. Plus, Buck and Levi will be here. I lost a whole day of work today, plus I have wedding details to go over. Besides, the FBI is closing in on the hacker."

Phoenix looked at Lucas.

Lucas said, "Her wolf and I won't leave her side and all the others will be in later. Go do your deposition. We will be fine. What time do you think you will be back home?"

"It could be nine or ten p.m."

Bella said, "I will stay with Lucas, I promise."

"I agree but only because I know the FBI is close to the hacker and Lucas would be as wild to protect you as I would."

Chapter 36
The Hacker

Gabe got home just in time to watch the late news report of Royce's attack at the ranch. They had all been shocked at NASA this morning when Bella messaged Seth.

Royce's face flashed on the TV screen. Then pictures and videos followed of Phoenix, Bella, and the wolf. Pictures of Bella, bloody with her shirt ripped, Phoenix with a bloody head wound, and Thor's face covered in blood.

The news sensationalized the fact that the wolf had killed Royce. Gabe was glad. Go Thor! Their trauma today made him wish his kidnap plan wasn't tomorrow. But then again, it might work in his favor. With Jasmine out with Kit, and the security detail out of commission, it would make it that much easier.

His plan was much less traumatic than today's ordeal.

At least until they all woke up.

As for NASA, they didn't know they would never see him again. And while Phoenix would never see him again either, he would never forget what he had done.

Bella would be gone by dark tomorrow.

Poof.

Chapter 37
Day of Deceit

Phoenix was sound asleep when Bella kissed him. Hungry. With instant response he shifted position and deepened the kiss as he pressed her into the mattress.

Bella wanted this kiss and met him passion for passion. She loved him beyond anything she had ever known. He was her soul mate, her hero, her rancher, and soon to be her husband in two more days.

She needed his kiss, and caress, after the terror of yesterday.

Phoenix felt the same need and loosened his restraint to let the fire rage a little hotter than normal. Bella responded with a heat that seared him back. But he groaned after a few minutes, knowing that he had to cool them down.

He looked at her, voice husky, and asked, "You were in the mood for a bonfire this morning?"

She licked his lips and pulled him back down to kiss her again.

Then Thor barked.

Phoenix moaned.

And Bella giggled.

Phoenix said, "We are putting in a doggy door."

Bella said, "As big as he is, you might as well leave a window open," and Phoenix chuckled as he sat up and looked down at her, still reeling from the heat.

"I love you," he said, and as he touched her lips, they opened for him.

He growled in anticipation, and said, "We are going to burst into flames after the wedding."

She bit his finger.

He warned, "Bella…"

She smiled and said, "Ok, I quit, but you better go let Thor out before he bites you too."

Thirty minutes later, Phoenix and Bella laughed as Buck sang old trail ride songs as he cooked steak and eggs, and bossed Levi around.

After breakfast, Lucas kissed Lili goodbye as she left for work in Wichita Falls. Then Buck and Levi headed to the barns with their instructions from Phoenix.

Phoenix said, "Ok, it's time to confirm when everyone will be here today. I need to leave at noon, and I don't want any questions in my mind on your security, Bella."

***

Bella texted Seth: Phoenix has a deposition in Dallas. What time will you and Ariel arrive? He is concerned about security.

Seth replied: Between seven or eight p.m. Is that, ok?

Bella replied: Perfect. Thanks! Look forward to seeing you tonight.

Seth replied: Are you ok?

Bella replied: Yes.

***

They all gathered again a few minutes later.

Phoenix said, "GP said that he would arrive around three p.m."

Lucas said, "I called Gabe and he will leave earlier since he is on vacation. He plans to be here by six p.m. and bring dinner since Jasmine is out with Kit."

Bella said, "That is so nice of him. I hadn't even thought of dinner."

Once security was confirmed, Phoenix and Bella made note of all the house damage from the attack yesterday. There were two bullet holes in the wall behind the dining table that Royce had meant for Phoenix. And another one on the back wall that went through Dante. Several walls needed to be repainted. A few stuffed chairs in the den were thrown out because of blood

236

stains. And there were two cracked windows that needed to be replaced because of Thor's ferocious pounding to get in the house.

Afterwards, Phoenix called the hospital for updates on Kit, Ryker, and Dante.

***

Jasmine answered Kit's phone and said, "Hey Boss. I have someone here that wants to go to work today."

Phoenix said, "I am not surprised. Would you put me on speaker please?"

He said, "Kit, what's the latest news from the doctor?"

"Hey Boss! The doctor just released me so I should be out of here in a couple of hours and will head to the ranch."

"No, Kit. The last thing you need is to be jostling that head of yours around on a horse or four-wheeler. Those pain meds make you feel better than you actually do. You just plan to be at the wedding on Saturday. After that, you might be able to do light duty while I am gone, and I mean only light duty."

"Yes, Boss. How's Buck today? He was upset when he came to the hospital last night."

Phoenix said, "He's doing you proud, as well as bossing Levi around. Would you believe that he even sang while he cooked breakfast this morning?" and they laughed.

Phoenix continued, "I must leave for Dallas in a couple of hours for that deposition that I told you about, but GP will get to the ranch later today in case Buck or Levi need anything. Lucas will be with Bella, so we are fine. Don't worry about anything."

Jasmine said, "I can come in to cook, Boss. I don't mind at all, and I need to cook for Kit anyway."

Phoenix said, "Thanks Jasmine, you're the best, but Gabe is bringing dinner with him tonight, so don't worry about it. Besides you have enough meals in our freezer to last us two weeks. You just take care of Kit because you know that if you come to the ranch, he will demand to tag along."

Jasmine said, "That's a fact."

"Take the break, Kit. Don't do like I did with my eyes and disregard the doctor. Take time to heal and get past it safely."

237

Phoenix called Dante, and he answered the phone with a grunt, and a groan, and said, "Hang on," so Phoenix waited.

When Dante got back on the line he said, "The nurse hates me," and Phoenix chuckled.

Dante said, "The doc said I can leave this afternoon. It sure is a good thing Royce shot my left shoulder instead of my right since I am right-handed."

"I hear that. Dante, do you have family around here? If you need a place to stay, the ranch is yours anytime, and I mean that."

"Thanks, Phoenix, really, but my sister is coming in from Fort Worth to take me home with her. I can stay there as long as I need to."

Phoenix said, "After Bella and I return from our honeymoon, I sure would like to talk to you and Ryker about general security options for the ranch."

"Sure. That sounds great, and speaking of Ryker, I tried to get in to see him and they wouldn't let me in."

Phoenix said, "The doctor let us in ICU last night for a few minutes. Ryker looked rough but he's going to be ok. Between lung surgery and the blow his heart took through the bullet proof vest, they wanted to monitor him. I'm going to call the nurse station shortly so I will ask them to let you in."

***

A little while later, Phoenix looked up and smiled as Bella walked into his office.

He pushed his chair back and pulled her on his lap and said, "Hello Dr. B, what can I do for you?"

Bella smiled and walked her fingers up his chest and said, "I came in to tell you that Lucas will walk me to my office, but now, I think I need something else first."

He happily gave her what she asked for.

Lucas rounded the corner to see what held her up and said, "Great. You leave your brother hanging in the den while you steam up the office. That's just wrong," and he winked.

Phoenix laughed and tickled Bella as she stood.

Lucas said, "You leave at noon for Dallas, right?"

Phoenix glanced at the clock and said, "Yeah, I need to change and hit the road before long."

Bella said, "I'll just stay here and wait then," and he said, "It's ok, I will drive by your office on my way out."

Phoenix followed them to the front door and watched them walk down the road to her office. He was impressed at how well she was doing after the nightmare with Royce yesterday.

On her birthday no less.

He went back to his desk and checked the honeymoon reservations, their rings, and the wedding license. Everything was ready. By Saturday at noon, they would be married. And they wouldn't be at the reception long.

***

Bella headed upstairs to her office with Lucas to check today's vet schedule. She had just unlocked the medicine safe when her phone rang.

***

She answered, "Hi Shiloh. I am so glad you called."

"Bella, I heard from Ranger Morgan yesterday, and of course saw the news, are you doing alright?"

"I am. It was horrific, and so many people got hurt, but they will be fine, thank God, and I don't ever have to see his face again. So, please, tell me that you are calling with good news."

"We are closing in on the hacker. I hope to know more by tonight or morning. I just wanted to give you a head's up that we are nearing the end of the trail. I figured that you needed something positive today."

Bella smiled and said, "Yes, absolutely!"

Shiloh said, "My next call to you will be to tell you that we know who the hacker is, and that we are arresting him."

"Thank you for all your hard work." Bella said. "I am grateful and look forward to that next call more than you know."

***

239

Bella gave Lucas the update and he gave a sigh of relief. Then she tried to call Phoenix, but he didn't answer, so she would tell him when he stopped on his way out.

After that, she focused on her medicine and supplies that she needed to treat five sick cattle. She filled two syringes with medicine for calves with intestinal issues, one syringe for a heifer with hoof issues, and a pain shot for a horse that needed a few stitches.

Bella filled the last syringe with a lethal dose of tranquilizer for one of the older cows. She had been bitten by a rattlesnake on the stomach and wasn't recovering. If she wasn't better by today, she would have to put her down.

She dropped that syringe in the lower leg pocket in her cargo pants. She never put the euthanizer syringes with the other medications.

Lucas said, "Phoenix is coming," and they went downstairs.

Phoenix pulled up in his King Ranch truck that had been repaired from hitting the deer. Bella whistled as he stepped out in slacks, shirt, and tie, and he grinned.

Eyeing him, she said, "I don't know, maybe I should have left my office in disarray and ran off with you to Dallas."

He winked and said, "Jump on in, gorgeous."

Lucas called out, "Don't forget to tell him!"

Phoenix said, "Tell me what?"

Bella told him about the call from Shiloh, and he said, "Yes! That's what I'm talking about. Hopefully by tomorrow the hacker will be behind bars for a long time."

Bella said, "Just so he's gone."

Phoenix drew her up against him, and she slid her hands up his shirt and said, "You sure look good."

He whispered, "I am good. Taste me…" and she did.

They made sure the memory of that kiss would last them all day.

***

Late that afternoon, Bella coaxed a heifer with a treat to take medication for a hoof issue. She smiled and gave her a neck rub. Then she sighed. She sure dreaded to see the cow with the snakebite. Maybe by now the cow had improved and she wouldn't have to euthanize her.

Bella heard someone call her name and turned to see who it was. It was GP and she smiled and waved. She hadn't seen him drive up.

He walked out to the corral with soft drinks, and she could see the worry on his face.

He said, "Are you really ok, Bella?"

She hugged him and said, "I am, GP. Don't worry."

GP said, "How's Phoenix's head injury?"

Bella said, "His thick hair hides the wound, so you can't even tell it. He barely flinched when the bullet grazed him."

GP frowned and said, "Royce was pure evil."

Lucas walked up and said, "I agree with that, GP," and they shook hands.

GP said, "Are you finished for the day?"

She said, "I have an old cow to check on. I'm hoping I don't have to put her down. She's at my office."

When they walked in the vet barn, the old cow was on her feet and mooed at them. She had eaten all her food.

Bella smiled and said, "You are one special cow old girl. Today was your lucky day."

They made sure she was fed and watered for the night and locked up the barn. It was close to six o'clock when Bella, Lucas, and GP walked back to the house.

In the distance they saw a blue SUV coming up the driveway.

Lucas said, "Who is that?"

Bella said, "I don't know that car."

GP said, "I don't either."

Lucas said, "Y'all go on in and let me greet them," and he unlatched his pistol cover.

Concerned, Bella said, "Lucas..."

He ordered, "Get inside."

GP escorted her inside and made her go into Phoenix's office and shut the door.

***

Gabe smiled from a distance as he watched Lucas stand outside, armed. He glanced at the clock, and it was two minutes after six p.m. Perfect timing.

He pulled up by the porch and Lucas smiled and gave him a thumb's up.

Gabe said, "Sorry, man, I didn't mean to startle you," as he got out of the car.

Lucas said, "No problem, did you get a new vehicle?"

"No, mine is in the shop, and I didn't want to wait around on it and be late getting here."

"That's great. We appreciate you coming. Phoenix was concerned about such a small crew with Bella."

"I understand. Can you give me a hand with dinner? It's ready to eat. I hope that y'all are hungry," and opened the back seat door to take out the bags.

Lucas' stomach growled and Gabe laughed and said, "Well, that answered that," and they headed inside.

GP opened the front door and shook Gabe's hand, meeting for the first time, and called for Bella.

Gabe followed GP's gaze and smiled as Bella came out of Phoenix's office. She looked beautiful in a red shirt and khaki cargo pants. The red shirt set off her bright blue eyes and black hair. He felt desire race through him when she smiled, a genuine smile, full of warmth and beauty, for him.

His mouth watered for her, but he pulled himself together and said, "Hey Bella, I hope that you are hungry, I have delicious BBQ brisket sandwiches, potato salad, cowboy beans, corn on the cob, and even hot peach cobbler."

They laughed as Lucas hurriedly called Buck and Levi to come eat, then unpacked the food, sampling as he went.

Bella said, "You are awesome to come early. You even spoiled us with a meal. Thank you! I can't believe that you gave up your vacation time to come."

Gabe said sincerely, "There is no place I would rather be. After yesterday, are you ok?"

She touched his arm softly, and said, "I am. My only concern now is for the ones that were hurt."

"I'm glad that Royce is dead, Bella," Gabe said in a voice that surprised her, and she nodded in agreement.

Buck and Levi came in, and Lucas said with a mouthful, "Y'all better hurry," and Gabe laughed.

Lucas handed Bella a small plate of food and she said, "No, I haven't been hungry today," and he frowned.

Gabe said, "Just eat a little, Bella. It's good. I ate on the way. You need nourishment after all you have been through."

She said, "Maybe later."

GP, Lucas, Buck, and Levi fixed their plates and dug in.

Then Gabe knelt and called the wolf over and said, "I even have a treat for this hero," and unwrapped some chunks of venison.

Thor licked his face enthusiastically and Bella said, "Thank you, Gabe. That was thoughtful."

Gabe said, "I admire him. He earned it," and the wolf devoured the meat.

Bella poured her and Gabe a glass of tea and they sat on the porch and talked as the sun turned the western sky purple, fuchsia, orange, gold, and pink as it set.

About thirty minutes later, Gabe looked at Bella's profile for a second, and knew that this moment of peace would change drastically in the next few minutes.

If only she had eaten the food like everyone else, she would have simply gone to sleep. Then he could have picked her up and carried her off without a scene. Now he had to have the confrontation with her here.

He glanced back through the window and all four men were collapsed in their chairs, drugged. The wolf was passed out on the floor.

Gabe glanced back at Bella and said with a smile, "Can you give me a hand to carry a few things in?"

"Sure. Glad to."

He walked down the steps and she followed him. Gabe made sure no one else was around and walked to the passenger side of his vehicle. He knew that Bella wasn't alarmed at all.

As he opened the door, he said, "I have a secret."

Playfully, she laughed and said, "What, a deep, dark, secret?" and he slowly turned to face her.

Bella stopped laughing. Startled at the lustful look on his handsome face, she stepped back. Fear filled her.

With an intensity that she had never seen in him before, he said, "It's time, Bella."

She was too scared to ask him what it was time for.

He stepped closer and said, "I am who you are searching for. I am the hacker."

Her mind grappled with what he said. But the shock, alarm, and terror pulsing through her reminded her of the danger she was in. She ran for the house and screamed for Lucas.

Gabe wasn't surprised. He understood self-preservation, but it was too late. There was no one to help her. He ran after her.

Bella flew up the steps, not sure why Lucas hadn't come to help her, but when she opened the door, she saw why. All four men, including Thor were passed out.

Gabe grabbed her from the back, and she fought wildly like he knew she would, and he smiled at her passion. Until she kneed him in the groin.

He dropped her with a painful growl.

When her feet hit the floor, Bella ducked back through the open door and ran toward the barns, aware that he would catch her, but she had to try.

In a minute, he tackled her. His blood pounded with thrill as he manhandled her and pinned her arms above her head. She laid on the ground, eyes riveted on him as tears ran into her hair.

He pressed his body onto hers and bit her ear, and said, "I have waited impatiently for this."

Crying, she begged, "Please Gabe, we trusted you. I trusted you."

He said, "I sure appreciated that," and kissed her.

Unable to move, fear consumed Bella as he ravaged her mouth. She thought, this was it, he was going to rape her right here on the ground, but he lifted his head and smiled.

Bella looked at the man above her. With thick black hair, blue eyes, dark skin, and a smile to win any woman, anywhere, why did he need to come after her?

She said, "Tell me why."

He knew they needed to leave but allowed her a few questions.

He said, "I am starved for you," and ground his body against hers.

She wished that she hadn't asked that question, but a thought flashed, and she said, "Then just take what you want, and leave me here."

His gaze turned dark, and he said, "Bella, hear well what I say, I will never let you go. My face is the only one that you will ever see above you."

She screamed and fought, and he kissed her again.

Somehow Bella realized that fighting him made it worse, so she calmed down and tried to think. He stopped kissing her and watched her curiously. She knew that he was no fool. He hadn't gotten this far without being clever.

He sat up and said, "Stop it. Your intelligence isn't going to find a way out of this. There isn't one. Now walk with me to the car and we will leave. If you continue to fight me, I will kill all of them while they sleep. They are only drugged, like you should have been if you would have eaten."

Gabe stood and pulled her up and said, "Give me your phone," and she pulled it out of her back pocket and handed it to him.

He turned it off and tossed it in the weeds.

He said casually, "Get in the car," and Bella looked at him with pure hate, and he slapped her across the face.

He caught her before she fell and lifted her chin to face him, and said, "That behavior will only get you hurt. Acceptance is wiser," and Bella listened in silence as her face burned from the slap.

She wanted to struggle as he led her to the car, but she didn't have a choice, she would have to find another way. She would never stop trying to get free, and she knew that Phoenix would never stop trying to find her.

It was dark as Gabe buckled her in the car like she was a child, and said, "If you can be civil, you can ride up here. If not, I can drug you and put you in the back."

She said hoarsely, "I'll be civil."

He checked her face for injuries and shut the door.

Bella looked through the dark windshield and cried for Phoenix.

Chapter 38
Kidnapped

The deposition in Dallas ended at six p.m. and by the time Phoenix left the attorney's office and got to his truck it was six-thirty p.m. He tried to call Bella and it went straight to voice mail. He got on the highway headed home and tried to reach her again and it still went straight to voice mail. Then he called Lucas and it rang until his voice mail picked up. Fear set in.

***

His phone rang and he quickly answered, "Shiloh, have you talked to Bella?"

She said, "No. I can't reach her. Listen to me, Phoenix. Gabe is the Hacker. The other guy was a false trail. It's Gabe."

Phoenix roared in agony and said, "No! He's with Bella!" and whipped the truck to the side of the road. Trying to focus through the fear, he yelled, "I'm leaving Dallas! Get the FBI to the ranch! Gabe is there! Hurry!"

She said, "Get to the nearest police station, Phoenix. Now! Do not drive home."

***

Phoenix called 911 as he roared away to find the police. He needed to get home fast and find Bella. Gabe was going to be a dead man when he found them.

In thirty minutes, the police dropped him off at the airport and Phoenix got on the helicopter that he had rented for the night. They had installed an app on his phone and gave him special headphones so he could use his iPhone while they flew. Shiloh called as the chopper took off.

***

Phoenix asked quickly, "Was Bella at the ranch?"

"No, and Gabe isn't there either. We have to presume that he took her."

Phoenix moaned and was consumed in genuine pain and horror as he imagined Bella's fear. He wanted to rip something to shreds to release the pressure exploding inside of him.

She said, "I know, Phoenix, I know, but listen to me. It appears that Gabe drugged the men, even the wolf, so Bella may be unconscious and not even know anything yet. We won't know more until all four men wake up. Gabe's phone isn't tracking but we have APBs out on his vehicle. And you need to know that GP, Lucas, Buck, and Levi are enroute to the emergency room. Where are you?"

"In a helicopter. I should be at the ranch in thirty minutes. What else can we do?"

Shiloh said, "Roadblocks are being setup everywhere, so we hope we have him pinned in. Texas Rangers and the Sheriff's Department are involved in the search. The FBI is on the way to the hospital to talk to the guys when they wake up. We search, follow leads, and pray. Call me when you land at the ranch."

***

As he ended the call, his phone rang again. It was Seth.

He answered, "Seth, I haven't had time to call, are you at the ranch yet?"

Seth said, "I have you on speaker. What is going on? Cops have all the roads blocked and are doing car searches."

Phoenix interrupted him, and said, "The Hacker is Gabe. He took Bella."

Seth and Ariel both exclaimed in shock, and Ariel began to cry.

Seth, voice ragged, said, "No! I brought him there. Oh, sweet Bella. I'm going to kill him!"

Phoenix said, "Get in line. I am on my way back to the ranch in a helicopter. Get there when you can. GP, Lucas, Buck, and Levi are at the hospital, they were drugged. Call and check on Lili. And pray we find Bella fast."

Ariel said, "Phoenix…"

Phoenix said, "Don't you leave Seth's side, Ariel, not for one second."

***

All four men were in different cubicles in the emergency room as doctors tried to counteract the drug they were given and wake them up. An FBI agent monitored all of them.

GP began to waken first but was disoriented and struggled to understand what was going on. When the agent questioned him about Gabe and Bella, he began to have chest pains and was rushed to ICU.

About ten minutes later, Lucas began to come around, and confused, fought to get out of bed. The doctor and agents tried to calm him down, but he got up.

Lili stepped in the middle of the men and got Lucas to focus on her.

Lucas said, "Why am I here? Where is everyone else? Where is Bella?"

The FBI agent interrupted and said, "Lucas. Gabe took her. He is the Hacker."

Lucas yelled, "No! And slammed his hands against the wall. I'm going to kill him!"

The agent said, "Lucas! Focus! We need information from you. What vehicle was Gabe driving?"

Lucas wiped his tears, and said, "A blue Suburban. He said his car was in the shop."

"Do you know what time it was when you last saw Bella and Gabe?"

"Close to six-thirty p.m. while we ate dinner. He had brought us food."

The agent glanced at the doctor. Now they knew how Gabe had drugged them.

Lucas continued, "But Bella didn't eat."

The agent nodded but knew that was not good. She had faced her kidnapper all alone.

Lucas looked at Lili and said, "We've got to tell Phoenix! He didn't even want to leave her."

The agent said, "He already knows. He's on his way to the ranch in a helicopter. We are searching for Gabe and Bella. Roadblocks are everywhere."

Lucas said, "What about GP?"

The doctor said, "He woke first, but had to be moved to ICU with chest pains."

"What about Buck and Levi?"

"They are still asleep."

Grief apparent, Lucas hugged Lili and said, "We have to get to the ranch."

***

As he drove down the dark highway, Gabe glanced at Bella. He had given her about thirty minutes of quiet to reconcile herself to her new situation.

Conversationally, he said, "If you want to know, it was pure chance that put Seth in my team at NASA."

Without thinking, Bella said, "You mean more like a nightmare."

He backhanded her and split her lip, and said, "That is your last warning to be civil."

She laid her head back against the seat and blinked the stars away. Her lip stung something fierce and throbbed. She felt as blood dripped down her chin.

He said, "Look at me," and she turned her head to face him in the glare of lights from the dash. He touched her lip and frowned, then said, "I prefer not to injure you."

Wisely, she swallowed her disbelieving laugh.

As he looked back at the road, she said, "May I ask a question?"

"Yes."

"What do you plan to do with me beyond sex?"

"We will have to live secluded of course. Sex will be the main focus so we will have children, and eventually fall in love. You will be mine for the rest of your life."

Bella felt the bile rise and glanced down so he couldn't see the revulsion in her eyes.

He slid his hand along her thigh and said, "It's going to be a hot and hungry night between us. I plan to make sure that you enjoy it. You're a doctor. You know that you can't stop that."

Horrified, Bella didn't respond. Then as he rounded a large curve, lights flashed up ahead. Gabe hit the brakes and turned to the right, on another road. Hope filled her. Cops were searching!

He snapped, "They might be looking, but they won't find you."

They looked at each other, and Bella's stomach twisted at the crazed hunger in his eyes. Again, she said nothing at all.

Gabe cussed a short time later and had to turn the car abruptly as lights flashed again in the distant darkness. His rough turn caused Bella to slide against the door. She reached down to reposition herself on the seat and felt something in her pocket. Without drawing attention to her movement, she brushed one finger against the lump. And froze. The euthanizer syringe for the sick cow was still in her pocket. She had a weapon.

She could do this.

She had to.

Before long, Gabe took a hard right without braking. Now they were on a very bumpy road and Bella's heart began to pound. It was simply a trail in the middle of nowhere.

And it was pitch black.

The only light anywhere were the headlights outside and the LED displays on the dash. Bella clenched her jaw and slid her hand over the syringe and tried not to think about the darkness.

She had plenty to think about already.

The syringe contained more than enough to kill three or four men. But to effectively inject him, he would need to be near or against her and she knew that she would only get one chance. She would have to do it fast and hard like a stab, to get the needle in before he could stop her. Even if she injected only a third or half of it, he wouldn't last long.

Hopefully she could survive before he died.

He might try to take her with him.

Gabe drove until the farm trail ended. He stopped, killed the engine, and turned on the inside lights. He turned to Bella.

She looked out the windshield into the darkness, and prayed silently, "Oh God. It's time. Help me."

He said, "I promise you that making love to me will definitely have its rewards."

She closed her eyes.

He continued, "I prefer you willing, but either way, I will have you."

She said with a whisper, "I never dreamed that my first time would be as a victim."

He laughed and said, "I wish it was your first time. Don't lie to me. You've been sleeping in Phoenix's room for days."

Bella said, "He had to move me in there for protection, not sex. We waited for the wedding," and she felt the immediate hot taste of rage strengthen her.

He turned in his seat and said, "Are you trying to tell me that you are still a virgin at twenty-seven?"

She wanted to slap him across the face and claw his eyes out but instead, looked at him and said simply, "Yes."

Gabe smiled and said, "How unexpected. I didn't realize that I would get to be your first, and only. I am glad that you told me. I will be gentle."

She almost gagged at his generosity. Then she focused on the syringe under her palm.

He said, "I have bedding and food in the back so when we get out, you can use the bathroom and clean up. I brought everything you need."

He lifted her chin and forced her to look at him, then said, "It's time to give me what I want."

She tried to hide the fear, and the fury, as she stared into his eyes. He really was a monster. And she wondered why the world always painted monsters as ugly on the outside. He wasn't, and it just made him more dangerous.

She didn't react so he let her go and reached for his door handle.

She thought only of her goal to survive, and said, "Can I have privacy to use the bathroom without you watching?"

He contemplated her simple request and said, "Stay by your door and I will agree. If you make me chase you, I'll tie you up and keep you naked."

Bella nodded and said, "Gabe. I must ask. Is there any way you would stop now, and let me go?"

He reached out and gently touched her wounded cheek and lips, before looking at her body, and said, "No. There isn't. So, hurry up."

Bella thought, so be it.

They both opened their doors and stood in the light of the car door to use the bathroom. Bella grimaced as she heard him pee. Then she unzipped her pants, squatted, and refused to look toward Gabe. As she used the bathroom, she slid the syringe out of her pocket and hid it in her hand.

When she stood, he said, "Meet me at the back of the car."

She hid the syringe under her hair behind her ear; like she would do in college with her pen or pencil.

She saw nothing but blackness around the car as she walked to the back; and focused only on the anger for all he intended to take from her. She had the right to defend herself. She had even offered him a last chance, and he didn't take it.

He would pay dearly for that decision.

Gabe lifted the tailgate of the Suburban as she reached the back of the car and laid the passenger seat down and quickly made a bed. Bella watched him emotionlessly, like he was just changing a tire, instead of literally making the bed to rape her.

But she knew she didn't plan to get in it.

When he finished, he turned and faced her. Bella's stomach knotted as she focused intently on him. The battle was here. Now. And the drive to survive took over. She would do whatever it took.

Gabe fondled her breasts and ran his hands down her body. He ripped his shirt off and dropped it.

When his eyes met hers, ravenous lust filled them. He flexed his bare chest muscles, and said, "Take the top off, or I will."

Without argument, Bella removed her shirt and bra and dropped them. Standing only in her pants, she knew that it was his distraction that would make her plan work.

He all but drooled as he looked at her bare chest. Then he unzipped his pants and stepped proudly out of them. She refused to look. Her heart pounded with fear, rage, and sheer adrenalin as she waited to attack.

He grinned, aware of her avoidance of looking at his body and stepped closer. Her time for avoidance was over, and he dropped his gaze to her pants.

He said, "Here, let me…" and reached for her zipper.

Bella raised her arms and crossed them over her head as if to give him better access. Now her right hand was draped near the syringe.

At her apparent willingness, he passionately kissed her and unzipped her pants.

She stabbed him in the neck above his left shoulder and shoved the plunger to inject the drug. Before she had time to move, he hit her hard and slammed her to the ground.

He yanked the syringe out of his neck, but she could see that he was too late. The syringe was almost empty. He raged like a wild man and kicked her in the thigh.

She gasped with pain and tried to scoot away from him.

He snarled and yelled, "What was in that syringe?"

Bella looked up at Gabe, naked and furious, and said, "Your funeral invitation."

He roared furiously and took a step toward her. Then a puzzled look crossed his face. He shook his head, jerked a few times, wobbled, and began to fall. Toward her.

She tried to get out of the way, but he landed motionless across her left arm and leg, and she screamed as rocks dug into her bare back and arm. Hand shaking, she reached for his neck to find his pulse.

It was thready and intermittent for a short time.

Then it simply stopped.

She took a ragged breath and laid back in the gravel. She looked up into the night sky, in the middle of nowhere, with a dead man on her, and only felt relief.

Oh, God.

I survived.

It took her a few painful minutes to get her arm and leg out from under him and she stood. The cuts burned something fierce on her back. She glanced around, amazed that the dark didn't seem to bother her at all anymore.

There were worse things.

She grabbed her shirt off the ground, zipped her pants and went to see if Gabe had a phone in the car. She found his pistol and a prepaid phone with signal and locked herself inside. She cried as she called Phoenix.

Chapter 39
Crime Scene

Phoenix hung up the phone with Shiloh as the ranch came into view from the chopper. The pilot had plenty room to land; and then Phoenix was out and running to the house. The FBI, Ranger Morgan, and Deputy Todd waited for him. His heart ached as he stepped through the ranch door at eight-fifteen p.m. His phone rang. It was an unknown number.

***

Hoping that it might be a ransom call from Gabe, he growled, "If you hurt her, I will kill you."

"Phoenix."

"Oh God. Bella, oh Bella, where are you? Are you hurt?"

"I killed him."

"Good! Just tell me where you are. I'm coming."

"With the darkness, I don't know. Just out in a field somewhere. But I don't think that I am that far away because he had to get off the road with all the roadblocks. The ground reminds me of the land close to the canyon."

Knowing that she couldn't leave the crime scene, but hoping that she was close, he said, "Does he have a gun there?"

"Yes. Should I shoot it to see if you can hear it?"

"Yes. I'm heading outside. I'll tell you when to fire."

Everyone rushed outside and Phoenix said, "Is there anything around you to shoot at?"

"A tree."

"Shoot it," and she fired.

From a distance, Phoenix heard the faint echo of a gunshot and said, "Yes, Bella! We heard it. We can find you. Lock yourself in the car and leave all the lights on. We are coming in a helicopter. Stay on the phone with me."

Bella sat in the car and watched the night sky out the windshield as Phoenix comforted her through the phone. In a few moments she could see a new light in the sky.

He said, "You should be able to see us any minute. I see your light."

She said, "I see you," and got out of the car and waited for him.

Phoenix watched the lone light on the backside of the canyon get brighter and brighter. Then he could see the shape of the car, and Bella as she stood there. Very still. Very small. Very brave.

He also saw Gabe's naked body on the ground behind the car. He clenched his jaw with rage. Too bad he couldn't die twice. Then he shook it off and thanked God that she had survived. Nothing else mattered.

Nothing.

When the helicopter landed, Bella was already running. Phoenix ran and caught her mid-air, as they kissed feverishly, and held on to each other.

After a few minutes, he moaned at her bruised face with bloody cut, busted lip, scraped arms and hands, dirty clothes, and hair.

He wiped her tears, not realizing his fell too, and said, "I need to kill him again, for hurting you."

She winced at her sore lip, and said, "That's why I did it for both of us."

***

One of the FBI agents interrupted them and said, "Bella, I need to get your statement. I talked to the pilot, and we can sit in the chopper to talk. The Rangers, the Sheriff's Department, more FBI agents, the coroner and first responders will be here soon."

Bella and Phoenix got settled in the chopper with his arm around her, and the agent climbed in and sat across from them.

The agent said, "To begin, do you know what killed Gabe?"

"Yes, I injected him with a euthanizer syringe that I had in my pocket. It should be on the ground near him."

255

The agent acted like he heard that comment every day, made a note, and continued, "Now, I'm going to have to ask many intimate questions. Are you able to answer them in front of Phoenix?"

She didn't hesitate and said, "Please let him stay."

"Ok. Start from when Gabe arrived at the ranch and tell your story. I will stop to clarify your answer if I need to."

Bella nodded and explained about the meal he brought, Gabe's hacker confession, everyone drugged inside, the physical and sexual assaults, the threats, the kidnapping with intent to imprison her, the traveling in the dark, about how she had discovered the syringe in her pocket, and how he evaded the cops until he finally turned down the trail to where they were now.

Phoenix was stricken for all she had endured.

The agent said, "Ok, Bella, you are doing great. Now I need to know everything that happened right here."

She said, "He stopped the car when the trail ended and began to discuss having sex and then gave me instructions. I told him that I was a virgin and asked him to please stop things before it went any further and he refused, although he did offer to be gentle," and Phoenix cussed.

She continued, "We each used the bathroom by our doors, and I slipped the syringe out of my pocket and hid it behind my ear."

The agent looked curious and said, "Why your ear?"

Bella said dryly, "Well, he was about to strip me, so I didn't have many options. I did it like when you put a pencil or pen behind your ear," and the agent nodded when she lifted her hair to show him.

The agent said, "Did you attempt to run?"

"Not here. He warned me earlier that if I fought him, he would drug me. And if I ran, he would tie me up. Bound and drugged would have made my situation worse than it already was. I had to be able to think."

The agent nodded and motioned for her to continue.

"Gabe told me to meet him at the back of the car, so I focused on the syringe and met him in the back. There was nothing but blackness around us. He made a bed, fondled me, and took off his shirt. He told me to take off my top. Then he took his pants off and found it funny that I wouldn't look at him. He stepped closer and focused on my body. I used his distraction and draped my arms over my head to put my hand into position. He took my move as a sign of willingness, kissed me, and unzipped my pants."

Bella knew that none of this could be easy for Phoenix to hear. It wasn't easy to say in front of him either, but at least she would only have to say it once.

"When Gabe was completely distracted, I stabbed him in the right side of his neck and hit the plunger. He hit me, knocking me to the ground, and removed the syringe from his neck. But the syringe was almost empty so I knew that he would die shortly. He was furious and asked what was in the shot. I told him it was his funeral invitation."

Phoenix smiled.

The agent didn't say anything, but he fought a grin.

"Then he yelled, kicked me, and came at me. But he began to feel the effects of the drug and collapsed on me. I felt for his pulse and held my finger on the artery until his heart stopped."

Phoenix squeezed her hand. It had been worse than a nightmare.

The agent was silent for a few moments and looked at her with respect.

He said, "I need to confirm - did he rape you?"

"No. He did not. I killed him before he removed my pants."

Then they all glanced up as the sirens and flashing lights that had been in the distance, finally arrived.

A female agent and paramedic took Bella aside. The paramedic checked her. And the agent took pictures of her injuries and kept her clothing and shoes as evidence. They found her bra under the car.

Once they cleared her to leave, Bella, dressed in paper clothes and flip flops, walked with Phoenix to the helicopter. He held her on his lap all the way home. They were both beyond grateful.

The chopper landed back at the ranch just before midnight. The house was surrounded by vehicles. Lucas met Bella in the yard, and it was an emotional time for brother and sister. Phoenix gave them a few minutes of privacy and then let Thor outside since he was howling and barking to get to Bella.

Bella turned when she heard Thor coming and knelt to receive his greeting, but he knocked her over and licked her. Phoenix finally heard Bella laugh.

Once inside, it was a tearful celebration as they grieved her physical condition and the trauma she had endured. Lili, Seth, Ariel, their Preacher, Ranger Morgan, Deputy Todd, Kit, Jasmine, Buck, and Levi were all there. GP was still in the hospital but doing better and knew that Bella was safe. NASA was even flying Pierce and Sterling up tomorrow. They had all been told that she killed Gabe in self-defense.

Amazed at her strength to survive, his death was the least of their concern. And then the Preacher that would marry them in two days, prayed for them.

A few minutes later, Shiloh arrived and told Bella about Gabe's investigation.

She said, "The FBI searched his home and found an office where he built the hacking robots. The robots were all labeled Troy, for the city of Troy they presumed, since the passcode to access the robots was Trojan. Unoriginal, but the names aptly fit the scenario.

"There were additional online videos of at least five other victims that he had targeted through his voyeur robots. Obviously, Phoenix's robot was intended for that same purpose, but Gabe became obsessed with you instead."

Then Shiloh looked at Seth, and said, "You can't blame yourself for Gabe getting to Bella. It was a freak coincidence that you were hired to work on the same NASA team, but he would have found another way to get to her without you. He had already chosen her."

Bella walked over and hugged Seth to comfort him. He couldn't hold back the tears. And neither could many of the others.

Shiloh continued, "Once he knew that he had physical access to Bella, he caused the destruction of the robot via the attack on her. Then he transferred the Trojan hacker files and framed another NASA employee. And…the rest you know."

Bella said, "You were concerned that it might take weeks because of all the false computer leads. Without you, it could have been hours before anyone knew that I was missing. How did you find him so quickly?"

Shiloh shrugged, and said, "I was smarter," and everyone clapped.

Then Shiloh reached in her pocket and handed Bella the figure of a black chess king.

She said, "You wanted me to kill his king in this hacker chess game. But it belongs to you. You took him down."

And the women hugged.

A few minutes later, Bella touched Phoenix on the arm, and said, "I'm ready to clean up."

He nodded and told everyone, "Thank all of you for everything. Make yourselves at home but Bella and I need to bow out."

***

Phoenix watched as Bella quietly walked into the bedroom. He wasn't quite sure what she needed emotionally or physically from him at this point. He intended to just follow her lead.

Bella gathered some clothes and said, "I may be awhile in the shower, will you stay close?"

He kissed her softly and said, "I'm not going anywhere," and she hugged him and walked in the bathroom, leaving a crack in the door.

Phoenix heard her move around and then the shower came on.

Bella knew the scrapes and cuts would burn but stepped into the shower anyway. She ground her teeth at the pain and let the water do its work as dirt, dried blood, the smell and touch of Gabe, the image of his naked dead body, and the memory of what she had done with the syringe, all ran down the drain with her tears. She stood a long while as the cleansing took place.

Bella looked in the mirror and the shower had certainly helped, but her poor skin was a mess. Her top lip was split. Her right cheek was bruised from the slaps. There was a cut over her eye from when he knocked her to the ground. Her left thigh had a large bruise from when he kicked her.

She turned around and grimaced at the wounds on her back, shoulders, and arms from getting smashed into the gravel without a shirt on.

She glanced at the large tub and decided to take a hot salt soak, and said, "Phoenix."

"I'm right here."

"Would you bring me one of my bikinis please?"

"Sure, I'll be right back," and in a second, handed it to her through the crack in the door.

Bella pulled on the bikini bottoms without a problem since her pants had protected her from the waist down. But the cuts and scrapes on her back were too tender to clasp the bikini top. She held it over her chest and turned on the water in the tub.

Phoenix said, "Bella? Are you ok?"

She said, "Come on in," and leaned over to pour the salt in the hot water. He walked through the door and expected to see her in the bikini but was not prepared for the damage to her skin, or the giant bruise on her thigh.

He moaned in sympathy as he walked to her.

She turned, trying to hold her bikini top over her chest, and said, "I know my back looks bad and it does sting, but it's superficial. I just can't take the pressure of the bikini top on the scrapes."

Phoenix held out his hand, and said, "I will be your husband in two days, you have more than enough to tend to," and she nodded, grateful for the man he was and handed him the top.

She looked at him and wondered if he would have a reaction to her partial nakedness. Especially, after her experience with Gabe.

He saw her insecurity, lifted her chin, kissed her softly, and said, "Bella your body is beautiful. A gorgeous gift to me. No wounds. No hacker changes that."

Relief flooded her and she smiled as he held her hand and she climbed into the tub. She laid to rest that inkling of fear that his desire might have been affected by all of this. Then she slowly lowered into the water until it reached the raw skin and she gasped at the harsh sting of the salt water.

He said, "Hang on, I'll be right back."

He returned, dressed in shorts, and climbed into the tub with her.

He said, "Why don't I drizzle some of the water on your back until you are acclimated enough to lower into it?"

Before long she was able to sit in the water up to her shoulders. They didn't talk but Phoenix sat near her and watched her soak.

After her body relaxed, and her skin felt more flexible, she turned and moved toward Phoenix. He drew her onto his lap. The love on his face was just what she needed, and she pulled his lips to hers.

Snuggled after the kiss, Phoenix said, "I have to ask you something. I want what is best for you. Should we push the weddi—" and she covered his mouth with her hand.

She understood how much love it took for him to ask her that, and said, "No. I don't want to wait any longer to be yours. I mean that."

"Thank God," he groaned, and kissed her.

He said, "What about the honeymoon? Perhaps we should make some changes, so you don't have to contend with commercial travel and vacation crowds. We just need each other. Where we go doesn't matter to me at all."

She kissed his chest, and said softly, "Can we? I just want to get in the truck after the wedding and go for a drive and find a place. Maybe even in the Wichita mountains across the Oklahoma state line. Just you and me. No timetable at all."

"I love the sound of that," he said. "You. A cabin. And a bed."

Chapter 40
The Day Before

Bella's phone rang and she groaned when she saw the early morning sun. Shiloh had returned her iPhone last night, but right now she wasn't so glad about that.

Phoenix checked her phone and said, "You might want to take this call, it's NASA."

***

Bella sat up, wide awake now, and reached for her phone and answered, "Hello," like she had been up for hours, and Phoenix laughed as she grinned at him.

A male voice said, "Dr. DelCaprio, I am Mr. Frost, Chief Director of Engineering at NASA. I hope that I haven't called too early."

"No, Mr. Frost, you haven't."

"I am calling on behalf of NASA to let you know that you and your family are in our prayers. It is a tragedy that one of our engineers created a criminal environment to harm you."

"Call me Bella, please, and thank you, Mr. Frost, for calling personally. I appreciate that but you didn't have to. NASA was in no way responsible."

"No, but several NASA employees, plus yourself, were affected. A tragedy. We wondered if there was something to make this time of recovery easier for you."

Bella said, "That is thoughtful, but no, I will be fine."

Mr. Frost continued, "Perhaps a donation to a cause important to you would be a good way to make something good come from a bad circumstance."

His idea caught Bella's attention and she glanced at Phoenix and said, "My future husband and I have plans to set up a foundation to help contribute to Dr. B's Animal Rescue, the Texas Wolfdog Project, as well as victims of eye injuries that result in blindness. These are all areas important to us. A donation to the foundation would be invaluable to those causes."

He said, "Consider it done. Who do we make the check payable to?"

Bella said, "Dr. Bella DelCaprio-Chandler and Phoenix Chandler. When we return from our honeymoon, we plan to set up the foundation. Thank you, Mr. Frost, and thank NASA for us."

He said, "God bless you, Dr. DelCaprio, and congratulations on your marriage."

***

Bella smiled at Phoenix, leaned against the door frame of the closet wearing only jeans and a very sexy grin.

He said, "Obviously, I need to include you in more business dealings at the ranch. I'm impressed, as always, with your interaction with people."

"What about my interaction with you?"

He walked back toward her. Then he crawled on the bed, kissing her until she was flat on her back with him over her.

He answered, "When it comes to us, impressed is only one of the many things that describe what I feel for you."

She smiled and snuggled in his arms, safe and loved. This was like a magnificent dream after the horror of yesterday.

He said, "You seem to be able to move around pretty good this morning. How do you feel?"

"My back feels so much better. Would you check it for me?"

Phoenix sat up, lifted the back of her shirt, and said, "It looks better! The redness is fading, and the scrapes and cuts look better too. What about the bruising and soreness?"

"The salt bath did the trick – I am barely sore."

Then she looked down at the large thigh bruise, and Phoenix growled.

She understood what he felt, and said, "I would feel the same way if it was you," and he kissed the large bruise.

Someone knocked on the door.

Phoenix called out, "Who dare enter this domain?"

Lucas laughed and said, "Open the castle, I want to see Princess Bella."

Bella laughed and said, "Come in, Sir Brother," and Lucas walked in with a cocky glance at Phoenix.

Then Thor ran in.

Then Lili, Seth and Ariel joined them.

Then Jasmine yelled down the hall, "Breakfast is almost ready!"

Phoenix laughed and got out of the way so everyone could check on her. Bella showed them her wounds and they hugged and loved on her.

After he was dressed, he headed to the kitchen. Lucas and Seth caught up with him. As they walked through the den, Phoenix felt the peace, and smiled.

All the threats were gone.

***

Lili and Ariel helped Bella put medicine on her back, and they dug around in her closet till they found a shirt that she could wear without a bra. She showed them her wedding dress and boots, and they lovingly touched them, like women always do.

Bella said, "Phoenix picked out the dress. He had me give him a fashion show at the bridal boutique. I bet the women from there dreamed about it for days. He was amazingly hot. For real. It was master class romance," and they laughed.

Lili said, "The boots are crazy gorgeous, did you get them from around here?"

Bella pulled them on and walked around and said, "Online. Aren't they fabulous? I can't wait to wear them naked," and both women laughed delightedly.

Ariel said, "Excellent idea! I will have to get some black thigh boots to wear naked whenever I finally allow someone to marry me."

Lili grinned and said, "I'm thinking red stiletto boots will work for my honeymoon."

Then Bella got quiet for a couple of seconds and said, "After this week it feels like a miracle to marry Phoenix tomorrow."

Lili solemnly said, "Are you ok? Have you processed at all yet? Two attacks in a row are simply unbelievable. I can't fathom it."

Bella nodded and said, "I have. I know it seems like I shouldn't be laughing this morning, but after the fear and heaviness all this time, the freedom to have that weight removed, brings joy and peace to the surface again.

"With Royce it was the fear of attacks, knowing that he wanted to kill me; then it was over and done. But Gabe was totally different. I spent time with him. He was welcomed into our lives and was trusted. When he told me he was the hacker, and took me, only then did he become the sexual predator I had feared.

"The time from when I found out who he was until I found the syringe in my pocket, were bleak and horrifying. But once I found the syringe, I knew that I had an excellent fighting chance. And while euthanizing an animal is sad to me, this was not the same. Killing him was my only way out of the imprisonment and torture he had planned for me.

"So yes, I really have processed. And now I look forward to the promise of all brides; for the man that loves me, and for babies that will look like him. Especially, after a wild passionate honeymoon, totally naked, wearing these very fine cowboy boots."

With that explanation, they laughed, and even the memory of fear faded away.

***

Phoenix heard the women laugh as they came down the hall and everyone in the kitchen smiled at the sound.

It was a good sound.

Then Bella walked around the corner, gorgeous in jeans and a black floral top with makeup that covered most of the bruises. But it was her sparkling blue eyes, fabulous smile, and infectious joy that made Phoenix walk over and kiss her breathless.

Everyone clapped and hollered like they were at a ballgame.

When Phoenix let Bella up for air, breathless, she said, "Right back at you, cowboy," and they laughed.

Then the breakfast buffet was on.

As they ate, Phoenix said, "GP is fretting to get home. He is being released sometime today from the hospital. His heart is normal. It was just the drug he was given and the stress considering his age."

Bella said, "It had to be shocking for him, I know Lucas and the crew said it was disturbing to wake up in the hospital for them too. How are Dante and Ryker doing? Have you heard from them?"

Phoenix said, "Dante's sister picked him up and he is in Fort Worth. He called this morning after the news aired about your kidnapping to make sure that you were ok. And as for Ryker, he is in a regular room now and hopes to be discharged in the morning since his heart tests show normal. His brother lives close-by so he will stay with him until he is recovered from the surgery. He hopes to make it to the wedding tomorrow."

Bella smiled and said, "That is great news. Those guys are amazing. We need to find some single women to snatch them up."

Kit spoke up and said, "I know a redhead from the Cattleman's Gala," and everyone laughed.

Then someone knocked on the door and Phoenix yelled, "Come in!" and four cowhands stepped inside from neighboring ranches.

Phoenix knew them and said, "Morning guys. How about some breakfast?"

The oldest one said, "Morning Mr. Chandler. We are here to help out on your ranch until Kit is up to par, and you and Dr. B are back from your honeymoon. My boss said to tell you he wasn't taking no for an answer so suck it up."

Phoenix laughed and shook their hands and said, "That means you have to get in the food line. Come eat! And thank you."

All four men turned to Bella and nodded in respect.

The oldest spoke for them again, and said, "Dr. B, everyone everywhere is glad that you are home safe, and mighty proud that a woman with courage like you, lives among us," and Bella smiled her thousand-watt smile as she tapped her heart and fought the tears.

They nodded in complete understanding and headed for the food.

Lili said, "Bella, if you show me your vet routine today, I have permission from the clinic to work here at the ranch until you return."

Bella hugged her and said, "You will love it, Lili! Thank you! We can head over to my office a little later. Guys, let us know if you need anything."

***

Phoenix's phone rang, and he showed the caller ID to Bella - it was Monique, his ex-fiancé, so he stepped away and answered, "Hello."

Monique said, "I just wanted to check on Bella, Phoenix, and make sure that she is ok."

"Thank you, Monique, she's had a rough week, but she's doing terrific. Would you like to talk to her?"

Monique said, "Oh, yes, thank you so much."

Phoenix tapped Bella on the arm, and she followed him outside and he handed her the phone.

"This is Bella."

"Bella, this is Monique, we met outside the restaurant."

"Of course, I remember you! How are you and the baby?"

Bella could hear the smile in Monique's voice as she said, "She was born yesterday. She is beautiful and healthy - and safe now thanks to your encouragement. But I wanted to check on you personally to make sure that you were ok. I was shocked to learn of the last two days, and I'm grateful you are home safe."

Bella said, "That is kind of you, and I am happy for your little girl. She has a good momma, I can tell. What did you name her?"

Monique said, "I named her after you. I hope that you don't mind."

Bella's lip quivered as Phoenix watched emotion wash over her, and she said, "I am honored Monique, and I mean that. Where are you staying?"

Monique said, "I'm not allowed to say, but we are in another state. But I would like my Bella to meet you one day."

"Yes, I would love that. Please let us know how you are. I will get Phoenix to send you my cell number. Don't forget to send a picture and I am proud of your choice. Take care and enjoy that baby."

***

When the call ended, Bella handed Phoenix his phone and said, "She named her daughter after me. Isn't that amazing?"

Phoenix smiled and kissed her forehead, then said, "No, because you are amazing."

***

Then Bella's phone rang, and she answered.

A male voice said, "Dr. DelCaprio, this is Dr. Thomas with The Texas State Board of Veterinary Medical Examiners. The coroner's office contacted us per regulations to inform us of the use of animal drugs in a human death."

Phoenix watched Bella's face pale, and she said, "I understand."

He said, "Don't be alarmed. I just need to let you know that you will need to provide a notarized statement and a copy of the police report to go with the coroner's report once it is complete. Please refrain from practice until this is done. This is normal procedure."

Bella said, "Yes, Doctor. I will let my employer know. In fact, we are marrying tomorrow so I will be sending in a name change for the license when we return from our honeymoon."

"Congratulations then, Dr. DelCaprio, and I know that you will be glad once all of this is behind you. I admire your ingenuity to survive," and she smiled.

***

Phoenix said, "Who was that?"

"The Texas licensing board. The coroner had to report the use of a euthanizer drug on a human, so I need to make a formal statement to go with the police report. He said it is normal procedure."

He said, "Are you ok?"

"I figured there might be some legality involved but it was still alarming. I'm glad that Lili is here to help the ranch. I will let her know of my restriction."

Phoenix said, "Why did you smile at the end of the conversation?"

"Dr. Thomas said that he admired my ingenuity to survive."

At noon Phoenix left to get GP from the hospital. After he left, Bella, Lili, Ariel, and Jasmine stood in the patio room and looked around. It was time for wedding setup. Lucas and Seth stood by with muscles ready to do what their women needed.

The women decided to arrange the patio tables and chairs on the south side of the pool with an aisle down the center. That way, Bella could walk out of the bedroom patio doors straight down the aisle to Phoenix. It would be an intimate wedding with close family and friends.

Bella let the girls decorate and smiled as they took control. Ariel arranged tropical plants where the wedding party would be and laid a large cowhide on the ground for them to stand on. Lili had brought large rhinestone bows for the center of all the guest tables. Jasmine set up a table for cake and champagne. The food would be buffet style in the house. It was beautiful and simple.

Ariel said, "What about music?"

Bella said, "Lucas will sing."

"Oh, that's perfect." Lili said. "I hope he sings for our wedding."

Bella glanced at Lucas who was behind Lili. He had heard Lili's comment and winked. Obviously, that was his plan.

Then he joined them and said, "When do you fly out for the Bahamas?"

Bella said, "We decided to change our honeymoon trip under the circumstances. We will save that trip for another time. He's going to take me on a drive. Just us. No commotion. No tourists. Maybe even to the mountains."

Lucas hugged her and said, "It sounds wonderful, Bella. But do you think Phoenix will give you time to eat cake before he runs off with you?"

"I can't make any promises."

Early afternoon, Phoenix arrived home with GP, who wanted to see Bella. He wrapped her in his arms and rocked her without words. Bella held on to him and felt the love and despair he had felt knowing that she had been taken.

A minute later he smiled and said, "I see you are preparing for a wedding tomorrow."

"I am so glad that you will be here, GP, and I have a question for you."

GP said, "Ask away."

"Would you walk me down the aisle?"

GP choked up and it took him a minute to respond, then he kissed her on the cheek and said, "It would be my greatest honor, Bella." and she hugged him.

Phoenix felt the arrow right to the heart. He was unaware that Bella had planned to ask his grandfather. There were no words to describe her. She just kept giving. It was just who she was.

Later that afternoon, Seth met Phoenix at the barn and said, "Phoenix, I know that it's old fashioned, but I wanted your approval to ask Ariel to marry me."

Not surprised at all, Phoenix said, "Absolutely yes. You're a good man. But I'm shocked that y'all haven't eloped yet. She is wonderful, Seth. But can you handle her? She is on the hot end of feisty."

Seth grinned and said, "There's not a doubt in my mind."

Phoenix said. "I'm happy for both of you. I know Ariel will say yes, even though she will make you work for it."

With a laugh, Seth said, "I wouldn't expect anything else."

Dinner had just ended when Pierce and Sterling arrived from Houston. Phoenix, Bella, Seth, and Lili met them outside with welcoming smiles.

Pierce, visually heavy of heart because of Gabe, stopped in front of Bella and said, "I wish there were words to express how sorry I am about—"

Bella gently said, "No, Pierce. I understand, but we were all deceived. Come inside and celebrate a new beginning with all of us. You are part of the family now," and Pierce glanced at Phoenix.

"It's the truth," Phoenix said with a handshake," and Pierce smiled in relief.

Sterling kissed Bella's hand and said, "If I could have taken your place, I would have Bella. It's an honor and a privilege to know you," and he fist bumped Phoenix and walked inside.

Seth and Lili followed them.

Phoenix stood with Bella on the porch as they watched the sun go down. She didn't tell him that she had done the same thing with Gabe last night before it all happened. Phoenix didn't need to know any more than he already did.

Phoenix said, "Some brides don't see the groom until they walk down the aisle. Is that a tradition that you would like to follow? I can easily—"

She stopped him and said, "No. I appreciate you offering but it isn't something that I want to do. Our relationship isn't traditional, it's exceptional, and I don't want to miss one minute of it. Especially after all that we have been through."

He answered her with a smile, and a long intimate kiss.

It was almost eleven p.m. when everyone headed to bed. Phoenix and Bella packed for their trip.

He said, "Why are you bringing all those high heels?"

"I can't tell you."

Phoenix stopped what he was doing and said, "Sure you can. Now I really want to know."

Bella said, "They are my lingerie."

Thinking he misunderstood her, he said, "You mean that you are wearing them with your lingerie?"

She shook her head with a seductive smile, and said, "No. They are all that I will be wearing."

Anticipating all her invisible lingerie, he drew her to the bed with kisses, and said, "Say it again."

Bella, eyes twinkling, said, "I'm going to be naked, modeling lots of high heels."

"Yeah, that's what I thought I heard. Be prepared to shop for shoes often."

Chapter 41
Wedding

The sun barely shone through the window shades when Phoenix felt Bella slide out of the bed. He watched as she ran in the closet. He wondered what she was doing and propped up on his elbow.

In a few seconds, she walked out of the closet still dressed in her pajama short set and posed against the doorframe wearing glitter stilettos.

He grinned and drawled, "Don't stop there," and she laughed as she took them off and ran back to the bed.

She said, "I was practicing," and he pulled her close as they faced each other.

He said, "Are you nervous at all about the wedding and honeymoon today?"

"Maybe that I might trip on my dress, or sneeze or something." Then she kissed his chest and said, "But I have never been nervous about making love to you. I am more than ready."

Phoenix whispered in her ear, "How ready?"

She whispered something private in his ear, and he groaned and crushed her lips against his.

In a few moments, he said, "Now I will think about that all day."

Bella scooted out of the bed and said, "You asked," and he grinned as she walked like a runway model all the way back to the closet.

The morning passed quickly. Phoenix loaded their luggage and personal belongings in his truck and tended to ranch business. Then he pulled the wedding rings and marriage license out of the safe on his way back to the bedroom to get ready.

He walked to the windows and watched Bella with Ariel and Lili make sure the patio was ready for the wedding. He unbuttoned and took off his shirt as Bella laughed at something Lili said.

Bella caught his gaze through the bedroom window and blew him a kiss. He acted like he caught it and laid it on his heart.

***

About forty minutes later, the cake and flowers were delivered, and the wedding and reception were ready to go. Bella spent a few minutes loving on Thor before Ariel and Lili ushered her into the bedroom via the patio.

***

After her shower, Bella sat in her robe and the girls gave her the treatment. Ariel and Lili worked the base makeup so that it covered her disappearing wounds. Then they accented her already fabulous eyes with shadow, liner, and mascara. The finishing touch was a stunning pale pink lipstick to cover her full lips.

And lastly, Lili loosely braided Bella's long hair and wove in the Boho flower jewelry.

Once they finished, Lili said, "You are gorgeous! Well, you are always gorgeous, but today we call it take-his-breath-away gorgeous."

Bella sighed in wonder as she touched her romantic braid and pursed her lips checking out her makeup.

She said, "You are terrific artists!"

Ariel said, "Honey, God was the artist. We just played with the makeup."

Bella led the way to the dressing room. She stepped into her wedding dress, pulled it up, and slipped her arms through the spaghetti straps. And that was it. No zipper. No hooks.

It hung from her shoulders with a draped V neckline and dipped low to the waist in the back. The gown's thin fragile material was white floral lace that flowed down her curves and laid delicately on her feet before it trailed behind her in a two-foot train.

She slipped her feet into the wedding boots and walked to the mirror.

She was ready for him.

Bella glanced at the clock, and they had less than ten minutes.

Lili looked outside and the guests were seated. The Preacher was in place. Phoenix and Lucas were up front. Everyone was waiting on Bella.

Lili said, "Everyone's ready. I'm heading outside to get in place by Lucas and Phoenix. This is it, Bella," and hugged her.

Ariel said, "I'll get GP."

A few minutes later, GP smiled as Bella held his arm. They stood behind the double patio doors and waited for the music to start.

Bella smiled, heart fluttering.

Then she heard the music and the doors swept open.

Phoenix forgot to breathe as his eyes met hers.

And then he smiled.

That smile that was just for her.

And he said her name.

And Bella smiled at him.

That smile that was just for him.

And she started up the aisle.

Phoenix thought he had imagined how gorgeous Bella would be at this moment. Especially since he had picked out her dress. But he barely came close. She was far beyond his imagination. What an exquisite vision she was. The fire of her beauty radiated with each step she took.

How he loved her.

How he wanted and needed her.

Bella watched him as he watched her. He was so handsome. So sexy. She loved that lock of hair that always draped above one of his eyes. She adored his grin that always started at the left side of his perfect lips. And she hungered for him as he stood, broad shouldered and strong, in a black tuxedo jacket, thigh hugging jeans, and boots.

Her man.
Her rancher.
How she loved him.

Phoenix grinned as she met his eyes again. And winked. And everything in the world was perfect for Bella.

She finally noticed all the guests that stood as GP escorted her down the aisle. She heard the oohs and aahs. She saw as Lucas swallowed to control his emotion, and as Lili wiped happy tears.

When Bella neared Phoenix, he stepped forward to draw her to him, and whispered, "My Bella."
Now he had her.
Forever.

They faced the Preacher, and he welcomed everyone to their marriage ceremony. He prayed, then talked about how extraordinary love can draw two people together for a lifetime of oneness. He spoke into their future and assured them that their faith would lead them there. He blessed them and led them through their vows, the exchange of rings, and pronounced them man and wife in the eyes of God.
The Preacher said, "You may kiss your bride."
Phoenix passionately claimed her lips. Then kissed her again as he dipped her. And still celebrating the moment, he lifted her till she looked down at him. Bella laughed and held his face in her hands. Then lowered her lips to his.

Afterwards, they greeted their guests. Ranger Morgan and his wife came, Deputy Todd, Shiloh from the FBI, the Detective from Louisiana, and even Ryker was able to make it. Several church friends, some business friends, and several neighbors came, including Ariel, Seth, Pierce, and Sterling, along with the ranch crew.
They cut the cake, and Phoenix licked icing off her lip. Then Phoenix wanted to throw the garter. He had insisted on a garter for all singles, men, and women.
Phoenix knelt and drew Bella on his knee. When he lifted the hem of her dress to get the garter, he saw her wedding boots and whistled.

He drawled softly, "I expect you to model them for me later," and she fluttered her lashes at him.

Ariel caught the garter and laughed. Then to everyone's surprise, Seth knelt on one knee and pulled a ring out of his pocket. Ariel gasped as he offered it to her.

Bold and passionately, Seth said, "Ariel, I love you. Will you marry me soon, and rock my world the way that only you can do?"

No one made a sound as they watched the love drama play out before them.

Ariel, beautiful in a pale pink jumpsuit, looked at him teasingly and walked around him like she was considering it. With a laugh, he pulled her down on his knee and thoroughly kissed her.

As the kiss ended, Ariel said, "Yes!"

Bella screamed and cheered with all the rest.

Lucas called out, "Wedding dance for the bride and groom!" and he sang while Phoenix and Bella flirted the whole dance.

When the song ended, Phoenix announced, "Everyone, stay and have a great time, we love you and thank you, but we are hitting the road," and Bella waved to everyone as he quickly escorted her through the patio doors to their bedroom.

Phoenix shut the door and smiled as he looked down into her gorgeous face and said, "You look deliciously mine."

She wet her lips and said, "I can say the same for you."

He kissed her and said, "How fast can we get out of here?"

She said, "Now, let's go like we are."

His hungry eyes followed the line of her dress and said, "Did you wear anything under it?"

With a teasing look, she said, "Of course not."

"Nothing?"

She whispered, "Just my boots," and he slid his hands firmly down her thighs and backside and groaned.

Bella wrapped her arms around his waist and slid her hands down into his back pockets, then pulled him against her.

Phoenix picked her up in a wild hot kiss, and said, "We have to go. We have to get in the truck now," and she smiled as he took her hand and pulled her down the hall, through the house, into the garage, put her in the truck, and peeled out of the driveway.

She watched him for a few minutes and said, "You're speeding."

He laughed and said, "You bet I am."

Bella, a little hot in the long dress and train, lifted the hem and exposed her legs and lowered the air conditioner vent to cool them.

Phoenix groaned and said, "Please tell me that you know where you want to go."

She crossed her legs in her fine boots, and said, "I kind of like the Medicine Park area by the Wichita Mountains Wildlife Refuge."

He pulled it up on his phone and said, "Why don't I call ahead for reservations?"

She grinned and said, "I already have," and he laughed in relief, and gave a fist pump.

Then he googled and asked, "How long does it take to get to Medicine Park from Wichita Falls?"

Google answered, "One hour five minutes with the toll road," and Phoenix smiled at Bella and pressed the gas.

A little later, Phoenix got a phone call. He said, "It's Rocking J Ranch."

Excited, Bella said, "It is about your bucking bull calf!"

***

"Phoenix Chandler here, I have you on speaker."

A man's voice said, "Phoenix, this is Jack at the Rocking J Ranch, we have a wedding present for you as I understand it. The calf your wife purchased will be ready to leave here in a week."

Phoenix smiled at Bella and said, "That is great news, Jack. It so happens we will be in Oklahoma for a week. I can bring him home with us."

Jack said, "Sounds great! Give us a call when you are on the way."

***

After the call, Phoenix said, "I am pumped but I still can't believe you bought that calf," and she grinned.

He said, "And that reminds me, I have a surprise for you."

277

"What?"

"I purchased a three-year-old female wolf husky hybrid with blue eyes, ready to breed. I think that it's time that we reward Thor with a mate."

She screamed softly, and said, "I am so excited! When can we get her?"

He said, "Why don't we pick her up on the way home as well. She's over by Lubbock."

Bella said, "Yes! I can only imagine their beautiful pups."

Phoenix looked Bella over, and said, "I can certainly imagine our children will look like their beautiful momma."

Bella smiled and said, "And their handsome daddy."

A little later, Phoenix and Bella both watched the mountains get closer. It wouldn't be long now. He entwined his fingers with hers. He was getting hot.

She squeezed his hand, squirmed a bit, and turned up the AC.

He grinned. She was hot too.

Once they hit the mountain range, it wasn't long before they arrived in Medicine Park. Their anticipation was off the meter.

In ten minutes, Phoenix parked in front of a two-story cabin that overlooked the lake and mountains. No other houses were around. He looked at Bella.

She was already breathless.

Every muscle in his body tightened, and he reached for her.

He whispered against her lips, "We are going to blaze hot, my Bella," and her response confirmed it.

Without taking his eyes off her, he shrugged out of his tux jacket and unbuttoned his shirt. Bella watched him and reached up and pulled her braid apart; black hair tumbled.

Bare-chested and ready, Phoenix got out of the truck and walked quickly around to get her.

To love her.

To make her his.

Bella's body sizzled as he came for her. She arched her back in uncontrollable anticipation, and he groaned when he saw her movement.

He opened the door and swept her up in his arms.

She clutched and kissed him as he hurried up the stairs. He keyed in the entry code, stepped across the threshold, and kicked the door shut.

Bella slid down him and stepped back. She ran her hands down her body in total abandon.

He unsnapped his jeans and reached for her. Ablaze with unbridled passion, Phoenix kissed her and backed her toward the bedroom. He rubbed his hot hands all over her, needing to touch her everywhere at once.

But just before they reached the room, he paused for a quick second. They gazed at each other with breathless excitement. With smoking eyes, he reached for the shoulder straps of her wedding dress.

And watched her dress hit the floor.

Bella licked her lips. She had wanted to see that look on his face, and posed for him, promising everything, wearing only her fancy boots. With a deep groan and a wild kiss, Phoenix scooped her up and carried her through the door.

And the fire raged.

The End

Epilogue
One Month Later

Bella ran as fast as she could to get away from the wolves. They gained on her with no effort at all, and she groaned and pushed harder.

Phoenix laughed as Thor and the new female wolfdog, Vixen, chased Bella playfully for the treats she held for them.

With a gasp, Bella slipped and landed flat on her back. She squealed as the wolves licked her face in affection, so she laid her arms out and opened her hands. The venison disappeared.

She heard Phoenix's laughter getting closer, then his handsome face grinned down at her.

"Were you just feeling frisky?" he asked.

She stuck her tongue out at him and he laughed again and helped her up.

She rubbed her backside, and said, "That was unexpected. What did I slip on?"

Phoenix looked on the ground behind her, and said, "A large cow patty as far as I can tell," and she grimaced and looked at her shoes.

He turned her around and checked.

"At least it's only on your shoes," he commented. "Come on, it's time to get ready for the wedding anyway. Ariel is already looking for you, and we need to leave in a couple of hours. Seth is sending the limo for us."

Bella smiled and said, "I'm so excited to go to a double wedding. I would never have believed that Ariel & Seth and Lucas & Lili would marry at the same time. As it is, I am still amazed we have already been married a month."

She grinned, as Phoenix slid his hand inside the back of her jeans and rubbed her tender backside.

He drawled, "I too, feel amazement, every time I have a moment like this."

Bella grinned and reached behind him.

He warned with a twinkle in his eye, and said, "Go ahead, but you know that we will be late for the wedding if you do that, my Bella."

"That is so very tempting," she said, and kissed him instead.

Ariel hollered across the field, "Get in here, Bella, and get dressed, I will need you in thirty minutes to help me!"

Bella yelled, "I'll hurry!" and glanced at Phoenix's hand still in her jeans, and after one more caress, he pulled it out.

She   laughed   and   ran   toward   the   house.

***

Phoenix watched her and knew that she was pregnant. He knew her body and behavior well and had seen the subtle changes. She grimaced at some smells. She ate less. She looked a little peeked the last few mornings. And she touched her stomach without being aware of it.

He frowned as he thought of the fall she had just taken in the pasture. He would have to ask her about pregnancy soon if she didn't tell him.

She rocked him. It was as simple as that. It wasn't just the sexual fire between them, he couldn't even list all the wonders she brought into his life. And to watch her bear their child, would be indescribable.

He prayed, thank you, God, for the millionth time.

***

Bella rushed through her shower, pulled her long hair up into a luxurious ponytail, put on her makeup and slipped on the pink strapless dress with jewelry and she was done.

She looked in the mirror and hoped she looked appropriate as Matron of Honor and then grinned and thought, well, she was really, more than likely, the pregnant Matron of Honor.

She didn't want to tell Phoenix anything until she had taken the pregnancy test. She would get one tomorrow after church. She rubbed her belly and knew that she was pregnant. She just knew.

And she knew that Phoenix was going to celebrate rancher style, exuberantly proud and bull-headedly protective. She was a blessed woman.

The first time with Phoenix on their honeymoon had been sensational beyond her wildest dreams. She knew that's when she got pregnant. No one would ever convince her otherwise. And their intimacy now touched everything about them. Dressing, sleeping, talking, working, arguing, playing, affection, communication, along with all the types of passion that they shared.

She would never look at another bride the same again. Bless them all!

Then she went to Ariel's room.

When Bella knocked, Ariel said, "Come on in," and Bella stepped in and smiled.

She said, "Ariel, that jewel headpiece is gorgeous in your short blonde hair!"

Ariel sighed and said, "Oh Bella, I'm nervous. And I'm never nervous. Why am I nervous?"

Bella said, "It's normal. I hadn't realized that I was nervous until I saw Phoenix down the aisle. When he smiled and said my name, I relaxed. You just need to see Seth. That's all."

Ariel said, "Ok. That's true. He makes everything right."

Bella smiled and said, "Can I help with anything? You look so beautiful already."

"No thanks, I can finish it. I just needed you here."

Bella said, "I understand. And I can't wait to see your dress!"

Ariel finished the last swipe of red lipstick and rubbed her lips together, then said, "I love, love, love, the dress but it's a stunner. Help me put it on," and she opened her closet and Bella gasped.

"Ariel! It is amazing. I can't wait to see it on you. That screams Hollywood."

They pooled the dress on the floor and Ariel stepped into it and pulled it up till the halter bodice was in place. They looked into the mirror.

"I have never seen a dress like that, and it is absolutely perfect for you," Bella said softly.

The dress was made of snug white satin. It had a low neckline and plunged into a super low V in the back. It showed off her lean, fit figure. The surprise was the open sides all the way to her hips. It reminded Bella of a one-piece bathing suit with large cutouts down the side.

Ariel looked at Bella and said, "It's a bit much for Wichita Falls, but Houston would have expected it."

Bella said, "Honey, Wichita Falls needs a movie star bride like you. Seth is going to love it! And especially, love taking you out of it," and Ariel finally laughed.

Phoenix knocked on the door and said, "It's me, Ariel."

"Come on in."

He stepped in, dressed in a black tux, and looked at Ariel and said, "Wow, Ariel! You look like a Hollywood star."

Bella said, "I told you!"

He smiled and said, "I couldn't be happier for you and Seth," and he hugged her.

Ariel said, "Do you think Seth will like it?"

He laughed and said, "Like is much too mild a word. Seth is going to go up in flames on the altar when he sees you in that," and the women laughed.

Then he walked over to Bella and kissed her bare shoulder, then nibbled her ear.

Bella winked at Ariel, and said, "Your turn's here."

Then they walked out to meet GP and headed to the limo.

Once they arrived at the church, Phoenix went to join Lucas and Seth at the altar, while Ariel and Lili met up in the bridal suite. Both brides fought tears. Which of course meant all their bridesmaids fought the tears too.

Bella hugged Lili and said, "You look like a bohemian princess. You are beautifully sexy. I can't wait till Lucas sees you."

Lili's dress was a white, sleeveless, empire sheath made from floral lace. An enchanting chiffon overlay fluttered to the floor. But the sexy, in the middle of all that feminine, was a slit from her thigh to the ground, leaving one leg bare. Her long brown curls were pulled up to cascade down her back and she wore a floral wreath around her head.

Lili said, "I wanted to surprise Lucas."

Bella said, "Honey, surprise is only one of the things that he will feel. Others are, panting, hot, and impatient fit much better," and they laughed.

When it was time, both brides lined up with their bridesmaids to begin the procession. In minutes the music started. Lili's procession went first and then Ariel's. The brides were totally stunning, and completely different, as they smiled and walked toward the grooms that loved them. The grooms watched their beautiful women come to them while they stood there, eager, and ready to love them even more.

Bella and Phoenix glanced at each other and smiled. They remembered their wedding just a month ago.

Before long, the reception was in full swing and packed. When they finished all their attendant duties, Phoenix drew Bella on the dance floor.

He smiled and said, "I wondered which pair of heels you plan to wear tonight, for lingerie."

Bella gave him, that smile, and rubbed her foot alongside his calf muscle, showing sparkly pink ankle strap stilettos.

He made a low sound in his throat, and said, "That looks delicious. Like cotton candy at the fair," and she laughed.

Then he whispered, "I have a question for you."

Bella whispered, "Ask away, handsome."

Phoenix looked at her and said, "When were you planning to tell me that you are pregnant?"

Bella almost stumbled so he pulled her against him to steady her.

Incredulous, she said, "I'm not even late yet! I planned to get a pregnancy test after church tomorrow. There is no way that you could possibly know."

"I'm a breeder and protector of pregnant females for a living. You don't think I know the signs? I've studied up on it, and I know you, and your body. You don't even notice the signs you give off. But I certainly do."

Excited, Bella said, "We will know for sure tomorrow!"

He laughed and said, "We can get the test on the way home, and we can know the minute that you go to the bathroom."

After they got home, Phoenix drew Bella down the hall to the bedroom. She smiled at his enthusiasm. She got ready to go in the bathroom and he tried to follow her in, and she pushed him out, took the bag from him, and shut the door.

He sighed and waited.

Bella took the test.

Phoenix said, "Come on, Bella. I'm dying out here."

She said, "Come on in, Daddy, I'm washing my hands," and he burst through the door and swept her off her feet.

She would never forget his smile.

Three days later, they waited at the doctor's office for an ultrasound confirmation.

Bella said, "They should be able to at least confirm pregnancy this early. I've read that some ultrasounds were very accurate at four weeks."

Phoenix said, "I've studied on it too. They'll know," and she grinned at his insistence.

The nurse called Bella's name and brought them to the back. She set her up on the ultrasound table. Bella shivered as the nurse began to rub the cold gel on her stomach. Phoenix squeezed her hand and smiled.

The ultrasound technician began to scan Bella's abdomen as she watched the fuzzy black and white screen.

Phoenix was impatient, and said, "Do you see one?"

The technician shook her head calmly, and said, "No. But I see two. It looks like you're having twins."

Bella laughed, and Phoenix yelled, "Yes!" with a fist pump, then scooped her up in his arms and kissed her.

About The Author

Patti was born and raised in Lake Charles, Louisiana, surrounded by lakes, rivers, and bayous. She loves the Cajun culture and cuisine and is always ready for a road trip to the Gulf of Mexico or other scenic areas. Family, faith, reading, and writing, fill most of her days.

You can find her blog at PattiArcher.com - and her author page at amazon.com/author/patticorbelloarcher.cajunlady.

Her next writing project is pending publication in the summer and fall of 2022. It is a romantic suspense trilogy based in Louisiana.

♥ If you enjoyed the story and characters of Double Target, no matter how you received the book, you can leave a review on Amazon. Simply go on Amazon – search Patti Corbello Archer – and all her published books will populate. If you click on the book you have read, then scroll to the bottom, there is a place for you to enter your review.

She would love to know! Thank you!